About the Author

T. S. J. Smith was born and raised in Birmingham and studied history and journalism at the University of Wales, Bangor. He spent several years moving around the UK and Australia before landing in Thame, Oxfordshire where this book was written. He now lives in Donegal, Ireland with his wife, Anne, and their three children. The idea for *Where Giants Walk* first came to him while searching for inspiration in the Cotswolds and in the hills of Donegal — both places alive with history, magic and mysticism. He is also the author of the acclaimed spy thriller, *The Soviet Comeback*.

BY THE SAME AUTHOR

The Soviet Comeback *(Jamie Smith)*

Where Giants Walk

T. S. J. Smith

Where Giants Walk

Pegasus

For Órla, Taidgh and Oonagh — all even more magical than Många
Världar

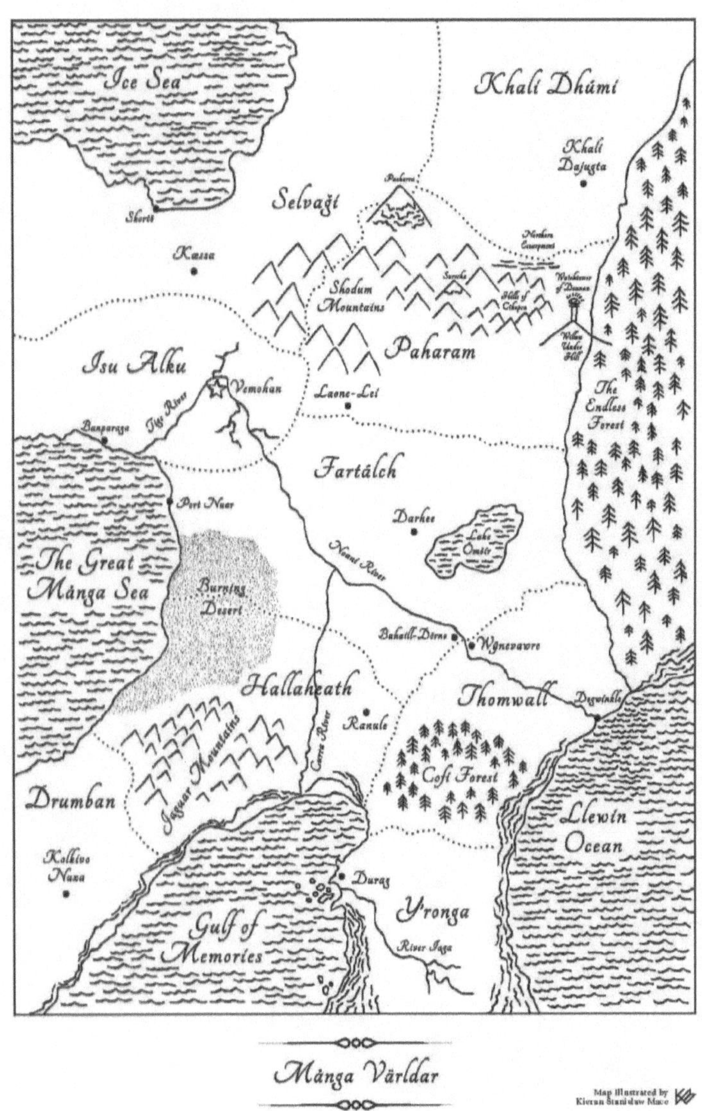

Map and front cover by Kieran Stanislaw Mace

CHAPTER 1

A Secret Garden

When Barry Birchwood walked out of school on Friday 21st September and made his way to work, he had no idea that in a few short hours his life would change forever.

But then, had he known what was coming, he might never have taken another step. Because what Barry really wanted was an easy life with his books, his stories and the constant opportunity for adventure. Only the *opportunity* for adventure, however, because he much preferred dreaming about them than the thought of actually having one.

Completely unaware of what was coming, he made his way through the residential estate of tightly packed, pale brick houses, down alleyways, and towards the rather neglected local high street.

He paused outside the bookshop as he passed and looked longingly in at all the books he couldn't afford. If there was one thing Barry loved, it was a good book.

But his window shopping was unexpectedly interrupted by a heavy thud against his back, and turning, he saw a group of boys from school, laughing. He pulled off his jacket and saw an old, greasy kebab sticking to the back of it. Tears stung his eyes but he fought them back as he looked up at them.

'Got summat t' say, bonehead Birchwood?' a short lad with pockmarked cheeks and an early attempt at a goatee said with a sneer. The boys with him all laughed encouragingly.

Barry shook his head silently. The short boy walked up to him.

'I didn't hear you, you loser,' he snarled in a strong Brummie accent, his face up close to Barry's.

'No, nothing to say. Sorry, Jordan,' Barry said meekly, looking at the floor. He was fourteen, but right now felt as small as a five-year-old.

'That's what I thought, a kebab would only improve that jacket you're wearing anyways. School uniform must be the best clothes you have,' Jordan laughed, walking past Barry and pushing him with his shoulder. He then pointedly trod on Barry's coat, which was on the pavement, and ground it into the kebab beneath.

Barry finally arrived at his destination, a pub with faux-Tudor black and white beams, embossed with the words The Golden Lion in peeling gold letters. Big Kevin, the landlord, a bearded man with an enormous beer belly, took no notice of his clear distress, and immediately put him to work scrubbing down the tables, and collecting glasses from the smattering of customers who had decided to get an early start.

Barry tried to ignore the loud, angry rumbling in his stomach, instead using his break to scrub down his coat. He was used to going without dinner. He tried to distract himself by imagining walking into another world full of magical creatures, of lands of elephants and pirates. This gave him a slightly vacant look as he ambled around the pub, clearing tables, emptying ashtrays in the garden and carrying out food.

Eventually, unable to take the noise in his stomach any longer, he sloped into the kitchen and cautiously approached the cook with a beseeching look. He was a huge, barrel-chested man with chest hair that curled out of the top of his buttoned chef's whites and bushy mutton chops covering most of his beetroot red face. Fortunately, he had a soft spot for Barry, and after one look at him cut him a thick slab from the remaining roast ham joint and added three fried eggs with a heel of bread.

Barry gave him a huge grin of gratitude and wolfed down the food. The ham and bread were dried out, and the eggs thick with grease, but to his stomach it felt like a banquet fit for a king.

He caught a glimpse of himself in a mirror on the wall by the table he was sitting at. His curly auburn hair was, as usual, a law unto itself; he had spindly arms and smooth skin interrupted by the occasional pimple. Of more concern to him, however, was the bit of kebab just above one of his pale grey eyes that must have been there all night. He wiped it away with a sigh, and allowed his daydreams to take him back off to his world of magical creatures.

By eleven o'clock that night Barry was on his last legs. His feet ached, his hands were raw from scrubbing and glass collecting, and his throat hurt from the smoke of the many candles stuck in old wine bottles to give the pub an olde worlde feel. His exhaustion must have showed as Big Kevin took a pitying look at him. 'Go on, you get yourself off home, it's slowing down now anyway.'

Barry didn't need telling twice. He grabbed a very old, brown, leather-bound book with silver lettering from one of the many decorative shelves around the pub, and within two minutes was outside in the cool night air. Traces of summer still lingered; the verges in the local park remained yellow-green, and he could comfortably walk without a coat, despite the hour. He breathed deeply and rolled his shoulders which were aching from lifting beer kegs all evening, enjoying the feeling of knowing not many others his age would still be allowed out and about. But that in turn made him feel a little sad and he no longer felt like going home. His mum might still be up and he couldn't face another row or more questions on his future, which was all she seemed to want to talk to him about these days. He loved his mum, but he was more than a little afraid of her. He just wanted to read his book.

He looked down at it and read the title for the first time. *Foraging for Fungus* by Jeremiah Stickleback. Barry groaned inwardly. Non-fiction was not his cup of tea; it was all a little bit too *real*.

But then, he reasoned, something was better than nothing. He opened it and started idly flicking through, holding his battered old mobile phone aloft over the pages to better see, already finding it more interesting than he had anticipated. Before he knew it, his feet had carried him past the turn off to the flat he shared with his mum above a minimart on Nearlywoods Hill, and onwards through a series of twists and turns, between houses and down alleyways. He got to the bottom of Puckle Lane and to a gap between two crumbling old red-brick warehouses. He shimmied through, holding the book out in front of him, and found himself on a short dirt-track lined with eons of fly-tipped rubbish. Broken bicycles, cardboard boxes, bottles and even a rusting bathtub lay long forgotten, and he could hear rats scurrying amongst the debris. It was a familiar journey for Barry, and some way down he left the track and stepped behind a bank of cypress trees to a wrought iron gate and his destination. His very own secret garden.

Well, not quite his own. It was a well-kept garden at odds with the track outside, and somebody obviously tended to it lovingly, though he had never seen another soul there. It felt like stepping out of the town and into the countryside. There was a little bird bath, a broad, aged ash tree, and a small pond, laden with waterlilies. The water was twinkling in the moonlight, giving the small garden a magical quality. The edges of the garden were banked with roses, cherry trees, dahlias, irises and even peonies, which Barry was vaguely aware should not be in bloom this late in the season. Surrounding the pond was an apple tree, bearing fruit, and an ancient willow tree, weeping over the water.

Barry settled himself on an old wooden bench facing the water, enjoying his small slice of tranquillity, and opened his book in the glow of the moon and his phone. Already he was discovering the rich tapestry of mushrooms that he could look forward to picking as October arrived. Anything to introduce some variety to his meals at home.

He was deeply absorbed by a chapter outlining a mushroom called chicken of the woods and where to find it when his concentration was broken by the sound of music. His head snapped up and he cast his eyes around, but could no longer hear it. He shook his head, and turned back to the book.

Suddenly, the church clock began striking midnight. Twelve long chimes. Again, it broke Barry's reverie, particularly as, when he looked at his flimsy, plastic wristwatch, it read only 11.17.

'Stupid thing,' he grumbled at it, tapping it firmly with his finger. The second hand continued to move steadily. Strange, it didn't seem to be running slow. He shrugged and turned back to learning about chicken of the woods, which, as he now knew, was also called Laetiporus sulphureus. It looked revolting, but according to Jeremiah Stickleback, was one of the tastiest wild mushrooms you could find.

This time there was no mistaking it. He could clearly hear the sound of somebody playing what he was fairly sure was the harp. But who would be playing the harp at this time of night?

Barry jumped to his feet, his eyes darting everywhere, trying to identify where the sound was coming from. He cocked his head to one side and listened carefully. It seemed to be coming from behind the willow tree on the other side of the pond.

'Hello? Who's there?' Barry called tentatively, but there was no response.

He edged slowly towards the pond, and the music grew louder. He could hear it more clearly now. It was a hauntingly beautiful yet heartbreakingly sad refrain and caused the hairs on Barry's arms to stand on end.

He reached the water's edge and saw his reflection stare back at him, dark and craggy in the moonlight. The boughs of the weeping willow blocked all sight of the far side of the pond and he began to edge his way towards it. His foot sank down to his ankle in a patch of thick mud and he cursed inwardly. It reappeared with a sloppy, sucking sound, and was caked in glutinous pond mud all the way up to his sock.

Barry pushed aside a dense thicket of purple irises, accidentally trampling several of them. He stood before the boughs of the willow, and there was a curious fog around the leaves, while the music seemed mere feet away.

As he reached out to move one of the low, pale green branches to one side, his hand swelled before him. He snatched it back and grasped it tenderly with his other hand.

Inspecting it, it looked perfectly fine and normal. He pushed his hand towards the mist which looked almost like a rain cloud, once more, and again saw it swell before his eyes, it felt stretched and uncomfortable. This time he held it there and pushed it forwards. The hand now appeared normal, but it was his forearm that was swollen, as if the haze was a barrier that caused everything to distort. Barry wiggled his fingers from the other side and everything worked as it was meant to. Retrieving his hand, he took a step back and saw that it was in fact a bonny little cloud blocking his path. He tried stepping around it, but the cloud moved to block him, and he felt, was almost laughing at him. He sighed, realising what he must do. With a deep breath, he pushed the branches aside and stepped into the space they left behind.

CHAPTER 2

The Tutelary

The world spun and Barry's whole body felt inflamed and engorged, like his head was about to pop. He felt like his body had been taken apart atom by atom and squashed back together again. But then, before he knew it, he was back on solid ground. He shook his foggy head, and a quick check showed that all of his extremities seemed to be as they ought to be. As he turned and looked back to the pond, everything appeared dark, cold and distant.

'You didn't really need to tread on my irises,' a stately voice said coldly.

Barry practically leapt out of his skin. He swivelled around towards the voice and nearly screamed.

Stood before him was a creature the like of which he had never even imagined in one of his stories.

A giant eagle sat upon a stool, with huge golden wings spread wide. But within its wings were slender hands grasping a harp, and it had long, slim legs which were stretched out in front of it, quite casually, displaying particularly knobbly knees.

Above the ink black beak was a long moustache which drooped down and hung below a feathered face. Its thick feathers were a deep red-gold that were glinting by the light of a small fire burning before the stool.

'Well?' the creature added, as Barry stood stock still and staring.

'W-w-well?' Barry stammered, bewildered and more than a little frightened.

'The least you could offer is an apology for crushing my irises. Have you any idea how hard I work to keep that garden?'

'The garden?' Barry said, turning slowly to point dumbly back at the other side of the willow.

'Yes, boy, the garden. Have you hit your head?' he asked, looking curiously.

'No... I...'

'Yes... use your words...' the eagle-man encouraged, gesturing with his arm, which made him look even more outlandish.

'What are you?' Barry spurted, then swallowed guiltily.

'Okay, ruuude,' the creature sneered, affronted. 'What are you? Certainly, a poor excuse for a man, this much is clear.'

'I'm sorry! I didn't mean to offend you, it's just... well... what...' He paused, following a warning look. 'I mean, who are you?'

'Well that's a little better. I suppose I should apologise for not introducing myself. I am the Tutelary.'

'A tutelary! I've read about them,' Barry said excitedly. 'You're a guardian...a watcher.'

'Excuse me,' the creature said, looking offended. 'I am not a tutelary. That implies that I am not singularly unique. I am *the* Tutelary, Kepheus. Watcher of the willow, guardian of the garden, and protector of the gateway to the realm of Många Världar,' he announced, puffing out his chest plumes proudly. 'I'm also an above average harp player, if I do say so myself,' he added smugly.

'The realm of Mango Vlabla?' Barry whispered, and looked beyond Kepheus, who rolled his eyes. It was dark, but the sky was clear and the nearly full moon shone brightly, revealing a tall hill climbing up behind him.

On the top of the hill was a mighty stone tower, standing proud and watchful over the lands beyond. Even from this distance Barry could see a flagpole reaching up from the tower and a flag hanging limply in the heavy, dead air of the late summer's night.

His eyes came back to the Tutelary. 'What is this place? Where should I go?'

'You should go nowhere but back whence you came unless you can answer a riddle of my choosing to gain passage to the lands beyond,' Kepheus said calmly, shifting the harp and preparing to play once more.

'A riddle? Isn't that a bit of a cliché?' Barry snorted. Kepheus raised a threatening eyebrow.

'But I've never been much good with riddles,' Barry protested.

'Then the secrets of Många Världar will remain a mystery to you.'

'Okay, what is my riddle then?' Barry asked tentatively.

'Very well,' Kepheus replied. 'Pay attention, as I don't like repeating myself.' He cleared his throat and stood up.

'Of bone and metal,
Wooden boards,
I am the song,
From peasants to lords.
It could be a major or perhaps a minor thing,
For I am music, though I cannot sing.'

The Tutelary finished triumphantly, an arm outstretched to add panache to his delivery, before then sitting down and inspecting his harp once more, seemingly oblivious to Barry.

Barry rubbed his temples. 'You're a song but you cannot sing? That doesn't make any sense,' he muttered to himself grumpily. 'You're a song for peasants and lords? But I don't know any songs from Morngla Vorbla.' He cursed, feeling like he was back in a lesson at school that he didn't fully comprehend. 'Can I have a clue?' he asked beseechingly.

Kepheus continued to ignore him.

'Now who's being rude,' Barry said archly.

Still no response was forthcoming.

'Very well, then my answer is a mime!'

And then, without warning, Kepheus rose from his stool and drew himself up to his full height, his wings spread out, towering over Barry. He began to squawk and crow with fire in his eyes, his arms clawing like talons. 'You have failed the test. Retreat or perish,' he boomed and his wings began to flap, creating a wind so strong it forced Barry to step backwards.

'Please, let me try again!' Barry protested, but there was no longer any reasoning with the Tutelary, who appeared possessed, and began to step towards him.

Barry was no match for the huge eagle-man, and with a last look up the hill at the lonely tower, he turned and fled back past the willow and to more familiar territory. He didn't stop running until he was safely back in his own bedroom, and he made sure the locks were firmly in place on his bedroom window.

He sat down on the end of his bed breathing heavily, his mind racing. He heard his mum stirring in the room next door and quickly pulled off his clothes and climbed into bed. The door opened and Barry closed his eyes and breathed slowly, doing his best to feign sleep despite his lungs hurting from the running. It seemed to work as moments later the door closed softly, and Barry lay awake long into the night, his mind replaying the events he was sure he must have imagined.

***

Barry was woken the next morning by the honks of car horns and the blaring of the call to prayer coming through the speakers at the mosque across the road. It always made Barry imagine that he was in some far off, exotic land and he dreamed of ancient sagas from Persia. But today he groaned and rubbed his tired eyes as he recalled the events of the night before. He swung his legs out of bed and stood for a moment, looking out of the window. Cars were moving slowly in the morning rush hour, and there was no sign that anything strange had happened during the night, just a world full of people who seemed to have a plan.

His mind was working in sprints that he could barely keep up with. Surely it must have all been a dream. He had read a lot of books, and he could say with confidence that none had ever mentioned sightings of half-eagle, half-man harp players with low hanging moustaches. Especially not in Briley Heath, the suburb of the big city of Birmingham that he lived in. It would have been all the talk in The Golden Lion. It must have been a dream, he told himself.

But yet it felt so real. He knew. To his core he really knew he had lived it last night. Just the thought made his head hurt. Maybe breakfast would help.

As he walked into the small kitchen, his bare feet cold on the linoleum floor, he saw a note pinned to the front of the rusty old fridge.

Barry,

I've been called in for an extra shift down the pound shop, won't be back before you go to work. You can scrape the mould off the bread and have toast for breakfast, which is more'n you deserve after coming in so late last night. See you tonight.

Mum

Barry tossed the note into the bin, and after inspecting the offering in the bread bin, scrunched his nose up and returned to his bedroom to get ready for work, hoping he would be able to scrounge some more food at the pub.

This was how it always was for Barry and his mother. Little money and less food. Just the two of them, with no father around and his mother reluctant to give him more than a smattering of detail about the man. 'He was awful tall, and handsome in his own way. And by God did he like to travel,' she would say when asked, 'and he must've liked travellin' more'n he liked us cuz one day he just buggered off.'

No one in the area could help fill in the gaps, as his mother had come there alone when he was only a year or two old, and had never given much away about where she'd arrived from.

Barry did his best to shrink into the shadows but still managed to get his fair share of black eyes and sore ribs from the other kids at school, with his patched clothes and a laptop that was almost an antique at this stage not helping. No matter how much he tried, he just didn't feel like he fitted in, and daydreaming was when he felt happiest.

That day none of the distractions he tried to use at work to divert his thoughts worked. Normally he quite liked conversing with the customers and hearing the gossip, but today he was just not present. Even a deep perusal of *Foraging for Fungus* struggled to engage him, although the discovery that worms didn't have lungs and were able to survive under water did manage to distract him while he tried to understand how that worked. But still his mind, inevitably, always returned to the garden, to the willow, to Kepheus, and to Många Världar. Just the thought of the tower enchanted him, and one thing was certain: he was going back tonight. He tried to fire up his laptop to take a look online during his lunch break, but the Wi-Fi was patchy and his laptop soon froze.

At one point he found himself staring blindly into space and Tracy Lackey had to call him three times to pass her order for another gin and tonic on to Big Kevin before he heard her. 'What's into you tonight, boy? Your head is up in those clouds even more'n normal,' Big Kevin told him, as he sipped on a strong pint of stout and leant on the bar.

'There's only one thing what gets a lad all distant like that, Kev, and that's a woman,' Micky Hancock, who the landlord had been chatting to, stated in a broad Brummie accent.

'Chance'd be a fine thing that a man round 'ere would think that 'ard 'bout a woman!' Tracy said bitterly, shaking her head and causing her peroxide blonde hair, which had been hair sprayed to within an inch of its life, to wiggle side to side.

'I'd give you a thought if you'd be prepared to give me something in return,' Micky said with a raised voice, winking comically, causing all those in earshot to laugh loudly.

'You shut your mouth, Michael Hancock, or I'll shut it for you!' she said, giving him a shove, although her eyes were smiling.

Their conversation was interrupted by the grandfather clock in the corner of the pub, which chimed eleven o'clock and Barry panicked.

He sidled up to Big Kevin as Tracy and Micky continued their banter and the laughter got louder. 'Kevin, sir, I'm really sorry but I don't feel well. I know you let me off early last night, but I really think I ought to go home.'

Big Kevin eyed him keenly. 'I don't want this to be a habit, mate. I gave you the job as a favour to your old mum, but there's many more what would like the work, and none of them would need me to tell the coppers they were sixteen if I was asked.'

'Yessir, I know, I don't want you to think me ungrateful.'

'Ah go on, lad, you're a good worker normally. Come back right as rain tomorrow and we'll talk no more of it.'

He'd barely finished the sentence and Barry was gone, grabbing his coat from a hook in the corridor behind the bar and charging out the back door. If he hurried, he could just make it.

It was 11.16 p.m. when he arrived at the garden according to his old wristwatch, and no sooner had he sat down on the bench than the clock began to strike twelve. It was another cloudless night and the waxing moon shone brightly, only a day away from being full, by Barry's estimations.

The harp duly began to play and Barry hopped up, moving confidently towards the willow, careful this time to not harm any of the irises, which all seemed to have miraculously become un-trampled overnight.

He reached the strange little cloud and paused. What if the Tutelary attacked him? He had been so angry, so furious that Barry had answered wrongly; what if he did not get a second chance?

There was no fighting it, Barry decided, he had to try again. He squared his shoulders and stepped into the haze, bracing himself for the sucking, squeezing, spinning sensation which became no more pleasant the more he experienced it. Again it spat him out and once more he was faced with the Tutelary, Kepheus.

Kepheus seemed to be ignorant of his arrival and continued playing his song, a sad melancholy tune of minor falls with a gentle melody that spoke of hope.

'Good evening, Kepheus,' Barry said boldly.

Kepheus continued to ignore him.

Barry cleared his throat loudly. 'Hello, Mister Tutelary… sir,' he said, moving closer.

The eagle-man sighed dramatically and relinquished the harp.

'You again,' he said wearily. 'Why are you back?'

'I have the answer to your riddle,' Barry proclaimed proudly. He had spent much of the day mulling it over and was confident he had it right.

Kepheus laughed, although through his beak it sounded more akin to clucking, and he wiped his eye to really hammer his point home.

'That's not how it works, boy.'

'But it's a piano!' Barry cried.

'Correction — it *was* a piano,' the birdman said. 'For that was yesterday's riddle. Each day a new riddle, and for each attempt failed, the next one becomes harder.'

'That hardly seems fair.'

'Fairness has nothing to do with it.' He shrugged, a movement that looked bizarre from his winged and feathered body. 'You're trying to cross into another world and them's the rules,' he added in a blasé tone that Barry found infuriating.

'Was I at least right for yesterday's?'

'Yes of course. It was very easy. If you couldn't get that I don't see how you're likely to succeed with any others.'

Barry screwed up his face and tried to control his irritation with the guardian. 'Can I hear the next one? There's no harm in trying.'

Kepheus surveyed him shrewdly, with a condescending smile in his eyes. 'Very well.' He cleared his throat again and rose to his feet.

'With rich green branches galore,
And foliage to spare,
I stalk through the world,
In hot water I prepare.
I'm super and rich, right to the fibre,
Dining with me will keep you regular.
My head is large and can be steamy,
If you don't know me, you'll know one of my family.'

Concentration had never been Barry's forte, but he was intensely taking in and absorbing every word Kepheus recited.

'Branches galore... super and rich...' he murmured absently, working his way through the lines of the riddle. His head hurt trying to process it, it just didn't make any sense. 'Okay, so it's obviously a tree or a plant, and something you can eat,' he reasoned, looking up at Kepheus for some encouragement, but the Tutelary's face remained impassive. 'Foliage to spare, so it must have leaves. It's got a large head...' His eyes brightened. 'I think I've got it!' he announced.

Kepheus turned his gaze to him slowly. 'Yes?'

'It's a cauliflower,' Barry said with complete confidence.

The confidence turned out to be horribly misplaced, as once again Kepheus's wings spread wide as the enraged fervour took over him and the squawks, clacks and sweeping of the wings returned. This time Barry did not hang around to argue and turned tail, leaping through the cloud and back into the relative safety of the secret garden, furious with himself for again getting it wrong.

The next day he didn't even make it into work, using up some of his precious phone credit by sending his apologies to Big Kevin by text on the mobile phone that was even older than his laptop. He holed up in his bedroom, stewing over another failed attempt to gain entry to Många Världar. Verbal reasoning had simply never been an area in which he shone. Nor had numerical reasoning for that matter, but for one who spent so much time in books, not being able to successfully pick apart a riddle stung Barry deeply. He kept going over the riddle from the night before, determined to understand where he went wrong, but his memory of the lines had grown hazy and distorted as time passed and he was no longer confident that anything he thought he remembered was true.

One thing was certain though, he would not give up. It felt like a force was driving him, a level of gumption, of get up and go that he couldn't recall ever experiencing before.

His concentration was interrupted by his mum coming back from work.

'Barry, why aren't you at work?' she asked, coming into his room.

'Oh, erm, Kevin didn't want me in until later today,' he lied unconvincingly, turning red.

His mum eyed him keenly, and he felt she was looking right through him. She was a pinch-faced woman with high cheekbones and a thin mouth, and surveying his room, rubbed her eyes and ran her hands through her dishevelled blonde hair. Books were scattered everywhere across the threadbare brown carpet.

'More stories? What happened to our talk about stopping with the stories, and starting to live in the real world?'

'Sorry,' he murmured.

'Sorry?' she exclaimed, throwing her hands up in dismay. 'Sorry, sorry, sorry. You're always sorry. Don't you want t' do summat with your life?'

'Yes, Mum, I want to write stories,' Barry replied and immediately regretted it.

'Stories don't pay the bills. Why can't you be like Maisie Conlan's boy, Jordan? Apparently he's planning to become a computer technician when he grows up. There's a great need for them in Birmingham these days.'

'But I don't want to be a computer technician, and Jordan Conlan is nothing but a school bully. Didn't you ever have dreams, Mum? Ever want to do something great that would change the world?'

Mrs Birchwood's eyes glazed over for a moment as if recalling some long distant memory, and she sighed heavily. 'Perhaps,' she admitted, her voice softening. 'But I will tell you what my father told me. Life is made up of two kinds of people, the dreamers and the doers. And right now, lad, you are living in dreams and doing nothin'. D'you want to work at that pub every weekend the rest of your life?'

Barry said nothing, looking at his feet.

'No more stories,' his mother said sternly. 'As of tomorrow it's time for you to commit to the real world.' She looked at him sadly and lifted her arm to embrace him before thinking better of it and walking back out the door, slamming it behind her, leaving Barry feeling more determined than ever to make it past the Tutelary.

***

That night Barry made his way to the garden under a full moon only just visible behind a smattering of ominously dark clouds. It briefly crossed his mind that maybe the gateway to Många Världar was only open at the waxing moon, but he dismissed it immediately, refusing to accept that his window of opportunity had closed.

When he arrived at the garden the time was only 11.10 and he fidgeted with nervous anticipation as he watched the seconds tick by on his watch infuriatingly slowly. The moon passed behind the clouds and a heavy rain began to fall. He cursed loudly, wishing he had thought to bring a coat, and was glad that no one was around to hear his bad language. It was a rain of large droplets, one that had a feeling of weight, like a cloud had been thoroughly punctured.

It was with great relief that Barry heard the clock chime twelve, particularly as his watch was now so wet it had stopped working. Moving towards the willow was difficult as the bank of the pond was now slick with mud. It was with no small amount of belligerence that Barry stumbled into the dark purple irises, crumpling several of them again. He instantly felt bad, as he did enjoy how they looked, but he was in no mood to dwell on it and was focused solely on answering today's riddle and getting past Kepheus.

The rain was crashing into the pond, creating a loud thrumming, rendering Barry unable to hear any harp playing. But then who wants to play harp in torrential rain, Barry reasoned, fervently hoping that Kepheus was a fair-weather tutelary, and he would be able to just stride through into the lands beyond without having to navigate an impossible riddle.

As he swept aside the willow branches Barry slipped and fell straight through the strange fog. Falling through a cloud that already takes you apart and puts you back together was not a pleasant experience and he momentarily lost any sight of what was up and what was down. Landing heavily on his hands and knees, Barry immediately retched, bile rising in his throat. He spat on the grass and coughed, noticing that the grass was soft and the ground completely dry.

'Such a barbarian,' he heard the voice of the Tutelary say pompously.

Barry looked up and saw the giant half eagle, half man perched as usual upon his stool, harp out in front of him. The sky above was clear and bright, although the stars looked different. There was even something that looked like the southern cross, but he dismissed that as his eyes playing tricks on him; the southern cross was a constellation on the other side of the world after all. The drumming of the rain on the water could still be heard faintly from the other side but the air in Många Världar was warm and still.

'What's the problem now?' Barry said wearily, stomping squelchily towards Kepheus.

'Where to begin? Your complete disregard for my irises, your revolting regurgitation onto the grass in front of me, your continuous wasting of my time and inability to answer simple riddles, or just your general impertinence. Pick any of the above.'

'Yesterday's was broccoli,' Barry said, ignoring everything the Tutelary said.

Kepheus tutted. 'Yesterday is dead, and so will you be if you fail again.'

'What do you mean?' Barry asked sharply.

'Three in a row is as far as you can go. Be wrong thrice and meet your demise,' Kepheus recited.

'Thrice and demise doesn't quite rhyme you know, Kepheus,' Barry pointed out.

'I'm not a violent creature, and I don't always enjoy my duties, but you irritate me greatly so dealing with you may not be a hardship,' he said loftily. 'The garden presents itself to a very special few, but I'm struggling to see why it would present itself to you.'

Barry gulped. The stakes felt a lot higher now. 'Can I hear the riddle and choose not to answer?'

The tutelary nodded curtly.

'Okay, then please give me the new riddle.'

'I'm always on the move and eat very well,
But sleep forever eludes me.
I have no eyes and cannot see,
But still sunlight blinds me.
I cannot drown yet cannot swim,
You wouldn't catch me out on a limb,
I love the cast offs, but not on the line,
Your friend, though much maligned.'

Kepheus finished with a smirk upon his face and began cracking his knuckles and stretching threateningly.

Barry sat down on the grass and ignored him, closing his eyes. A lightbulb felt like it was dimly flickering in the back of his mind but he was struggling to fully illuminate it, the switch just out of reach. It rang a bell but he could not quite place where from. The lines were echoing around his mind and he broke them down. *Something that eats very well but does not sleep*, he recalled, *something blind. Something that cannot drown.* The lightbulb quickly began to shine a little brighter. He had read something recently… *Foraging for Fungus. Something in the book had no lungs so it could not drown, and they also do not sleep or have limbs…* 'I know it!' he shouted jubilantly, breaking the silence.

Kepheus looked up from a comically deep lunge he was doing, his head swivelling to the side like an owl. 'I have heard you say that before so forgive me if I don't stop preparing to disembowel you.'

Barry laughed gaily. 'Oh shut up, bird man. You will listen to me and you will grant me entrance to the realm beyond,' he said, trying to allow disdain into his voice for the first time in his life.

'That will remain to be seen, human,' Kepheus spat. 'Answer wrongly and die.'

'The answer,' Barry began softly, the hairs on his neck tingling, 'is a worm.'

CHAPTER 3

Många Världar

Barry readied himself to leap back through to the garden, to escape the awful wrath of the guardian, and dropped to an awkward crouch.

Kepheus rose to his full height, his wings spread and dark eyes flashing. Barry visibly quailed and his hands trembled.

'Welcome to Många Världar,' the Tutelary said clearly and somewhere Barry heard a chime, as if a spoon had tapped a large glass. Kepheus sank to one knee and opened his wing, to give him entry, while his hands began plucking at the harp, picking out a complicated melody but one that his fingers were clearly familiar with, a tune of welcome perhaps.

A deep sigh of relief escaped Barry's lips and he closed his eyes with a soft chuckle as he felt some of the tension lift. The past three days had been far more adventure than he had ever really wanted, but again he felt a strange compulsion deep down in his gut driving him forward.

With a brief nod at the pompous guardian of the realm, who was pointedly ignoring him and focusing on his harp, Barry walked tentatively forwards and into the land beyond.

Up ahead the hill was blocking the moonlight and Barry could barely see his feet as he moved forward carefully, unsure what to do. On the crest of the slope was the tower, looking formidable and resolute against the backdrop of the starry sky.

It was the only landmark to aim for, so Barry set his feet in that direction and began to climb the long, steep grassy hill, which was bereft of trees, giving the tower a clear view in all directions.

As he climbed a sheen of sweat gathered at the bottom of his back giving him a deep chill as the growing breeze blew against it. He wished he had brought a torch, and now felt very aware of how unprepared he had been for actually getting past Kepheus, with no spare clothes and no message to his mum.

Undeterred, he continued to climb and the tower eventually came into clear focus. It was surrounded by a wall, set back from the tower by around a hundred metres, with a single large gate set in the boundary opposite the entrance. Moving quietly towards the wall, he looked up at the tower and saw that the flag raised up from the rampart was faded and torn. The strands fluttered impotently in the wind, which had now become quite strong.

Near the foot of the flagpole was a small parapet, surrounded by the familiar crenelated walls of a battlement. But that was not what drew the eye of Barry. A lone woman stood gazing out across the realm and her thick black hair shone in the light of the full moon. Barry's feet carried him up towards the boundary wall, his eyes fixed on the woman in the tower.

She turned her head to one side and their eyes met, or at least Barry felt they did, but it was difficult to say from the distance. Certainly, she was looking at him and her beauty was overwhelming. He felt himself blush despite his best efforts not to. He raised a hand, and she raised one back, her face unreadable.

'You would do well to stay away from the wall,' a low voice said, causing Barry's heart to skip a beat, and he leapt into an odd position with his arms flung out to his sides as if he was surfing.

Barry looked at the source of the voice. A hooded figure, cloaked entirely in black, was watching him. At least he thought they were, but their face was shrouded in darkness and hidden by their hood. Despite the cloak billowing around the figure, he could tell they were slim and strong, which was only reinforced by the tip of a sword he saw appear from below the cloak as the wind lifted it up slightly.

He was grateful they did not laugh or mock his jumpiness; instead they moved swiftly towards him. He stood up straight and lifted his chin defiantly, trying to give a look of confidence or one that suggested he belonged to this new and strange land.

As they approached, moonlight fell upon the chin and mouth and he saw with some surprise that it was the face of a young woman, with smooth skin and full lips. The eyes remained hidden in shadow.

'Who—' Barry started, but the woman placed a finger over his mouth.

'Not here, it is not safe,' she whispered quickly. 'Follow me.'

She led him round the wall towards the gate, and as the wall crested the top of the incline Barry's breath caught in his throat.

Stretched out in front of them was a broad valley stretching for miles and miles, as far as a line of hills in the distance, small and dark under the night's sky. Down a long slope lay a village, with barely a light to be seen at the late hour. It was clustered near the foot of the hill and looked like something from an alpine postcard, with neat wooden roofs and stone cladding.

To their left lay a forest of spruce and pine, towards which Barry was being led. He felt confused, and much as he didn't like to admit it to himself, a little frightened. As they reached the sloping trees, the woman shoved him into a thicket and held him up against a tall pine tree, pinning his head to it with a forearm across his throat. A knife appeared that she held to his cheek.

'Who are you, stranger?' she said darkly, in a low voice. 'Talk quickly or I will carve out your eye.'

'I'm Barry Birchwood,' he spluttered, unsure what else to say.

'That is not a real name. Methinks you are a minion of Iovixa, or a Cikavac spy.'

'A minion of what? What's a chickenvat spy?' Barry choked, as the arm pressed against his neck increased its pressure.

The woman paused and inspected him closely. She smelled vaguely of wild berries and woodsmoke but her shadowy face was fierce, like a hawk. The pressure on his neck lessened a fraction, but the knife remained firmly in place, and a knot on the tree trunk was digging painfully into his shoulder blade.

'Nobody is so stupid as to pretend not to know those names,' she whispered to him.

'You're choking me!' He gasped. The pressure re-intensified on his neck as her eyes blazed. 'Please, I don't know what you're talking about, I'm not from Många Vlablar!' Barry cried. The woman released him and he fell to the ground, drawing big rattling breaths, rubbing his throat. He could feel a trickle of blood snaking its way down his cheekbone from the sharp knifepoint.

'Not from Många Världar?' the woman said sharply. 'Then where are you from?'

'I'm from a town called Briley Heath, in Birmingham, not that it's any of your business,' he replied, climbing to his feet and rubbing his neck. 'Now how about you tell me who you are.'

'You are from… the other side?' she whispered. Her hood fell back to reveal wide, slanted, almond shaped eyes. She seemed alarmed, rather than angry.

'Well, yes,' Barry said weakly.

'You give this information away too freely,' she whispered.

'How about you tell me who you are instead of telling me off and pinning me to trees and threatening to cut out my eyes,' Barry said, starting to feel an anger brewing up in him.

'Very well,' she said. 'Follow me, and I will explain.' Barry nodded, and she began snaking her way through the trees.

'I am Zosime,' she said curtly.

'Okay, Zosime, where are you taking me?'

'To someone who will know what to do with you.'

'What do you mean, what to do with me?'

'If you are truly from the other side, then this could be something we have long been waiting for. I cannot tell you any more. I will take you to Willow-Under-Hill—'

'Willow-Under-Hill?' Barry interrupted.

'The village,' she answered dismissively. 'I must get you to Tchyglock, and he will determine if you are a friend, or if you are an agent of the usurper.'

'Nothing that you're saying makes the slightest bit of sense to me.'

She said nothing, and they walked onwards in silence.

The densely packed trees they walked through were tall and their footsteps were muffled on the mossy, pine-strewn forest floor. As they moved downhill a mist started rolling across the ground giving the place an ethereal, magical feel.

Then, out of nowhere, there was a sudden whooshing sound as an arrow lodged itself in the tree just next to Zosime's head.

'Poachers!' she cried, as another arrow pinged off a branch above Barry. He threw himself to the moist forest floor, following Zosime's lead.

Zosime held a finger to her lips, and they listened cautiously. He strained his ears but could not hear a thing. Zosime made a series of gestures with her fingers, but seeing Barry's blank look, rolled her eyes and crawled silently over to him.

'Why are poachers coming after us?' Barry whispered furiously. 'We can hardly be mistaken for partridges.'

'Their game is people. These woods are out of bounds after nightfall, and they collect a coin from the suzerain for each body, dead or alive, found breaking the curfew.'

She held a finger to her lips once more and cocked her head to the side.

'Two of them, over there,' she whispered into his ear, 'at nine o'clock. Follow me, keep low and use the trees as cover. We can still make it.'

'My nine o'clock or yours?' Barry whispered frantically, but she was already moving into a low crouch and darting off.

He leapt to his feet and tried to catch up with the figure disappearing into the misty gloom. An arrow lodged itself in a tree just ahead of him, and with a panicked yelp he found himself running as fast as he could, veering away from the direction the arrow had come from. More arrows started whizzing past, but within seconds he had gone too far to be spotted. He hurtled through the trees, low branches grabbing at his face and clothes as his feet took him further downhill.

He chanced a glance behind him and ran full pelt into the thick trunk of a tree.

***

It was still dark when he regained consciousness, so he was unsure if it had been seconds or hours that he had been lying on the floor, but the damp had seeped into his bones, and his teeth were chattering. Looking down there were strange insects crawling over his legs; a caterpillar in the shape of a cross with four legs going in different directions and a tiny head in the middle, a ladybird that was purple with yellow spots, and a vibrantly orange beetle.

Disoriented and cold, he wished fervently that he had taken the Tutelary's advice and not returned after failing the first riddle, and that he was back in the warm, welcoming Golden Lion. Back on his feet, he shook off the dirt clinging to him, and tried to decide which way to go. He needed some food and some warmth; the mist was rising around his feet as the night grew old.

The trees felt less magical now, but rather menacing and dark, and the stars were hard to see through the brushy tops of the trees. He briefly considered climbing a tree but quickly ruled it out. He was not athletic to start with and trying to climb a tree with barely any branches felt foolish beyond belief. He pulled his blocky mobile phone from his pocket but it showed no signal, and the battery was almost dead. It felt strangely out of place in this world.

Remembering the rough layout of the landscape he had seen from the top of the hill by the tower, he decided to head further downhill, and back in the direction he had come from. This time, he worked his way through the brush slowly, keeping low to the ground and his ears firmly on alert for the sound of any poachers.

Barry had been walking for well over an hour in a crouched position when he finally saw some signs of life. His back was cramped and his knees and thighs complaining loudly when he at last came to the edge of the trees and saw the village ahead of him.

Lights were twinkling with the promise of warmth and he let out a sigh of relief. The tree line sat a hundred yards back from the nearest edge of the village and the moon, still glowing brightly overhead, was illuminating the cleared stretch of grass better than streetlights.

He stepped out towards the houses before quickly darting back behind some trees as he saw a guard, armed with a bow and arrow, appear on the right side of the clearing. As Barry watched, he saw another guard appear down the slope on the left side of the village, between them covering the whole stretch of the clearing.

Barry shrank back into the shadows, remembering Zosime's warning about the out-of-village curfew. The mere memory of the poachers still made him shudder with fear, the twang of bow strings and whistling of arrows ringing in his ears.

The guards met in the middle, nodding to each other as they passed and continuing in their respective directions. Barry waited, hoping they would both disappear back around the corners and the coast would be clear, but he was quickly disappointed as more guards appeared around the corners, ensuring all areas of the clearing were covered.

Barry groaned, unable to consider a way through. He followed the edge of the trees with his eyes to see if the gap was narrower at any point but was again disappointed. The forest had been thoroughly pushed back from the village. With no visible way to make it to the village, he collected as many pine needles as he could to protect himself from the cold, damp forest floor and nestled up against a tree trunk a safe distance back from the tree line, preparing himself for a long night.

As his eyes began to droop shut, Barry was woken abruptly by a loud explosion. He leapt to his feet and ran back to the edge of the clearing, peering cautiously from behind a bushy spruce.

Smoke was rising from a building on the north end of the village and the guards were all running towards the source of the commotion. Seeing his chance, Barry ran swiftly in the opposite direction to the explosion, keeping within the shadows of the forest, dancing between trees and logs and feeling rather proud of himself.

As the last of the guards disappeared around the corner, he decided to make a run for it across the clearing, pumping his arms and trying to force himself into hitherto unknown speeds. His bones and muscles were cold from the chill of lying on the misty forest floor, but they were soon burning as he charged across the clearing towards the opening to a street. He could hear shouts and calls in the distance as smoke rose from the far end of the village, but no guards could be seen. The stone walls of the village rose up before him and at last, with his lungs burning, he made it into the apparent safety of a narrow alleyway.

Barry leant against a wall breathing heavily, sweat dripping from his temples and his shirt sticking to his back. He had never been an athlete and never aspired to be one, it simply didn't fit into his life of stories and doing as little as he could get away with. Now, however, he regretted his life of idleness, as his lungs felt like they might burst into flames and a painful stitch was jabbing him sharply in the side. He felt faintly sick but forced himself to stand upright and take in his new surroundings.

The cottages were made of a rough, grey stone but the upper floors were clad with a pale wood that leant forwards over the street. The buildings felt rustic and cheery, but there was an oppressive stillness all around. The walls were high and the alley down which he walked carefully was almost pitch black. The ground was smooth with tightly fitted flagstones. Ahead he could see some light and eagerly made his way towards it.

The alleyway opened out onto a wide street with cobbled stones, lit by flickering gas lamps lining both sides of what looked to be the main thoroughfare of the village. No one appeared to be abroad at this time of night and Barry cautiously continued ahead. The houses followed the same chalet style as he had seen in the alley, and combined with the gas lights and broad boulevard-like street, it gave the impression of a wealthy little village.

Barry relaxed a little, feeling more comfortable and safer away from the forest poachers and curfew guards with their bows and arrows. The street bent around a corner and through the arches of an unguarded tower. Barry wondered if its watchers had also been drawn away by the commotion on the other side of the village, but shrugged and walked through the arches and on into what looked like the centre of the village.

Little shop signs jutted out from the walls. An apothecary, and a greengrocer. There was a butcher's, a baker's, and next to them, to Barry's great enjoyment, was even a candlestick maker's. It was picturesque and idyllic, the gleaming cobbles and stone walls glowing in the moonlight. Empty wooden stalls and sailcloth flapped in the breeze, the signs of a market stall that was no doubt busy by day, but looked a little forlorn by night.

Then, his eyes finally settled on what he had been looking for, the familiar territory of a pub.

The old wooden sign was creaking in the wind and had the faded words The Dog written on it in peeling golden letters, sitting beneath a picture of an odd dog that looked to be a cross between an Alsatian and something quite small, with large ears upon a large head, and a small body covered with lots of gold and black hair.

Coals were glowing feebly in braziers standing on either side of the entrance, and to Barry's great relief, he could see light dancing on the drawn curtains. With a deep breath he pushed open the heavy wooden door, studded with black iron, and entered.

CHAPTER 4

An Unlikely Moniker

Warmth and noise greeted Barry in equal measures, an assault on his senses after the long, cold walk through the oppressively silent forest and village streets.

A large fireplace was burning merrily, accompanied by the hum of drunken conversation across the cosy room, stretched either side of a bar which stood down some steps in the centre of the inn. Shadows danced on the walls, and the smoky room smelled of beer, stale sweat and roasted meat. Despite the hour the inn was busy but not full, and the patrons leant over their drinks to talk, as if afraid of being overheard. The further into the room Barry walked, the heavier the air became and the few faces that turned towards him looked suspicious and world-weary.

Behind the bar was a man who appeared to be the result of someone tall breeding with a bulldog. He had sagging, droopy cheeks and hangdog eyes, and very short auburn hair seemed to grow evenly everywhere except his face. His shoulders were large and muscular and he had a rounded potbelly, on which his bristly hands were currently resting.

'What kin I git yous?' he grunted, his gruff tone at odds with the small smile on his face.

'Could I get a pint, please?' Barry replied sheepishly, expecting to be laughed away.

'Ay, yous could at that. But a pinta wot?" the barman replied seriously. 'I've a grand elixir of clumpyberry, a lively essence of tomfoolery, there's a wee bit of distilled pensiveness back here somewhere, and just fresh in, the juice o' a kelpie from the hinterlands.'

Barry laughed, but stopped when he saw the deadly serious look on the bartender's face. 'I'll, erm, take a bit of the pensiveness please.'

The barman grunted and bent down behind the bar. There was the sound of clattering and banging, and Barry was almost sure he heard the cry of an eagle. When the barman reappeared there was a clay tankard steaming in front of him, the smoke drifting from the top of it hiding whatever it was inside.

'Tha'll be a five bit, lad,' he said.

Barry shoved his hand into his pocket. 'Ah, I'm afraid I don't have a five bit, I'm not from around here.'

The barman's face darkened.

'Will any of this suffice?' Barry said, pulling some coins from his pocket.

The barman picked up a pound coin and held it up to his eye. His eyes promptly widened and he threw it down onto the bar. It clattered on the wood until Barry held it still.

'What manner of thing is that?' he said. 'Where're yous from?'

'I'm from a town called Briley Heath, you know, in the other world.'

'Seven suns, boy, keep your voice down,' the barman whispered angrily, his eyes wide. 'Come round the back now, before anyone hears.'

But it was already too late.

'Eer, Dog, did ee just say ee was from Briley?' a man with a grubby face who was sitting near the fire pit just behind Barry said.

All at once the barroom became deathly silent as everyone turned to stare at Barry. He noticed now that their clothes seemed worn and run down, and their eyes haunted.

Barry felt his face go red, a problem he'd endured since childhood and been unable to shake.

Whispers started murmuring through the bar and Barry caught words like 'Other side', 'Briley', and most concerningly, 'It's him at last!'. They got louder and louder until the barman barked, 'Enough!'

Silence descended on the inn once more.

'You, come w'me,' he said, pointing at Barry. 'Nob, watch the bar,' he added to the man with the grubby face.

Not knowing what else to do, Barry obliged and went through a door to the side of the bar, following the barman down a dingy corridor and into the bowels of the inn.

The building was deceptively large, and there were some twists and turns before the barman tapped on a door and turned the handle.

It revealed a simply furnished room with a narrow bed, burning fireplace and large bay window, covered by heavy drawn curtains.

Before the fire sat a tall man who looked older than he probably was. He had the air of a Christmas tree that had been kept over from the previous year, with not much left but the bones and the sense that it hadn't expected to live this long. His greying hair was long but only in patches, and deep lines creased his once handsome but now leathery face, which had a bristly, short, salt and pepper goatee. He was skinny, but lithe, the main clue that he was younger than his face suggested. One thing was clear to Barry: this was not a man to cross.

'I require nothing more tonight, Dog,' the man croaked, looking up at the two of them as they entered. As his eyes settled on Barry they seemed to widen momentarily in shock, but the impassive look returned so swiftly to it, Barry was not sure if he had imagined it. He shifted uncomfortably on the spot.

'Sir, this lad just walked in tay the bar...' Dog said nervously.

'And...' the man prompted.

'And well, he's after sayin' he's from over... from Briley Heath,' the barman finished with a tone dripping in apprehension.

Barry fully expected another deafening silence, just as he'd experienced in the bar, but if the man seated was surprised, he did not show it.

'Very well, take a seat please Master...'

'Birchwood, Barry Birchwood,' Barry answered the lingering question.

'Take a seat please, Master Birchwood,' he said, in a tone that left Barry in no doubt about following his instruction. He obligingly sat down in a second chair next to the fire and instantly felt the warmth seep into his skin, making his cold hands tingle.

'Are you Tchyglock?' Barry ventured.

'I have been called many things, and you may call me that one,' the man said. Still no expression crossed his face and it made Barry uncomfortable, unsure if he was being mocked.

'You don't seem very surprised to see me,' Barry said, trying to fill the awkward silence.

'Unfortunately, I am not surprised at all,' he said.

Barry started to speak but the man held up his hand to stop him, and pulled an odd-looking pocket watch from within his patched and frayed cloak. He inspected the multiple whirring hands and nodded, and then the door opened.

Zosime strode into the room, her eyes wild as she pushed back her hood. Long dark hair fell back in a military-tight ponytail as the hood fell, and now, in the light of the room, Barry saw that her eyes were a curious violet colour, while her skin was pale. She was younger than he had previously thought, and couldn't be too much older than he was. Her face had a tautness about it, like it had been drawn into a scowl for too long, like it had seen too much, like it was angry. Yet beneath that, there was a raw, rough-edged beauty. Barry realised he was staring and promptly tried to look anywhere else.

Her eyes fell on him and her face softened just a fraction. 'You made it,' she said with relief. 'I was afraid the poachers had taken you.'

'My route here was a little roundabout,' Barry said cautiously, still not sure whether the duo was friend or foe.

'Did my diversion help?' she asked eagerly.

'Were you the cause of the smoke? If so then that was a very great help, I wouldn't have been able to get to the village otherwise.'

Her mouth had been thin and tight but relaxed into the hint of a smile. 'I am glad,' she said and pulled off her cloak to reveal that underneath she was wearing jet black, leather clothing and a curved sword hung from one hip. In a sheath at the other hip was a dagger that felt all too familiar. Barry found himself rubbing his cheek, suddenly conscious of what a mess he must look.

She sat on the edge of the bed, the only place left to sit.

'You knew we had met?' Barry asked Tchyglock.

'Evidently. Now I would hear your story from your own mouth.'

'Oh, well, okay. It's not a very interesting story though,' Barry warned self-consciously.

Neither of them said anything, so Barry proceeded.

'Well, I'm Barry, as I said before, and I work at The Golden Lion most of the time, but my mum is always on at me to find a vocation in life. I'd like to write stories, but mum doesn't think much of that idea either. Anyhow, I often go to this little garden to read my stories, and when I did the other night, I heard a harp playing. I followed the sound and came up against the Tutelary, Kepheus, who didn't seem to like me too much. I got the riddle wrong twice, but then on the third time I knew the answer was a worm because I'd just read about them in a book.' He took a breath before ploughing onwards. 'Well then I walked up the hill, saw the girl on the tower and Zosime took me into the woods before cutting my cheek and accusing me of words that meant absolutely nothing to me,' he said, looking crossly at her. 'Well, then the poachers came, I lost sight of Zosime, ran away from the poachers and…' He paused and decided not to tell them he had knocked himself unconscious on a tree. 'Well then I found the village and when the smoke started up I made a break for it into the woods. I found this inn, and well, you know all this anyway I guess,' he finished meekly.

Zosime was staring at Tchyglock. 'You cannot think that he is—'

'That I'm what?' Barry asked slightly indignantly.

'He's a man child!'

'Oi!' Barry said tamely.

'Look at him, Tchyglock. He's a wet blanket, a fawning slackhound—'

Zosime was silenced by a raised hand from Tchyglock. The man seemed to have a natural authority that oozed out of him. 'Not all presents are gift-wrapped, Zosime,' he said. 'Did you expect a ready-made warrior? No such person exists on the other side.'

A slow smile began to appear across her mouth and it lit up her whole face. 'Then the prophecy is true? He is the one?'

Tchyglock turned to Barry. 'You have done well to get this far, all things considered, Master Birchwood. We have been waiting for you for a very long time.'

CHAPTER 5

The Luellason Dynasty

'Now it is time to tell you something of us,' Tchyglock said, interlocking his fingers and resting them on his lap.

Barry was too busy glowering at Zosime. He didn't know what a slackhound was, but it didn't sound good.

Tchyglock's face cracked and creased into what looked like an attempt to smile but it showed far too many teeth. 'You said you liked stories, boy. I'm about to tell you a story that will whisper throughout eternity. Nobody is forcing you to stay, but hearing a tale never did any harm.'

Barry swallowed his anger at Zosime's insults and nodded.

Tchyglock drew his patched cloak around him and began speaking in a strong and clear voice.

'Long, long ago, the empire of Många Världar was beset by war. It is a land of many creatures, and not all of them are creatures of good intent.

'The giants who roamed in the south western lands of Drumban were many and they fought long and hard against the armies of the emperor Nuvua Luellason the First. They were cruel and wanted nothing but anarchy and man-meat. But the emperor was mighty and after many bloody years of war and violence, the giants were forced back to Drumban, across the Jaguar Mountains, in the far south-west of Många Världar.

'The eight kingdoms prospered under the rule of the first Luellason dynasty. She had restored peace, and all of the races and creatures lived together harmoniously once more, caring little for the differences that made them all unique and interesting. When Nuvua eventually passed, a succession of great emperors followed. All were just, fair and much beloved, and the land was whole.

'Years and generations passed and Många Världar was prosperous, with all the normal ups and downs but none too high or too low. But then, fourteen years ago, some eight hundred and twenty years after the end of the Giant War, rumblings started growing in the north. There was talk of a gang of warlocks playing with dark forces that they should have known better than to meddle with. They began to stir up trouble in the kingdom of Y'ronga, which had long felt forgotten by the distant capital of the empire. The warlocks turned the people in the far-flung land against the folk in the other member nations of Många Världar with easy talk of mindless patriotism and pointing fingers of blame at other peoples and nations for anything that they were dissatisfied about in their own lives. Once the warlocks had filled Y'ronga with poisonous lies that soured the hearts of people throughout those lands, they renamed it the Y'ronga Republic. The emperor at the time was Malásso Luellason, proud descendant of Nuvua, and she was determined that the empire would not descend back into war under her rule. She travelled south to Y'ronga to speak to the people there and meet with the gang of warlocks, to mollify them and ensure peace was kept throughout the realm.'

Tchyglock grew still for a moment as his face darkened. The flames of the crackling fire in the hearth seemed to shrink back. Zosime's eyes were closed and a pained look sat heavily on her face.

'When the emperor crossed the Cofi Forest and entered the land of Y'ronga, her party was set upon by bandits under the command of the warlock gang and all but the emperor were slain. Fire and rage burned in the pit of the emperor's heart, but still she put the people first and tried to sue for peace. She was taken to Durag, the capital of Y'ronga, in chains and paraded through the streets like a circus animal. The people jeered and threw rotten fruit at her, but she held her head high and did not bow when greeted by the gang of warlocks at the city walls.

'It was there she discovered the truth of the poisoning of Y'ronga,' Tchyglock stated bleakly. 'The gang of warlocks had been seduced by an offer of power, and their minds overthrown by a single powerful sorcereress. A sorcereress named Cikavac.'

He paused to let his words take effect, taking a deep drink from a pewter tankard beside him before continuing.

'Cikavac had black eyes and a power to rival that of even the ancient magic of the throne. Emperor Malásso offered unprecedented concessions to the sorcerer, a freedom from the crown that no other protectorate had ever enjoyed. But Cikavac laughed and shouted for more. The emperor could offer no more without risking rebellion and chaos throughout the empire and she asked to withdraw. But Cikavac had never had any intention of parlaying with the emperor, and even less intention of releasing her. Instead, she set her mind against Malásso, calling dark forces from the underworld to her side, and the very earth shook beneath them with the awesome power she called forth.'

'Sacrilege,' Zosime muttered and Tchyglock nodded softly.

'But no matter what she tried, she could not break the fortress that was Emperor Malásso's mind,' he continued. 'Realising now that she could not reason with the madness of Cikavac, who was intent only on destruction and power, Malásso began to plot her escape. But alas, she had not reckoned on the power base Cikavac had already built, and as she began to draw in her magic, the wall behind Cikavac began to slide sideways. Into the room marched a man the size of a castle. Cikavac had summoned Iovixa, the lord of the giants, and a fearsome hunger was visible on his brutish face. Again, the emperor gathered her power and prepared to fend off the leader of the giants.'

Tchyglock paused to take a sip of water before continuing.

'But then Cikavac joined her sorcery with the power of the gang of warlocks, who had gathered behind her. As the mighty emperor turned to face her gathered foes, intent on incapacitating them swiftly, she was swept up from behind by the long, veined arm of Iovixa. Before she had chance to defend herself...' Tchyglock gulped audibly, 'he ripped her cleanly in two.'

Zosime wiped a tear from her tightly drawn cheek, and the light in the room seemed to dim as if out of respect for the memory of the fallen Emperor Malásso Luellason.

Tchyglock coughed and took a sip from a flask next to him before continuing. 'Många Världar never knew it had to defend itself, did not know its emperor had fallen, did not know that the giants were coming once more. They had no time to gather their armies, no time to prepare for war. Much of the empire fell swiftly, and the poisoned minds of Y'ronga spread across all of the realm. Not content with claiming the title of emperor, Cikavac named herself suzerain of Många Världar, or almighty overlord. To us she is known only as the usurper. We have lived in darkness, under the black heart of the usurper Cikavac ever since.'

A silence fell upon the room, as Tchyglock sank further into the folds of his cloak, and Zosime gazed firmly at the fire.

Barry cleared his throat. 'That's a terrible story and I'm very sorry for you both and your empire. But forgive me, I still don't quite understand what it has to do with me.'

'You remember the tower we met next to?' Zosime asked.

'Of course,' Barry replied.

'Imprisoned in the Watchtower of Donnau is the last remaining member of the Luellason royal bloodline. Malásso's husband, Emperor Consort Curlan, and her children, Princes Oshin and Sesanda, were slain in the brave but fruitless defence of their lands. Only one remained. Princess Lahlia was too young to fight and had been kept protected by the most loyal of royal guards, right to their bitterest end as the giants overran them all. Cikavac and Iovixa took power, and instead of granting Lahlia the release of death to join her family beyond the clouds, they trapped her and forced her to watch the destruction of everything she held dear. Once a watchtower to warn of oncoming trouble, now all it watches over is fear and decay. It is a fate worse than death.'

'But it means she's still alive! And the bloodline can take the throne once more!' Barry exclaimed.

'That,' Tchyglock said, 'is where you come in.'

'You want me to give Lahlia her throne back?' Barry said incredulously.

'To give implies ownership. Get it back though… perhaps,' Tchyglock said, a faint smile again playing on the corners of his mouth. Barry was beginning to find him more than a little condescending.

'I think I can say with total confidence that you have the wrong man,' Barry said.

'There is another part of the story that I omitted.'

'Wonderful,' Barry muttered, loud enough for the pair to hear.

Zosime looked at him disparagingly. 'Tchyglock are you sure—'

Again Tchyglock cut her off with a raised hand. Barry was also beginning to find that particular habit rather irritating.

'Before the fall of Emperor Malásso she was visited by a warlock. Not one of the gang of warlocks, but by one of the honest warlocks of Många Världar who stayed true to the code that binds them. This warlock was known well to the crown for he was of an ancient royalty himself. The warlock told the emperor that he had been visited by a prophecy that had come to him and invaded his dreams. The message was clear — if she went to Y'ronga, Många Världar would fall to the giants once more. The emperor scorned him for believing there is truth in dreams, for she had become too confident in the strength of her hand. But there was another part of the prophecy that had descended on the old warlock. It spoke of the fall of Många Världar, the misery the gang of warlocks would spread, and of their only chance of victory against the dark powers in the west — a saviour from beyond the willow tree, a saviour from the other side. The voice that spoke to the warlock said the saviour would come at the darkest hour and could save Många Världar,' Tchyglock finished emphatically.

Barry could not help himself. He began to laugh. He laughed until his sides hurt. Just when he thought it was subsiding, he thought of telling his mother that he was the saviour of a magical land, and he tumbled into laughter all over again.

Finally, the laughter stopped and he wiped tears from his eyes. He noticed that neither Tchyglock nor Zosime seemed to see the funny side.

'Come on, surely you must see how absurd it is to think that I am the saviour,' Barry said. 'Just look at me,' he said, tugging at his muddy, soggy clothes and skinny legs.

'The most important strength is not in the size of muscles, nor is the quality of a man in the clothes he wears. Tell me, how many attempts did it take to get past Kepheus?'

'Three,' Barry said sullenly.

Tchyglock nodded. 'Yet after failing twice and facing his wrath you did not turn away, you persevered. I wonder why that was.'

Barry shrugged.

'Did you feel compelled? Like there was something greater than yourself driving you onwards?'

'I did actually,' Barry admitted.

'And once you gained entrance to our lands, despite being faced with a heavily guarded tower, being threatened and cut by a hooded woman, shot at by poachers in the forest, and knocking yourself unconscious—'

'I never told you that!' Barry exclaimed, his hand going unconsciously to his tender head, where he could feel a tell-tale egg-shaped lump blossoming.

'And despite that,' Tchyglock continued, ignoring Barry, 'you still managed to find your way through a vast forest and gain entrance to the village after curfew.'

'That was only because of Zosime distracting the guards,' Barry protested feebly.

'You are rather whiny, and clearly spend too much time indoors—'

'Say what you really think, why don't you,' Barry interjected.

'You're scrawny and weedy—'

'Oi!' Barry objected.

'And have no respect for your elders or the plight of the land you have entered,' Tchyglock finished. 'But you do have courage and determination, and I see in you a lifetime of potential just waiting to be fulfilled. It is you the prophecy spoke of, and we would ask for your help.'

Barry bowed his head and rubbed his tired eyes. It occurred to him that he'd missed out on an entire night's sleep.

'Look, I'm so sorry for what has befallen Många Världar, I truly am. I do respect your plight, but like you said, I'm scrawny, I spend too much time indoors reading stories, I never wanted to be in one, not really. I'm sorry, but I don't think I can help you,' he said and got to his feet. 'If there's somewhere I could sleep until curfew is lifted, I will be on my way back to where I belong in the morning.'

He nodded politely to the impassive Tchyglock and a visibly seething Zosime, and pulled open the door. The sound of loud singing could now be heard from the direction of the bar. Barry walked back along the corridor and into the comparatively bright lights of the bar room. There was a huge cheer as Barry entered the room, and he was immediately pulled into a rough embrace by the grubby man that Dog had called Nob.

'Praise be to t' seven suns, the Cloud Runners and everyone else. The saviour's here!' he announced to the whole bar, with tears in his eyes.

Another huge cheer erupted and everyone leapt from their seats to rush towards Barry.

'No, I'm sorry, there's been some kind of a mistake,' Barry tried to say.

But Nob just hugged him again, and cried ''Ere, lads, 'e's awful modest too!'

Another cheer, and Barry's arm was wrung nearly out of the socket by tearful and smiling faces that looked like they had done nothing but frown for an age. Dog pushed the pint of distilled pensiveness into Barry's hands. It was still smoking slightly, but he could just about discern a forget-me-not blue liquid beneath it.

Everyone stood back as if to expect a speech and Barry flushed again, his face turning a deep beetroot red.

'Look, everyone, I don't know how to tell you this...' he started timidly.

Someone shouted, 'Drink!' from the back of the room, and everyone laughed and banged their tankards and glasses upon the tables and stamped.

Barry laughed in spite of himself. He peered at the distillation of pensiveness dubiously.

'Don't look at it, boy, drink it! Nobody said the saviour had to be sober!' a woman near the front of the throng crowed.

He grinned sheepishly and took a sip. It tasted like an autumn day, like leaves falling from old chestnut trees and crunching beneath his shoes. It was incredible. He raised it back to his mouth and downed the whole lot, pushing the crowd into a frenzy of cheering, clapping and stamping.

Barry wiped his mouth and opened it to continue his apology. The words seemed to stick in his mouth. Immediately all of the thoughts about what to do seemed to be happening at the same time in his head. The pros, the cons, the shame, the pride, the dreams and the fears.

He set the clay tankard down on the bar with a dull thump, and held up his hand to silence the crowd, immediately feeling as irritated at himself as he had been towards Tchyglock for doing it.

Before he'd even processed his pensive thoughts, he found himself needing to talk. 'I don't know what I can do to help, but I am at your service,' he said simply, going bright red.

He saw Tchyglock and Zosime appear behind the bar and a smile had managed to find its way to both of their faces, but both were lost to him as the crowd swept him up once more, with drinks pushed into his hands along with all kinds of food, some of which looked like nothing he had seen before. A calm contentedness fell upon Barry, and to his great surprise, for the first time in his life he felt like he was exactly where he was supposed to be.

CHAPTER 6

A Very Small Journey

It was still dark when Barry was shaken roughly awake. He was lying on a long, thinly cushioned bench in the bar and someone had thrown a moth-eaten blanket over him.

Tchyglock's face loomed over him, and he put a finger to his lips to silence Barry who had jumped at the sudden arousal. He beckoned to Barry to follow him, and led him again through the rabbit warren of corridors through the back of the inn and up two flights of rickety wooden stairs that spiralled upwards, downwards, at times sideways. Eventually they entered a room with a doorframe so small that Barry had to squat right down to enter.

Zosime was standing at the window of a small room with an uneven floor, looking out at the dark street below, and did not turn around. Barry was faintly aware of a distant banging.

Tchyglock moved straight to the opposing wall and murmured something indistinguishable to it. To Barry's amazement the entire wall became completely transparent. He could see outside, over what felt like a precipice, and he noticed that they were a lot higher up than he had realised, and far higher than the inn had appeared to be from the outside. It was raining heavily, his head was very sore, and he fervently wished he could have been left a little longer under the moth-eaten blanket.

'Zosime, come here,' Tchyglock commanded in the hushed tones people always use before dawn. She turned, walked over to them and stood before him expectantly. From within his cloak Tchyglock produced what looked like a tobacco tin. When he opened it there was a series of tiny jelly-like creatures that were muttering in high pitched squeaks, and unmistakably, farting repeatedly.

'You know what to do,' said Tchyglock said, looking at Zosime

She nodded, picked up one of the farting jelly creatures, and to Barry's total disgust, popped it into her mouth and began chewing.

If it bothered her, Zosime did not show it. She gave Barry a wink and promptly disappeared.

Barry let out a distinctly unmanly squeal, before Tchyglock clamped his hand over his mouth.

'Do not move your feet,' he said and pointed at the floor where a tiny woman clad in black was running towards the opaque wall.

'Barry, listen carefully,' Tchyglock said, coming uncomfortably close.

Barry wondered briefly if he was still asleep and rubbed his eyes as his brain tried to compute what he was seeing.

Tchyglock slapped him on the face. 'I said listen carefully,' he snapped again, as Barry felt rage course through him. 'We do not have much time. We must travel by waterway; it is the only safe way to travel. I would prefer to give more explanation, but the giants are coming and we must make it to the nearest headquarters of the resistance. Eat one of these,' he said, pointing at the jelly creatures whose farts smelled strongly of eggs. 'It will shrink you down to insect size for the duration of our trip. You must stay close to me; if not, you will certainly die.'

'I'm not eating one of those things,' Barry said flatly, and promptly received another sharp slap to the face. 'I swear to our merciful lord—' he started furiously.

'Talk less and cop on to yourself, boy,' Tchyglock snapped, and shoved one of the creatures into Barry's mouth. He clamped a hand over Barry's mouth, leaving him with little choice but to chew on the tiny farty creature. At first it tasted like one of the jelly sweets he used to buy with his earnings on a Saturday morning from Mrs Griffith's Supa Scoops Sweet Shop in Briley Heath before it had gone out of business like so many of the shops had, but then the flavour of eggs and vomit kicked in and he nearly retched.

The retching caught in his throat, however, as the world became blurry and he felt his body contracting inwards. It wasn't painful but was certainly not pleasant either as the low ceiling rushed away from him.

Barry landed flat on his face on the hard, wooden floor which now felt the size of an ocean to him. Every tiny bump in the grain of the floorboards felt like a hill he had to climb. He pushed himself up and immediately threw himself sideways with a scream as he saw something huge rushing downwards towards him.

As he cowered on the floor and found that he hadn't been attacked he looked up. Standing beside him was Tchyglock, looking perfectly calm, and perfectly tiny.

The door that had seemed small before, now looked like a wall of wood stretching to the sky, and the windows looked like they would fit in the biggest of cathedrals.

Barry felt lightheaded and swayed on the spot, but Tchyglock caught him before he toppled over again.

'I realise it can be a bit of a shock to the system the first time you eat a splodgeworm, but the nausea will wear off quickly.'

Barry answered by being sick on Tchyglock's shoes.

Tchyglock did not seem to care, instead grabbing Barry roughly in the crook of his arm and forcing his head up to meet his gaze.

'The nausea will pass, but the next few hours may not be very enjoyable. Can you swim?'

'Well I did get my green stripe for swimming a length…' Barry started.

'Perfect. Just go with the tide, stay close to me and you should be okay.'

'I dislike the word *should* in that sentence,' Barry said suspiciously. 'Where exactly are we going swimming? We're on the top floor of a pub.'

'Come,' Tchyglock said simply and began to march towards the transparent wall of the pub which now felt a long way away. Barry ran to keep up, his tiny legs pumping and feeling like they weren't making much headway.

When Tchyglock reached the wall, he didn't hesitate and simply strode right through, with a faint 'plop' sound. Barry pressed a hand to it and it seemed to bounce back, as if the wall were made of rubber.

He tried to do as Tchyglock did and walk into it, but again his body bounced back, landing him on his backside. Tchyglock's head stuck through the wall, giving him a strange, disembodied appearance.

'Focus not on the wall, but on the other side,' he said, before plopping back out of sight again.

Barry swore loudly at Tchyglock but tried to do what he said. He looked beyond the wall. He could see shadowy buildings beyond, rain pelting down heavily and the drains overflowing with water. There was a ledge beyond the wall and he ran towards it.

Rubbery pressure pushed at him momentarily, but with his eyes firmly focused on the outdoors it quickly gave way, and with a sucking pop he was standing on the ledge and instantly getting very wet. Each raindrop felt like a pond emptying on top of him and he found himself trying to jump between them.

'Over here!' Tchyglock yelled, from the edge of the ledge, and Barry ran over to him. The crashing of water onto the stone was almost overwhelming; it felt like standing behind a waterfall.

When he reached Tchyglock, the man was soaked to the bone and windswept. He shouted something at Barry.

'What?' Barry screamed. He could see Tchyglock's lips moving but could not hear a word over the roar of the gutter next to him, which looked as fast flowing and broad as the Amazon River. 'I can't hear you!' he yelled at Tchyglock in frustration.

The older man rolled his eyes in irritation and Barry did not need to be a lip reader to understand the nature of what he was saying. Tchyglock looked intently at Barry, as if weighing him up, and then, without warning, grabbed Barry and shoved him, head-first, into the gutter.

Barry sank deep into the water and immediately felt his body being dragged along by the rapids, as the gutter sloped downwards and the rainwater rushed with it. Something hit him hard on the shoulder, winding him, and he saw the stem of a leaf float past him. It was as big as he was.

With the wind knocked out of him, he involuntarily gasped for a breath and inhaled a mouthful of water. Mercifully, a pale green leaf floated beneath him and he used it as a springboard towards the surface, soaring above the water, coughing and spluttering as he went.

He splashed down on the surface of the water and grabbed hold of a passing twig. It looked like the size of a tree trunk to Barry in his new micro-sized form and it helped him keep his head above water in the rainwater rapids.

'Hold tight,' he heard Tchyglock's voice yell from somewhere behind him.

Rushing towards Barry was the reason for Tchyglock's warning. The gutter sloped sharply down towards the gaping black hole of a drainpipe.

Barry frantically tried to push himself backwards from the log, fruitlessly swimming against the tide. Tchyglock floated idly past him, astride something that Barry didn't have time to process, and gave him a wink. 'Don't fight the inevitable,' he shouted and disappeared into the black hole. Barry could have sworn he heard the sound of laughter, and then all went dark.

Roaring filled his ears and he covered his head as he was pelted with gutter debris being washed away in the torrential rain. He noticed he was screaming.

It was pitch black, he felt oddly weightless and the drop seemed to last forever. Another leaf floated idly past him and he grabbed it, desperate just to have something to hold on to as he plunged to what he was sure would be his death.

At once the roaring of the water grew even louder and was mixed with a crashing and splashing sound that almost deafened Barry. He dared to look down and saw some daylight, but his relief was quickly replaced by terror as the iron grate of a storm drain swam into focus. Hitting the metal would mean certain death, but being buffeted and pelted as he dropped, it was near impossible to know if he would make it through one of the slats. Holding onto his leaf, he tried to manoeuvre it to become a sort of parachute. It was too broad for him to hold either side, but by merely holding the tip it felt like the drag it created gave him a tiny element of control.

He pulled on it, feeling the speed of his descent slowing ever so slightly, and swung his legs to try and pull himself to one side. The weight of the water on him was suffocating as he swayed in and out of the main stream pouring down the centre of the drainpipe. The grate rushed up towards him and with all his might he swung himself to the edge of the pipe, and as he felt the brief opening of daylight fall upon his face, he pushed off the side of the metal drain and propelled himself, head-first, into one of the gaps in the grate.

The darkness now was complete and his other senses were on overdrive. Roaring water filled his ears, the taste of mulch, mould and things Barry tried not to contemplate were on his tongue, and the smell of rotten foliage overpowered his nostrils. He knew where the rain gutter was taking him down towards and he didn't relish the thought. The increasingly foul smell the further down he got only confirmed his suspicions.

He sensed more than saw the end of the drain as it opened up into the huge sewer below and clamped his mouth shut before the drop came, inwardly cursing the moment he had trusted Tchyglock.

As the bottom fell away beneath his legs, an arm grabbed him and pulled him to the side. For the first time since the rooftop, he felt solid ground beneath his feet.

Barry looked up and saw the grinning faces of Tchyglock and Zosime. Barry promptly threw up on the ledge in front of them and their smiles faded.

They looked wet and windswept but none the worse for wear, unlike Barry who was caked in mulch, leaves, twigs and all manner of other debris.

'What in God's name did you do to me?' he spluttered furiously. He had never felt rage like it. They didn't answer. 'I'm tired, cold, soaking wet and I stink. I'm pretty sure I have a hangover from whatever I was drinking last night, and not to mention the fact you've reduced me to the size of a peanut and thrown me into a drain that nearly killed me at least a dozen times, with no explanation.'

'We needed to see what you were made of,' Tchyglock said.

'And?' Barry said, fighting down another wave of nausea.

'You have done well, boy,' he said gruffly. 'It is not many could survive the journey from the secret room to the sewers.'

'Forgive me if I don't celebrate,' Barry responded caustically.

'Using a leaf to glide through the grate… I have not seen that before,' Zosime said, with almost a faint hint of admiration in her voice.

Barry looked at her hesitantly. 'That? That was just a desperate attempt to use physics in my favour. I read a book once—'

Tchyglock held his hand up again, making Barry's blood boil all over again. Before he could explode the mysterious man started talking.

'The giants are coming, we believe, to destroy Willow-Under-Hill. We had to get you out before they descend on the village once more.' As if on cue, a booming sound seemed to shake the very earth they were surrounded by. 'None from the inn will talk to anyone of your arrival,' Tchyglock continued, speaking faster now, 'but it is vital we keep your identity a secret until you are ready.'

'Ready for wha—'

'We must take you to Burroha. From there we train, and we will answer all of your questions. The safest way to travel is splodgewormed.'

Barry's face scrunched up as he thought of the jelly like creature he had eaten.

'They reduce us to this size allowing us to move freely,' Zosime added. 'But when this size, the fastest way to cover ground is by water.'

'Come, we must keep moving. It is a long journey to Burroha,' Tchyglock said. 'Follow me.'

He began walking along the ledge and another thick pipe appeared overhead. It was a deep copper colour.

'The water in here is clean and fast flowing,' he said. 'Once we are in the pipe, the key is to sit astride a leaf and pull the front up, to use it like a toboggan.'

Not waiting for a reply, Tchyglock grabbed hold of a bolt at a pipe joint and hoisted himself up, scrambling on top of the pipe before hastily disappearing.

'Why didn't he tell me that before pushing me into the gutter?' Barry asked Zosime furiously. 'I nearly died countless times.'

'Like he said, we needed to see what you were made of,' Zosime said matter-of-factly. 'Some of us still do,' she added, an edge in her voice.

Barry ignored her and tried to follow Tchyglock, but struggled to pull himself up. With Zosime watching on, he felt painfully aware of how spindly his arms were. She put her hands beneath his feet and launched him upwards.

He nearly slid straight over the pipe and down into the stream of sewerage below, but managed to hook a hand onto the edge of a small hole in the pipe. Even in his micro size form, Barry still had to wriggle to fit through the hole, which to his normal size eye would have appeared as little more than a crack.

The sound of the splash as he dropped into the icy cold water echoed all around as he again fell into pitch black darkness. He rose to the surface spluttering and trying to tread water. A more graceful plop told him Zosime had joined him.

'Here, take this,' Tchyglock's voice said right next to Barry, making him jump out of his skin. He felt something leathery being pushed into his hands, and the loss of his hands momentarily sank his head back beneath the surface. The water here was much colder than in the gutter and Barry could feel it starting to chill his bones.

He kicked himself back above the water and tried to move the leaf Tchyglock had given him into position. It was incredibly heavy and did not seem to want to move where he wanted it to.

'Are you both ready?' Tchyglock asked, his voice echoing back at them in the dark metal pipe.

'Yes,' Zosime said.

With a superhuman effort Barry splashed and kicked and forced himself up onto the leaf, and was supremely grateful that the darkness kept the other two from seeing the singularly ungraceful position he had assumed.

'Ready,' he grunted.

'Barry, lie flat on the leaf and use your arms to propel you forwards. The pipe slopes steeply downwards shortly, at which point you will need to sit up, pull the front of the leaf up to prevent it from driving underwater, and use the stem as a rudder.'

'Super,' Barry said in a voice dripping with sarcasm.

Very soon his shoulder muscles were screaming at the exertion and it was with huge relief that he felt the pipe begin to slope downwards and the current pick up. He then found, to his great surprise, that he began to rather enjoy himself.

As his eyes became more accustomed to the darkness, he was able to make out the shadowy shapes of his companions, as well as the larger obstacles of leaves or stones to steer himself around as their leaves whizzed along on the ever quickening current. Every now and then he'd hear Tchyglock shout 'Left, left, left!' or 'Right, right, right!' when the pipe forked, and he would nudge the stem of his leaf deftly one way or the other and follow the stream to who knew where. The booming from above ground grew louder, the pipe itself shaking at one point, before it slowly began to fade away.

Barry lost track of time completely down there in the subterranean watery rollercoaster, but when the pipe finally opened out onto the real world many hours later, the sunlight was blinding.

The pipe had led them out onto the side of a low hill and into a stream that had carved a path for itself into a dyke passing between two much larger hills. The dyke was picture perfect, with the stream broadening out and becoming a small river running through the centre of the valley, which was covered with wildflowers, weeping willow trees and ancient oaks, and birdsong chittered peacefully on the warm breeze. On the banks of the river sat a collection of idyllic chocolate-box cottages, hewn from logs, with thatched roofs.

The three of them floated on through the valley in silence, absorbing the tranquil scene before them after their hours navigating the dark sewers. After a while their surroundings grew wilder and more remote as the hills became mountains and no sign of habitation could be seen.

Night had fallen when they reached a towering, peaked mountain and Tchyglock, who was floating a few yards ahead of the other two, signalled to the left and Barry saw a tributary of the stream leading, to his bitter disappointment, through an opening back into the mountainside.

This time, however, the tunnel was less dark, and seemed to be illuminated by a greenish glow on the walls. The sides of the passageway were wet and mossy, and when Barry reached out to touch it, the luminescence came off onto his fingers. 'The moss is glowing,' Barry exclaimed, to himself rather than anyone else.

'Well spotted,' came Zosime's dry response.

Barry ignored her, too entranced by the glowing mountain. The tunnel began widening out and the roof of it got higher as they floated along on their leaves, surrounded by the echoes of dripping and the weight of the mountain pushing down on them.

They veered around a corner and the tunnel opened into a bowl that looked manmade. On the right-hand side stood a harbour of sorts, with a short jetty jutting out into the water. Tchyglock led them over to the harbour, which looked ghostly in the green light, and Barry and Zosime both steered their leaves to follow.

Barry stepped off the leaf and onto some stone steps that had been carved to lead up to the jetty and almost fell over. His legs had cramped up from the hours of sitting uncomfortably and concentrating on his steering. Zosime pulled him up and he shook his legs and massaged them to get the feeling back properly.

'Welcome to Burroha,' Tchyglock said, and signalled for him to follow. He led them towards the shadowy back of the wall to where a crack appeared all the way up to the roof, large enough for them at their full size, but hidden from view when on the water. It led to a walkway, that when full-sized would be a narrow squeeze, but felt cavernous to Barry, reminding him he stood little higher than an earwig.

High above him torches burned in brackets, casting shadows on the smooth walls of the tunnel. The path sloped upwards.

After walking for what felt like an eternity on their little legs they arrived at a huge black door, with an iron door knocker hanging high above them.

CHAPTER 7

A Hollow Mountain

Lahlia Luellason stood on the parapet of the tower and watched the giants come. The Watchtower of Donnau afforded her views through the basin of land which stretched as far as the low Cthopsa Hills and beyond across the kingdom of Paharam, lands that her family had once ruled over.

The first tinges of dawn were creeping in, as the sky moved from black to a dark blue. The ground shook.

They were coming.

Bursts of fire shot across the valley, momentarily illuminating figures so huge and vast it was beyond comprehension, even at such a distance. Then it began to rain. Large droplets at first, before becoming a heavy, sheeting rain driving down from the heavens. Lahlia heard thunder, but dismissed it as the steps of giants until a fork of lightning cracked down from the dark sky, lighting up the whole basin. Her breath caught in her throat.

There were giants everywhere.

Huge, shaggy giants, larger than oak trees, were throwing flaming torches taller than her at farms and crops. The rains were saving many of the crops, but the houses of innocent civilians burned.

As the lightning faded all that was left was the sooty glow of bonfires spread as far as the eye could see.

Lahlia sobbed helplessly, forcing herself to watch as what was left of her family's realm burned before her eyes. The giants were marching steadily towards Willow-Under-Hill, becoming even vaster the closer they came, and as the sky grew lighter. She could hear their roars and laughter now as the grey day rose and the rain drove ever harder.

Another flash of lightning and Lahlia saw something that struck even greater fear into her heart. Riding at the head of the giants was a horned black beast with huge shoulders. Stood astride it was a woman wearing a flame red crown. As the lightning whipped down the woman pointed at the ground before her and opened a huge crack in the land. She pulled the crown from her head and held it aloft. The lightning struck it and she was set ablaze, surrounded by a crackling white nimbus. She leapt from the beast and channelled the pulsing electricity surrounding her, sending a huge torrent of it into the crack in the earth. The horned beast roared and charged mindlessly into the crevasse as the nimbus around the suzerain faded.

The princess watched on in horror as from the crack a swathe of red flame, redder than the crown upon the suzerain's head, swelled out, and the unmistakable sign of clawed hands appeared on the lip of the crack.

Giants, the suzerain, and the hordes of hell. They were all coming.

***

'How are we ever going to get through that?' Barry asked, his heart sinking at the sight of the immovable black door before them.

Tchyglock winked at him and pointed to the floor where a tiny version of the main door lay horizontal on the ground. Tchyglock lifted the knocker and banged it seven times.

A hatch opened up in the ground.

'Who goes there?' a dry voice called up from beneath the ground.

''Tis I, Tchyglock, and I bring with me Zosime and one other who is new to the cause.'

The hatch slid shut and the door swung inwards into the rocky floor of the tunnel. It revealed some steps which Tchyglock led them down.

'Welcome back, sir,' a man said in the same dry voice they had heard through the gate. He was even tinier than them, and stood in chainmail, belted at the waist, with a deep green scarf at his neck.

'Thank you, Krimor,' Tchyglock said, nodding to him.

Krimor opened a door behind him, and light blazed in. 'Here, sir, you'll be needing these,' the guard said, passing a vial of lurid yellow liquid to each of them.

Barry immediately realised how parched his mouth felt and he unscrewed the cap to take a sip.

'Not here,' Zosime snapped, pulling Barry's hand sharply from his mouth, and yanking him through the doorway.

The room they entered more closely resembled a hall. It was a vast cavern, with an arched and buttressed ceiling giving it the feel of an enormous cathedral. The area they had walked into was two metres wide and penned off from the rest of the hall.

'Now you can drink it,' Zosime said, as she drank her own vial.

Barry upended his thirstily but nearly spat it straight back out. It tasted even worse than the splodgeworm, like fish on the turn.

He retched violently and then was surrounded by a blue nimbus. He gazed at his hands as lumps began to appear beneath his skin. The same thing looked to be happening to Zosime, and it was only the calm expression on her face that kept him from screaming.

There was a loud pop that sounded like it came from within Barry's own head, and all of a sudden, he was back to full size.

Zosime and Tchyglock both appeared next to him with a pop and smiled at the wild-eyed expression on his face.

'Please warn me before these things happen to me,' he rasped pleadingly. The sour taste had not been lost amid his sudden growth spurt.

'Where's the fun in that?' Tchyglock asked, his face as expressionless as ever. Barry found him incredibly difficult to read.

Tchyglock stepped over the now miniscule pen and out into the cavern beyond. There were people milling about everywhere. Silence fell upon the hall as eyes turned to see Tchyglock striding across it. The eyes all slid from respect at Tchyglock, to smiles towards Zosime, and a mixture of curiosity and mistrust as they settled on Barry, whose face turned a familiar shade of red.

On one side of the hall stood a mass of rough-hewn benches next to what looked to Barry like a street food vendor. Hordes of people sat eating and talking at the benches and Barry's stomach gave a timely rumble.

He was therefore disappointed when Tchyglock led them past it and into a maze of streets cut straight from the mountain itself. On the sides of the streets were small, roofless houses, and people waved at Tchyglock from the windows, smiles on their war-hardened faces. But not everyone resembled people in the way Barry was used to them. There were people with furry paws instead of hands, some with gills, and outside one house sat an elderly couple in chairs, and both had forest green skin. Barry wanted to look in every direction at once, and had to actively pinch himself to check that he wasn't lost in one of his daydreams.

Tchyglock led them towards one of the tunnels leading off from the cavernous room. It led them around a tight bend to a large shaft that seemed to reach high into the darkness of the mountain above. A wooden platform sat on the rocky floor amidst a series of ropes and pulleys.

A boy, not more than ten, stood next to the platform. He was wearing shorts, with socks pulled up to his knees, and a cape over a string vest.

'Mornin', babs, allrroyte? Off upstairs?' he said, to Barry's extreme surprise, in a broad Brummie accent, which didn't make any sense at all, but gave him a sharp reminder of home. Unlike everyone else they had walked past he didn't seem in awe of Tchyglock at all.

'That we are, Darvagh,' Tchyglock responded, his eyes twinkling.

'Well chop chop quick as you loike, on yer pop,' the lad said, clapping his hands to hurry them along. 'People takin' lunger and lunger about it recentlay, I won't 'ave it.'

The three adults silently obeyed, and Barry had to bite his lip not to laugh as the sandy haired boy with a young freckly face aimed a kick at Zosime's backside to hurry her along.

The moment they were all standing on the platform, Darvagh nonchalantly pulled a narrow rope next to him, and it set into motion a series of pulleys, but they didn't move.

'It doesn't seem to be working,' Barry said to the boy. Darvagh gave him a wink and waved, and it felt like someone had put a hook behind Barry's navel from out of nowhere as the platform shot upwards at high speed.

It rushed upwards like a hydraulic elevator but without the comfort of a ceiling or walls. Without thinking, Barry reached out a hand to run it along the wall as they rocketed upwards but Zosime grabbed it back.

'Are you trying to lose your hands?' she asked sharply. Barry kept his hands firmly in his pocket after that.

It was only seconds later that the lift lurched to a halt next to another opening hewn right out of the mountain.

To Barry's dismay there stood Darvagh once more, looking unruffled and picking his nose.

He gave a nod of recognition to Barry. 'Allrroyte?'

Barry was rendered completely speechless, particularly because it didn't seem to have phased his two companions. The three of them stepped off and walked to a door in an alcove of the opening.

'Actually, Zosime, on reflection, I think you can leave us here,' Tchyglock said to the young woman.

She looked as if she was about to reply, before pursing her lips and nodding. She turned and got back onto the platform.

'Gordon Bennet, love, make yer mind up,' Darvagh said, rolling his eyes.

'I've got the key here somewhere,' Tchyglock said, rummaging through the many pockets of his cloak. 'Ah, here we go,' he said, pulling out what looked like a wooden peg with various spikes along the shaft. He wiggled it around in a distinctly non-key-shaped hole, and after much metallic screeching, the lock clicked and the door opened inwards.

Suddenly they were bathed in sunlight and the sound of birdsong. The door swung shut behind them, and turning, Barry could no longer see any sign that a door had ever been there.

'I have a lot of questions,' Barry said, his head hurting as he looked around what appeared to be a large farmer's kitchen, complete with cast iron stove. Pots and pans hung from hooks around an island in the centre of the kitchen, and floor to ceiling windows gave a panoramic view of the land all around. They were on top of the mountain.

'That is to be expected,' Tchyglock said sagely. 'Come, take a seat.'

Barry sat at a high chair at the kitchen island and gazed out of the huge window in front of him, as Tchyglock busied himself with a kettle. Clouds were scudding with unusual speed across a pale blue sky, and in the far distance he thought he could make out Willow-Under-Hill and the tower beyond, but he couldn't be sure. Huge plumes of smoke distorted the miles of fields, like a patchwork quilt, stretched out between their vantage point and the long journey they had travelled. Many of the fields looked blackened from this height, Barry noticed with confusion. When he looked out of the other window, however, the view was obstructed by mountains that dwarfed the one they sat astride. High white peaks broke through the low clouds, and a vast glacier ran across and through them, towards the highest peak of them all. Rainbows danced along the mighty glacier, and Barry had never felt so small.

'Spectacular, isn't it,' Tchyglock said, putting down a steaming mug in front of Barry, and a slab of bread and cheese.

'It certainly is,' Barry said, inspecting the contents of the mug.

'It's jauce tea,' Tchyglock said, watching Barry. 'It's an excellent analgesic, anti-inflammatory and will keep you regular.'

Barry flushed. 'I'm not in any particular pain.'

'Trust me, after the ride you've been on today you will be sore tomorrow, and I need you to be fighting fit. Drink it.'

Tchyglock had a way of talking that left you in no doubt about doing what he said, Barry noticed. He sipped the tea. It was bitter and sour, and he screwed his face up. But no sooner had he swallowed than he felt a warming sensation spread through his whole body, making his fingers and toes tingle. He immediately took another large slug of it, and tore off a chunk of the bread and soft white cheese with his teeth. Even the flavours of that felt stronger and more potent than what he had ever experienced before.

'Pace yourself, boy, your body is not used to such things. A bit of a departure from diet coke, Chinese takeaways and Mars bars.'

'We could never afford takeaways,' Barry said absently, then stopped. 'Wait, how do you know about those things? They are all from my world.'

Tchyglock gave him a bleak look. 'That is a story for another day, boy.'

'And what about that lift operator boy? How did he get to the top before the lift?'

'Do not be deceived by Darvagh's appearance, he is older than you know. Older than me, perhaps older than the mountain itself, although that may be pushing it, and magic courses through him. Now we must focus. Word of your arrival will quickly spread among the Sonphea, and they will expect much.'

'Who are the Sonphea?'

'The Sonphea is the resistance. The people living in the mountain below are the resistance, or at least a large part of it. The Sonphea is all those opposed to the usurper and her gang of warlocks, and of course, the giants. We have been forced to hide and can only find safety and protection in each other. We have this base, Burroha, and the territories stretching across Paharam and Khali-Dhūmi in the north, for which I am the commander, and other bases around Många Världar, although none as large. The ultimate leader of the rebellion is Xhaffa, and he will want to meet you, as will the other base commanders, if they can find their way here. You see the minions of Cikavac are everywhere, and while she sits upon the throne in Vemohan, they are moving through the land destroying anywhere they find resistance. Do you see the smoke and blackened land out there?' he asked, pointing out the window at the fields. 'The giants have burned, maimed and destroyed everything in their path. We believe that even this morning, Willow-Under-Hill was destroyed by the giants. It is a miracle we were able to get you out.'

'Then why did we leave? We might have helped to save it!' Barry exclaimed, thinking of all the people they had spent the night with in the pub.

'You are more important than a village,' Tchyglock said simply.

'Me? Are we back on this saviour thing again? Because I don't think I'm any match for an army of giants or gangs of warlocks.'

'There are many things we must do, but you have to be trained first, otherwise you will be killed before we have even left the mountain.'

'Wonderful,' Barry said dryly.

'You would prefer to die?'

'I would prefer to be at home in bed with a good book,' Barry said, under his breath.

Tchyglock slapped him again. 'You are a selfish child. Too long you have sat coddled in your world of stories, of cowardice and avoidance of life, boy. Become a man and live the stories you read about. Too much depends on you, too many lives have been lost, and so will countless more unless we turn the tide of the battle and depose Cikavac and her minions. You complain much, and do little. Look out there, at the blackened land. Farmers have lost their livelihoods, families have lost their homes, children have lost their parents. And all you can say is you want to be at home with a book. For shame.'

Barry felt a multitude of emotions. He had never met anyone who drove him to a white-hot fury as much as this strange, expressionless man who everyone revered, who rudely held up his hand all the time, and most aggravating of all, kept slapping him across the face. But the man's words had stung him more deeply than he ever remembered Jordan Conlan managing, than his mother or Big Kev at The Golden Lion. He hung his head as the shame sank in, making his heart feel heavy.

'I'm sorry,' Barry mumbled.

'Despite all of that, I believe you are the one we have waited for. And I am here to teach you,' Tchyglock said more softly. 'If you will be taught.'

Barry looked him straight in the eyes and felt a calm descend upon him. 'I will,' he said, more clearly now. 'I am ready to do what must be done.'

Tchyglock clapped his hands. 'Good. Then let us start.' He stood and walked over to the window facing the glacier and beckoned to Barry to follow.

'Do you see the mountain at the end of the glacier?'

'The one we can't see the top of?'

'Yes. That is Pæharra. The tallest mountain in Många Världar. They call it the path to heaven, as it reaches so high that you can touch the gods themselves.' Tchyglock squinted up at the peak disappearing through the clouds. 'People say a lot of foolish things. But one thing is true, at the top of that mountain is the Sonphea's chance to save the soul of Många Världar.'

'What do you mean?' Barry asked, nonplussed.

'For some time, we have had reason to believe that Cikavac, the giants and the gang of warlocks are not working alone. That they are channelling the occult, meddling with dark forces… That they have opened the gates of hell themselves,' Tchyglock finished and looked at Barry, who scoffed loudly.

'Come on, giants are one thing, but everyone knows heaven and hell aren't real. Heaven and hell are spurious notions created eons ago to control us all. There isn't any Devil or God, there's just life and then nothing. Fact. I watched a whole TED talk on it.'

'You sound like you know a great deal about it,' Tchyglock said, seeming impressed.

'Well, you know I do like to try and broaden my mind, and facts are facts, science is science,' Barry said with false modesty.

'Gosh, you must be like a cat with nine lives,' Tchyglock exclaimed.

'No, just the one life,' Barry replied, confused.

'But you must have died at least once to know with certainty that there is no afterlife, no heaven or hell, of course. How did you reincarnate?'

'Well… I haven't died exactly, but you know… it's science…' Barry floundered.

Tchyglock smiled triumphantly. 'You have fallen into the same trap that so many from your world do. They believe nothing other than what they can see and hear. What they can google on the interweb,' Barry let that one go, 'or what you can prove with science. Isn't the beauty that we don't have any idea what happens when we die? Isn't the most wonderful thing about having a conscious mind that we have an imagination? It means that in the absence of there ever being an answer to the question of death, we get to choose what we want to believe, without any fact at all?'

Barry was stumped. He also wondered how Tchyglock, this crotchety, ageless man with such a bad haircut, knew so much about the world he came from.

Tchyglock patted him condescendingly on the head. 'You are not the first and you will not be the last to fall into the trap of absolutism on this subject. But remember, you are not in Britain now — you are in Många Världar! The world is very different on this side of the willow, and there is so much you don't yet comprehend.'

'All right, don't go on about it,' Barry complained. 'I put myself at the disposal of your clearly vast and unending reserves of knowledge.'

Tchyglock raised an eyebrow and scratched at the patchy stubble now on his cheeks, spreading from his usual goatee.

'We'll get to manners in due course,' he said blithely. 'But now that Cikavac has accessed the forces of hell, we must harness the power of heaven. It is the only way to turn the tide of the war and reclaim the land from the evil that possesses it.'

'And how exactly does one go about harnessing the power of heaven?' Barry asked dubiously.

Tchyglock pointed at the sky. 'We must speak with the Cloud Runners.'

CHAPTER 8

A Bit One-Eyed

'Cloud Runners?' Barry asked, feeling, not for the first time that day, a bit thick.

'I forget all the reasons people from your side of the willow come up with to explain clouds,' Tchyglock said with a chuckle. 'Something to do with water vapour, if I remember correctly. An ingenious idea, but another example of science trying to find rational explanations for irrational things. Do you ever notice how science is always meant to be absolute fact, but people keep making new scientific discoveries, that just disproves what had previously been "fact?"'

Barry rolled his eyes. 'So, you're disputing that clouds are created from evaporated water now?'

Tchyglock pointed at the sky, where fluffy white clouds were scudding across the sky. 'Do they look like water to you?'

'Well no—'

'Exactly. They are light, and fluffy and free of worry.'

'Clouds have worries?'

'No, that's exactly my point. And do you know why?'

'I feel like you're going to tell—'

'Because they are souls.'

'Souls,' Barry said incredulously.

'Yes, all of the souls of humans, animals, giants, banshees, vampires and all the rest rise up from the earth when they die, and they are shepherded by the Cloud Runners. They then decide what to do with them; they either get sent on to heaven, or turned to water and rained down where they seep through the ground to the underworld. We're seeing a lot of storms lately, because there are an awful lot of people who have gone over to the dark side.'

'Okay, so if I take every single thing you're telling me as the truth; that clouds are souls, they are ferried around by people living up in the sky and that rain is people being sent to hell…' He looked at Tchyglock with a raised eyebrow. 'Assuming I take all of these outrageous suggestions as gospel, how exactly are you proposing that we "speak with the Cloud Runners"?'

'For that, we must climb among the clouds,' Tchyglock said simply, and looked out towards the huge, immovable peak, which even at the distance they were from it, felt overwhelmingly vast.

'You're not serious!' Barry exclaimed. 'You'd have to be a highly trained mountaineer to even attempt that.'

'Where better to train in mountaineering, than in a mountain-dwelling community?' Tchyglock smiled. 'Which is why we need to get you started right away.'

Barry had his head in his hands. Climbing the highest mountain in a magical realm had never even featured in any of his books so far as he could remember.

'You ask a great deal,' Barry said. He felt heavy with the weight of expectation that had been suddenly landed on him.

'I ask what I must for the sake of the people,' Tchyglock replied. 'For too long the good of the world has been diminishing, the brotherhood of man reduced to hiding in mountains for fear of attack from a darkness too evil to comprehend. Nothing truly worth having ever comes easily, Master Birchwood, and the only journeys really worth taking are those where reaching the destination is an achievement.'

Barry nodded slowly. 'And what of the princess? I thought the goal was to save her?' The woman had rarely left his thoughts despite all that had happened to him in the past twenty-four hours.

Tchyglock studied him shrewdly. 'All in good time, boy, all in good time.' He clapped his hands. 'Now come, we have little time to get you trained and ready for your journey to the skies. If we can get the heavens to join our cause, then there may yet be hope for Många Världar.' He rose. 'Do you fancy travelling a different way?' he asked Barry with the faint hint of a smile.

'That depends which way it is,' Barry replied cautiously, climbing to his feet and following Tchyglock.

Before opening the door, Tchyglock turned to Barry. 'Trust me, you'll enjoy it,' he said, and pressed what looked like a doorbell on the inside of the house.

The floor opened beneath Barry's feet and he found himself falling into darkness.

After a few feet he felt his whole body land gently on smooth rock beneath him and he began sliding rapidly downwards. He realised he was in a giant stone chute and his body slid down, faster and faster.

The chute threw him around corners like he was a bobsled, gathering pace on the smooth, well-worn rock. Around him caves opened up, with stalagmites, stalactites, glowing walls and pitch darkness. At one point his descent disturbed a cave full of bats, but he had little time to worry about them as the slide swept him onwards and downwards.

Once he got over the initial shock, he found that he started to enjoy the ride. It was like being on a particularly extravagant slide at a waterpark. The deeper he got into the mountain, the lighter it seemed to get as he got towards the homes of the Sonphea. Holes opened up in walls showing the caves of families sitting in candlelight, children playing on crudely carved streets, and the air began to grow warmer as he neared the heart of activity. The chute squeezed into a hole carved into solid stone, casting Barry into pitch darkness, before flattening out into a brightness, and he skidded to a stop.

'Watch out!' Tchyglock's voice came from behind him and Barry quickly scrabbled out of the chute and leapt to the side just in time. Tchyglock came shooting out of the rockface and slid straight past where Barry's head had just been, before grinding to a halt some yards further forward.

'That was *awesome*,' Barry said, a huge grin plastered across his face.

'It does lift one's spirits,' Tchyglock agreed, hopping to his feet nimbly. 'Come,' he said, as he began striding to the opening of the cave they had landed in. It led them back to the main cavern they had arrived in earlier, but this time Tchyglock kept to the edge, until a narrow opening appeared on his left. Barry followed him into it, and along a well-trodden tunnel. The floor was softer than elsewhere in the mountain, with what looked like sand muffling their footsteps.

It opened out into a low, long ceilinged cave that was brightly lit by torches in brackets along the walls, and it smelled of sweat.

In front of Barry was undoubtedly a training facility for the Sonphea. Pens with sandy floors were separated out by wooden fencing, and within them were pairs of people sparring with hands wrapped in cotton, sword fighting, lifting weights, climbing ladders and more besides with the air full of grunts, groans and the occasional cry of pain.

'Welcome to the training academy,' Tchyglock said, lifting his arms out proudly. 'This is where the revolution begins.'

They began walking along a path at the side of the cave and Barry saw battle hardened men and women, with rippling muscles, scars and the same expressionless faces that Tchyglock sported — the faces of people who had led hard lives, and seen too much.

They came to a stop next to a pen where a stocky woman was circling an even stockier man. Their eyes bored into each other as they weighed each other up. The man was shirtless, with a thick carpet of black chest hair and an angry red scar from his armpit to his hip, looking like his body had been sewed back together. The woman was shorter but her legs were as thick as tree trunks and she wore her pale hair in a long braid down her back. Suddenly the man darted forward towards the woman and his hands moved at lightning speed.

The next thing Barry saw was the man lying face down on the floor with the woman sitting on top of him.

Tchyglock clapped. 'Very good, Matildh.' She nodded in his direction.

'What happened?' Barry asked. 'One moment the man was attacking, and the next he was on the floor. I didn't see anything happen in between. It doesn't make any sense.'

'You may have been watching, but you clearly weren't looking,' Tchyglock said cryptically.

'What do you mean?'

'Both Matildh and Rito are excellent fighters, and both have survived many battles. But Matildh is far superior because she has mastered the Oran.'

'Which is what?' Barry asked, exasperated at having to tease every detail out of his companion.

'In your world I understand that mindfulness has become very popular, yes?'

'Yes, Sally Parsnip down the pub was going on about practising mindfulness recently. It's like meditation.'

'Exactly. Well Oran is along the same lines, but it goes further and contains far more power. It is finding your inner calm, detaching yourself from the noise around you, but also allows you to rapidly speed up your perceptions, almost altering time itself. Matildh is a master of the Oran; she is totally calm and able to see things in slow motion, allowing her to react faster than an idle onlooker's eye could perceive.'

'I want to master the Oran,' Barry said firmly.

Tchyglock chuckled. 'I'm sure you do, boy. But it is no mean feat. It takes discipline, dedication and incredible determination.'

'Perhaps you underestimate me,' Barry said slowly.

Tchyglock said nothing but gave him a strange look that was half condescension and half curiosity. At that moment a man walked towards them. He was missing an eye, the skin over the empty socket was puckered and sunken, and the teeth he had left seemed to point in different directions. His face was grizzled and weather-beaten, and he looked as tough as old meat.

'Maurice, it is good to see you,' Tchyglock said, walking towards the man and shaking his hand firmly.

'And you also,' the man rasped. 'You survived your foray into the big bad world then.'

'Yes, but we only missed the giants and the hordes of Cikavac by an hour or two. The hour is almost at hand,' Tchyglock said sagely.

Maurice raised his eyebrows and looked past him to where Barry was standing awkwardly. 'Are you sure about that?' he croaked.

'I believe there is more to this one than may meet the eye. We need your help and all of your skill to mould him into a fighter and a climber as quickly as possible.'

'Hello,' Barry said quietly, not making eye contact.

Maurice walked to Barry, who held out his hand. Maurice ignored it and inspected Barry uncomfortably closely. He smelt of tobacco and sawdust.

'The boy smells like a new-born babe,' Maurice said to Tchyglock, and then began poking Barry in the arms, chest, and legs. 'And he's as soft as one too.'

'Oi!' Barry exclaimed, jumping away from the old warrior.

'Maurice is the Ohjaaja, the head of training for the Sonphea, Barry. There isn't a thing he doesn't know about warfare, fighting techniques, mountaineering, swimming and anything else we need our army to be capable of in the fight against the hordes of evil.'

'Barry sounds like the name of a horse,' Maurice said, his eyebrows furrowed. 'He's a soft, lavender soaked foal, Tchyglock. I'm good, but I can't polish a turd,' he said, rudely dismissing a very offended Barry and walking away to inspect two young men fighting with padded flails. Even with the padding, the thought of being struck by one of the huge balls of iron swung on a chain made Barry rather need the toilet.

Tchyglock marched after the training instructor. 'Maurice, be reasonable,' he implored.

'Reasonable doesn't come into it, Tchyglock, as you know. I train people to survive, to fight, to take on danger and live to tell the tale. That wet blanket wouldn't know danger if it bit him on the arse.'

'Now wait just a minute,' Barry said, his temperature rising.

'What?' Maurice said, walking over to him and poking him hard in the chest. 'Have you ever stood up for anything in your life?' he said, poking him even harder, forcing Barry to take a step back.

'I'm sorry, but I'm asking you not to poke me again, sir,' Barry said meekly.

'Or what?' Maurice sneered, this time shoving Barry backwards so that he stumbled into the wooden pole at the side of the pens.

Barry could feel his temperature rising, and the hairs on his arms were standing on end as he glared at Maurice.

'I said, or what, you pathetic popinjay,' Maurice crooned, and then gave Barry a slap around the face just as Tchyglock had done multiple times.

It all caught up with Barry at that moment. The snide comments of the Tutelary, the knife held to his throat by Zosime, the poachers' arrows, the terrifying splodgeworm drainpipe ordeal, the constant slaps and interruptions by Tchyglock, the general lack of sleep, and now this crusty old man insulting him, poking, shoving and slapping him.

Barry saw red.

He started grunting like a warthog and then released all of the rage inside of him and charged full pelt at the old warrior, driving him into the wall.

Caught completely by surprise, the wind was driven out of Maurice, and Barry took advantage of it and slapped him as hard as he could on both cheeks, 'How... do… you… like… it?' he yelled, slapping Maurice's cheeks during every pause, and finishing by poking him hard in the breastbone.

The old man dropped to his knees wheezing, his face beetroot red.

The anger fell away from Barry as quickly as it arrived and now he felt ashamed, embarrassed and very aware that people in the pens behind him had stopped what they were doing to watch, stunned, at how the events had unfolded.

'I'm really sorry, I went too far…' Barry said, leaning down and putting a hand on Maurice's shoulder. Before he could even take a breath, Barry found himself on his back with Maurice's knee in his chest and a knife at his throat. Barry had no idea how or what had happened, other than the fact that the hand he had placed on Maurice's shoulder now hurt intensely.

The Ohjaaja looked down at him, his one eye boring into him. Then, to Barry's surprise, his face broke into a big, craggy grin.

He looked up at Tchyglock. 'Maybe there is some hope for the wee runt yet,' he said to his leader, whose face had now split into a natural grin for the first time since Barry had met him.

'Please,' Barry spluttered, 'I can't breathe.'

Maurice removed the knee from his chest and instead of offering him a hand to pull him up, walked over to the pen and gazed out at the onlookers. 'What are you all looking at? I didn't call an end to training,' he barked, and everyone leapt back into their respective workouts.

'It will be hard, and you will feel more pain than ever before,' he said, before Barry realised he was talking to him. 'But if you follow my instructions exactly, I will give you a better than average hope of surviving.'

'Inspiring words,' Barry muttered under his breath.

'I'm not here to inspire, boy, I'm here to make you good. Be here at dawn tomorrow,' he croaked, nodding at Tchyglock and walking off to a pen to begin barking orders at an older woman shooting arrows at a target.

CHAPTER 9

Dynrym's and Dead-Nettles

'Remember to bend and breathe,' Zosime reprimanded him. 'You look like you're about to burst a blood vessel.'

Barry let out the desperate breath he had forgotten to release in his concentration, while trying to contort his body into what he considered an unholy position. He bit off the retort brewing in his mouth. 'Yes, Master,' he said through gritted teeth. Her insistence that he refer to her as master while she taught him the Oran had been difficult to take.

'Good, now breathe,' she said, with what Barry felt was an unnecessary amount of condescension.

The past few weeks were a blur to Barry. He didn't remember ever being so sore and bruised.

Each morning he would be woken before dawn by Zosime sneaking into the dark cave he had been assigned high in the subterranean metropolis in which the Sonphea resided, and she would then tickle his feet with a feather. Sometimes she varied it by throwing a wet flannel at his head. Neither were pleasant and more than once he used language his mother would cuff him around the head for.

After his unpleasant awakening, the two of them would go straight down to the training pens for an intense two hours of Oran drills. He was kept away from others in a walled pen where nobody could see his progress. They said it was so Barry could concentrate, but he suspected it was more so nobody could see how bad he was. Zosime worked him through a series of complex shapes, not dissimilar to the yoga that Barry had seen middle aged women practicing in the Briley Heath town hall on Tuesday evenings. But this was harder, much, much harder. While its focus was on inner calm, peace and controlling your breathing, it required you to go a step further and physically slow your heart rate while speeding up your awareness. All of that while bending and moving in a series of complex shapes and moves designed to make you a powerful fighter that used the enemies' strength against them.

Zosime was incredible at it. Her lithe body bent and shifted in ways Barry couldn't even come close to, and at first Barry could not follow her movements, they were so blindingly quick. To her credit, Zosime was unerringly patient with him, with only the barest exasperated tut escaping her lips giving the occasional indication of any frustration at the speed of his progress.

But he was improving. Zosime told him he had reached fifty percent Oran, whatever that meant.

He could now slow things down around him, and his body was becoming more supple and flexible by the day, while his muscles were hardening and his puppy fat was slipping away.

After two hours of Oran, Barry was allowed to go and get himself some breakfast and today made his way up to the dining hall, feeling wide awake despite the early hour.

It was his favourite time of day, as he would grab a big bowl of porridge and bacon, and a cup of a strange juice he had become partial to, and sit at one of the rough wooden tables, watching as the Sonphea filtered down.

For the first week he had sat alone on a table at the edge of the dining area, keeping his head down and trying to remain invisible, much like he always had during school dinner times. But then word had slowly spread through the caves like an echo, of the coming of the saviour. He continued to eat alone, but now had to endure the wide-eyed stares and rude inspections of onlookers.

He would hear the whispers: 'Is he really the saviour?' 'He looks like a stiff breeze would blow him over.' 'I'd imagined he would be bigger and better looking', and on it went, but what was even worse were those who bowed to him, treating him like a celebrity. He didn't know how to respond to it, and felt even more alone.

It had been with great relief, then, when all the tables had been filled one morning and a teenager with a small afro haircut and large ears was left with no choice but to join him.

'All right if I sit 'ere?' the boy grunted awkwardly in a strange accent that was somewhere between cockney and the west country.

'Please do,' Barry said brightly, sliding his plate and cup in to make space.

The surly young man sat down and began shovelling his fry up down his throat, avoiding any eye contact with Barry. He shovelled too quickly, however, as he began to choke on a large chunk of sausage. He clutched at his neck and his eyes bulged as he tried to clear his airways, to no avail.

Barry leapt to his feet and began hitting him on the back with increasing ferocity. Finally a piece of pork and leek mush shot out of the gasping boy's throat and landed in a pool of saliva in Barry's bowl.

'Are you all right?' Barry asked, concerned, noticing that everyone had stopped to stare at the two of them.

The young man noticed the staring faces himself, and looked deeply embarrassed, taking huge gasping breaths.

'I'm fine,' he said, returning to his former surly self and gluing his eyes back to his half-finished plate.

Barry awkwardly sat down opposite him. He looked disconsolately at the half-masticated piece of sausage sitting in the centre of his porridge, and as delicately as he could, spooned it up and set it on the tabletop next to his plate.

Noticing it, his dinner companion's ears darkened as he blushed again.

'Sorry 'bout that,' he apologised with a nod to the drooly sausage. 'Fanks for saving my life and that,' he added awkwardly through a more appropriately sized mouthful of breakfast.

'Oh, no problem, we've all been there,' Barry said with a jovial wave of the hand. 'I'm Barry,' he added, nervously holding out his hand, hoping he wouldn't be left hanging in front of the usual cast of starers.

The boy cast his eyes around apprehensively, and then sighed dramatically. With a shrug he shook Barry's hand. 'I'm Dynrym, but everyone just calls me Dyn.'

'Good to meet you,' Barry said. His eyes fell forlornly onto his watery bowl, and he pushed it to one side. To his mortification his stomach gave an enormously loud rumble.

Dyn grinned. 'Hungry, are we? Let me get you some grub,' he said, shovelling a last recklessly sized mouthful of food into his mouth and pushing himself to his feet.

'Oh no, don't worry, I'm fine.'

'Ah come on, 'smy fault your brekky's no good, ain't it. Follow me, I'll sort you out with some proper grub instead of this greasy slop.'

Barry hesitated, aware that he didn't have long before he was due back down in the training pit for his morning drills and another few hours of thankless exercise. His face hardened. 'Lead on,' he said to Dyn.

Dyn led him through the network of streets in the great hall and to a tunnel that felt more natural than most of the others, as if it had been there for millennia and not hewed from the rock by the hands of the Sonphea.

His companion stopped some way down the tunnel next to an alcove which Barry would have walked straight past. Steps disappeared upwards into the darkness and as Barry followed Dyn, they spiralled around until it came to another narrow street. Walking past several holes in the wall revealing the homes inside, Dyn stopped outside one that was blocked by a large round stone which stood in front of the entrance.

Dyn set his shoulder against it and rolled it to one side. 'I seem to be the only person in the Sonphea who values his privacy,' he said, seeing Barry's questioning look. 'I only just got my own hole, and without this stone I'd never get a moment's peace.'

They moved inside and Barry saw that Dyn's home was a lot smaller than the one he had been given. It was little more than a single cave carved out of the mountain, and they hadn't got as far as removing some of the stalactites and stalagmites, some of which had things hanging from them. A rug showed the place where he slept, and clothes were thrown haphazardly around the room. For a brief moment Barry was transported back to his own room in Briley Heath, and with a pang he thought of his mother and the worry she must be feeling. He resolved to get word to her that he was safe and well.

'It's not much, but it's mine,' Dyn said grinning. 'It was a relief to get outta the hole I was sharing with my dad, we were drivin' each other mad. He just didn't get me if you know what I mean? Not a lot of room in these mountain caves.'

'Don't know who my dad is actually,' Barry said, before realising it might sound a bit much. 'But yeah, can see why you'd do each other's heads in.'

'Well join the club, cuz I've no clue who my ma is,' Dyn said cheerily. 'Who needs two parents anyway, better off without them I reckon. Anyway,

I promised you some grub dint I,' he added, seeming more confident now he was in his own surroundings. He pulled open a small cabinet near the back of the cave and pulled out some meat and cheese.

'No one other than the refectory cooks are allowed to actually cook, what with us being in a windowless rocky hole with nowhere for smoke to be an' all, but cold food can be good too. Look 'ere, I've got some delicious cheese. Cheese is a bit of an 'obby o' mine if I'm honest, I know it's not what teenagers normally like, but there you go. People round here are only interested in fighting and dying, but sometimes you need summink else in life I reckon. Some lovely cured pork to go with it too,' he said, holding his tub of food out to Barry.

'I can't take this,' Barry said.

Dyn's ears darkened again. 'Why, what's wrong with it? You won't tell anyone about my cheese hobby will ya?'

'No, course not. It looks great, but I can't take your secret hobby cheese.'

Dyn's face brightened. Barry could already tell he was the sort of person who showed every emotion he felt. 'Mate, it's the least I can do after you saved my life down there. What a way to go that woulda been, while everyone else round here is dyin' in battle against giants, I pop my clogs eatin' a sausage!'

Barry snorted with laughter and stopped, embarrassed. Dyn looked at him and they both burst into a fit of laughter together.

'How long have you been here?' Barry asked once they had sat down and tucked into Dyn's food.

'We joined up two years ago,' said Dyn through a mouthful of a hard, salty cheese. 'Only a few of us were left after the giants came and destroyed our city, and Tchyglock come and gave us a home. Good of him on the one hand, but on the other hand we have to live inside a mouldy mountain and chances are we'll still get trod on by a giant anyways.'

'I'd probably prefer to choke on a sausage,' Barry said with a wink. 'What do you do around here? I've not seen you in the training pit.'

'They'll let me in when I turn fifteen next week,' Dyn said with enthusiasm. 'I mainly go out in the foraging teams at the minute, getting fruit and berries and what not to feed us all. I'm ready to fight though, especially now that you're...' he stopped suddenly embarrassed.

'Now that I'm here?' Barry said with a raised eye. 'I wouldn't bank on that changing anything.'

'But aren't you… you know…' Dyn said cautiously.

'Aren't I what?'

'You know, everyone's saying that you're the saviour,' he finished awkwardly.

'So people keep telling me, but do I look like a saviour to you?' Barry asked, holding his arms open.

'Heroes can come in all shapes and sizes,' Dyn said falteringly.

Barry sighed heavily and absently popped a chunk of a fragrant, semi-soft cheese into his mouth. 'I've never felt like a hero, I just liked reading about them. I didn't know this is where my adventure would lead me, people are expecting a lot and I'm just an ordinary lad truth be told. I'm a few weeks into my training and I'm only at fifty percent Oran,' he finished disconsolately.

Dyn nearly choked again, this time on a chunk of salami. Managing to get it under control himself this time, he finished chewing as quickly as he could. 'You're at fifty percent in just a few weeks?' he exclaimed.

'Yeah, I know it's not great when I'm meant to be a saviour and everything.'

'No, mate, nobody gets to fifty percent that quickly.'

'I'm sure that's not—'

'Nobody does. Seriously.'

'Really?' Barry said, surprised.

'Even the best trainees, the ones who really get the Oran, you know what I mean? Even they would take at least six months to get to fifty percent.'

'That can't be true,' Barry said, dismissing it but feeling an unfamiliar tinge of pride. 'I'm the least sporty, active person you've ever met. They didn't even let me play football in PE at school I was that bad, they'd just send me off to run laps.'

'What's football and PE?' Dyn asked curiously.

'PE is a lesson at school where we get taught sports, and football is the biggest sport in the world. I can't believe you've not heard of it,' said Barry.

'I forgot you're not from Många Världar,' Dyn said. 'What's it like in your world? Tell me about football,' he said eagerly, sitting cross legged on the floor and scooping up another handful of cheese and meat.

'Football is a game where there are two teams of eleven players, trying to kick a ball into the opposition's goal. There are different positions and clubs all over the country. My favourite is Aston Villa.

'Doesn't sound very exciting, not like the Combination Games,' Dyn said. 'Not that we've had them for ages,' he added sullenly.

'What are the Combination Games?' Barry asked curiously.

'You have competitions in each of the eight kingdoms of Många Världar, where competitors take part in multiple events like sword fighting, mead drinking, kelpie riding—'

'What's a kelpie?' Barry interrupted.

'You know, they're river horses, water spirits. They definitely do not like to be ridden either,' Dyn said with a chuckle.

'Anyway, there's all sorts of events, an' when you win in your kingdom you go through to the Många Världar Combination Games and compete to be the best in the world. They last for weeks, and the atmospheres amazin'. We all go an' set up tents in huge villages, an' cook on fires, tell stories an' sing songs, was always the happiest I ever saw my old man. The usurper outlawed the games as soon as she came to power, sent round leaflets telling everyone that the games are a way some of the rebellious groups use to leech off those true to her, an' people just seemed to lap it up. She likes division, you see, she likes things that push people apart, not bring them together,' he said philosophically, then grinned. 'Thank the gods you're here, eh? Fifty percent Oran in two weeks.' He laughed and shook his head.

And so it was with an extra bounce in his step that Barry strode down to the training pit. A belly full of cheese, new friendship and confidence that he might yet be able to live up to the expectations of him made him happier than he had been in a long time, and he completely forgot that he was over an hour late to the pits.

That was until an ice pick came speeding towards him, missing him by mere inches.

'What...?' Barry exclaimed, throwing himself into the second Oran shape to dodge the deadly weapon.

This time a crampon flew at him, and the spikes wedged themselves in his backside.

'Ooooooweeeee,' yowled Barry yowled, extricating the spiked shoe from his bottom. He saw Maurice lining up another crampon to throw at him, 'Stop!' he cried, holding his hand up to the training master.

The man's craggy face was fixed into a scowl. 'Has somebody died?' he asked.

'What? No. Not that I'm aware of anyway,' Barry replied, confused.

'Then you are sick? Are you dying?'

'No, I'm fine but—'

Another crampon shot towards him, whistling past his ear.

'Then you have no excuse for being late to your lesson,' Maurice said coldly.

Barry hung his head. 'I'm sorry, Ohjaaja, I have no excuse.'

'It is as I thought — you are not the saviour, you are not even worthy of licking the boots of the saviour,' Maurice spat.

Barry felt the now familiar heat rising within him. 'I can't be that bad to be the quickest person to get to fifty percent Oran,' he shouted.

Maurice burst out laughing. 'You're right, you must be so special! All of the great people were famous for being halfway good at something.' He stopped laughing abruptly. 'Understand this, Barry Birchwood. You have achieved nothing yet. You have done nothing. So far, you are nothing special.'

'How can I prove to you that I can be?'

'You must take what we are doing seriously. I do not instruct just anyone. I have others who train the masses. My time is precious and you must understand the value of it, I will not be around forever. Dedicate yourself to the crafts you are learning. I have no interest in anyone content to be fifty percent good at something. If you are to fulfil your destiny then you cannot settle for being good, you have to pursue perfection.'

'Perfection sounds impossible.'

'Of course it's impossible. But all of the greatest people throughout history never stopped striving for it, and you must do the same.'

Barry dropped to one knee. 'You are right. I have not had the focus needed to be the best. But I place myself fully at your service, Ohjaaja,' he said respectfully.

Maurice nodded, pleased. 'I hope you had a big breakfast, because today we will not be stopping for lunch. Double mountaineering followed by double sword fighting.'

Barry groaned inwardly. 'Very well, Ohjaaja.'

Mountaineering was one of the hardest disciplines that Barry was being made to learn. Maurice would take him out into the mountains for hours at a time, complete with crampons, ice picks, rucksacks and thick, down-filled clothing. At first, they would traverse steep, rocky ground where grip was minimal and the drops precarious.

Then, the pair would climb to the snowline where Barry's breath rose in frosty clouds before his face. They would clip on their crampons and he would try his best to keep up with the wiry one-eyed Ohjaaja. He was taught the art of ice climbing, placing ice screws, fixing ropes and heaving himself up the freezing cliffs with ice picks. His arms and shoulders would scream at him as he yanked his body up the slippery, frozen cliffs, working hard to never look down. More than once vertigo threatened to overcome him with dizziness, putting his ice screws and ropes to the test.

Throughout it all Maurice would kick him, poke him, throw water and snowballs at him, and try anything else he could think of to put him off and test his nerve. Barry wasn't sure he had ever hated anyone so much, yet something inside him made him persevere, craving the approval of his master, always looking to the Ohjaaja for a nod or a smile. He was yet to receive either.

Barry had quickly learned that the climb was far from the most dangerous part of mountaineering; it was during the descent that he really felt most terrified and out of control. His feet would often lose their grip, and more than once he had to rely on the strength of Maurice and the rope that connected them to save him from losing control and tumbling thousands of metres to a very grisly death.

Today, though, Barry felt a renewed drive. His newfound friendship with Dyn made him feel more of a sense of a belonging to the Sonphea, and along with Maurice's hard but true words, had given him a greater connection with the responsibility upon his shoulders. The more he understood about Cikavac, the more he understood the importance of stopping her. That day he climbed higher than he had ever done before. The air was tighter in his chest and his nose began to bleed. But as he stood on a narrow, icy precipice, clinging to his ice pick, which was buried in the frozen wall behind him, he looked out and understood for the first time why people climbed mountains for pleasure. Snow-capped peaks rose all around him, but through a gap between two slopes his gaze stretched for what felt like a thousand miles, to green meadows, forests and rivers. The sun bathed everything in a golden light and he could see it all from his own silent, untouched place on a mountain.

'It's beautiful,' Barry whispered to himself, his face shining.

'What are you doing up there?' Maurice barked from the foot of the ice wall they were climbing.

'Breathing it all in, Ohjaaja,' Barry called euphorically.

'Breathe it all in on your own time, because we won't be breathing for long at this altitude. Make your way down, it's time to head back.'

'Yes, Ohjaaja,' Barry said dutifully. He cast one last look at the scene before him and up at the skies. White fluffy clouds peppered the deep blue sky and felt closer than he had ever been to them. Suddenly a smaller cloud spun and scudded across the sky, bouncing into a much larger one which quickly absorbed it. It had moved faster than any of the other clouds, and against the wind.

'I saw a cloud move up there,' Barry said to Maurice once they had climbed below the snow line.

'Congratulations. I saw some ice up there.'

'The cloud… it moved strangely, as if it had been flung by something… or someone,' Barry added.

'Your hunch is right, boy, it was the Cloud Runners,' Maurice said, glancing up at the sky. 'They are the shepherds of the sky, and should be left well alone.'

'But my task—'

'Your task is an abomination,' he said with sudden venom. 'Gods and angels are not there for idle conversation, and they do not dabble in the affairs of mortals.'

'Then why train me? You know what I must do.'

'I know what you have been ordered to do, and I too must follow orders. My orders are to ready you for everything that is ahead of you, which I will do. But my skills are in earthly matters, things I can touch and feel: the point of a sword, the path on a mountain, the strength of an arm.

The heavens have their own rules, and I cannot instruct you in them, and would not even if the entire Sonphea demanded it of me.'

'Then you would send me to my doom?'

'Perhaps. But if you are indeed this saviour you tell me you are, then perhaps it will be something else. I will say no more on this now, boy.'

They climbed in silence for the remainder of their descent and back to the training pits, and Maurice said nothing to him as they parted ways before Barry's next session. His body ached and groaned as he sat on the floor. He leant back against the wall of the training pits, and quickly wolfed down some dried meat, washed down with a pink fruit they had picked on the mountain that Barry did not recognise. He had barely swallowed his last mouthful when his next session began.

***

Sword fighting was one area with which Barry felt that he had a natural affinity. In much of his training, he felt out of his depth frequently, scared, useless and, more often than not, a combination of all three. But with sword fighting, it felt like something he had always been meant to do. Almost immediately, from the first rusty short sword he was handed, the blade felt like an extension of his being. As his body hardened from the mountaineering training, and became supple and fluid from the Oran, it all came together for his fighting training in the pits. His tutor for the sword fighting was a woman of middling years who called herself Dead-Nettle. Her body was covered from head to toe in tattoos of wildflowers and her raven black hair hung down the length of her back in a tight plait, and she, like several others Barry had seen in Burroha, had thin gills on her neck. Unlike his other tutors, Dead-Nettle was upbeat, cheerful and encouraging, and Barry found that he was flourishing under her tutelage.

'Good, really good,' Dead-Nettle said to Barry later that day, as he lay on his back in the dirt, dripping with sweat, as her sword point pressed gently against his torso.

'I'm not sure being killed is considered really good,' Barry grunted, pushing the sword aside.

'Many would consider being slain in battle to be the most honourable of deaths,' his tutor said, pulling Barry to his feet.

'You know what I mean. If we were in a real fight, I would be lying dead in the dirt,' Barry said. 'Hardly a mighty end, and hardly what will help the Sonphea defeat Cikavac.'

'You put too much pressure on yourself, Barry-Bacch,' she said, using an affectionate, if slightly condescending, term she had adopted for him. When she said it the sound seemed to roll right out from her stomach. 'You are only a few weeks in, and already you are the equal of many sword wielders under the mountain.'

'I cannot afford to be anyone's equal, I have to be their better. Tchyglock and Maurice demand it of me.'

'They make many demands, but sword fighting does not bow to demand, only to practice. The only way to achieve mastery is to become one with your weapon, to not only deliver the thrust but to have planned it in advance, to know your opposition's move before you do.'

'Sometimes I almost feel like I do, but when I fight against you, you're always a step further ahead,' Barry said sullenly.

Dead-Nettle laughed, a throaty, dry sound. 'You are good, Barry-Bacch, but you should not compare yourself to me. I am the best in the Sonphea, perhaps the best in all of Många Världar. If you defeat me, then perhaps you really are the saviour. For now, be content that you have come a very long way in a very short space of time. I believe in you,' she said, and using her own blunted training sword, flicked his up off the ground, where Barry plucked it out of the air. 'Now, little one, we go again.'

Barry drew himself into a fighting stance, his legs spread and knees bent, lowering his centre of gravity. The duo circled one another, sword points angled downwards, treading carefully.

Barry eyed Dead-Nettle, looking for any sign of weakness, any hint of what she was planning, any chink in her armour, but there was none. Her face was impassive and she had lowered herself into the mind of Oran, analysing her opponent dispassionately. Barry worked to do the same, slowing his heart rate and absorbing all the information around him, all the energy from the still, dry air of the training pit under the mountain, and channelling it all into his focus on the sword in his hand and on his opponent.

A fly flew between them, seeming in slow motion to Barry, but his momentary distraction as his eyes flickered was all the opening Dead-Nettle needed. She pounced at him and would have drawn blood had Barry not leaned backwards and caught her sword with his own. Sparks flew as the swords grated off each other. More blows rained down towards him as he stumbled further backwards, barely parrying them. There was no gleam in Dead-Nettle's eye, no look of triumph, just calm and considered thrusts, hitting every opening her opponent gave her.

Realising he was being boxed in against the wall, Barry feinted to the left before darting to the right, and found himself with a sudden opening. As Dead-Nettle swung around to follow him, he ducked back from the momentum of her sword swing and darted forward with his own sword. His tutor bent her body at an incredible angle and his sword missed her hip by millimetres, but he didn't stop to admire the move, and instead tried to press home his advantage. Now it was her on the back foot, and he stepped forward into every dart of his weapon, forcing her back towards the wall of the pen. A tiny sheen of sweat was barely visible on her upper lip, but Barry knew he was testing her more than he ever had before. He felt like he was flying as they both darted around the pen at incredible speed. Suddenly, as she tried a counter-blow to a powerful lunge, Barry saw his opening for victory, like watching moves on a chess board. He parried her slice of the sword, spun and brought a blow that would have drawn blood from her shoulder. But in the act of spinning, Dead-Nettle threw the sword into her other hand and pressed it firmly against Barry's chest.

'Nice try,' she whispered, breathing heavily.

'No!' Barry cried. 'I thought I had finally had you!'

'You took me closer than ever before, Barry-Bacch, but you made the fatal mistake of turning your back on me.'

'It seemed the best way to pull off the killer blow,' Barry said glumly, slumping to the floor and breathing heavily, as sweat began to soak his shirt.

'If the only way to make the killer blow is by turning your back, then you are rushing it, forcing something that isn't there. In battle I would have killed you.'

Barry nodded. 'I really thought I had you.'

'Your skill is fearsome, and the move you did to turn the table of our contest was brilliant. But your main issue remains the same, you are impatient. How far are you with the Oran?'

'Zosime said fifty percent.'

Dead-Nettle nodded. 'That is very impressive, young man. But you fight like one who is at fifty percent. When you master the Oran, you will master your patience.'

'Everything takes so long here,' Barry said. 'Back home I would just watch a video online and be good to go.'

'What's a video online?' Dead-Nettle asked curiously.

'It's like moving pictures that anyone around the world can see.'

She tutted. 'That is no way to learn a thing, and impossible to understand and master a thing.'

With a shrug, Barry picked up his sword. 'Then let us go again, for I *will* master this thing.'

Dead-Nettle grinned, pounced at him once more and they disappeared behind a shower of sparks.

CHAPTER 10

Playing Politics

By the time Barry reached the dining hall that night he was battered, bruised and could barely lift his arms. After collecting a plate of what looked like the cook's interpretation of beef goulash from the counter, he scanned the benches and his eye was drawn to Dyn's hand waving cheerfully at him.

He smiled broadly and weaved his way through the benches, ignoring all the usual brazen stares of people as he passed, and sat down heavily opposite his new friend.

'You look awful,' Dyn said with wide eyes, his very large ears glowing orange from the candlelight behind him.

'Thanks,' Barry replied wryly. 'You try a day of Oran, followed by double mountaineering with Maurice, rounded off with double sword fighting with Dead-Nettle and see how you look.'

'Tough gig being the saviour, huh?'

'You've no idea,' Barry said, trying to close his fingers around a knife and fork. After being ripped to bits mountain climbing, and then enclosed tightly around the hilt of a training sword, they had fixed themselves into a claw shape.

'Maybe a spoon'd work better,' Dyn said kindly, passing his own chipped spoon. Barry smiled gratefully and propped the spoon in his claw. He was too weary to care how it looked as he shovelled the goulash into his mouth, splattering a lot of it down his shirt. Dyn didn't comment, which Barry appreciated almost as much as the spoon.

'So only a few days until you come down to the training pit then?' Barry asked conversationally, shamelessly talking with a full mouth.

Dyn's face brightened. 'Yeah, can't wait. Maybe you can help me with the Oran, being as you're at fifty percent and all.'

'Don't say that too loudly. You should've heard Maurice this morning. "You're only halfway good at something",' Barry said, trying to mimic the Ohjaja's gruff voice. 'But course I'll help you, want to join me in the morning with Zosime?'

'I wish,' Dyn replied wistfully. 'They know rightly who can go down there and who can't. You can't learn the Oran until you're of age.'

'Being the saviour has to count for something though, right?' Barry said with a wink. 'Let me talk to her.'

A grin spread across Dyn's face. 'Excellent! The better I get, the longer I'll survive before a giant treads on me.'

Barry laughed, then stopped. 'These giants, they're pretty big then?'

Dyn looked at him, his eyes quizzical. 'Erm the clue's in the title, Barry. Giant-s.'

'Yeah, but how big are they really? Twice our size?'

'Twice our size?' Dyn exclaimed condescendingly. 'Bloody hell, I wish. We might stand a chance then. You need to think much, much bigger'n that. Lemme think.' He paused, a finger tapping his chin thoughtfully. 'You seen the Watchtower of Donnau?'

'The one where Princess Luellason is being held?'

'That's the badger. Well, one of your more vertically challenged giants could wear that tower like a jumper.'

'Good one, Dyn.' Barry grinned, rolling his eyes. 'I wasn't born yesterday you know.'

'Who's laughing, mate,' Dyn said seriously. 'They're bigger'n houses, as tall as the tallest oak trees you ever seen. Their hands are the size of doors, their feet like longboats, and their teeth better represent garden shovels.'

Barry paled as Dyn described them.

'Long story short, they're flippin' terrifyin',' Dyn finished.

'How can we hope to beat such things in a battle?' Barry whispered.

'Not a clue. You're the saviour, you tell me!'

Barry wanted to cry, scream and hide all at the same time. What use was he, Barry Birchwood, against an army of giants? At that moment he felt every ache and pain in every single muscle tenfold, and he just wanted to go home.

'Now you see why I've accepted my fate of death by giant boot,' Dyn said sagely, and patted Barry on the arm.

Barry gave a weak smile. 'Is squashed by a boat-size boot better or worse than squeezed by a hand the size of a door?'

'Good question,' Dyn replied thoughtfully, before spotting Barry's grin and laughing. 'That's the spirit! Gotta be able to laugh at these things.'

'Easy for you to say, the hopes of an empire aren't resting on your shoulders.'

'Yeah, that'd be a bummer al' right, 'choo gonna do though, eh? What's for yer won't pass yer. But to answer yer question, obviously a hand is worse than a boot.'

'Ridiculous! At least you can try to wriggle out of a hand,' Barry said, and they lost the next half an hour to a debate on the best way to be killed by a giant. It was the first time Barry could remember properly laughing since arriving in Många Världar, and some of the dread began to drain away.

Dyn was just in the midst of explaining precisely why drowning in giant bogies would surely be the very worst way to go, as Barry howled with giggles, when his face suddenly darkened, eyes widened and he stopped mid-sentence.

'What's up?' Barry said, getting his laughter under control. 'Realised it's still not as bad as suffocating in their armpit?'

'Suffocating in an armpit is no way to go,' a proud, clear voice said from behind him. Barry whipped around to see Tchyglock looking down at the pair. It was only then he noticed that people at the surrounding tables had stopped talking and were looking reverently up at their leader.

'Oh, Tchyglock, hi,' Barry said feebly. 'This is Dyn,' he added to fill the awkward silence, signalling to his friend who appeared to be trying to shrink below the height of the table.

'Well met, Dyn,' Tchyglock said with a nod.

''Lo sir,' Dyn croaked, barely audibly.

Tchyglock smiled knowingly and turned back to Barry. 'If you are finished dining, might I ask you to join me?'

'Sure. Can Dyn come too?' Barry asked, throwing a glance at his friend who was giving him dagger eyes.

Tchyglock looked as if he were about to say no, before pausing and eyeing the pair keenly. 'Why not. Yes... why not,' he said with a curious look. 'I'm interested to hear more about how exactly you could drown in giant snot,' he added, causing a mortified Dyn to slide even further down in his seat.

The pair followed their leader away from the refectory and back into the maze of streets under the mountain.

'What's this about?' Barry asked, jogging to keep up with the man who was striding out ahead of him, his long loping legs covering the distance much quicker than Barry's or Dyn's could hope to do.

'Not here,' the man said shortly.

The trio walked in silence, and Barry was surprised when Tchyglock didn't lead them to the elevator up to his house atop the mountain, instead taking them down a passageway away from the main hall which angled upwards. It opened then into another large cavern, albeit much smaller than the one they had just left, and here the walled streets seemed tidier, more orderly. The cavern was much emptier, and it seemed as if people spoke in muted tones. A wooden sign hung at the entrance to the cavern, stating in formal letters, Métier District.

'What's a métier?' Barry asked, but was stopped by Tchyglock holding up an infuriating hand to silence him. Barry felt his temperature begin to rise.

'It means occupation or business district,' Dyn whispered in his ear.

Tchyglock strode to the door of a building that was larger than the others which had a polished brass sign fixed to the door: CHAMBER OF COMMERCE AND WARFARE.

It struck Barry as an odd combination of things to have in one chamber, but the thought was quickly pushed to one side as he entered a surprisingly lavish building. It seemed at odds with the largely frugal and functional nature of all the other Sonphea buildings he had seen so far.

A plush crimson carpet covered the floor, while gold painted cornices lined the plaster-covered stone walls. Rather than look impressive, to Barry it just seemed garish and out of place in a house underneath the mountain. The air was warmer than the usually cool, moist air of the caves, and it was dimly lit with glowing braziers.

They walked to the end of the stuffy corridor, passing a number of doors, until the passage turned a corner and opened out to a large alcove. A bespectacled man with a bald head and bushy white hair sticking out above his ears looked sternly up at the trio, and if there was any surprise at Dyn's presence he did not show it. His head was glowing in candlelight, making him look like a hairy egg full of yolk.

'She is ready for you, sir,' he said to Tchyglock in a crinkly voice and gestured to the door next to him.

'I should hope so,' Tchyglock replied, not breaking stride as he opened the door.

Barry and Dyn hovered at the door, unsure whether they should follow. Inside they could see an ornately decorated room, with a woman sat behind a huge desk.

'Hello, Tchyglock, thank you for accepting my summons,' the woman said throatily. She stood up and rounded the desk to shake his hand. Her salt and pepper hair was slicked back into a tight knot, and her voluptuous frame had been squeezed into a suit at least one size too small. Her face was proud and a faint smirk seemed to be a permanent feature. Barry could almost feel Tchyglock bristle at her choice of words, but he did not show it.

'Good evening, Phula,' he replied, shaking her hand briefly.

The woman looked past him to where the two teenagers stood awkwardly. 'So, which of these two frightened rabbits is meant to save us all?' she asked curiously.

Tchyglock turned and rolled his eyes dramatically. He beckoned them in. 'This is Barry, and this is Dyn. Boys, this is Phula Crabapple, and she is… involved, when it comes to Sonphea decisions around commerce, and some military operations.'

'Interesting turn of phrase, Glocky,' she said, smirking as she walked around him and grabbed both boys by the cheeks, inspecting them closely.

Dyn winced, while Barry took her hand firmly and pulled it away from his cheek. She smiled, a smile that didn't extend to her watery brown eyes, and looked intently at him.

'So you are the one,' she whispered, giving Barry a curious look, her hand now resting on his shoulder.

The silence lingered in the room just long enough to become uncomfortable, and Tchyglock coughed awkwardly, reminding her of his presence.

'Why is it you asked me to come by, Phula?' he asked with obvious irritation.

'I was eager to meet this one in whose hands you intend to place the fate of us all. He's barely off his mother's breast, and is hardly an impressive looking young man,' she said. 'No offence, dear, but a lot of our lives are depending on Glocky here making the right call.'

'Why on earth would I take offence at that?' Barry said sarcastically.

'Well, quite,' she responded, either not understanding the sarcasm or choosing to ignore it.

'At the moment what Barry is or isn't is not the concern of the Chamber of Commerce and Warfare, Phula, and I have better things to do than while away the hours bandying words with you.'

'Remember that no act of war can be taken without my consent, Tchyglock,' Phula snapped, her tone shifting dramatically. 'You may like to be a lone maverick, but you are not the leader of the Sonphea and you making the wrong call on something like the saviour could get us all killed.'

'There may be some truth in what you say, but I remind you that I am nonetheless the commander of Burroha. If you have any concerns you can of course speak to Xhaffa, or the Council, otherwise we will bid you good day,' Tchyglock said with a forced calmness, but the meaning of his words was clear.

All four of them stood silently, and the two senior members of the Sonphea eyeballed one another, the air in the room frigid with tension.

It was Phula who broke it. 'There was one more thing, *Commander.*'

'Yes?' Tchyglock snapped impatiently.

'Word is that the giant hordes may be coming our way after they annexed Willow. If that is true our supply lines will suffer, and you should be aware of our stock levels.'

'Yes, you make a good point,' Tchyglock conceded with obvious reluctance. 'How long can we last with our current levels?'

'We are confident to last for the long haul, but not forever. I estimate that with rationing we may be able to last with no new supplies for six months, although there would be a detrimental effect on our numbers, and it does not account for any increase in the people we need to feed here in Burroha.'

Tchyglock nodded pensively. 'Very well. I will need to speak to the quartermaster, Sasha Wellbelieve, on this. Can you provide a report of your conservative estimations?'

'I would be happy to present to the Council myself,' Phula said, a little too eagerly.

'Just the report please, Phula,' Tchyglock said firmly. 'But I will let them know you compiled the report,' he added kindly, seeing the frustrated look on her face. He turned to look at Barry and Dyn who had been standing silently near the door.

'Come, let us not take up any more of Phula's time,' he said commandingly. 'Phula,' he added with a final nod at her. 'I will look forward to your report.'

She said nothing, only nodding coldly as the three of them filed out of the office. Tchyglock led them in silence back along the ornate corridor and back out into the Métier District cavern. A refreshingly cool breeze blew over them, which was welcome after the stuffy confines of Phula Crabapple's office.

Tchyglock released an explosive sigh, followed by some equally explosive expletives.

'What's her problem?' Dyn said.

'An excellent question, Master Dyn,' Tchyglock said, leading them deeper into the large cavern. 'What do you think?'

Dyn flushed. 'Er, well she seemed to want to be more up with Xhaffa.'

Tchyglock laughed. 'Yes, you are absolutely right. She certainly does want to be more up with Xhaffa. And you, Master Birchwood, what did you deduce?'

'She seemed to me like a spider wanting to catch everything in her web, including me.'

'Well put, Master Birchwood, Phula is incredibly ambitious. Ambition is no bad thing; it's what motivates it that is the important thing. I have ambitions of the Sonphea overthrowing Cikavac, Dyn has ambitions to begin his training, and you have already exceeded your own ambitions of having an adventure. It's the motivation behind the ambition that is the important thing. Phula craves power, and the ostentatious office she created was designed to stand out and look impressive. She should not be underestimated, or indeed undervalued, as she is a good administrator for Sonphean commerce and central to our survival, which she well knows, thus I must accept her summons. But her political motivations remain unclear other than they are self-serving. Always question the motivation behind your ambitions, only then can you know if achieving them will give you what you are searching for,' Tchyglock finished, eyeing Barry closely. Dyn trailed along behind awkwardly.

'Now,' said Tchyglock, clapping his hands. 'I need you both to come up to my house with me. I take it neither of you have any pressing engagements this evening?'

Barry was longing to soak his aching body in a tub, but fixed his face into a willing smile and nodded.

'You need me too?' Dyn asked hesitantly.

'Yes of course, very much so,' Tchyglock said gently.

Dyn's face brightened and he nudged Barry, giving him a wink. 'Wait 'til I tell my old man I went to Tchyglock's gaff,' he whispered excitedly.

They walked back through the heart of the Sonphea's mountain base to the lift where Darvagh was waiting for them.

'Allroyte, chook?' he said with a grin to Tchyglock, then looked at Barry. 'You've had a few less cakes, ent yah, eh?' he said, poking Barry in the belly. 'A roit fatty you woz the other week.'

'Lovely to see you too, Darvagh.'

'Ah, don't moind me, mate, just havin' a likkle joke. Who's this then?' he said, looking at Dyn, as they all climbed into the lift and he yanked the rope, setting the pulleys into motion.

'I'm Dyn,' Dyn replied quietly.

'Eh? Speak up, not all of us has ears big enough to hear a whisper,' he said, chuckling.

Dyn's looked like he was about to give an angry response, but it turned into a high pitched squeak as the lift suddenly kicked into gear. They rocketed upwards through the mountain and Dyn's face paled.

Within seconds the elevator juddered to a halt. As they staggered out, and onto the landing ground, Dyn fell onto all fours and retched heavily.

'Lesley, we 'ave a vomiter!' Darvagh called into the empty lift, and out of thin air appeared a stocky person with fairy wings and a thick black moustache, wearing a pink tutu and high heels. They were holding a mop and bucket and were grumbling under their breath.

Lesley kicked Dyn roundly in the side, who rolled over and stood up hastily, wiping his mouth and looking deeply ashamed of himself. Lesley, meanwhile, had not acknowledged any of them and continued to grumble.

Barry distinctly heard the words, 'I am not a slave,' and 'I have a life you know,' as they slopped what appeared to be already grimy water over the chunks of reconstituted beef goulash, and something that looked like it was once cheese from his cave, and sloshed it back and forth with a mop that had seen better days.

'Don't mind Lesley,' said Darvagh, 'don't loike bein' pulled away from their very active social life.'

Barry let Tchyglock steer him and Dyn away towards the house atop the mountain.

'See yer, tubs and ears!' Darvagh shouted after them before grabbing Lesley and jumping back into the lift.

'I'll give him ears,' Dyn said through gritted teeth.

'Yeah, you really showed him,' Barry said with a chuckle. Dyn scowled at him in reply. The scowl was short lived, however, when they entered Tchyglock's home.

This time, instead of blazing sunshine illuminating snow-capped peaks and lush green valleys, very little could be seen from the windows. It was gloomy outside, but beyond that you could see little else as thick clouds roiled around the building, giving everything a dusky glow.

A peat fire was glowing lazily in the hearth, and Tchyglock stoked it, coaxing some flames from the embers and bringing a wave of warmth.

Dyn was looking around with a mix of amazement and deep sadness.

'What is it?' Barry asked him.

'It's the first proper home I've seen since the giants destroyed my city,' he said with sadness.

'Degwinkle was a great loss, not only strategically,' Tchyglock said kindly. 'It was a place I always enjoyed visiting, always full of laughter and merriment.'

'The last thing I remember before the screams is the laughter an' dancing,' said Dyn numbly.

'What happened?' Barry asked softly.

'Ours was a large city far south of 'ere, in the Thomwall Kingdom, next to the Noani River and Llewin Ocean. The sun shined nearly all the time an' the air tasted salty, I can still taste it now actually. We were a small city but didn't want for much cuz we knew the waters better than most an' could catch the finest fish, an' command the highest prices. I can still hear the songs we would sing when sorting through the day's catch on the pebble beach. We were singing them on the day the ground began to shake.'

'An earthquake?' Barry asked.

'It might as well have been,' Dyn said wanly. 'A whole army of giants came out of nowhere, with no warning at all. They trampled, maimed 'n' destroyed everything. Our crops torn up, our houses broken down to their foundations, my friends killed in the most 'orrible ways imaginable. I managed to get a few of us away,' he said, looking at the ground, 'but then we had to watch from the hills as our land was taken from us in the blink of an eye. Only time I've ever seen my old man cry, an' he weren't the only one at that.' Dyn stopped and tears came to his eyes. 'I really miss my home,' he said simply.

Tchyglock was looking at Dyn strangely, his eyes lost in thought.

Barry felt a tightness in his throat as he looked at the boy he now called a friend.

'We will get your land back, Dyn,' he said earnestly. 'Everyone should have a home.'

Dyn wiped his eyes roughly and grinned at him. 'As long as we don't get squished first!' Barry couldn't help but laugh at the complete inappropriateness of the joke.

'I do not understand the humour of you boys,' Tchyglock said. He went and rummaged in a cupboard, bringing out three dusty bottles, and passed two to the two young men.

'No way, Orlaberry Moonshine!' Dyn exclaimed. He pulled out the cork and took a swig, and a look of ecstasy fell over his face. 'Now that takes me back to festivals on the beaches,' he said, another tear coming to his eye.

'To your homeland,' Tchyglock said, raising his bottle.

The three of them raised their bottles and sat in silence for a moment. Barry took a sip of the dark purple liquid, which seared his insides but left a gurgling warmth all the way down into his stomach. It seemed to ease the pain throughout his aching body, and he felt a gentle contentedness settle over him. In the silence he thought of the horrors Dyn had faced, of the lands destroyed, the thousands of people turned into refugees in the blink of an eye, trying to find a way to reclaim their shattered lives. Yet again he felt the resolve harden deep inside him to try and help.

'Now,' Tchyglock said, 'to the reason I've asked you here.' He paused, as if picking his words carefully. 'Dyn, lad, you will know of Xhaffa and the Council, but Barry, you are less familiar. Xhaffa, the leader of the Sonphea, will be arriving here at Burroha two weeks hence. He will call together the Council, which I sit on, and we will sit for a week. You, Barry, will be the main area of discussion and they will be deciding your next move.'

'Do I not get a say in my next move?' Barry asked curtly.

'That will depend how strong you are amidst their politics. Many will seek to use you for their own gains.'

'But isn't it already decided that I should go to convene with the Cloud Runners?'

'That is indeed the conclusion I hope the Council will come to, but the ultimate decision will be Xhaffa's. He is wise and strong, but he can be obstinate and unyielding, and will not have his decisions questioned.'

'What's that like,' Barry said with a wink at Dyn.

Tchyglock did not smile. 'This is serious. It is essential to the survival of the Sonphea, and to Många Världar generally, that we secure the support of the Cloud Runners. Of that I am convinced.'

'And er, why am I here then, sir?' Dyn said awkwardly.

A faint smile touched the corners of Tchyglock's mouth. 'Because you will be going with our bookish saviour here.'

Dyn's eyes nearly popped out of his head. 'But I ent trained up or anything, I ent even started.'

'Barry, in the kitchen you will find some bread and cold meat. I think we could all use something to eat.'

'I'm not too bookish to run your errands then,' Barry mumbled as he trudged into the kitchen.

The moment his back was turned, Tchyglock strode over to where Dyn was standing near the window.

'Barry is going to need you by his side,' Tchyglock said in a low voice, looking fixedly out of the window at the swirling cloud.

'I dunno how much help I can be to 'im,' Dyn said hesitantly.

'The greatest strength does not come from muscles, fists or swords, Dynrym Romalliosson. True fortitude comes from within,' Tchyglock said, poking Dyn in the chest. 'We can train him, and we can train you, but being a leader, in a position of responsibility is a lonely one. Do not underestimate the power of friendship.' Tchyglock looked at Dyn out of the corner of his eye. 'I think you might just find your own strength too. The Sonphea is relying on you.'

The thick cloud parted, and a ray of deep, golden sun bathed the two of them for just a moment, as the setting sun sat on the distant horizon.

'He is an unlikely source of our hope, but Barry is, I think, our only hope,' Tchyglock finished simply.

Too soon the clouds swept away the sunshine once more and darkness fell over their faces again.

'Well I've not exactly known him long,' Dyn said awkwardly. 'But yeah, anything I can do to help him, I will,' he finished with more strength in his voice.

Tchyglock smiled knowingly, and turned as Barry walked back into the room with plates of food.

'I thought perhaps you had got lost on your way to the kitchen,' Tchyglock said, enjoying the way Barry visibly bristled.

Barry dropped the plates onto the table heavily, scowling.

Ignoring him, Tchyglock sat on a high stool and began to eat, and signalled to the two young men to do the same.

'Now, there are seven members of the Council. I am one, and the leaders of the other Sonphea bases also sit on the Council. They are Rummy Goliasson of the Endless Forest division, Shengju Pli who oversees our base in the capital, Vemoham, and Adger Godfrey who leads what's left of the resistance on the Noani River in the south. There are other small pockets of the Sonphea, but none with a seat at the Council. The other members of the Council are the Sonphea's quartermaster, Sasha Wellbelieve, the chief warlock, Nox, and special advisor, Langellis Mirnok.'

'Okay…' Barry said slowly. 'Is the hard part remembering all those names?' he added with a smile.

'Be serious!' Tchyglock snapped. 'Each of these Council members has the potential to make your life very difficult. Every day that your journey to the Cloud Runners is delayed marks another village crushed by Cikavac and her evil hordes.'

'Okay, okay, sorry,' Barry said, holding his hands up apologetically. 'Tell me what I should do.'

'Every member of the Council brings something different, with their knowledge and skill sets, and all have great experience, but experience does not always bring wisdom. There are different motives, with some focused only on the good of the Sonphea and vanquishing the usurper, but others, like Phula, are more focused on personal gain and playing at politics. They know that I have the ear of Xhaffa, and that I found you, so those who oppose me may also choose to oppose you and we must be ready. Now, Dyn, who do you think we should be most wary of?'

Dyn had been twiddling his fingers and gazing out of the window. 'What? Oh erm, well I've heard the odd whisper about the Mirnok fella...' he said tentatively.

'Go on,' Tchyglock said encouragingly.

'They say that Xhaffa listens to him more'n he should.'

'Exactly right!' said Tchyglock. 'What else?'

'People seem suspicious of Nox, but I dunno, maybe that's just cuz of his magic...' He paused, but seeing an encouraging look from Tchyglock, he continued. 'And well, I heard Rummy ain't the quickest.'

'What you've heard isn't overly far from the truth, or at least bears some resemblance to how I myself perceive things,' Tchyglock agreed. 'Rummy has been a valiant warrior, and has protected our people well in the woodland, but a very hard life has left him a little too fond of things that dull the senses. But he is a good man, and when he has a clear head, is very astute. I do not think he will oppose our cause. I have a strong friendship with Shengju Pli and Adger Godfrey and though they will favour anything related to their own realm, I am confident they will support our proposed mission. Sasha Wellbelieve is an excellent quartermaster, a practical woman and will ask some searching questions. She might be difficult, but as long as we prepare, I believe she will understand the reason behind my plan. You were right, Dyn, to say that we should be wary of Langellis Mirnok and Nox. But one who you omitted to mention was Xhaffa himself.'

'But surely as the leader, Xhaffa is wise and will understand why we must go?'

'Power and wisdom are not mutually exclusive. Xhaffa is certainly cunning, but he has grown comfortable in his position and does not like to be questioned.'

Barry was tempted to ask Tchyglock if that's where he got it from but managed to hold his tongue.

'If you're planning for us to do the quest anyway, what difference does it make if we get their permission or not?'

'You are of the Sonphea now, and there is a chain of command. As the saviour many will be looking to you to lead. Those who are more worried about their position in the Sonphea than the reason the Sonphea exists in the first place — to reclaim the land — will see you as a direct threat. As such, they may look to supplant you, or at least discredit you.'

'Why should I care what they think? I don't answer to them, I'm just trying to do the right thing and what people keep telling me I was born to do,' Barry said crossly.

'And that answer, in a nutshell, is exactly what Xhaffa will fear. That you are a mercenary, answerable to no one, one who does not respect his or the Council's authority,' Tchyglock said. 'You are learning much in your training, but you are from another world with no understanding of our land or our ways. If you do not educate yourself in a people's customs or reasons, you will always dismiss them and at best be ignorant, at worst be considered stupid.'

Barry bridled. For too much of his life he had been called slow or stupid, just for thinking differently.

'Dyn, I am tasking you with teaching our friend here the ways of the Sonphea. He has been training hard — and well,' he added seeing Barry open his mouth, 'but alongside his physical training, he must begin the mental learning. For that he needs you to immerse him fully in the culture and history of Många Världar and the Sonphea.'

'I'm not really a teacher, I dunno that much to be honest,' Dyn said awkwardly.

'I have every faith in you,' Tchyglock said with his best attempt at warmth. Barry thought it looked more like a leer, but Dyn's smile suggested it had worked.

'No problem!' He glowed.

Tchyglock clapped his hands. 'Good, I am relying on you. And you will begin your own training in the pits tomorrow, I will let Maurice know. Now it is late, and Master Birchwood, I know you must be very fatigued. It was important that we had this discussion, however. The Council meet in two weeks and we must all be ready. Good night,' he said with finality, and turned back to gazing at the dark mists outside.

Barry barely remembered the journey back to his cave that night; his eyes were drooping and his body ached from top to bottom. He was sound asleep within seconds of his head hitting the pillow.

CHAPTER 11

A New Shadow

arry's sleep was restless and his dreams confused. The face of the girl in the Watchtower of Donnau flitted in and out of his thoughts, her whispered words just beyond his reach. Her golden hair glowed as if in a setting sun, but she was surrounded by darkness, and his body felt like it was burning every time her face appeared.

When dawn at last arrived in his dark cave under the mountain, Barry awoke drenched in sweat. He felt stiffer and wearier than when he had gone to bed. For a moment he was in the confusing purgatory between dreams and reality, and he shook his head as his lodgings came into focus.

The mountain was still around him, and even the usual echoes of movement that reverberated around the caves were lost in the deep silence that sits just before daybreak. Barry peeled off his sodden clothes, and shivering, tiptoed to the shallow stone basin carved into the rock at the side of his room. He picked up a large jug stood next to it and poured it into the bowl. With great reluctance he readied himself for the splashes of icy cold water.

But just as he moved to thrust his hands into the basin, he jumped as if stung and let out a suppressed yell. He was sure he had just seen the face of the woman who had haunted his sleep. He rubbed his eyes and it was no longer there.

'Come on, Barry,' he said firmly to himself and slapped both his cheeks 'This place is crazy enough without imagining things too.' He thrust his head into the freezing water and as quick as he could, patted the water over himself in a hurried attempt to feel clean.

Once dressed, he trudged down to the canteen, tousle haired and rumple clothed, feeling more than a little sorry for himself, and tried to work out some of the knots and tightness in his muscles along the way. It was with some surprise that he saw an equally dishevelled looking Dyn sitting cradling a hot mug of coffee and staring into its depths, lost in thought.

He was the only one there aside from the kitchen crew and their muffled sounds, and the area was warm with the smell of baking bread and sugared lemon cakes.

'What are you doing here this early?' Barry asked.

Dyn jumped from his reverie. 'Flamin' 'ell, don't sneak up on me like that,' he exclaimed, clutching his heart.

Barry chuckled. 'You not get much sleep either?'

'Nervous weren't I. A lot's gone on recently.'

Barry nodded, and walked to fetch some of his usual strange, sweet juice and a cake, and returning, sat down opposite Dyn. He shifted awkwardly on the bench. 'Listen, it's not too late for you to back out. You must be regretting coming to sit with me in the dinner hall…'

'Are you mad? You lost the plot? Meetin' you's the best thing what could've happened to me.'

'Really?' Barry said, surprised.

'Course! There I was, sat eating cheese on my tod, whilin' away the months until I could start my trainin'. Even my old man forgets my name half the time… though that could be the bump on the head he got from a giant's toenail,' he added as an afterthought. 'Point is, now 'ere I am, startin' the Oran before I'm even fifteen, teaching the saviour, hangin' out with Tchyglock, going on,' he lowered his voice, 'secret missions. Bet my old man won't forget who I am now, eh?' he finished with a broad grin.

'No chance,' Barry said seriously.

'Plus, you know, it's all right… being mates with you,' Dyn said gruffly, looking firmly at his mug.

Barry grinned. 'Well, you're not the worst person to hang out with I suppose,' he said, and threw a crumb of cake into Dyn's face.

'Oi, leave it out!' Dyn grumbled, brushing cake from his hair, but he too was grinning. Then Dyn's smile faltered and he looked across at Barry. 'Bit nervous about the Oran, truth be told. Not my natural forte, that stuff.'

Barry let out a self-mocking laugh. 'You think it's my natural forte? If I can do it anyone can. Back in the forests by Willow I couldn't even climb a tree to escape the poachers when I needed to. So if I can pick up the Oran, I mean it when I say anyone can.'

'You really think so?' Dyn asked hopefully.

'Course,' Barry said intently.

But over the next few days it seemed Barry's confidence in Dyn's athletic abilities may have been misplaced. He watched from afar across the pit as his friend struggled hopelessly with the very basics of the Oran, and his sword fighting was more of a risk to himself than anyone else.

'Can you not give him a hand, Master?' Barry demanded crossly of Zosime one morning as the quiet of their Oran training was interrupted by an eruption of swearing from Dyn. Through a crack in the wall of his isolated training cell, Barry could see that Dyn had twisted himself into knot attempting the second phase of Oran, something he had been able to master right away.

Zosime sighed and stood upright. 'If you are noticing outside noise, you are not centred on the Oran,' she said drily.

'But you know how important it is for Dyn to master these things,' Barry whispered furiously. 'He needs your help.'

'His teachers in the pit are fully capable. You cannot rush the Oran. There is nothing unusual about your friend's struggle, it takes time… usually,' she finished looking at Barry.

'But we don't have time!' Barry exclaimed. 'He will be joining me on my mission, and he needs to be able to defend himself.'

'I understand he is not terrible at the mountaineering,' Zosime offered.

'That is something,' Barry admitted. 'Please help him?' he pleaded.

Zosime huffed. Her ponytail had come loose during the morning's training and she brushed it back from her face. 'Okay, fine. I will do what I can. But only if you focus on your Oran, I have seen little progression in the past two days. Not befitting the saviour,' she said in a voice laced with sarcasm.

Barry scowled, but lowered himself back into the Oran and zoned out the fresh wave of howls from Dyn.

While Dyn was struggling with the physical elements of his training, similarly Barry was having his own difficulties with the more traditional parts of his training. He found that by the evening when Dyn was showing him around the Sonphea, and trying to teach him the ways of Många Världar, he was so tired that he was not absorbing most of what Dyn told him.

'What did I just say?' Dyn snapped one such evening as Barry tenderly prodded an ugly welt he'd picked up that day in a sparring session with Dead-Nettle.

Barry paused guiltily. 'Erm, something about a river?' he offered tentatively.

'I dunno why I bother!' Dyn said crossly, massaging his own marks from the day, a purple and yellow bruise that had blossomed across much of his left shin. 'Not doing this for the fun of it, you know.'

'I'm sorry,' Barry said earnestly, sucking his teeth. 'I'm just so tired. Tell me again about the river.'

Dyn took a deep breath and closed his eyes, before continuing. 'The Noani River's one o' the most important things in the whole of Många Världar. It runs right across the empire from Vemohan, the capital city of the empire, in the north, and down across four member nations of Många Världar to the Llewin Ocean in the south. People live off it, with the fish an' the transport, an' it cuts the whole empire in half. I hear you can't hardly even see the other side in places it's that big.'

'Is it still in free country, or is it controlled by Cikavac's forces?'

'No idea, ask Tchyglock on that one. But they must've taken some of it at least cuz my home is right on the river an' that definitely ain't free country.'

Barry looked down at the map of Många Världar in front of him. 'Well if they came from Y'ronga and your city is around here, and they took Willow-Under-Hill when I arrived, that means they must have the whole of the east border.'

'There's a lot more'n what's on this map to Många Världar. I couldn't even tell you where it ends. The clue's in the title of the forest,' Dyn replied, prodding the words Endless Forest at the edge of the map.

'Then what's the point in this map if it only shows us some of it?'

Dyn shrugged. 'Can only teach you what I know about, can't I.'

Barry tutted. His head felt like it was being squeezed tightly, giving him an uncomfortable flashback to his splodgeworm experience. He found himself longing for his soft bed back in Briley Heath, his books and absence of any responsibility, just his own little world. Once more his mind drifted to his mum. He wondered if she was worried, or pleased he had left, or, with a knot in his stomach, if she had even noticed.

'Can we leave it there tonight?' he asked, suddenly feeling homesick for the first time in his life.

'Are you okay?' Dyn asked, concerned.

'Yeah… just tired is all,' Barry said, suddenly wanting to be on his own. He climbed to his feet.

'I'll walk with you,' Dyn offered.

'No, it's okay… I'll see you tomorrow,' Barry replied hurriedly, leaving before Dyn could tag along.

Despite his body being exhausted, his mind suddenly felt wide awake and wired, and he decided to take a walk to clear his melancholy thoughts. The realisation of how selfish he had been to leave without a word to his mother had dawned on him and he felt bile rise at the back of his throat.

He followed his feet without paying attention to where he was going, ambling through the dark, green-hued network of passageways that wound through the vast mountain. As he walked, a deep humming began to intrude on his lugubrious musings, a sound that seemed to grow louder the deeper into the mountain he delved. Before long the rock itself seemed to vibrate around him with a deep resonant choral humming that was cascading all around the tunnels.

Barry quickened his pace until the tunnel he was in narrowed and shrank, forcing him to bend almost double and edge towards a dull light vaguely visible on the walls. The tunnel, which had been angling downwards, suddenly arrowed sharply upwards, forcing Barry to drop to all fours and scramble up uncut rock towards an opening.

The dark tunnel opened out into a gap just wide enough for him to fit through. Poking his head through, he gasped; the passageway had opened into a sheer rock face that dropped down fifty feet to the floor of a large cavern, the ceiling of which was held up by huge iron buttresses driven deep into the walls. The cave was lit by burning torches, the flames flickering in the breeze being generated by the singing of hundreds of people who were lying on their backs on the floor.

Barry clung tightly to the rocks in the tunnel, fighting a sense of giddiness from the dangerous precipice his head was sticking out of. He realised that what he had previously thought to be a humming was actually a deep and guttural choral singing being generated by hundreds of voices as they gazed at the buttressed roof. It was one of the most moving sounds he had ever heard, as the voices overlapped in harmonies and counterpoint melodies, fusing into the resonant hum that stirred something deep inside Barry.

Even from his perch amidst the buttresses he could identify several members of the Sonphea that he recognised, and was surprised to see Zosime, eyes closed, singing intensely. Dead-Nettle, too, was there along with Matildh and Rito, the fighters he had first watched in the training pit. There were chefs, cleaners, warriors and more whom Barry had seen moving around Burroha, all united in their powerful chanting.

It felt religious to Barry, but there was no obvious leader or preacher, rather a sense of equal togetherness and shared warmth. It was unlike anything he had ever encountered before, either within Många Världar or back in his own world.

Gradually the singing slowed to a halt as the torches burned lower. Eventually the people in the cavern began to get to their feet, and Barry carefully squirmed his way back down the passageway, trying to retrace his steps back to his own cave. It took a painfully long time, as every rocky passageway seemed to look the same, and it was only by walking towards the distant sounds of the main Sonphea cave that he was eventually able to find his way to more familiar terrain. Almost crawling his way back to his bed, he fell asleep fully clothed with his mouth half open and drooling, as the now familiar image of Princess Luellason took over his dreams.

***

'Zosime...' Barry ventured tentatively.

She ignored him, resolutely staying focused on a complex stage of Oran movements. Barry followed her movements, stretching into them with increasing ease. He noticed that his body was recovering increasingly quickly from the arduous days of training, and he barely felt any soreness from the exertions of the day before.

'Zosime?' he asked again a bit louder.

She again ignored him and he tried to bite his lip and refocus on what he was doing but could not help himself.

He forced a small cough. 'Master, I need to talk to you about something.'

Zosime rolled her eyes slowly and moved out of the rapid lunges she was moving through to stand upright facing him.

'What is it that is so important that it can't wait until after your Oran training, which is apparently so vital to the Sonphea that I have to train with you every single morning?' Zosime asked pointedly.

'Well, last night I went for a walk…' he started, trying to pretend he hadn't noticed her tone.

'Congratulations. I'm not seeing how telling me that was urgent.'

'There's more. I was walking around the mountain minding my own business when I got a bit lost—'

'Your story is believable at least,' Zosime interrupted caustically, beginning to stretch again.

Barry scowled at her. 'The tunnel I was in had a sort of dead end, in that it opened out high up in the wall of a cavern with nowhere to go, and well, I saw something I don't know if I was supposed to or not.'

Zosime stopped her stretching and looked at Barry curiously. 'What did you see?'

'I saw… you, and lots of other people, lying on the floor and singing.'

Zosime's face was unreadable. 'What did you think of it?'

'It was utterly beautiful,' Barry said simply.

She gave a hint of a smile at the corner of her lip. 'I'm glad your head isn't completely full of dragon swill. Perhaps there is some hope for you yet.'

Barry remained nonplussed, particularly in light of a rare almost-compliment from his Oran teacher.

'What was your question exactly?' Zosime asked patiently.

'Well… what was going on?' he blurted.

'It is as you said, we were singing.'

'Yes, but why were you singing? Where I come from it is not usual for people to lie on their backs in caves and sing together.'

'Things will always seem strange if they aren't what you have grown up experiencing,' she said enigmatically. 'Surely this has been covered in your studies with Dyn?'

'Erm,' Barry started uncomfortably.

'He mentioned your cultural education was not going very well.'

'What a tattletale!' Barry exclaimed crossly, thinking of exactly how he would repay Dyn for revealing that to Zosime.

'Stop that. I understand, there is a lot of pressure on you and your studies are having to proceed at a rate that some would not approve of,' she said sternly, leaving him in little doubt as to where she stood on the matter. 'What you witnessed was the worship of togetherness.'

'You mean like a religion?'

'We would not call it that. Religion is a word too often used to justify prejudices; it is a method used by Cikavac to control her hordes and deprive them of independent thought. The worship of togetherness is none of those things. There are no rules. You can eat what you want when you want; you can choose if and how you connect to God or Gods, and everyone can interact with it in whatever way they wish. Nobody is made to join in; nobody is born and told what their relationship with it is; it is a spirituality and a connection with the whole.'

"So… you don't believe in Heaven or God or any of those things?'

'Personally, I do not. I believe in the beauty of nature and the world I can see and touch, but many believe in the Great Almighty and the Cloud Runners, and others believe different things altogether, all of which are fine. We are not a very secular society. Or at least we weren't… but that is not important to the Worship of Togetherness.'

'I don't understand,' Barry confessed.

Zosime sat on the sandy floor with her legs crossed. 'Come, sit with me,' she said, brushing dust off her leather garb. 'When you lower yourself into the Oran, what are you doing?' she asked.

'Don't change the subject,' Barry protested.

'I'm not, I'm trying to explain.'

'Okay, okay,' Barry said. 'I am slowing my heart rate, focusing on my breathing, centring my awareness,' Barry recited.

'Yes of course, those are the physical things you are doing, but what is the result of those physical changes?'

'Well my heart rate becomes slower—'

'No! You're not that dense. It isn't physical, think!' Zosime pressed.

Barry rubbed a hand over his weary face. 'I… I… see everything more clearly. I notice things more.'

'Good, what else?'

'I can feel the breath travel down my throat and into my lungs, feel the hairs on my arms. Once I felt like I could even see each flap of the wings of a fly.'

'Exactly! And what have you noticed about your surroundings?'

'My surroundings?' Barry said, nonplussed.

'The air, the rocks, the sand, the mountain!' Zosime almost shouted, more animated than he had ever seen her.

'They're… they're… just there,' Barry replied tamely.

Zosime visibly deflated.

'What did I say wrong?' Barry asked.

'Nothing, you said nothing wrong. I expected perhaps too much, but this is a key part of the final stage of the Oran. Everything around us is alive, and when you can sink deep enough into the Oran and open your mind fully, you will see how absolutely everything is alive and is connected. The whole of Många Världar is connected, and a master of the Oran can access that connected power and use it for good. And that is the togetherness that we celebrate in song. We give thanks and pay respect to the awesome power and spirituality of the world.'

Barry was silent as he thought on her words.

'It is hard to understand when you have not seen it.'

'Then can you teach me how?'

'Come.' Zosime stood and gracefully moved to the walls at the side of the training pits. 'Take the position of Kabukka,' she said, 'with your hands pressed against the wall.'

The position always reminded Barry of getting on his marks for the hundred metre sprint at school as he knelt down on one knee, with one leg thrust behind him. But unlike the pre-running pose which had only led so often to him coming last in at school, he thrust his arms out in front of him, and setting his lower back, lifted his upper body from the floor. Unlike the usual Kabukka where he must hold his upper body upright with only the strength of his core, he was able to distribute the weight to his arms and legs as he pressed his palms against the cold rock of the mountain.

'Good, now lower yourself into the Oran, but slowly, and take notice of everything happening to your body as you go.'

Barry closed his eyes and began his slow breathing, feeling the ground below his feet, the air in his lungs, all of the places in his body where there were aches, pains, twists and knots. He let his mind drift over all of them and focused on his heart. It was thudding quickly, but he imagined the breath washing over it like cool water and noticed it relax and slow. As always with the Oran it felt like a curtain was slowly being drawn in a darkened room, revealing a window full of light that bathed his whole body in warmth.

'Now push your mind outwards,' he heard Zosime say as if from a distance. He began to feel outside his body with his mind, like tentacles of light venturing out from him, touching and exploring the air around him. He could hear Zosime's breath, the flutter of her eyelashes as she watched him, felt the unmoving coldness of the rock against his hands, the solidness of the ground beneath his feet. He noticed the sounds emanating from the training pit, the clang of swords, the grunts and groans, and twangs of bows releasing arrows.

'Now focus your thought on the elements around you,' Zosime's voice whispered in his mind.

He drew his mind back in closer to him and concentrated his will on the rock beneath his hands. It was resolute, cold and hard, and some of the nobbles stuck into the skin of his hands. With a shallow breath, he pushed his mind into the rock itself.

He let out an involuntary gasp. He could feel the mountain. The rock was alive. A sense of eons filled Barry's mind, the slow moving of endless time, the desperate longing to reach for the sky, the desperate dragging of the ground beneath it. He could suddenly sense the feeling of the Sonphea in its belly, of the birds that nested on its crags, the weird and wonderful insects of Många Världar that called its soil home. His mind roamed through the rock, feeling its world and its connection with the world around it, the endless life that depended upon it. As his mind reached the peak, he gazed out across Många Världar. He took a deep breath and prepared to jump, to see the world.

But suddenly the shadow of Zosime was beside him on the mountaintop. She shook her head sternly and beckoned him back.

His mind was too detached from his emotions to show any surprise, but he reluctantly followed her awareness back into the mountain, through the rock and tunnels, past thousands of creatures that resided within the mountain and back to the training pits. He looked down and could see his body from above, and with no mirror for the past few weeks, was surprised by his appearance. He was almost unrecognisable from the doughy and pale boy of Briley Heath. His muscles were developing some definition; his face was tanned from his mountaineering training, and his deep red hair had grown longer. Zosime stood cross-armed looking up at the space where his consciousness hovered, tapping a finger impatiently. He noticed a large candle burning in a bracket on the wall and without thinking, blew hard at it. It flickered and went out, and he let his mind drift back into his body and slowly eased his way out of the Oran, and stood up straight.

Zosime's face was aghast.

'What's happened?' he asked, concerned.

'How did you do that?' she said, her eyes wide.

'What do you mean? I did what you asked me to, and it was incredible! The mountain is alive around us!' Barry breathed excitedly.

'The candle! You blew it out!' she said, pointing at the large candle which was spewing a trickle of oily smoke from the extinguished wick.

'So?' Barry shrugged.

'So? So that should be impossible! Your body can blow out candles, but you did it with your mind.'

'I dunno, I was just messing about really—' Barry began, but she quickly cut him off by grabbing his hand and pulling him.

'We must go to Tchyglock immediately,' she said.

'Can't it wait?' Barry asked irritably, half resisting her pulling him along. 'I want some breakfast, I'm famished!'

'This is more important than breakfast,' she grunted, pulling him roughly.

'Maybe to you it is—'

'Shut up. Do you not realise what this means?'

'That the Oran really burns through the calories?' Barry said whimsically.

Zosime looked as if she might punch him.

'Fine, what does it — please stop pulling me, I'm coming, I'm coming!' Barry complained, trying to extricate his wrist from her vice like grip. He managed to free it and stood still. 'Now I'm not moving until you tell me what's going on and why it's more important than a bacon sandwich.'

Zosime closed her eyes and began counting to ten over and over.

'Stop that!' Barry said crossly.

'It's important,' she said through gritted teeth, 'because what you did should be impossible for you. The warlocks cannot even manage such a thing with spells. You turned your mind into substance.'

'Great! Might save me having to schlep up the mountain to chat with the Cloud Runners then, can just lob my mind up there and away we go!' Barry grinned.

Zosime cursed loudly at him and began dragging him again.

It was almost half an hour later when Darvagh deposited them on the rocky landing platform at the top of the elevator outside Tchyglock's door. Zosime knocked and they waited. After a minute nothing had happened, so she knocked again. Once more there was no response and Barry thudded heavily on the door, impatient as the rumbling in his stomach grew louder.

Another minute passed and still nothing. Zosime sat on the floor, frustrated.

'We can come back after breakfast?' Barry ventured tentatively. 'Maybe he's having a lie-in.'

Zosime rolled her eyes again, something Barry was beginning to find almost as irritating as Tchyglock holding up his hand.

The sound of the elevator clunking into action roused them and Zosime got to her feet.

Darvagh jumped out with a grin. 'Here we are, bab,' he said, leading a dishevelled looking Tchyglock out.

'Why didn't you tell us he wasn't home?' Zosime demanded.

'Do I look like your flamin' messenger?' Darvagh said, half serious.

'What are you two doing here? Barry, shouldn't you be at breakfast before your training with Dead-Nettle?' Tchyglock asked pointedly.

'I would love nothing more than to be at breakfast,' Barry said irritably. He had never coped very well with hunger, despite growing up with an often-empty belly.

'Tchyglock, I need to speak with you,' Zosime said, giving him an intense look.

He raised his eyebrows and unlocked the door to his mountaintop home. 'Very well, come in.'

'Sounds interesting,' Darvagh said. "'specially if there's some brekkay going,' and he made to follow the other two in. To Barry's surprise Tchyglock let him follow them into the house.

The sun was just coming up on the horizon, giving the world a blue and gold tinge that was quite spectacular.

'What is it, Zosime?' Tchyglock asked as soon as the door was closed. Darvagh immediately moved into the kitchen and began opening cupboard doors and pulling out bits of food. Barry, with great difficulty, resisted the urge to join him as his stomach gave another loud gurgle.

Hearing it, Tchyglock rolled his eyes in a look greatly resembling Zosime's, and walked to the kitchen, kicking Darvagh in the backside. 'Out of the way, I'll fix us some breakfast.'

'Allroyte, allroyte, old man, keep yer wig on,' Darvagh said, dodging another kick as he moved to the breakfast bar next to the kitchen.

'Zosime, start talking,' Tchyglock commanded.

'This morning while Barry and I were training he asked me—'

'He broke Oran to ask you a question?' Tchyglock interrupted.

'Yes but—'

'Then he is further behind than I had hoped,' Tchyglock said irascibly.

'I am here you know,' Barry said.

'Tchyglock, that isn't the important part,' Zosime said, her own irritation beginning to show, both of them ignoring Barry.

'Nothing is more important than Barry mastering the Oran,' Tchyglock responded stubbornly.

'Would you please just let me finish?'

Tchyglock opened his mouth but bit off the retort and nodded. 'Please do.' He put down a plate of suspicious looking meat on the counter in front of them. Darvagh immediately dove in, his small hands grabbing fistfuls of the pinkish meat. Barry eyed it cautiously before his hunger got the better of him, as well as the fear that Darvagh would eat it all if he didn't get in quickly. Whatever it was, it tasted like fishy chicken and he chewed it distastefully.

'This morning while Barry and I were doing the Oran, he asked me—'

Tchyglock tutted but said nothing.

'He asked me,' Zosime continued, raising her voice, 'about the worship of togetherness which he had come across by chance during a late night walk the previous evening.'

'Well, I'm pleased to see his cultural learnings are coming along, but I don't understand how that's urgent.'

'Would you let the poor girl finish, old man,' Darvagh exclaimed through a mouthful of food.

Tchyglock looked furious but bit his lip.

'I explained to him about the ritual, but found it better to show him as part of the Oran.'

By Barry's reckoning he was now on chew number thirty-six of the piece of fishy chicken in his mouth, which was showing a great reluctance to being digested. Tchyglock nodded, again clearly fighting the urge to speak, instead scratching his stubbly beard.

'It is when I showed him the next stage of Oran that something impossible happened.'

'Nothin's impossible darlin',' Darvagh said, his small teeth apparently having no problem getting through the meat.

Zosime ignored him. 'I walked him through it as he lowered himself into the Oran, but encouraged him to draw his focus closer and push his awareness into the mountain, so as to better understand the foundation of the worship of togetherness and push him forward with his Oran. You know the process.'

'I do,' Tchyglock agreed.

'After he stopped responding to my prompts, I lowered myself into the Oran and followed his awareness through the mountain to the high slopes and called him back. I quickly raised myself back to full consciousness, but Barry was going more slowly. As I stood in the training pit waiting for him to return, I felt his consciousness blow out a candle on the wall, and then he returned.'

Barry had expected Tchyglock to burst out laughing at the absurdness of Zosime's story.

Instead, total silence descended on the room. Darvagh had frozen in mid chew. Tchyglock's mouth was open. Barry finally swallowed his mouthful with great difficulty and looked around at his companions, bemused.

'Master Birchwood, is what Zosime says true?' Tchyglock asked.

'Yeah, I guess so. I don't understand what the big deal is,' Barry said, braving another chunk of the meat.

Darvagh was staring at him through his wide child eyes. 'You know what this means,' he muttered.

'It means nothing, what she is saying is impossible.'

Darvagh fixed him with a disparaging look dripping with condescension. 'Tchyglock—'

'Darvagh, what he's suggesting goes beyond the realms of ordinary magic. Not even the warlocks can affect the mortal world with their apparitions.'

'Maybe the young man is anything but ordinary,' Darvagh responded, swishing his cape and returning to the plate of meat. Barry was not sure how he felt about being called a young man by someone who looked like they weren't yet old enough for high school.

'Can you give us a demonstration?' Tchyglock asked Barry.

'Happy to if you have something better to eat afterwards,' Barry said.

'Many people consider hedgehog a delicacy,' Zosime said, a tiny hint of a smile playing at the corner of her mouth again.

Barry spat his mouthful out. 'Hedgehog? What's wrong with you people?' he said, pulling bits out of his teeth.

'More for me,' Darvagh said, grinning through his small, pointy teeth.

'Come, let us see this miracle,' Tchyglock said, moving chairs back to clear a space.

'Fine,' said Barry, pleased for any distraction from the taste of hedgehog in his mouth. He moved into the middle of the space, and moving into the simple, comfortable starting position of the Oran, began the ritual of moving his consciousness slowly inwards. Within minutes he was looking down at himself from somewhere near the ceiling. He looked longingly out of the window, eager to see if he could float his shadow on the wind towards the increasingly sun-drenched horizon. Moving his consciousness outside he noticed an eagle was soaring above and he wondered if he could hitch a ride on its wings.

Darvagh suddenly appeared next to him, or a version of Darvagh as a very wizened old man. He was crinkly and wrinkled, but wearing Darvagh's clothes which made him look utterly bizarre. 'Maybe bring it back inside,

Baz,' he croaked. His age clearly hadn't affected the strength of his Brummie accent.

With great reluctance Barry turned his shadow around and looked back through the windows to where Tchyglock and Zosime were sitting, looking at Barry's prone body expectantly. Darvagh, back to his schoolboy self, looked out of the window and winked. Unable to help himself, Barry walked to the window and rapped on it with his knuckles.

The reaction was better than he had hoped. Tchyglock jumped out of his skin and fell off his chair theatrically. Zosime also jumped, and spun towards the window. Unsure if they could see his shadow or not, Barry waved, before reducing his shadow back to a stream of awareness and pulling his thoughts back into his body. On the way back he knocked the plate of hedgehog meat off the counter and onto the floor, before standing up, back in control of his physical form.

'Oi! I was enjoying that!' Darvagh complained, pointing at the meat on the floor, apparently no longer impressed by Barry's newfound abilities. Tchyglock on the other hand, had remained sitting on the floor, holding himself up with his hands behind him and legs outstretched. His face was bleak and his lips had tightened, thin and grim.

'You can leave to get some breakfast now, Master Birchwood,' he said, turning away in disinterest.

'What?' Barry asked dumbly.

'Leave us now, your training is more important than this distraction.'

'Tchyglock, you can't be serious?' Zosime started, looking stunned and angry.

'A minute ago you said it was impossible, but I've just done it. Why is it suddenly not important?' Barry asked crossly.

'Enough!' said Tchyglock. 'Barry, leave us to get on with your day. Do not mention this foolishness to anyone. Zosime, Darvagh, you can stay if you wish.'

With a furious glare around the room, Barry stormed to the door and pressed the button, releasing the trapdoor and disappearing from sight. He was sick of Tchyglock's constant patronising and belittling of him, especially in front of Zosime who had been so difficult to convince of his worth.

As Barry zoomed down the slide away from Tchyglock's house, a thought came to him. Putting his feet down to slow himself to a stop, he quickly lowered his mind into the Oran and sent his consciousness spiralling up through the mountain, following the slide. It lifted up through the floor and into the apartment where Zosime, Darvagh and Tchyglock stood talking.

'He must not be allowed to know. He is not ready,' Tchyglock was telling the other two intently.

'He must be told!' Zosime exclaimed.

'He is not ready, Zosime. He is too young, and carries a heavy enough burden already.'

'It means he is a—'

'He is also listenin' in,' Darvagh said calmly, interrupting Zosime and pointing to the empty space near the ceiling that Barry's mind was watching from.

Tchyglock's eyes flashed. He whipped his hand up and muttered something Barry couldn't identify. Without warning, Barry's awareness was pushed from the room and could not get within ten feet of the door. He brought his awareness back to his body and slid down to the breakfast hall, his mind racing. What was Zosime about to say? What was it that Tchyglock did not want him to know? And what had Tchyglock done to be able to remove his invisible shadow from the room?

CHAPTER 12

The Game

Each morning Barry tried to extract the information from Zosime, who infuriated him by telling him to ask Tchyglock. But he had not seen Tchyglock out and about in the mountain, and the intensity of his physical training and night-time lessons kept him from having the freedom to venture up the mountain to ask the leader of Burroha himself. Which, Barry suspected, was exactly the intention.

Anticipation began to build through the mountain ahead of the big meeting of the Council, and efforts to spruce up their rudimentary home were notable. Barry had received more than one crack around the ankles with a broom handle when he'd dropped some crumbs on the floor at mealtimes. His training had intensified, and by the night before the arrival of Xhaffa, Barry was feeling more confident than he ever had in his abilities. His lessons with Dyn had also improved, despite the regular breaks Dyn would take for them to have cheese and biscuits.

'Where do you even get all of this stuff? I haven't seen too many dairies in the mountain,' Barry joked that evening.

'Ask no questions an' I'll tell no lies,' Dyn said, grinning through a mouthful of Stilton. 'Special occasion, ain't it, what with you meeting the main man tomorrow an' all.'

'Was every other night a special occasion too then?' Barry asked, chuckling.

Dyn grinned, but then his face grew serious. 'You feeling ready for the Council meeting then?'

'I think so,' Barry said cautiously. 'But I don't know how much there still is I don't know, if that makes any sense.'

'Course. You only know what you've learnt. But they can't ask any more'n that. I'm not exactly a teacher, am I. I've not seen much of the world, can only share with you what I've come across myself.'

'Well you know plenty more than me, so it's a good start,' Barry said kindly.

There was a tapping outside the entrance to Dyn's doorway. Dyn looked at Barry quizzically, who shrugged.

Dyn rolled back the rock covering his doorway, and it revealed a young girl with deep green skin and raven-black short and spiky hair. Barry recognised her as one of the tribes that he'd learned had once lived in the Cofi Forest far in the south, one of the first places to be annexed by Cikavac's forces.

'What d'you want?' Dyn asked brusquely.

'Sorry, sir,' the young girl squeaked, her green cheeks flushing. 'I'm… supposed to get the sav… that is I'm supposed to get Barry Birchwood to come with me,' she finished falteringly.

'Who is it that sent you?' Dyn demanded.

Barry stepped in front of him. 'It's okay, I'll come with you now,' he said gently. 'I'll see you tomorrow,' he added to Dyn.

The girl smiled gratefully at him, and scampered on ahead, clearly nervous to talk to him.

'Hey, slow down!' Barry said, jogging to catch up with her.

'Sorry,' she said, looking down at the floor.

'No need to be sorry,' Barry said moving into stride alongside her. 'What is your name?'

'Felanne,' she said in a small voice.

'Nice to meet you, Felanne, I'm Barry.' He offered her his hand, and with a nervous smile she placed her small hand in his and shook it. 'Is this your first mission for whoever sent you?' he asked seriously.

She nodded silently.

'Well, you are doing a wonderful job so far,' he said kindly.

'Really?' she asked, grinning broadly.

'You really are, Felanne. Were you nervous to meet me?'

'Maybe a bit, but not much,' she said more confidently, increasing her walking speed and puffing her chest out.

'Well, you're very brave. Everyone else in the Sonphea seems to be scared to ever speak to me. It can be very lonely.'

She stopped and looked at him seriously. 'Everyone should have some friends. I can be your friend if you want. But not your best friend, because I already have one of those.' Her voice had a curious accent, as she almost rolled her Rs, but it came from further back in her throat.

'Oh?' he said, amused.

'Yes, Ruby and I are best friends,' she said, very matter of fact, and continued walking.

'I will take just being friends,' Barry said smiling. 'Do you know why everyone is afraid of me?'

'Well...' She paused awkwardly.

'It's okay, you can tell me because we're friends.'

'They say you're the saviour...' She started and stopped, clearly unsure how to proceed. 'But... maybe not everyone thinks it is true.'

Barry nodded. 'I think you are right. Maybe they will be nicer to me once they believe I am the saviour?' he said, almost to himself.

'I think they will,' Felanne said. 'I will tell everyone to be nice to you,' she added, her face serious again.

'Sometimes I don't even believe it myself.'

'You don't believe in yourself. But look,' she pinched him, 'you are completely real!' she said smiling.

Barry laughed in spite of himself. 'I can't argue with that. Tell me, Felanne, who are we going to see?' he asked, as she led him into the main hall.

She looked at her feet. 'I was told not to say,' she said uncomfortably.

'I can keep it a secret because we're friends, and friends don't tell on each other,' he said as they walked down the main thoroughfare, and the usual procession of people avoiding eye contact with him and moving out of his way ensued.

'Well... okay,' she said, convinced. 'It is the lady Phula Crabapple,' she said as they moved into the tunnel leading to the Métier District.

'Is it now,' Barry said, again to himself. 'It looks like the politics are already beginning then.'

'What's politics?' Felanne asked.

'Oh, it's just a silly game that adults play, nothing that you or I should be interested in.'

'How do you win the game?' she asked curiously.

'Nobody ever really wins the game of politics. In the end you always lose, that's why it's better to just not play in the first place.'

'Sounds silly, why would anyone play a game that you can never win?'

'A very good question, Felanne, but sometimes you have to play just a little so that you don't get overlooked.'

His mind was whirring as Felanne led him into the Métier District. 'I wonder, would you be able to deliver another message? If it isn't too late for you?'

She lifted her chin defiantly. 'I can stay up for ages yet!'

'Well, you must be very grown up then. Do you think that ten minutes after I go in to see Ms Crabapple that you could come and knock on the door to deliver me another message?'

'Who is the message from?' she asked curiously.

'It will be from Tchyglock, you know who he is?'

'Of course, I know who he is, silly! One time he spoke to my daddy for a whole minute.'

'Your daddy must be very important then.'

She nodded sagely then stopped. 'Why do you need me to give you the message if you already know it.'

'I'm very forgetful you see, so I'm very lucky to have a friend like you who can remind me of these things. I bet you have a brilliant memory.'

'I do, even though my daddy says I always forget what he's told me to do. But,' she leant towards Barry conspiratorially, 'I do hear him, I just don't want to do my chores,' she whispered, looking around as if her father might leap about from behind one of buildings in the business district of the mountain, that rose up like giant stalagmites.

'I need you to remember this message, and say it exactly like this when you come and knock on the door. Are you paying attention?'

She nodded eagerly.

'Say, Lord Tchyglock has asked to see you immediately on an urgent Council matter. He asks that you come alone,' Barry finished carefully. 'Now can you remember that, Felanne? It's important that you say it just like that.'

She recited it twice, and on the third had got it perfected.

'Perfect, so remember, come and knock in ten minutes, okay?'

She nodded, looking around nervously.

Barry felt bad involving Felanne in his plan, but he could not risk becoming entangled in Phula's web.

He entered the gilded building and as he approached her door he thought he heard voices coming from inside. Her doddery secretary did not appear to be at his desk, so assuming that was whom she was conversing with, he knocked loudly to announce his presence, and giving it a couple of seconds, opened the door.

To Barry's surprise there was nobody in the room except for Phula Crabapple, who had the look of a woman who was trying to act natural. She stood from behind her desk and smiled.

'Ah, Master Birchwood, thank you for coming,' she began.

'Who were you talking to?' he asked curiously.

She laughed. 'Oh dear boy, I was talking to myself. Sometimes in this place it's the only way I can be sure of an engaging conversation.' She smiled a gleaming smile, and Barry decided to let it drop, not wanting to get side tracked.

'What can I help you with?' he asked politely.

'Can I offer you a drink?' she asked him, again flashing her fixed, toothy smile and walking over to a large wooden globe which she swivelled to reveal a drinks cabinet.

'Erm, no thank you.'

'Well you won't mind if I do?' she said, and poured herself something pink and sparkly from a crystal decanter without waiting for Barry to respond.

'Please, sit down,' she said, putting an arm behind his back and steering him towards an impressive wooden chair before her desk. Depositing him in it, she returned to her side of the desk and sat in a chair that more closely resembled a throne. It was raised up so that she would always be looking down on whomever sat across from her. It made Barry feel even more insignificant than normal, which, he reminded himself firmly, was exactly what she wanted.

'So, tomorrow is the big day of Xhaffa and the Council's arrival.' She smiled. Barry noticed that it was only ever her mouth that smiled; it never extended to the rest of her face.

Barry nodded but said nothing.

'I expect you're looking forward to meeting them. I don't doubt they are as intrigued about you as I am.'

'Intrigued?' Barry asked, trying to remain non-committal.

'Well of course, Tchyglock tells us all that you are the saviour, and it will be interesting to see if in Tchyglock we all trust.'

'You don't trust Tchyglock?' Barry asked, feigning confusion.

Phula's glassy grin was now oddly fixed in place. 'As Tchyglock made clear the other day, what I think is not as important as Xhaffa and the Council.'

'I don't think he believes that what you think is not important,' Barry said, feeling the need to pacify her.

She laughed very briefly. 'You're a dear boy. And you should not have to carry such a burden on your own, on such young shoulders.' She stood up and leant on the back of her chair, her face only just visible over the top of it. 'Sometimes I find that a problem shared is a problem halved, wouldn't you agree?'

'I don't know what you mean,' Barry replied honestly.

'Of course you do, Master Birchwood. Tchyglock has a plan for you, something he will take before the Council tomorrow. If you are seeking to overthrow the suzerain, I can make your life a lot easier. Or…' she opened her hands.

Barry smiled brightly. 'Well of course, I know how important you are to the Sonphea and that you would only ever do what you could to help the resistance.'

'Exactly, my boy,' she said condescendingly and she moved to pour herself another drink. 'So it really is in both of our interests to cooperate. Tell me, what does old Glocky have planned for you?'

Right on cue there was a small knock on the door and Felanne entered.

'What is it? You have already done what I commanded,' Phula demanded, allowing her irritation to show.

Felanne faltered under her stare and tears welled in her eyes. She looked at Barry who gave her an encouraging smile, and her back straightened.

'Master Birchwood, Lord Tchyglock has asked to see you immediately on an urgent Council matter. He asks that you come alone,' she chirped breathlessly.

Barry rose. 'Apologies, Ms Crabapple, we will have to finish this chat another time. I've found it isn't a good idea to keep our commander waiting.' He bowed slightly. 'I thank you for your concern, it is good to know you are here if I need you,' he said earnestly.

The fixed smile had disappeared from Phula's face to be replaced with something akin to a sulky pout. She waved him off and returned again to her drinks' cabinet, turning her back to them.

Once they were outside Barry picked Felanne up and swung her around in his arms, making her giggle.

'You did perfectly, Felanne!' he said.

'Did you win at politics?' she asked seriously as he put her down and they fell into stride alongside each other.

'I got a little win, and that's enough for now,' Barry said, smiling. 'Now it is getting very late, I think you should run along home to your parents.'

'Okay,' she said with a shrug. She ran off, her green body disappearing into the gloom of the tunnel ahead. 'See you soon, friend,' her voice echoed, fading with her.

CHAPTER 13

The Council of the Sonphea

That night Barry again tossed and turned, feeling caught between sleep and waking dreams. Over and over the face of the princess appeared to be talking to him, pleading with him, but he couldn't hear her words. He was shouting but couldn't hear his own voice, which was getting lost in the vast distance between them. He felt his consciousness begin to lift out of his body, begin to try and run over the hills and vales to hear what the princess was trying to tell him.

'Barry, Barry…' A woman's voice entered his dreams but it wasn't the voice of the princess. His eyes snapped open and he started, confused. He could feel his awareness moving back into his body; he felt momentarily blinded and terrified.

Slowly Zosime's shadowy face came into focus, hovering above him.

'Are you okay?' she asked, sounding worried.

'What? Huh?' It took Barry a moment to remember where he was. His shirt was again plastered to his body with sweat and he felt freezing cold. 'Oh sure, I'm fine.'

'You were shouting… Who were you shouting to?' she asked.

'Dunno, just a dream,' he said dismissively, leaping to his feet. He had to put a hand to the wall for a moment as a wave of dizziness swept over him. Why was this woman, whom he had only seen once from a distance, haunting his dreams?

Zosime moved to help him, looking concerned, but he shook his head and splashed some cold water on his face.

'Can you look away while I change, please?' he said self-consciously, desperate to get out of his sweaty clothes.

She smirked slightly and turned her back to face the entrance to the cave. He quickly slipped out of his clothes and yanked on anything dry he could lay his hands on.

'What are you doing here?' he asked as he pulled on a top. 'Why have you woken me up? What time is it?' Barry noticed the sounds of the mountain coming to life and worried he had slept too long.

'It is still before daybreak, but the people are excited this morning. I know we do not have any training together today, but I thought perhaps some light Oran might help to clear your head before the events of the day unfold.'

'Sure,' Barry said. Already he noticed that his brain was reciting the details he had been taught about the members of the Council, his conversations with Tchyglock, and of his teachings with Dyn, Zosime, Dead-Nettle and Maurice. 'There's a lot going on in my head.'

'Nothing better than the Oran to help make sense of dark night-time thoughts,' she said, walking to the entrance to his cave and looking out. Barry joined her, and could see the twinkling lights of candles, oil burners and lanterns flickering in the caves of the Sonphea as they came to life, and the smells of cooking drifted up a conical chamber that rose through the centre of the mountain.

But the Oran did not come easily that morning. Barry's thoughts continued to stray to the anguished face of the princess. He wanted so badly to help her that it overtook any thoughts of the Council, or even of his strange experience with Tchyglock's suddenly changing mood after his Oran demonstration. He looked at Zosime who was moving slowly into a pose that rested her entire weight onto one arm. She always made it look so easy. Nothing here was ever easy for him, he thought grumpily, and sat down with a huff.

Zosime opened one eye, and with a sigh, returned to a standing position. 'Are you okay?'

'There's a lot of things that I don't understand,' he said.

'Not all things are meant to be understood,' she said cryptically.

'What happened at Tchyglock's house? Why did he suddenly decide what I could do was not important?'

'Ask Tchyglock,' she said, reeling out her staple response.

'Come on, Zosime, just tell me,' he pleaded.

Her shoulders slumped slightly. 'It seems that I… was mistaken,' she said, avoiding eye contact.

'I don't believe you.'

'You will know everything that you need to know when you are ready to understand it. Today you must focus on the Council. It is important that they approve our mission.'

Their conversation was interrupted by the sound of trumpets blaring through the mountain.

'Xhaffa is here,' Zosime said. 'Come, we must go to celebrate his arrival.'

As they joined one of the biggest tunnels running towards the main cavern they were joined by hundreds of others, all marching to welcome the arrival of the leader of the Sonphea.

The throng carried them along to the main cavern which was almost unrecognisable. Long forest green banners showing a circle of shining people of every race leaning their hands together to form a tower, with a midnight blue tree rising from the centre, hung in streams down the walls of the enormous cave.

'What is that banner?' Barry asked Zosime.

'It is the flag of the resistance, the true flag of Många Världar,' she replied, 'the flag of our nation before it was replaced by the usurper.'

The cavern was packed with people but a route had been kept clear through the centre, and over the heads of the people in front of him Barry could just make out a column of warriors marching through.

Leading them was a muscular man of medium height and blood red hair in long dreadlocks down his back. He wore a white shirt with leather straps criss-crossing his barrel chest, out of which the hilts of several knives were clearly visible. His face was deeply lined, but his eyes were small and sharp.

In the centre of the cavern he was greeted by Tchyglock. They embraced, and Tchyglock stood back.

'All hail Xhaffa, leader of the Sonphea,' he called, his voice echoing around the now silent chamber. 'All hail!'

The crowd burst into rapturous applause, and the silence was lost amidst the cheering, clapping and whistling of the assembled masses. Xhaffa raised his hand to acknowledge them all, though his face remained grim. He then allowed Tchyglock to lead them to a broad tunnel at the opposite end of the cavern towards the Métier District, and the troops followed on. Their armour did not match, appearing mostly to have been pieced together with rust spots burnished out as best as they could to give an air of consistency. A uniform was not a luxury the Sonphea could afford. However, all wore identical steel helmets that ran smoothly back from the forehead to a point behind their heads which then curved down to the nape of their necks.

The crowd began to disperse and Barry looked to Zosime to continue their conversation, but she had slipped away with the crowd.

Feeling at a loose end, Barry looked for Dyn for some company and found him training hard in the pits. He watched him for a short time as he practised with throwing stars. He was learning how to throw the small, pointed metal rings called shuriken in arcs towards a target thirty metres away and Barry was impressed by how far he had come in a short space of time.

Wandering idly away, he cast his eyes around for Dead-Nettle or the Ohjaaja to distract him with some training or conversation but neither could be spotted amidst the hundreds of bodies thrusting, shouting, stretching and clanging across the long, low-ceilinged cave.

All of a sudden, a deep gong rang out through the mountain, making the very walls shake and dust fall from the ceilings. There were a number of cries of frustration from around the pits as fighters distracted by the noise were overcome by their opponents.

Barry heard the scampering feet of Felanne before he saw her, and he turned to be met by the small, green girl who was out of breath and had clearly been running full pelt to him.

'Good morning, Felanne!' he said. 'Are you okay?'

He put a hand on her back as she doubled over, completely out of breath and trying to talk to him.

'Mess-age… for… you…' she panted.

'It's okay, take your time,' he said and fetched her a cup of water from a nearby basin hollowed out in the wall. She gulped it down gratefully and took a deep breath.

'The gong… started the Council. They want… you to join them,' she said, her panting growing less frequent.

***

Barry stood outside a plain wooden door flanked by two guards in steel breastplates and the smooth, pointed helmets of the Sonphea warriors. The door sat within a large bulge in the rock that ran outwards from the side of the Métier District cavern. The guards opened the door and Barry could see that the bulge had been hollowed out to create a large chamber.

Within it was a round table and seven pairs of eyes turned to gaze at him.

Barry could feel his heart racing, and briefly imagined entering an executive boardroom like he had seen on television back in Briley Heath. He tried to stop his face turning red, but to his fury felt the tell-tale warmth.

'Welcome, Barry Birchwood,' Xhaffa said in a strong clear voice. He was seated at the far side of the round table, but the spaces either side of him left nobody in any doubt who sat at the head.

'An honour to be here, sir,' Barry said deferentially, with a small bow of his head. He had never felt so uncomfortable in his life.

'If everything Tchyglock has just told us is true, then the honour is all mine,' Xhaffa said. His voice sounded like the ringing of a bell; clear and true. 'Please join us,' he added, signalling to an empty chair directly opposite him.

'Perhaps we should begin with some introductions,' the man to his right said, a slim, silver-haired man with a goatee, pale white skin and sharp, narrow eyes.

'A good idea, Langellis,' Xhaffa said.

The silver haired man gave a small cough. 'Master Birchwood, I am Langellis Mirnok, special advisor to our leader,' he said in a honeyed and considered voice, bowing slightly.

Barry nodded politely. Next to Langellis Mirnok was a woman who, in contrast to the pale Langellis, had skin the colour of coal, and a stern face with a strong jawline.

'Sasha Wellbelieve, quartermaster,' she said in a clipped, matter of fact tone, but her eyes glowed with warmth.

'I am Rummy Goliasson,' the broad shouldered but corpulent man sitting next to Barry said. He had rosy cheeks and wore a leather shirt spotted with rust from the chain mail frequently worn over it. He was balding and had tufts of hair sticking out at odd angles around his head. A twig was lodged in one tuft. He had the appearance of one who had once been strong and handsome, but had gone slightly to seed. A square jaw and high cheekbones were just visible amidst the veiny nose and stubble, and his deep liquid brown eyes had a doe-like quality about them. 'I am the commander of the Endless Forest division.' He smiled broadly at Barry before taking a long drink from a polished goblet before him, knocking a huge broadsword which had been resting against the table next to him to the ground in the process, with a huge clatter.

Barry returned his warm smile and turned to his left, to look at Tchyglock.

Tchyglock did not smile, but said to the room, 'As you're aware, Master Birchwood and I have met. I am Tchyglock, commander of the Burroha division.'

Tchyglock had told him to not seem too familiar with him during the Council, but Barry was nonetheless taken aback by his cool formality.

To Tchyglock's left was a tall, willowy woman with dark hair that reached down to her waist. She sat with an incredibly straight back, and was dressed in the practical black leather garb that Zosime often favoured, and had similarly slanted, almond shaped eyes.

'A pleasure to meet you, sir,' she said in a low, throaty voice. 'I am Shengju Pli, commander of the Vemoham division, our resistance in the capital, and throughout the kingdom of Isu Alku, up to Selvaği and the Ice Sea.' Her face had remained quite expressionless and Barry wondered if it was a peculiarity of her people, wherever they hailed from, to have an air of aloofness, or if it was simply a peculiarity of Zosime and Shengju.

He smiled warmly at her regardless, remembering that she was likely one of his allies in the room. She gazed at him but did not return the smile.

'Adger Godfrey, of the Noani River and south lying territories, and you are very welcome indeed,' a heavily tattooed man chirped before Barry had even moved his gaze onto him. Godfrey had narrow gills on his neck and a completely bald head, while his face had a bluish tinge from the tattoos laced across it. He had left the dome of his head uncovered by ink, making the unblemished skin look almost like a cap. He was wearing a white vest, and Barry could see he wasn't so heavily covered in tattoos as Dead-Nettle, and his inky designs seemed more haphazard. Looking closer, Barry saw that the tattoos were covering a huge number of scars. He seemed to exude a cheerfulness at odds with his ferocious body, and Barry liked him instantly.

'Nice to meet you,' he responded politely and received another grin in return. He moved on to the final member of the circle. An elderly white man, with severe wire-rimmed spectacles and heavy bags under his eyes, gazed mournfully at the table. He was leaning back, his head resting on his chest which was enveloped in heavy, wine-red velvet robes that looked like they would cost more than Barry's house.

'I am Nox,' he said curtly, without looking at Barry.

After it became clear that he was going to say nothing more, Rummy laughed nervously. 'That's a warm welcome by our magician's standards,' he said to Barry, and several people chuckled lightly.

'Warlock,' Nox said gruffly, fixing Rummy with a cold glare.

Rummy shrugged and chuckled, leaning back in his chair and taking another sip from his goblet.

Xhaffa cleared his throat and they all fell silent.

'We all know why we are here. The prophecy once delivered to Emperor Malásso by one of Nox's ancient order spoke of a saviour coming to us in our darkest hour and turning the tide of the war. Tchyglock believes he has found that saviour.'

Barry felt his face redden again as all eyes turned on him, and he was aware of the mix of looks that ranged from delight through to scepticism and ending with Nox who was looking completely disbelieving.

'No pressure,' Shengju said dryly, causing a snicker from Adger Godfrey.

'Tchyglock, please present your case,' Xhaffa said coolly.

Tchyglock stood and scratched his stubbly chin.

'Master Birchwood arrived in Många Världar some weeks ago. As you all know, the portal is visible to only a precious few, and none for decades. Zosime, a captain here I believe you are all familiar with, first encountered him at the wall surrounding the Watchtower of Donnau, and escorted him into the Endless Forest, questioned him and decided to bring him to me in Willow. They were set upon by poachers and got separated. Despite that, he was able to escape the poachers and find his way into the village, in spite of the fact it was after curfew.'

'No mean feat,' said Sasha Wellbelieve, impressed.

'Indeed. He found his way to The Dog Inn, and being unfamiliar with the ways of Många Världar, stood out rather quickly. Dog brought him to me. After questioning him, I realised he fitted the prophecy perfectly. He had arrived from the other side, passing the willow tree and the Tutelary. That night the forces of Cikavac descended on the town so I had no choice but to bring him to Burroha by splodgeworm. He handled the journey admirably and has been in intensive training since his arrival. His development has been...' he looked at Barry and rolled his eyes, 'impressive,' he finished, clearly hating praising Barry in front of him.

'Is that it?' Nox said, aghast.

'Excuse me?' Tchyglock said, arching an eyebrow.

'I think what our learned friend means is that we were expecting rather more proof than your word. The fate of the resistance and the entire nation does depend on your being right, after all,' Langellis Mirnok interjected.

'Why would I lie?' Tchyglock demanded, his temperature rising.

'No one is accusing you of lying, my dear man! But how do we know he is who he says he is? For all we know he could be an agent of the suzerain,' Langellis replied. 'I wouldn't be doing my job as special advisor if I didn't ask these questions. All we have is his word, and yours.'

'And since when is my word not enough?' Tchyglock retorted.

'What Langellis says has merit.' Sasha Wellbelieve interrupted them. 'Nobody questions your word, Tchyglock, but for such a huge claim as the coming of the saviour, we need some proof. Putting our hopes in the wrong person would be nothing short of disastrous.'

Langellis opened his hands and raised his eyebrows as if to say *Exactly*.

'In just the time since he arrived in Burroha, he has almost completed the Oran,' Tchyglock said.

'Already?' Shenju Pli said, looking shocked.

'Indeed,' Tchyglock said with some satisfaction. 'I do not call him the saviour lightly. I well know its implications. If you assume that my word is correct, I think you would all agree that he meets the terms of the prophecy, and as such I have a mission—'

'One should never assume,' Nox said pompously, 'especially in the face of such a mighty foe.'

'Wait, did you say he's nearly completed the Oran? In just a few weeks?' Rummy interjected with a delayed reaction. 'That is unheard of,' he bellowed. 'Sounds like the saviour to me, Glocky!'

Tchyglock nodded appreciatively as others smiled at Rummy in spite of themselves.

'Perhaps we should hear from the boy himself,' Sasha Wellbelieve said, and all eyes turned back to Barry.

'I am happy to answer any questions you have for me,' Barry said meekly.

'Well, boy, do you think yourself the saviour?' Xhaffa asked brusquely.

'I have absolutely no idea,' Barry said and there was much awkward shuffling in chairs. Tchyglock's brow furrowed deeply.

'Excuse me?' Xhaffa said.

'Well for a start, would you follow anyone who called themselves the saviour?' Barry said, and Adger Godfrey chuckled. 'A month or so ago, I was a nobody in a town on the other side of the willow tree, more interested in reading about adventures than living them. More than that, I didn't want an adventure. I had never heard of any prophecy, but what I can say is that when I discovered Kepheus, the Tutelary, I suddenly felt compelled into action more than ever before. I know I'm new to Många Världar and still learning the ways of your people, but whether I am the saviour or not, I'm here to help in whatever way the Council sees fit. It feels like what I was born to do.'

Tchyglock gave him the tiniest of nods.

'I admire your courage, Master Birchwood,' Xhaffa said, leaning forward and resting his chin in his hands. 'And if what Tchyglock says about the Oran is true, then you clearly have an extraordinary ability, the likes of which the Sonphea have possibly never before seen. But there is a big difference between courage and talent, and the horror of war, of being able to act when all seems lost or when the courage of others has failed.'

'Might I make a suggestion, my lord?' Langellis Mirnok said coolly.

'Careful,' Tchyglock whispered softly to Barry from behind his hand.

'Of course, Langellis,' Xhaffa responded cordially.

'I think we all want to believe that our young friend is the saviour, including our young friend himself. And we all know the value of Tchyglock's word.' He paused and gently lifted an eyebrow. 'But as you wisely pointed out, it is essentially a lack of experience of using his newfound skills in a live environment that remains the concern. It is a concern that should certainly be put to bed before we risk such a valuable addition to the Sonphea on any missions.'

'Well said, Langellis. What is your suggestion?' Xhaffa asked.

'I think completing the Trial of the Broken Viaduct would be the perfect demonstration that he is indeed the saviour.'

'Outrageous!' Tchyglock exclaimed, jumping to his feet. 'Nobody has taken that trial in decades. It may even be impossible to cross now, and the viaduct is only the beginning, if anything what awaits him on the other side is even more dreadful.'

'Langellis, that is as good as a death sentence,' Adger said, shocked.

'Hear me out before you string me up,' Langellis said, looking a little hurt. 'I know it seems ludicrous, but to unite the rebellion behind the symbol of the saviour, every single person will need convincing absolutely that he is who we claim.'

'It *would* remove any doubt about Barry's status,' Shengju said.

'Shengju, you can't seriously think this suggestion has merit,' Tchyglock said, wide eyed at his friend's words.

'I do not doubt that Barry is the saviour, but the fact remains that many will. For people to have faith in him, they need a demonstration that puts your claim beyond all dispute.'

'Master Birchwood, as you can see this is a decision that the Council must take and it would be better if you were not present,' Xhaffa said, as everyone fell silent. 'We will summon you once a decision has been reached on the trial.' He did not smile or offer any warmth, and it was clear there was no disputing his order.

Begrudgingly, Barry climbed to his feet. He tried to make eye contact with Tchyglock, but the older man's face was red with anger and he was looking furiously at his feet. Barry turned and left the room, back past the guards.

Unsure of how long it would take the Council to reach a decision, he decided to head to the food hall where he would be easy to find, and was pleased to see Dead-Nettle sat alone, slurping up some noodles in a dark broth.

He plonked down heavily opposite her and she nodded through an enormous mouthful, chewing it quickly.

'Aren't you supposed to be at the Council?' she said after eventually swallowing.

'They kicked me out,' Barry said, pouting slightly.

'You must have made a wonderful first impression,' she said with a grimace.

'They didn't all believe I am who Tchyglock says I am. They're deciding if I should do some trial.'

'Oh yeah? To be expected I suppose. What's the trial? I hope it's not sword fighting,' she said with a wink as she shovelled another enormous mouthful of noodles and broth into her mouth.

'Don't know what's involved. Something about a broken viaduct, any idea what that is?'

'You're joking, right?' Dead-Nettle gasped, eyes wide and spraying bits of food over Barry. 'They definitely said the Trial of the Broken Viaduct?'

'Yeah, that's the one.'

'That's outrageous!' she exclaimed.

'That's what Tchyglock said,' Barry replied. 'Is it really that bad?'

'It's worse,' Dead-Nettle replied. 'It's a ridiculous suggestion, there's no way that the Council will agree to it, Barry-Bacch. I didn't think it even still existed.'

***

It was more than two hours later that Barry was summoned back to the Council chambers. Dead-Nettle had done a good job of calming his nerves about the Trial of the Broken Viaduct, but he remained apprehensive about what else they may decide to press upon him.

When he entered the mood was sombre, and again Tchyglock did not meet his eyes. Everyone was silent as Barry took his seat.

'Master Birchwood,' Xhaffa began slowly, 'it is the will of the Council that you complete the Trial of the Broken Viaduct. If you are successful you will become a full member of both the Sonphea and of this Council. The trial has been set for midday tomorrow. Courage, young man. We look forward to welcoming you onto the Council—'

'Xhaffa, this is lunacy,' Tchyglock interrupted, and he saw several Council members nod in agreement. Even Nox looked perturbed.

'Enough, Tchyglock. I have made my decision. That will be all, Master Birchwood.'

Barry looked around the room. Adger Godfrey was shaking his head, and Sasha Wellbelieve's lips were drawn thin. Eye contact was hard to find among any of the other members, with the exception of Langellis Mirnok, who eyed Barry with a scarcely concealed smirk, and a deep dislike in his eyes.

He left the room and decided to head back to his cave to think and get ready for whatever awaited him the next day. He had barely arrived when Tchyglock appeared at the entrance, looking wild and somehow more powerful.

'You cannot go through with this trial, it is madness.'

'How could I say no?' Barry asked. 'You know as well as I do, they would think me a spy if I didn't and would lock me up. I'd rather try my chances on the trial.'

'You don't even know what the trial is!' Tchyglock exploded.

'I'm guessing it's something to do with a broken viaduct...' Barry began. 'How bad can it be?'

'Boy, your foolishness knows no bounds. The Trial of the Broken Viaduct has not even been attempted in over fifty years; it hasn't been completed in an age and many think it now impossible to traverse. It is an ancient bridge that crosses two mountains, hovering over a drop of thousands of feet. A frozen waterfall falls over it and it is barely held together. The slightest movement could cause the entire thing to crumble into the abyss.'

'So I just have to get across a rickety bridge?' Barry said with a nonchalance he immediately regretted.

'A rickety bridge?' exclaimed Tchyglock, almost beside himself. 'If you fall, you die. If you slip, you die. If the bridge breaks, you die. If the waterfall is unpassable, you die. Are you getting the theme? And I've not even mentioned the gale force winds. To set foot on the bridge is death. And even once you're across, the journey has only begun, as you still have to navigate the Klazak Pass and the creatures that lie in wait for you there. Once through the Pass, you must then find your way back to Burroha, but cannot return the way you have come,' he paused, 'not that you would want to,' he added as an afterthought.

Barry swallowed, beginning to understand the magnitude.

'Are you frightened?'

'Yes,' Barry admitted quietly.

'Good. You should be,' Tchyglock fumed, looking down at Barry, eyes blazing. 'Rickety bridge,' he muttered, rolling his eyes.

'Can you help me?' Barry asked.

'On the trial? No. But I will do my best to prepare you for it. I could curse Langellis, his argument was a compelling one, but it means now that we cannot escape on our mission to the Cloud Runners. If we flee nobody will ever believe you are the saviour.' He shook his head. 'I will be having severe words with Shegju Pli, it was her words that swayed our leader…' He stopped as he saw Barry's terrified face. 'But that is of no moment. Let us get to work, we have a long night ahead, and I will send Maurice tomorrow.'

It was deep into the night when Barry was finally able to get some sleep after Tchyglock had taught him new fighting moves and challenged his Oran. He was roughly woken the next morning by the scarred, one-eyed face of Maurice.

'Ohjaaja,' Barry mumbled sleepily. 'There's no class today,' and he tried to close his eyes to return to sleep.

'Wake up, boy, there is no time to waste,' the trainer said gruffly, yanking Barry fully up by his collar and landing him on his feet with a strength that defied his age.

'Oi! Gerroff me,' Barry complained grumpily. 'What's the problem?'

'Keen to die today, are you? Ready to plunge to your death?'

'Has nobody around here ever heard of dressing up the truth? Ignorance is bliss?'

'Ignorance will get you killed nice and quickly if that's the sort of bliss you're after,' Maurice said flatly. He walked over to Barry's basin, filled a jug from the icy water and threw it over Barry before he'd realised what was happening.

Barry yelled a list of expletives but stopped as Maurice threatened him with a second jugful.

'It's time to go. Get changed and meet me at the training pens.'

Barry was still shivering and cross when he arrived in the pens, but was grateful for any distraction from the certain death he kept being told he was facing later that day.

'What did Tchyglock go through with you yesterday?' Maurice asked, skipping any greetings or platitudes.

'He tested my Oran, taught me Chen's Five Mountain Fighting Movements as well as he could in the time, and some other basic survival tips.'

'All useful, but not enough to give you a chance.'

'That's a nice confidence boost.'

'Focus, boy. We do not have long. I was there the day the Trial of the Broken Viaduct was last attempted. I was only a boy, but I had nightmares about what I saw for years after. You have to be more focused, vigilant and canny than you can possibly imagine. Most of all you have to be lucky.'

'How can I be lucky?' Barry asked crossly.

'Knowing me is a good start.' Maurice handed him a device that looked similar to a crossbow but much smaller and with a strap at one end. 'This is a mountain arrow and has only one use in it, but if you are falling push the release trigger and an iron dart connected to a strong rope will jet out, similar to a grappling hook but much more reliable. Use it wisely.'

'Thank you, Ohjaaja,' Barry said sincerely.

'I've invested too much time in you to lose you to this foolish bit of posturing by Xhaffa. In days gone by people would only attempt the trial with much more equipment, but Xhaffa has let us know that it would be *inappropriate* for you to be given too much aid,' Maurice said with a single eye roll. 'Now, moving on, what do you know of mountain griffins, screaming wolves, ice fravashis and highland silkies?'

'Erm…'

'Nothing at all?' Maurice said, exasperated.

'We don't have such things in my world, and it never came up in your mountaineering classes,' Barry protested.

Maurice looked like he was chewing on something unpleasant. He regained his composure with obvious difficulty. 'Right, so they're all dangerous and they're all lying in wait for you in the Klazak Pass if you defy all the odds and make it across the viaduct.'

'This trial is the gift that keeps on giving,' Barry said, feeling increasingly hopeless and wishing Dyn were there to cheer him up.

Maurice slapped him around the face.

'Oi!' Barry yelled furiously. 'Is face slapping a requirement for senior positions around here or something?'

'I don't have time for you to feel sorry for yourself. Concentrate, your life depends on it.'

Barry nodded but continued to look angrily at his mentor.

'These creatures are all lethal, but like everything they have their weaknesses. You need to identify them and do it quickly, because they will not hesitate to kill you. Highland silkies are the saw-toothed seal folk who occupy the mountain lakes, so drink from their waters at your peril. Mountain griffins are half lion, half eagle and are incredibly intelligent and not easily bested. But they are proud and arrogant, and easily distracted by gold. Screaming wolves sort of speak for themselves, I think, don't they?'

Barry merely gulped.

'They are pack animals with a blood curdling scream, and are quite fearsome and territorial, and usually hungry. Not a lot of grub for them up there on the glaciers, you see,' Maurice added, becoming almost conversational. 'Now, let me see, what else was there?'

'You mentioned something about ice fravashis…' Barry began.

'Ah yes. Ice fravashis.' Maurice grew silent for a moment as his face darkened. 'Ice fravashis are… quite terrifying.'

'Handy that all the others sound like cuddly teddy bears then,' Barry retorted, unable to stop himself, but was quick enough this time to dance out of range of Maurice's slap.

'Of all the magical creatures that live in the high places of the mountain, and there are more than you think, ice fravashis are by far the most dangerous. They are fallen souls of the ancient kingdom; unable to control their powerful magic, it turned inwards on them, blackening their hearts. The ancient monarchs doomed them to live in the barren high places, caught between the heavens and the living. They are wholly evil, dark spirits that serve none but themselves and nobody is ever known to have bested one. If you spill blood, they will come.'

'But it seems likely that I'm going to get a cut or two along the way, assuming I get that far.'

'Try not to. If faced with one, it is better to fall on your sword than to let them defeat you. They will not give you an easy passing.'

Barry was beginning to feel quite sick. There was a heaviness on his shoulders as the reality truly sank in of the awfulness of what lay in store. A nation of people wanting him to save them, and those same people driving him to his death. He felt trapped and helpless and for the first time, genuinely wished he had never left the safety of Briley Heath. Now he found that his mother didn't seem so bad.

He thought again of how worried she must be about him, and promptly vomited onto the floor of the training pit. At first, he thought Maurice might slap him again, but instead he looked at him with great concern.

'What they hope to achieve by this I do not know. Only Xhaffa would take someone prophesied to save our people and send them to the Trial of the Broken Viaduct. But you have shown enormous promise and resilience, and you know I do not say such things lightly.' He gripped Barry's shoulder briefly, before turning and awkwardly looking away. 'Come, you will need equipping.'

It was several hours later that Barry sat in his cave with Maurice, Tchyglock, Dyn, Zosime and Dead-Nettle. He was clad in brown leather that felt unfamiliar but oddly empowering. His hands were covered by gauntlets that were soft leather on the palm and delicate but strong rivets of steel across the back of his hands and wrists, and he had the mountain arrow strapped to his left forearm. A light sword was strapped across his back, as Maurice said it would throw his balance off if buckled to his hip. Across his chest was a long thin pack containing some bare essentials for the trial, should he make it across the bridge, and on his feet were stiff leather shoes with dozens of tiny spikes drilled into the soles. A thick belt was strapped around his waist, and fixed to it were two ice picks, some throwing stars, and other small essentials. They had opted against a bow and arrow and focused on lightness and mobility for the crossing of the viaduct, but it did leave Barry feeling more vulnerable, particularly when he thought of the terrors that awaited him if he somehow made it across the sky-high bridge.

'You look the part if nothing else,' Dead-Nettle said to him with a smile.

'Thanks,' Barry said nervously. 'Thanks for your help, everyone.'

'Don't mention it,' Dyn said grinning.

A gong sounded deep in the mountain and a guard appeared at the entrance to the cave.

'It is time for the trial, sir,' he said politely.

Maurice gripped Barry by the arm. 'Luck, boy. If anyone can do it, you can. If you remember nothing else, remember this: if you manage to cross the viaduct, do not stray from the road. Lose the road, and you will not find it again. Understand?'

'Do not stray from the road, got it,' Barry said, relaying it to himself.

Dead-Nettle gave him a huge hug and a faltering smile as she fought back tears, but turned and hurried from the cave, unable to speak.

Zosime's face was unreadable as she approached him, and to Barry's great surprise, gave him a heavy kiss on the cheek. He felt his face flush.

'Have heart, Barry Birchwood,' she said intensely, and followed Dead-Nettle from the cave without a backward glance.

'Dyn and I will accompany you to the trial,' Tchyglock said gruffly.

Barry felt like he was walking to the gallows as they made their way through the mountain in silence, which suddenly felt cold and oppressive rather than cosy and safe. Dyn kept looking at him with very unsubtle sidelong glances. The absence of Dyn's laughing and joking made things feel infinitely worse.

When they reached the main hall it was thronging with people all walking in the same direction, abuzz with anticipation. When they saw Barry, a silence fell over the hall and the crowds parted to let him through.

The three of them walked through, Barry feeling thousands of eyes on him, and was surprised to see that many of the faces looked sad or concerned.

Felanne ran out of the throng to Barry, her tiny feet pattering on the sandy floor. Barry knelt down to her eyeline as she passed him a small red flower. 'This will bring you luck,' she said in a small voice and patted him gently on the cheek.

'Thank you, Felanne,' he whispered, feeling his eyes fill with tears as he fastened it to a button on his leather jerkin. She gave him a small smile, raised the back of her fist and pressed it against her forehead in a gesture Barry was unfamiliar with, and ran back into the mass of people.

'Good luck, Barry Birchwood!' someone shouted from back in the crowd. It was followed by more cries of 'Courage, Barry!' and 'You can do it!', and a warmth began to emanate through Barry's body.

The cheers all began to merge into one as one by one the crowd all joined in with a chant of 'Barry! Barry! Barry!' It grew in volume as Barry, Dyn and Tchyglock passed through them and every hair on Barry's body tingled.

'D'you see what you mean to the people?' Dyn said to him. 'Whether the Council see it or not, you are their saviour.'

Barry smiled gratefully at him, aware that the sick feeling in the pit of his stomach had not lessened, but his hands felt steadier and he walked just a little taller.

As they reached the far side of the hall Xhaffa stood at the entrance to the next tunnel, flanked by the rest of the Council. He looked sour faced at the chants, and Barry wondered if they had ever cheered for their leader as they did for him.

The chanting fell away with a raised hand from Xhaffa.

'Well met, Barry Birchwood. It is time for the Trial of the Broken Viaduct,' he said in a booming voice full of authority.

Without waiting for a response, he turned, and along with the Council, led the way into the large carved opening behind him. Ahead of him was a detachment of soldiers carrying burning torches. Barry and his friends followed the Council, and the entire crowd of people followed on behind them.

The walk felt like an eternity to Barry; the thud of thousands of feet walking through the same tunnels created a drum beat that felt like it could be his racing heartbeat as they stomped higher and higher.

As they reached a particularly steep part of the tunnel the crowd began to disappear up near vertical stairways carved into the sides of the mountain, and Barry felt he could detect the sweet smell of fresh air. He imagined this must be what it felt like to be a football player waiting in the tunnel ahead of the kick off to a huge match. The only difference was they didn't have to worry about dying horribly.

The silence was replaced by the loud hubbub of a crowd up ahead as the now small group moved past a line of Xhaffa's guards preventing any of the throng from following them. A large opening appeared up ahead initially showing nothing but snow and pale blue sky, but as they moved out into the open Barry's stomach dropped several metres and he had to place a hand on Dyn's shoulder as a wave of dizziness threatened to topple him. Ahead lay the Broken Viaduct.

CHAPTER 14

The Viaduct of Rümen Tor

Two huge craggy peaks reached up towards the heavens, and stretched between them was what had once been a mighty bridge. In the age of the ancient kings and emperors it had been powerfully reinforced with vast stone pillars driven into the mountainside to support a broad road in an incredible display of construction and architectural prowess.

But little of the bridge or its buttresses remained. Time and weather had taken their toll, leaving nothing but a thin strip of road clinging in places to the remaining buttresses. There were large gaps here and there in the crumbling remains of the road where bird nests were visible, safe from any predator. In some parts it was piled high with snow, and right in the centre was an enormous pillar of ice that descended from a rocky outcrop high above. It hid a large portion of the bridge from view and enormous dripping icicles hung beneath it.

What was once an indomitable viaduct was now barely a ruin.

'Seven suns,' cursed Dyn as the full weight of Barry's task became clear. Tchyglock threw him an angry look and Dyn clamped his mouth shut, but it no longer mattered to Barry; a feeling of overwhelming inevitability was slowly consuming him.

The Council led them along a narrow path that showed signs of recently being cleared of snow and ice. It took them around the side of the mountain towards the bridge. Up above them stood the massed Sonphea in makeshift terraces that didn't look much safer than the bridge and had probably been created around the time the viaduct stopped being a road and became a trial. Upon seeing the arrival of Barry into their midst the chants began once more, but Barry was only faintly aware, his attention fixed upon the death trap before him.

At the mouth of the ravine Xhaffa and the Council stopped and turned. Sasha Wellbelieve looked concerned, Adger Godfrey looked close to tears, while Rummy Goliasson was shaking his head — whether from the drink or disbelief that the trial was happening, Barry was not sure. Nox remained impassive, but his eyes were boring into Barry's, unlike in the Council chambers where he had avoided eye contact with anyone. Shengju Pli shifted uncomfortably on her feet and whispered something to Rummy who renewed his head shaking. Barry could have imagined it, but he thought he saw her mouth the word *Mistake*. Langellis Mirnok was bouncing on the balls of his feet, while Xhaffa appeared to be in his element, standing proudly at the head of the Council and facing Barry and the crowd. One of his personal soldiers handed him a trumpet shaped object and he raised it to his lips. Silence fell as the crowd waited expectantly.

'The Viaduct of Rümen Tor once stood as a symbol for a united Många Världar,' Xhaffa boomed, his voice loudly amplified throughout the frigid mountain air by the trumpet. 'The impossible bridge between the mountains, allowing merchants to pass through the realm as it prospered, a centre for trade and beauty.' He paused as the crowd hung onto his every word.

'But like our fair empire it has become rotten and decayed and is in need of saving. Who better to forge a path across it and on into the forgotten land beyond than the long-prophesised saviour?' he said, lifting his hands. The crowd cheered and applauded, putty in their leader's hands.

'I've heard words like "impossible" used for the trial. But all things seem impossible until someone breaks the belief barrier. And we, the resistance, the Sonphea of Många Världar, know all about overcoming the impossible.'

Another roar from the crowd. It occurred to Barry that the Sonphea had probably had precious little to celebrate for a very long time. He heard Tchyglock mutter, 'Get on with it,' under his breath.

'We are here to witness the first attempt at the Trial of the Broken Viaduct and the Klazak Pass beyond for an age. To be successful Barry Birchwood must return to Burroha by the last light two days from now. Barry Birchwood, do you accept the challenge with a full understanding of the depth of the risk involved?'

'I do,' Barry said in a shaky voice, trying to look anywhere but at the bits of stone that resembled the remains of the bridge.

'Say it into the amplifier for all to hear,' Xhaffa said firmly, handing him the trumpet.

'I do,' Barry said with more conviction this time. It did little to cover up the churning in his stomach. Dyn looked on the verge of tears which did not help. Total silence greeted Barry's acceptance of the challenge. Looking up at the massed crowds teetering in the precarious looking stalls, he saw them as they one by one raised fists and pressed the back of them to their foreheads, elbows jutting out to the sides, in the same gesture Felanne had shown him in the hall.

Xhaffa's face was stony as he saw the silent gestures, more powerful than any words as the wind whistled around them. He was wearing a black coat of a rich material that reached the length of his body and stretched over his hefty muscle. He was a forbidding figure, particularly when coupled with the other-worldly scenery around them.

He lowered the trumpet and spoke directly to Barry. 'Take this,' he said, handing him something that looked similar to a balloon, but of a different material. 'Should you reach the other side of the viaduct, inflate this and release it to alert us of your progress. Now, please make your way to the starting line and Nox will signal the beginning of the trial. Good luck, Barry Birchwood,' he said nodding, and led the Council along the ancient road to where several large seats had been set directly facing the foot of the bridge.

'What does that mean?' Barry whispered to Tchyglock, nodding to the gestures of the crowd.

'It is the Bu, the Sonphea sign of defiance, revolution and hope. It is the greatest sign of respect you could receive. The people believe in you.'

'But I haven't done anything yet,' Barry muttered.

'To even attempt this trial commands respect. To do it when so young and new to the Sonphea, even more so.'

'I'm afraid,' Barry admitted to Tchyglock in a small voice, trying to fight back tears.

'Then you have the wisdom to match your courage. Only a fool pretends to not know fear, but by seeing it and naming it you use your head to understand and conquer it,' Tchyglock said.

'That doesn't make me any less afraid,' Barry said, instead of what he really wanted to say, the thought fixed in his mind. *I don't want to die.*

'I know, Barry, but believe in yourself as I do,' Tchyglock said with uncharacteristic tenderness, as if understanding. 'With a little faith you give yourself the possibility of doing something remarkable. If it feels overwhelming just close your eyes, take a deep breath and let all the world slow down around you, and release all of the anxiety when you breathe out. Courage, I will look for you at sundown two days from now,' he said, putting a firm, calloused hand on Barry's slight shoulder.

Barry turned to Dyn, who grabbed him into a bear hug. 'You can do it, Baz,' he said into Barry's ear. His two companions walked away; Tchyglock to take his seat by the Council and Dyn to climb up into the stalls, leaving Barry all alone.

The rocky path turned to ice as he warily stepped towards the edge of the bridge. Stood atop a plinth high to his left was the warlock, Nox. He was much taller than Barry had first thought, and he looked resplendent in robes of emerald green flecked with silver, with the backdrop of the white and blue mountains behind him. Nox began to glow and the sky grew dusky black, until nothing but the glowing warlock could be seen. The blazing man slowly faded, cloaking the entire ravine in pitch darkness.

There was a deafening thunderclap overhead and the sky erupted in a blazing shower of golden stars. Gasps and cheers bellowed from the audience, giving the cascading flecks of gold a thunderous rhythm.

The stars faded into nothing, the sky returned to its proper colour and the single peal of a bell rang through the mountainside. Then, total silence settled over the makeshift arena. Barry allowed himself a last look over his shoulder and saw that the entire crowd had risen to their feet and as one were giving him the Bu. Shengju Pli also stood from her seat and followed the crowd in pressing the back of her clenched fist to her head. The rest of the Council followed her lead, except for Langellis and Xhaffa who both remained firmly seated. Barry turned properly, and returned the Bu, but fixed his eyes on Xhaffa who refused to return his gaze.

Barry set his jaw and clenched his teeth, and turned back to the whistling viaduct before him. To his great surprise when he glanced to his left, Nox stood on his plinth, fist raised to his face, and he gave him a sombre nod, his face expressionless.

CHAPTER 15

Trials and Tribulations

All sound fell away as Barry had eyes now only for the impossible death trap before him. It was so vast, and now he stood on the edge of it, the impossibility of it all descended on him fully. He shifted forward slightly, feeling tiny amidst the giant mountain peaks and the remaining huge blocks of stone.

Due to the frozen waterfall, he could not see the other side, and was almost grateful for the fact; it allowed him to take the viaduct in more bite-sized chunks.

With a deep breath he took his first step away from the mountain and onto the stone of the bridge. He winced, expecting the rock to give way completely, and felt the collective drawing of breath from the crowd behind him. To his great relief the stone held and did not complain as he moved his full weight onto it, but a strong wind made him sway on his feet, feeling lightheaded. The first ten metres of the bridge were relatively undamaged, insofar as the full width of the bridge remained, and with growing confidence Barry shuffled across the first few metres, keeping to the middle which he hoped was the strongest part. His pace slowed as he reached the first point where the width of the bridge had begun to fall away.

The ancient stones were mottled and mossy, with thin sheets of ice streaking across them. The raised stones on the sides that offered protection from the drop were no longer there, and in the next few metres, the bridge narrowed considerably. It was impossible not to notice the drop of thousands of feet beneath the crumbling stones. He could see the enormous buttress curving out of the mountain to hold up the section of bridge beneath, and Barry felt increasingly aware of the strong wind, and a lot less certain on his feet.

He stretched out a foot to test the strength of the stone, but his foot hit black ice and his whole body jolted forward. There was an audible gasp from the massed crowd. He fell forward into a crouch, his hands placed on the ground. For a bizarre moment he was transported back to getting on his marks in the hundred-metre sprint on school sports day, and the situation he now found himself in felt even more ludicrous. He had always hated school sports day, never winning anything, but now fervently wished he was back there with every fibre of his being.

The ancient stone was cold under his hands, and close up he could see the black ice that had nearly caused him to slip over the edge. 'Focus, Barry,' he murmured to himself and carefully pushed himself back to his feet.

The bridge was about two metres wide, and paying close attention now to the icy rocks, he edged himself forward. Barry wasn't sure if it was his imagination playing tricks on him, but it felt like the stone was creaking under his feet. His breath rose in billows as he moved forwards trying to master the feelings of disequilibrium and dizziness that were striving to overwhelm him.

With a big lunge he made it to a section of bridge that opened back out much wider and breathed a sigh of relief. He heard the crowd behind him do the same and wished he did not have an audience for the trial.

The widened section lasted for another ten metres before, he could see, things would begin to get particularly difficult. He walked more firmly forwards and without warning, the yellowed stone fell away beneath his feet.

Barry felt himself falling before he realised what had happened, and his arms frantically flailed for a grip. Swivelling in mid-air, his arms landed on the rock of the remaining part of the path that hadn't crumbled away. His legs hung beneath him, dangling into the abyss.

This section of the bridge looked like someone had taken a huge bite out of it, as the rock had simply fallen away beneath Barry's body. He was faintly aware of the sound of screaming in the distance. His forearms were resting on the remaining rock, but it was slipping and he could feel himself slowly sliding backwards, with nothing to place a foot on.

Slowly, and with great care, he began to pull himself upwards, digging his fingertips into stress lines in the rocky pathway. There was no denying a creaking and cracking in the rock, as pebble sized pieces of stone fell away beneath him. He could not hear them land.

As his body climbed over the edge, he lay flat and silent on the ground, his face pressed into the stone. His breath was coming in great gasps and he felt the urge to cry at the hopelessness of it all. Aware of the eyes upon him he worked to suppress the feeling, but felt a great reluctance to move. He had only come about twenty-five metres across the bridge but felt like he had run a marathon.

He raised his head and looked ahead. If he thought things had been difficult so far, they were about to get much, much worse.

There was now a gap between the part of the bridge he was lying on and the next part of the bridge of any substance. All that was left of the next section was a strip less than half a metre wide. Barry would have to leap diagonally and land perfectly on the long narrow walkway. The slightest error would leave him with nowhere to go but down.

He got carefully to his feet but stayed in a crouch, trying to distribute his weight as much as he could. Rolling his shoulders, he weighed up the move. There was a gap of about a metre to the strip. Not a big gap, but one that felt infinitely bigger when hovering over such a huge drop and with freezing winds whipping around him.

Just the thought of it turned his stomach. Keeping his low position, he shuffled closer to the edge and flexed his increasingly numb fingers. It was so very cold and the wind was beginning to sting his face.

He crouched on the edge, refusing to look down, and tried to ignore the shaking in his legs. Eyes fixed on the point he wanted to land, he sprung into the air.

But as he pushed off his foot lost its purchase, slipping as the tiny spikes on the soles of his boots failed to grip on the icy surface and skidded. He just about had the power for the distance, but not the height, and his face smashed into the side of the stone, before grinding its way up and over the lip of the path. He howled in pain as he scrabbled with his hands to make sure he didn't fall. He swung his legs up and over the side and again lay face down, breathing into the freezing cold and unwelcoming stone. He had spun and was facing towards the crowd as he sat up and gingerly touched his heavily bleeding face.

There was a big groan from the crowd as his bloodied face was revealed to them all. Blinking through grazed eyelids, Barry could see Tchyglock watching on, his face pale and eyes drawn. His hands were white knuckled on the arms of his chair. Next to him, Adger Godfrey again looked on the verge of tears.

Barry carefully moved himself around and looked at what lay ahead. He could barely concentrate; his face was on fire with pain and blood was dripping from his chin and down his clothes. His top lip felt like it had exploded, and from the whistling sound coming from his nose, he was fairly sure it was broken.

Looking along the straight thin strip that was all that remained of the bridge, Barry surveyed what was to come. Snow drifts were piled in places as the path reached most of the way to the middle of the bridge where the frozen waterfall lay. Moving incredibly carefully, Barry began sliding along the strip on his backside, legs straddled either side of the path for balance. As he reached the first snow drift, he gratefully plunged his face into it and let out a silent scream.

It set fire to every part of his ruined face and he felt bits of skin pull away as he removed his head. His right cheek felt particularly gritty, and he ran handfuls of the stiff, frozen snow down it, gently rubbing away some of the dirt and fragments of stone. His hands became so cold it stopped feeling worth it. He needed feeling in his fingers a lot more than he needed a clean face right now.

Blinking away tears of pain, he focused instead on brushing the snow to one side to allow him to continue and discovered, to his horror, that the snow had hidden the fact that for the next few metres the strip narrowed even further. He flexed his fingertips, raised himself, and moved forwards on his hands and feet, edging along the tiny precipice that was all that stood between him and the frozen ravine.

He felt incredibly foolish, crawling like a beast in front of the thousands of onlookers, but he reasoned, he would rather look foolish than look dead.

Stone began crumbling beneath his hands, and he again heard the terrible sound of creaking. He increased his pace, and felt the bridge begin to sway beneath him. He stopped moving, frozen with fear as the entire length of the bridge to the waterfall began to shudder.

A desperate grinding sound emitted from somewhere deep below, and with a reluctant glance downwards, what he saw caused his heart to stop beating.

A giant balustrade that curved out of the depths of the mountain and up to hold in place the long strip of bridge he was on, was cracking. The pillar was as thick as a shed and had stood the test of time, of storms, sub-zero temperatures and more, but inexplicably the weight of a teenage boy was the final straw. A deep fissure was widening along the length of it, and ear-splitting cracks began to explode through the peaks. The bridge was now shaking violently, but Barry remained frozen in terror, unsure of whether to move quickly or stay still and not speed up the bridge's destruction.

An enormous grinding from beneath him made his decision, and now throwing caution to the wind, he leapt to his feet and began sprinting along the narrow length of stone. The bridge began to fall away beneath his feet as a resounding scream of stone and metal from below told him the buttress had completely given way, but he dared not look down, focusing only on keeping ahead of the falling stone.

He began to get closer to where the waterfall enveloped the centre of the bridge and desperately looked for somewhere within it that he could get back to a safer footing, but saw nothing, just a resolute sheet of ice. Out of nowhere, a humungous slab of ice broke away from somewhere higher up the waterfall and crashed straight through the bridge in front of Barry, leaving an insurmountable gap for him to cross. He skidded to a halt but the falling bridge caught up with him and he felt himself falling helplessly, with nothing to grab hold of and nowhere to go.

Time stood still as Barry felt himself standing on air, before gravity began to play its part to force him downward to his death. With a desperate cry, Barry pointed his left fist at the waterfall, some twenty yards away, and smashed the trigger of the mountain arrow fixed to his wrist with his other hand.

The small iron arrow hurtled from his arm like a bottle cork and flew straight and true, burying itself into the side of the waterfall sheet ice, dragging a thin cord behind it. As the cord reached its limit and tightened, Barry felt his arm nearly pulled out of its socket, as he swung wildly in an arc.

Hanging there beneath the remains of a long-abandoned viaduct, with vast mountain peaks all around him, Barry felt like a tiny, insignificant spider who had found himself in a place where no one should go. In the distance he could hear screams and cheering from the crowd, but no longer cared. He just wanted to stay alive.

The mountain arrow had buried itself deep within the ice, which seemed to be taking his weight without complaint. From his new vantage point from below the viaduct, Barry could see how the middle section had stood for so long despite the weight of the waterfall pressing down on it. The bridge below the waterfall was held up by not one, but two enormous buttresses that reached up from somewhere within the darkness at the bottom of the ravine. How the ancient people had built such a thing Barry could scarcely imagine, but he said a silent prayer of thanks to them for their ingenuity.

He waited until he had stopped swinging in wide arcs and then began to try and haul himself upwards. Despite his gloves, the cord cut into his hands, drawing more blood to match his tattered face. A steady dripping of water from within the frozen waterfall was not as refreshing as he would have imagined.

Barry had pulled himself up about halfway when the arrow first slipped in the ice. Only an inch, but enough for Barry's breath to catch in his throat, as a numbing fear climbed through him. He couldn't see it clearly, but if the arrow had slipped, that meant that the ice had begun to crack. If the ice cracked, there would be no way back for him.

He stayed perfectly still, and when no further slips were forthcoming, Barry very cautiously began to climb once more, heaving himself up with straining arms, and propping his foot in a loop of the cord as Maurice had shown him to do.

Another slip.

Barry froze. This time the rope had jumped down a full metre. He could hear a sharp cracking sound from above, and with five metres still to go, the realisation began to hit Barry that the ice would not hold his weight.

He was not going to make it.

Barry closed his eyes and took a deep breath. His arms were beginning to tire and his wrist had now joined the rest of his bleeding body from the mountain arrow strap cutting into it. He felt battered, bloody and defeated and allowed himself a moment to absorb the beauty around him.

There were far worse places to die, he reasoned. The glistening peaks stood all around him, mighty and reaching for the stars. Perhaps now he would get to meet the Cloud Runners, albeit not in the way they had intended. The water trickling steadily from beneath the bridge was almost soothing, transporting him to the summer riversides and babbling brooks of happier times.

He found himself focused on the bright red flower Felanne had given him for luck, and laughed bitterly at the irony of it in his current situation. He lowered himself into the Oran, intent on connecting with the surroundings that would soon consume him. There was a freedom to hanging there under nothing but untouched space.

'I'm not the saviour after all,' he said loudly to himself, disappointed, 'just a boy who likes books.'

His breathing slowed and his heartbeat eased off the full throttle it had been pounding through since he first stepped onto the viaduct. As he slipped into the Oran, he was vaguely aware of another lurch of the rope. It would not be long now.

Without his urging, his awareness began to float out of his body, like a trapped animal finally freed. He floated on the surprisingly warm thermals and his heart almost burst with joy at the feeling. A condor floated down on vast, silent wings and surveyed Barry's still body curiously, realising it wasn't yet quite ready to be picked at, and circled away, looking disappointed.

Barry moved his awareness up to the bridge and absently inspected the ice waterfall. A huge column of ice was splitting away from the rest, with a spiderweb of cracks spreading outwards in ripples from where the arrow had buried itself. Barry's weight was slowly pulling the arrow free from its icy tomb.

Free from the emotions of his mortal body, Barry eyed the ice curiously and saw that it was indeed hopeless. He could never make it up to the bridge, the arrow would slip away the next time it was pulled. He sighed as he looked back to the crowd, more aware now of the volume of roaring.

He looked for his friends and spotted Dyn and Dead-Nettle, their arms around each other, both sobbing helplessly. Maurice had turned his back, unable to watch. Zosime's eyes were glistening, a single tear snaking its way down her perfect cheek.

Tchyglock was pacing frantically back and forth, wringing his hands and cursing. Xhaffa's face had a curious look that was somewhere between sadness and relief, while Shengju Pli had her face in her hands. Rummy Golliason was drinking and Adger Godfrey had joined him.

Barry wished he could talk to them, tell them all it was okay, that he didn't mind because he had found his courage in the face of death.

He sank his awareness into the bridge itself. It was old and angry. Angry at being bothered, angry that it wasn't the viaduct it once was, angry that it had been left to rot. But there was strength still left in it, more than Barry had realised. If only he had been able to reach the waterfall, he may have just had a chance to make it across.

A loud, sharp crack reverberated through the bridge as the cracked column of ice began to separate itself from the rest of the waterfall and his body began to fall.

Without thinking, Barry flung his awareness down and solidified his consciousness. He grasped the falling cord in one hand, and one of his body's arms with the other. With an almighty roar he used a strength he didn't know that he possessed and launched his deadweight body upwards and over the lip of the viaduct. The pillar of ice, which was higher than a house, slowly began to topple like a felled tree, and swung over the side of the bridge, silently falling through the empty air. It was a long time before there was a distant crash far, far down in the darkness thousands of feet below, but the impact juddered right up through the mountain.

Barry flew his awareness back to his body, which lay limply on the wet stone where the icy column had been just moments before.

He opened his eyes and screamed.

CHAPTER 16

A Cascade of Rainbows

Pain such as Barry had never experienced coursed through the whole left side of his torso and arm. His shoulder was the epicentre of the hurt, and it was burning with a white-hot fire. Looking down at it with great reluctance, Barry saw why: it had been completely dislocated from the socket and hung feebly at his side.

The whole shoulder joint looked distorted and engorged as the ball of his arm had created a large lump behind his shoulder, and he was reminded of *The Hunchback of Notre Dame*, one of his favourite stories. The ice must have yanked his shoulder out of the joint when falling before the arrow became fully free.

He knew how to fix the shoulder, but he was afraid to do it.

He unstrapped the mountain arrow strapping from his forearm as it was weighing it down and pulling painfully on the loose ligaments. He sat back and propped himself against the ice. He looked up at the crowd in the distance and saw that there was total silence. It was difficult now to see the expressions on people's faces clearly, but the prevailing mood seemed to be complete, utter shock and stunned silence. Barry thought back to Zosime's reaction the first time he had been able to affect the world through his Oran consciousness, and Tchyglock's odd response when he had proved it. He wondered if he had done something wrong, but dismissed it as he recalled how he would be dead at the bottom of the ravine had he not acted. The only movement in the distance was coming from the Council who had climbed to their feet and appeared to be in a heated argument. The wind was whipping around Barry's head, making any attempt at hearing their discussions impossible, but Tchyglock's allies appeared to have finally joined together as the commander had hoped, with Shenju Pli, Sasha Wellbelieve, Rummy Goliasson and Adger Godfrey all gesticulating wildly to Xhaffa and pointing at Barry. Langellis Mirnok seemed more animated than normal and was arguing in return, while Nox was saying little, a look of shock on his usually impassive face. Xhaffa was attempting to pacify the Council and looked conflicted.

Tchyglock threw up a hand in anger, and Xhaffa seemed to relent with a small, curt nod. Rummy slipped on the ice and Sasha Wellbelieve and Adger Godfrey both turned their focus on trying to help the now thoroughly drunk commander back to his chair, all three of them slipping over in what would be a comedy sketch, if the situation hadn't been so far from funny.

Meanwhile, Tchyglock had stormed down to the edge of the bridge, followed by Shengju Pli, both of them shouting something and gesturing to Barry. Whether from the pain, the roaring wind, or something else, Barry could not hear anything they were saying but they appeared to be signalling for him to stop.

Tchyglock's face was as white as the surrounding mountains, and Shengju Pli looked thoroughly distressed. Their meaning soon became clear: stop the trial, we are coming to get you.

Barry forced himself to stand up and nearly passed out from the pain as his arm wobbled limply at his side.

With great reluctance he shook his head, and with his good arm, waved to signal a clear no. He knew there was no going back. He could not give up the trial now in front of the crowds, no matter what had happened. There was only one way back, and that was forwards. He turned and leant sideways against the ice.

His eyes were watering even at the thought of what he now had to do, and his breathing grew rapid and shallow as bile rose in the back of his throat. Barry pulled the collar of his shirt up between his teeth so that he didn't bite through his tongue, and grabbed his bleeding left wrist firmly in his left hand. Wincing, and with eyes screwed shut, he lifted his right arm in front of him and pulled the arm forwards.

He roared loudly, the sound whipping around the mountains as the shoulder joint slowly began to move back into place. Tears of pain were flooding down his cheeks and he had never felt so lonely in his life, despite the eyes of thousands upon him. With a roar that turned into a scream he felt the joint pop back into place and collapsed to the floor, his breathing ragged and laboured.

Feeling began to return to his body, but the white-hot burning in his shoulder did not reduce. He knew he should fashion a sling to help the shoulder to heal, but balanced on the edge of a precipice with another half of the viaduct still to go, he couldn't risk losing the use of an arm, no matter how much damage he may do to the joint in the long term.

He sat down, deliberately keeping his back to the crowds, the Council, and the presumably livid Tchyglock, and began to tear the leather strap that had once held the Mountain Arrow. Carefully pulling it into a long strip, he tied it around the top of his arm to support his painful shoulder as best he could and pulled it into a knot with his teeth. Barry muttered a silent prayer that it would hold his shoulder in place.

The sound of some shouting and bellowing came to him as the wind dropped, and unable to resist, Barry threw a glance behind him. Dyn and Dead-Nettle had now joined Tchyglock and Shengju at the start of the bridge and were shouting to him, remonstrating for him to stop.

'Barry, wait there,' he heard Dyn shout as the wind dropped completely and a wall of roaring met Barry's ears. 'The trial has been called off. We're going to come and get you.'

It was so tempting. Just sit it out by the waterfall and return back to the mountain, to get his shoulder seen to, having proven that he was courageous, that he had determination, and perhaps people would now believe he was the saviour. It was the *perhaps* that stayed his hand.

To return now would win many over, but not all. The face of the princess appeared in his mind as it so often did, and he knew to rescue her, to parley with the Cloud Runners, all of it would only be possible if his position as the saviour was beyond any doubt.

'I'm sorry, but I have to finish,' he yelled back to the best friend he had ever had, the friend he had only even known for a few short weeks.

'What?' Dyn replied, cupping his ear as he strained to hear. The wind was picking up again.

'I'm sorry,' Barry yelled, but again his friend could not hear. Barry stopped trying to shout. With tears in his eyes, he shook his head. 'I'm sorry,' he whispered, the wind whipping it away. He raised his fist in the sign of the Bu, and turned his back.

He pulled one of the ice picks from the belt at his waist and with a determined sigh, began to hack at the huge block of ice in front of him.

***

After three hellish hours of relentlessly hacking and chipping away at the solid ice Barry began to hear the sound of running water. He was drenched with sweat from the exertion of the constant hacking, the pain from his shoulder was blinding, and his hands were blistered from the repetitive battering. He had been sucking on ice chips for liquid, but despite that his throat felt dry and parched, and the sound of water felt heaven sent.

He pressed his ear against the sheet of ice and the rushing water sounded close. With what felt like a super human effort, he began throwing his entire weight behind the ice pick and on the third hack the metal pick broke through. The success gave him a renewed energy and began chipping away to widen the hole. He tried to avert his eyes from the blurry reflection of his tattered face in the thin sheet of ice, focusing all his energy on breaking through.

Soon he had an opening large enough for him to squeeze through. With a look up at the towering block of ice, he hoped that the structural integrity of it remained in place.

'Crushed by a frozen waterfall or dropping thousands of feet, which is a better way to go?' he muttered to himself wryly.

He hesitated, feeling the temptation to look back, but did not trust his resolve to hold. He was so desperate to return to his companions, to warmth and food and safety. More than anything he wanted to be off the mountain.

Barry ground his teeth, and forced his way through the narrow hole in the ice. He did not look back.

He found himself in a large hollow running directly through the ice, and clear water was cascading down from long icicles above him. He held back against the edge, keen to avoid being soaked with the frozen water, but instead dropped to a knee and began scooping up mouthfuls from ice-cold puddles on the floor. He felt instantly revived, and massaged some of the water onto his shoulder, which numbed some of the pain coursing through it.

More than anything, Barry was glad to be away and out of sight of the crowds and his friends. Surviving the trial was hard enough without worrying about looking a fool in front of thousands of people.

He knelt for a few minutes, resting his aching body and building up his strength. Looking around, he saw how beautiful his surroundings were. Light was being refracted through the ice in a myriad of colours, filling the hollow with a cascade of rainbows, dancing across the walls and bouncing off the puddles. He smiled, feeling more relaxed than he had since he had been told he was doing the trial. It was just him now, and he was used to being alone.

As he explored the hollow, he found that the running water had, over the decades, forged a stream through the ice, where it was released to the ravine below. He was delighted to find that it had created a large opening on the far side of the waterfall through which he would be able to fit easily without getting too wet.

He knelt next to the stream and gently splashed the freezing water on his face, grimacing at both the intense cold and the pain as his hands rubbed away grit from wounds that had begun to scab over. The water ran red with his blood as he gently mopped at his swollen and battered face and forearm. Deep, angry grooves had been cut into his wrist from the mountain arrow strapping, but as it had saved his life, he decided he could live with the scars with which it would leave him.

With another deep drink of the water, he squatted and left the waterfall behind.

'Half down, half to go, come on, Baz,' he announced loudly now, enjoying the freedom of not being watched. The condor floated past again, and seeing that Barry was alive and well, gave a forlorn cry before lifting itself up and away on the mountain air.

Before Barry lay the second half of the bridge, and it followed a similar theme to the first. The weight of the waterfall had completely eaten away at a large section of the stonework, with only the top of a giant supporting column showing in front of him. Barry imagined a column of ice, similar to the one he had experienced on the other side, may have been the culprit for destroying an entire segment of the path.

Beyond that, the bridge narrowed into a slim track, which was broken in places. He felt keenly aware of the fact he had used his mountain arrow already, and that his shoulder would not survive another yanking upwards from whatever his Oran-self was.

He sat down on the edge of the cracked path, his feet dangling beneath him. It was only a two-metre drop to the buttress, but it was iced over and had no sides. He also had no idea if it would hold his weight. It was four metres across, and he felt sick at the thought of having to pull himself up on the far side.

'Come on, lad,' he mumbled, finding comfort in the sound of his voice, and lowered himself down.

He dropped to a squat to prevent his feet from losing their grip on the ice and squatted for a moment, absorbing his new surroundings. The mortar on the underside of the viaduct ahead was crumbling and loose. It was unlikely to take his weight for long, he realised with a depressed sigh.

Keen to limit the amount of weight he put on his near-useless shoulder, he decided to take a running jump.

From his crouched position, he dug the spikes of his shoes into the slippery surface, and with both ice picks in his hands, propelled himself forwards, sprinting across the top of the buttress, and leapt with all his might up towards the lip of the viaduct above.

His hands slid forward over the lip, and learning from his mistakes, he stopped his face short of smashing into the stone. He allowed his momentum to carry his torso onto the bridge and dug the ice picks into the crust of ice. They caught between some ancient cobbles, and his shoulder began to scream again. He tried to shift his weight onto his right arm and drag himself forwards, but soon realised it was impossible without using both arms. He dropped the pick from his left hand and began to push himself up with it, pulling on the ice pick with his right. The shoulder joint was slipping and Barry could feel the loose tendons slowly failing to keep the joint in place. With another roar he forced himself upwards and rolled onto his back, clutching his shoulder. It had not dislocated again, but the pain was unbelievable. Barry wondered if they had ibuprofen in Många Världar and laughed bitterly at the ridiculousness of the notion.

The sky was a pale periwinkle blue, with the only clouds visible across the sky high up, small and white as the shadows grew longer from the sun getting lower in the sky. The wind was less strong now, but whistled in his ears in the way wind does at that height. The viaduct was cold against his back but the temptation to just lie there and close his eyes was strong.

He climbed to his feet, refusing to get caught in a cycle of feeling sorry for himself. He wanted to put the viaduct behind him once and for all.

With his feet planted wide, he tried to distribute his weight as much as possible, remembering the crumbling mortar he had seen from below. The narrow track of stone was even slimmer than on the first half of the bridge, barely reaching a yard across, and ran in a zig-zag for at least thirty metres before widening out again. Speed was his only option, he reasoned. If the mortar failed and the bridge collapsed, there would be nothing to cling to or throw himself onto.

With a deep breath, he began moving across the slippery stone as quickly as he could without losing his footing.

Barry could feel the tiny spikes on his shoes crunching into the black ice of the bridge. Every now and then the spikes would fail to get a proper purchase and his shoe would slip. He felt like he was running across a tightrope, with no safety net to stop him toppling. He glanced below and thought that in the far distance he could see a river snaking its way through the valley and a spate of vertigo overcame him. He crouched down and clung to the sides of the rock, fearing the dizziness would see him fall.

The world swayed around him and he promptly vomited over the side of the bridge, unable to keep it down.

Closing his eyes and breathing deeply, he felt his balance begin to return.

'I just want this to be over,' he said to himself, feeling thoroughly dispirited as he wiped the watery vomit from his mouth.

Looking firmly ahead, for the first time he allowed himself to notice the end of the bridge. Ignoring the obstacles he could see along the way, he was overwhelmed with a sudden feeling of elation. Maybe, just maybe, he might make it.

He pushed himself upwards and began moving forwards, trying hard not to look down into the ravine again. He jogged ahead, and then heard the unmistakable sound of mortar crumbling away from the bridge.

He paused. All was silent. He pushed onwards, keeping his pace high.

When the crumbling began again, he did not stop. When the rumbling deep within the stonework began to shake his legs, he did not stop. When the crashing started behind him, he began to run.

Barry did not risk looking back, but focused on the bridge and his feet, throwing himself forwards as fast as he dared. As he closed in on what he hoped was the safety of the wider bridge he saw that there was a large gap between the narrow strip and the broader section. Without pausing to think, he leapt off the strip and soared over open air to land with a long skid on the other side.

As he slid to a stop, Barry turned to look behind him. The narrow track had not disintegrated entirely, but sections of it had fallen away, leaving thin tendrils of stone and large gaps between the more solid remains. The trial would be impossible in the future, and Barry was glad that if one good thing came out of his enduring it, it was that no one else ever would ever have to again.

The section he was on felt more solid, and some eagles clearly thought so too, with various huge nests balanced in some of the nooks and crannies of the bridge. A large mother eagle looked at him through fierce eyes, protecting a nest of birds that were almost ready for their first flight.

'It's okay, eagle mother, I come in peace,' Barry said, holding his hands up in obeisance.

She squawked loudly at him and took an angry step towards him, spreading her wings wide.

Barry stepped nervously around her, keeping as much distance as he could between himself and the giant bird of prey. This was her territory and he had no business being there.

When he was a few sidesteps past her, the eagle seemed satisfied that Barry was not interested in a fight and returned to her nest, but continued to eye him suspiciously.

Barry turned and focused on what was ahead of him, and his heart dropped considerably. There was simply no more bridge between him and the mountain ahead.

The wide bridge stopped abruptly, about thirty metres shy of the mountain he must reach to survive. There was no going back, but no way forwards either.

All that had endured were the remains of what looked to have once been a mighty tower that in its pomp would have stood tall and proud above the viaduct. Now all that remained was a tendril of stone that angled upwards for twenty metres before curving down to land on a vast plinth on the mountainside. It was less the tower, more the archway that had once supported it, and it seemed entirely flimsy.

It looked like a fast track to a certain — and horrible — death, but Barry did not need to be a rocket scientist to realise it was literally his only option. There was no going back across the dismantled viaduct; the only way was to scale the last remaining raised archway on the bridge that had managed to endure long beyond all the others that had presumably once lined both sides of the bridge.

There was nothing for it.

Barry surveyed it quickly, and realised he could not risk driving pitons into the stone as he would when mountaineering, for fear that the entire structure would give way. The archway itself was triangular in shape, with a flattened underside angling into a pointed top. He realised that it meant that he would have to climb the arch from underneath.

With a grimace he wrapped his legs and arms around the thick base. With a last look at the eagle who continued to stare at him, he began to pull himself up with his looped arms, and push up with his legs, squeezing the freezing stone tightly.

He didn't bother to inspect the sturdiness of the archway; it was, after all, his only option regardless of its structural integrity. He screwed his eyes firmly shut as he shuffled his way upwards. The sharp edge of the arch was cutting into his arms, but he did not slacken his hold. Leg push, arm pull, leg push, arm pull. He focused on the rhythm, but could not help but notice the narrowing of the archway.

He opened his eyes and saw that he had almost reached the tip of the arch, but that it was now so thin it was a miracle that it had not already given way. Right before his eyes, the now all too familiar hairline cracks began to lace their way through the stone.

The eagle mother began emitting loud cries, but her warning came too late. With a gulp at the vast abyss he was hanging over, Barry released his legs from the stone and started swinging his body backwards, using his arms as a pivot. On the third swing he felt his legs touch the opposite side of the archway, but his foot failed to grip it.

He swung again as a large crack began splintering down the stone between his arms, and again his feet failed to grip. The stone now began crumbling from between his fingers, and with a final huge swing, he ripped the chunk of stone he was holding completely out and was momentarily horizontal above the drop with nothing to hold onto. But the fifth swing had been just enough and his legs wrapped around the opposite side of the archway which still held firm.

He was dangling upside down from the angled ancient stone structure and could feel his legs slipping but the archway was curving away and was out of reach for his arms.

Blood was rushing to his head and again dizziness threatened to overwhelm him with the world upside down, the mountain air thin, and only the strength of his thighs between him and the drop. He forced the dizziness to one side with sheer adrenaline, and squeezed with his legs, feeling blood trickling up his thighs towards his midriff, pulling his body to the icy cold stone.

His fingers closed around the jagged, weatherworn stone and for a moment he lay upside down, hugging the archway, and he had nothing to stare into but the enormous abyss. As the daylight began to grow dimmer the foot of the ravine was even harder to distinguish, but he could see pine trees that appeared the size of ants from such a height and he felt like his stomach might drop out of his mouth. His hands were beginning to slip and his shoulder was screaming furiously and would not hold him much longer.

The pain was blinding and he vomited again, some of it splattering across his face as it fell. He screamed at the mountains in sheer fury and frustration. The anger at his plight forced him into action but his hands lost their purchase completely and his bleeding, aching thighs again had to take his full weight. His strength was beginning to fail him. He felt so very exhausted.

The ground was now in sight and he focused his attention on it to distract from the dizziness. He was going to make it. He was going to complete the viaduct.

His jubilation was quickly interrupted by an almighty crash behind him. Twisting his head awkwardly, he saw that what remained of the first half of the archway had completely fallen and taken a vast swathe of the wider part of the bridge with it. He was pleased to see that the eagle nest had remained unharmed on the only remaining part of that section, but his pleasure turned to horror as he saw cracks running right up the frozen waterfall.

Barry began to awkwardly shuffle down as quickly as he could, trying to grip as best he could. As the lines in the waterfall widened with ear-splitting cracks and huge chunks of frozen ice began to fall from far up the mountain, Barry threw caution to the wind, loosened his hold on the shuddering archway and slid all the way to the foot of it.

He threw up his arms to protect his head as he crashed into the ground and somersaulted forwards with the momentum, rolling up onto his feet. *It's a shame nobody saw that move instead of all the clumsiness they did see,* he thought to himself. He stood fully upright on the snowy pathway cut into the side of the mountain, and the relief was unbelievable. But it was mixed with horror as he beheld the pandemonium unfolding before his eyes.

From way up high, the waterfall was collapsing in upon itself. Slabs of ice the size of trucks were tumbling from the mountain. He saw the eagle mother shepherding her chicks to the edge of their remaining piece of bridge and urging them to take flight. They looked scared and Barry could not blame them. One by one they dropped off the edge of the broken viaduct, and Barry held his breath as one by one he saw them tentatively manage to take flight, encouraged by their mother. Barry began to furiously blow up the balloon Xhaffa had given him and released it, but it had barely made it to the tip of the archway when a shard of ice plummeted straight through it, taking what was left of the archway with it. The Viaduct of Rümen Tor was no longer broken, it was destroyed.

With a crack that almost burst Barry's ear drums the frozen waterfall began to implode and a pillar that reached up a hundred metres broke away and was angling for Barry.

He needed to move. Fast.

Turning tail, Barry looked around and began wading through the deep snow that had not been touched in decades. He threw a panicked glance behind and saw that the pillar was hurtling towards him. It would instantly crush him.

With a final roar, he threw himself forwards as the icy pillar crashed just inches shy of him, shaking the entire mountain around him.

Once more he found himself lying face down in the snow, breathing raggedly, every fibre of him hurt and exhausted. He commando-crawled forwards as the barely distinguishable road curved around a bend, hiding the viaduct from view, though it did not lessen the deafening destruction of the ancient viaduct by the disintegrating waterfall.

Despite the chaos unfolding, he could not help but allow himself a tiny smile. Despite all the odds stacked against him, he had made it across the viaduct and he now stood at the entrance to the Klazak Pass.

It was getting darker now and Barry began to wonder what his next move should be. But those thoughts were quickly put to one side as a different noise became audible. It wasn't the crashing, booming sound of the waterfall, but was a series of whumph noises that were getting louder. Barry cocked his head to one side to better hear, and noticed a flock of birds flying overhead, tweeting and chirping loudly, arrowing outwards from the mountain. The whumph noises were soon replaced by a deep roaring that sounded like it was coming almost from within the mountain itself and was getting louder and louder.

Soon the noise had completely blocked out the sound of the breaking waterfall, and filled Barry's head with a roaring, whooshing sound. The mountain began to shake and shudder. With a renewed horror Barry realised what was happening, but he was already too late.

He turned slowly and saw it.

An avalanche was coming.

CHAPTER 17

Avalanche

From high on the mountain vast slabs of snow were falling and hurtling down the untouched slopes, gathering momentum and destroying everything in their path.

From afar it must have looked beautiful, but stood directly in its path, Barry had never seen anything more terrifying, including the viaduct.

Huge plumes of powdery snow were being driven in every direction as the avalanche gathered rock, ice and snow to grow exponentially in size, racing at Barry at a terrific speed.

Snow drifts covered what had once been the ancient road that Barry stood on, with the mountain slope on one side, and a downward slope on the other. There was nowhere for him to go, nowhere for him to hide.

He looked around frantically, and began running as best he could, but the snow came up to his knees. Getting more desperate, he could feel his heart pounding in his chest as if determined to get in a lifetime of heartbeats in just a few seconds before the end of it all. A feeling of overwhelming powerlessness engulfed him, as the roaring and shaking filled his entire body.

The wall of white was just seconds away, towering high above and blocking out the pale moon that had appeared low in the sky. He screwed up his eyes and thought of his poor mother who would never know what had become of him. Of Tchyglock who had put so much faith in him. Barry threw himself face forward into a deep snow drift and tried to burrow into it, feebly hoping the avalanche would pass over his head.

And then it hit.

The force was phenomenal. It was like being punched by a thousand people at once as the entire snowdrift Barry was lying in was lifted into the air and thrown forwards with incredible power.

The world turned upside down, as Barry was tossed into the air, before the whirl of snow plucked him back into its midst and lurched him forwards. Rock and chunks of ice whipped around him, cutting him, banging him.

Remembering the only advice Maurice had given him for an avalanche, he started desperately swimming the breaststroke against the tide of the snow, to try and get on top of it, but had no idea which way was up, which was down. It felt completely hopeless at first, but he noticed that he was moving slightly away from the tip of the avalanche, and more importantly from the worst of the debris, and deeper into the tsunami of snow. The force of the avalanche was so strong that every sweep of his arm felt like trying to push against a bag of bricks. Barry had never felt so out of control in his life.

The world was white and the sound was deafening. He could feel himself crying, but the tears were freezing on his already ruined face.

A pine tree appeared out of the fog, appearing ghostly in the white vortex, and Barry desperately tried to grab hold of it, before realising it had already been torn up by the avalanche. He could not tell if he was high in the air, or low to the side of the mountain. There was a renewed thrust as he was bundled head over heels, spinning out of control. Something huge hit him on the back of the head and all went black.

Barry wasn't sure if he was unconscious for seconds, minutes or hours, but when he opened his eyes the pace of the avalanche was definitely slowing, and he began to see patches of sky. His eyes were thick with blood from a wound on his head, and his shoulder had dislocated itself again. Beyond pain now, Barry's body felt loose and slack, letting itself get tossed to and fro as he gave up trying to swim against the tide.

There was a sudden lurch and he felt momentarily weightless, as if the avalanche had tumbled into nothingness, and with an almighty *flump*, he landed heavily and was buried in snow.

Everything went from white to completely black.

Barry felt completely suffocated, couldn't breathe and began to panic.

With great caution, he tried to wiggle his fingers and toes and was relieved to find that he was able to. With his right hand he carefully moved it upwards and dug out an air pocket around his face, and breathed deeply. He felt sick from the blow to his head, and could taste blood in his mouth. All was quiet now.

Unaware which way was up and which way was down Barry tried to consider his next move, but found it difficult to concentrate as the terror at his predicament and the pain coursing through his body threatened to overwhelm him. He forced himself to slow his breathing.

'Deep breaths,' he said to himself, finding comfort in the sound of a voice.

There was the sound of some shifting snow beneath him, and he made the decision to try and move in that direction, fervently praying that it was the way to the surface.

The cold was seeping into his bones, but he was grateful that it was numbing some of the pain in his dislocated shoulder. He twisted himself around and began cautiously, slowly and methodically digging and wriggling his way through the complete darkness.

Time lost any meaning as Barry determinately dug, one handed, into the darkness, alone with just the terror that he was digging to his death and would never be found. Eventually, the darkness began to become less oppressive, and tinges of lightness slowly began to appear through the snow.

He thanked his lucky stars for picking the right direction to move in and dug faster, dolphin-kicking with his legs, while remaining careful not to disturb the snow too much or restart the avalanche.

After what seemed like an eternity, his head broke the surface.

The world had been cloaked in a sea of white. His head poking out was the only thing to break up a colourless landscape. Twisting around, he blinked, blinded by the brightness of the snow against an inky black sky.

Behind him was the cliff from which the avalanche had hurtled , rising at least a hundred metres up. His core temperature had plummeted and he had pins and needles in his nose, which he knew was a sign of frostnip, the early stages of frostbite. After all he had endured, Barry was not prepared to lose chunks of his nose as well. Casting his eyes around, he spotted the beginnings of a tree line in the distance and instantly knew that his survival for the night depended on him reaching it.

He fanned his arms out and slowly began to push himself forward with his arms, trying to spread his weight as much as possible over the powdery snow. He rolled onto his back, and with an exhausted scream, yanked his shoulder back into place. This time there was a deep grinding sensation, but he put any thoughts of what it might mean from his mind. Survival was all that mattered now.

As he worked his way across the enormous snow drift, he began to see the roots of trees poking up, the remains of animals that had not been as lucky as him to survive the avalanche. He whispered an apology to each of them that he passed, feeling responsible for the avalanche, and once again wishing he had never discovered the entrance to this magical and brutal world.

The snow was fluffy and not well packed, and more than once Barry disappeared back into the snow before clambering back out. Eventually he reached firmer ground and was able to see the full devastation of the avalanche.

The entire mountain had changed shape, losing vast swathes of ice, rock and snow. But Barry had bigger problems than the changing shape of the mountain. He had lost the road.

"Do not stray from the road. Lose the road, and you will not find it again."

Maurice's words echoed around his head, and alone on a barren stretch of uninhabited mountain, Barry felt like his doom was closer at hand than at any point on the broken viaduct.

He began to trudge towards the tree line, but frequently stumbled as his feet were completely numb. He rubbed furiously at his face in a bid to stave off frostbite and knew that above all else, he must keep moving.

With the tree line only two hundred metres away he started dreaming of a warm fire and lost concentration. He tripped on a rock and fell over a steep six metre drop he had not seen amidst the endless white surroundings. He landed heavily and began to roll uncontrollably down the mountain. He frantically tried to grab at something to stop his fall, but lumps of snow just came away in his hands.

Mercifully the terrain flattened out just ahead of the trees and he came skidding to a halt just shy of an anaemic looking spruce tree.

There was no use wiggling his fingers and toes as he could no longer feel them anyway. He set about gathering any loose wood he could find and walked further into the forest where the temperature was a marginally warmer.

Lighting the fire took some time due to the numbness in his hands which prevented him from setting his stone to flint, which he was grateful had survived in the small pack of essentials strapped tightly to his chest. The wood was not as dry as he would have liked, but eventually, after great effort and patience, he had a merry, if smoky, fire blazing before him. Before allowing himself to relax, he dragged some fallen boughs around him, and using his knife, cut large sprigs of pine and spruce to form a makeshift shelter.

As the fire brought back some feeling to his body, so too it brought enormous amounts of pain. There was an intense burning in his foot, and on closer inspection he was fairly sure that he had broken at least two toes. As he tried to stand, he found that he could add some broken ribs to the list too. But none of them compared to the agony of his shoulder.

Getting close to the light of the fire, he peeled off his shirt and saw that the entire shoulder joint was swollen and inflamed. A black bruise was spreading around the joint towards his neck and chest, and there was a clicking, grinding sensation whenever he tried to lift the arm.

He had placed a rock with a deep indent in it next to the fire and shovelled snow into it, and soon drank deeply, but his belly longed for some food.

He lay down on a snowless clearing next to the fire, pulled the boughs around him and the sprigs over him, and allowed his eyes to close.

Sleep was fitful and hard to come by despite the overwhelming weariness. His stomach was cramping in hunger, and his body screamed every time he moved. Each breath hurt through his ribs and the frozen ground beneath him crept into his battered joints despite the fire, which he regularly woke up to throw more wood onto.

In his fevered sleep Princess Lahlia appeared once more. This time she appeared more solid, and he could hear her voice. It was soft and lyrical.

'Barry Birchwood,' she whispered, like a voice on the wind.

'Help me,' he pleaded, his body on fire.

'You are stronger than you think. You must survive, we are all depending on you.'

'I can't, I want to give up,' he moaned.

'Everyone who has a hard life wants to give up at some point. It takes huge resolve to continue,' she said gently, her face beatific, 'and you have that resolve.'

'I don't!'

'I believe in you. I believe you will rescue me, I have seen it in our dreams.'

'Do you mean this is real?'

She smiled. 'Nothing is more real than our dream bond.' Her expression suddenly changed. 'Barry.' she said sharply.

'What,' he groaned.

'Wake up.'

'I don't want to.'

'Wake up now!' she shouted.

Barry's eyes snapped open and his ears were filled with screams.

CHAPTER 18

Rhew

He leapt to his feet and his own screams joined those echoing around the mountainside as his whole body protested furiously.

Through the pre-dawn darkness he could see the whites of enormous eyes darting through the trees. Barry quickly stoked up the fire and pulled a blazing branch from it, sweeping it back and forth around him.

The torch illuminated the shadowy shapes attached to the luminous eyes and the high-pitched screams. A pack of the screaming wolves Maurice had warned him of were scampering through the forest around him. They had large, jutting lower jaws, and elongated canine teeth that curved over their lips. In the flickering darkness their piebald fur made them appear as streaks of evil, flitting through the trees and opening their huge jaws wide to screech at the night sky. The sound was piercing, and without thinking, Barry dropped the torch and covered his ears.

Seeing their chance, a pair of the wolves leapt into the clearing. Barry quickly grabbed the blazing branch and swung it in their direction, forcing them back. Around him he could see the wolves growing bolder, closing in towards him.

He drew his slender sword with his free hand, holding the torch with his weakened arm, barely keeping it aloft. Now that they were closer, he got a better look at the wolves and was struck by how ugly they were. They were smaller than the wolves he was more familiar with, but their screams, fangs and powerful lower jaws made them even more terrifying, while their dappled hides and bulbous large eyes made them appear sickly and diseased.

'Get back!' he roared, hoping to frighten them off, but was unsurprised when it was greeted with nothing more than another chorus of ear-splitting screams.

A wolf leapt at him from the side, and with a rapid thrust of his sword he impaled it. Its screams died with it.

Seeing their fallen comrade, the pack smelt blood and screams began to be intermingled with snarls. More of the ragged, starving creatures ran in to attack him, and Barry struck swiftly and ruthlessly, whirling the burning branch around him wildly to prevent any attacks from behind. The bodies of the fallen wolves lay in front of him like a barrier, but casting the fire around he could see that there were tens of others prowling the edges of the clearing, waiting for their opportunity. He could not defeat an entire pack of starving wolves. The wolves sensed the same thing, and a dozen of them all hurtled at him at once.

He stumbled backwards and tripped, dropping his sword. As he scrambled to reach it, a wolf landed on his face, and from the size of it and the fact that the pack stepped back slightly, Barry sensed it was the pack leader.

It filled Barry's nostrils with the smell of rotting carrion. The wolf's weight on his chest was suffocating him as his broken ribs ground together, and the beast almost seemed to grin at him as it opened its huge jaw, preparing to crush his skull. Barry struggled feebly amidst the cacophony of euphoric screams coming from the surrounding pack.

Then, without warning, the screams turned to yelps. The pack leader's jaw clapped shut, leaving rancid drool dripping onto Barry's face, as the wolf's head snapped around. With a frightened yap he leapt off Barry, hurtled out of the clearing and disappeared into the forest, the pack following.

Silence descended onto the clearing as the screams grew further and further away. Barry was both confused and immensely grateful. *Why would they suddenly disappear*, he asked himself, before pushing himself up onto his elbows and taking stock of his situation. Water was easy enough to produce on a snowy mountain, but his body needed food to recover and he wondered if roasting one of the fallen wolves would provide him with any nutrition. The thought made him gag slightly.

'On a long forgotten mountainside, a weary child did reside,' a cold voice whispered.

Barry nearly leapt out of his skin. He snapped around and saw a lone man in a full-length crimson velvet coat stood atop a large boulder. Despite the red coat, everything about the figure burned blue-white. The hair, short and spiked all over, was whiter than the snow, while his eyes burned with azure flames. His skin had a pale blue, translucent quality, while the teeth closely resembled icicles, as they hung clear and colourless, with sharpened points. He exuded evil, and the disappearance of the screaming wolves now made a great deal more sense.

'Who are you?' Barry demanded, scooping up his sword.

'The child has demands, but I smell the blood on his hands,' the man replied, sniffing menacingly.

Understanding dawned on Barry with a slow horror as again the words of Maurice replayed in his mind. 'If you spill blood, they will come.' He looked at his bloodied hands, his battered body and gently touched his tattered face. He had been careless in the face of the Ohjaja's advice, but there had been little alternative.

'You are an ice fravashi,' Barry said. It was not a question.

The man laughed giddily, and everything around them seemed to grow colder. His eyes blazed an intense blue and suddenly the fire sputtered and died, bringing with it an even more intense chill that hurt Barry's broken bones.

Illuminated by the waxing moon, there was nonetheless a darkness surrounding the faintly glowing figure that seemed inexplicably deeper than the night sky, as if it was beyond night and into nothingness.

'Little did the child know, this was as far as his journey would go,' the fravashi chanted.

'I'm not a child,' Barry said furiously. 'Tell me your name, fravashi.'

'The child comes to high places, full of demands, forgetting the smell of blood on his hands. Those who enter the Klazak Pass are few, and none can best the fravashi named Rhew.'

He spoke his name with a long exhale, and it seemed to summon an arctic wind that rattled through the trees around Barry. The shadowy figure licked his blood-red lips with a leer, and jumped down from his boulder, landing lightly as if carried by the breeze.

'I do not want trouble,' Barry said, feeling ice cold sweat beading its way down his body and taking a step backwards.

Rhew began to idly saunter towards him, smirking. He was slender and wiry in appearance and looked human, but Barry knew there was nothing human within the dark spirit.

'To consume you is no trouble, it is no trouble at all, for tonight I will welcome another lost soul to my hall.'

Remembering Maurice's teachings, that ice fravashis could not be bested and to lose was a fate worse than death, Barry turned tail and ran.

He dashed out of the tree line and back to the vast expanse of white. The road was completely lost from sight, and he no longer had any idea if he was even in the Klazak Pass, or some other pass, valley or even a different mountain.

'Run, run, he runs away, but your time is up, Rhew will not play,' the icy shade chided in his high, breathy voice from right behind Barry.

Barry spun and swung his sword, which is what saved his life as, with a bell-like peal, the sword clashed with the blade of the fravashi which had been rushing with an overhead swing down at his back.

For a moment the pair's eyes locked, the pale grey of Barry's determinately boring into the cold blue of the eons-old spirit cursed to roam the high places of the mountains. The eyes were beyond cold; they were icy and piercing with hate and it chilled Barry's soul. The staring contest ended as quickly as it had begun as Rhew scraped his blade along the length of Barry's with a spiteful leer, before jumping back and sweeping it down with frightening speed.

Barry only just managed to parry it, and it was followed by a flurry of blows that hurtled at him, the fravashi's arms almost a blur as he rained blow after blow down on him. Desperately fielding them, Barry was forced backwards, unable to see any opening to make any kind of offensive move himself. Unlike in his training with Dead-Nettle, there was no underlying knowledge that whatever happened he would in fact be okay and relatively unharmed. This was a fight to the death, and Barry desperately clung to life, forcing his weary body into a battle that he could not possibly win.

As he backed further up the slope, Rhew began to break through Barry's defences and soon he could feel hot blood dripping from shallow slices in his arms and thighs. Rhew was cackling, and Barry realised he was playing with him. Furious, he gritted his teeth and began to swing aggressively at the fravashi, determined to go down valiantly and not as the plaything of the evil spirit. Rhew parried his blows with ease and laughed.

'The child's teeth have no bite, much too weak for a fravashi knife fight,' he jeered, lithely spinning to fend off a clumsy jab Barry had made for his ribs. Barry had a sudden idea, and darted inwards as the fravashi lifted his sword with another body-juddering crash, and once more their eyes were locked, mere inches apart, Barry's breath rising in clouds around their heads in the freezing night. A single tear snaked its way down Barry's cheek as the pain threatened to overcome him. However, while their eyes were locked, his fingers numbly fumbled with his belt.

'It's all too much for the child, time to say adieu. There is no shame in falling to the fravashi named Rhe-aaaargh!' The creature screamed in pain and rage and staggered backwards.

Barry had stuck one of his throwing stars straight into the ice-cold eye of Rhew. There was a hissing sound from the eye, like the sound like a balloon going down slowly, as the fravashi leapt around on the spot clutching his face and screaming.

Then he grew completely still and pulled the small throwing star out of his face. There was nothing but an intense flaming blue where his eye had once been, and gloopy droplets ran down his cheek like glowing tears. His one remaining eye flashed with an intense hatred that made Barry's blood run cold.

Now Rhew approached him slowly, any sense of fun and games gone completely. Without breaking stride, he began raining blows down on Barry with renewed vigour. This time he didn't strike to maim, but to kill.

The slashes came with whip like precision and Barry was forced quickly backwards, stumbling and swinging desperately to fend off the swordsmanship of his opponent's narrow blade. The fravashi was silent now, and no hint of a smirk touched his red lips, a red so dark they almost looked like they had been painted.

Barry threw another star, which Rhew easily dodged, and he tried to start working his way onto the fravashi's blind side. In his attempt to move sideways, Barry's foot slipped on the loose shale of the mountain. Before he knew it, he was falling.

The mountain angled down sharply and Barry was rolling rapidly. He tried to claw at the ground to stop his fall but his momentum was too quick.

As swiftly as he had fallen, he came to a stop as he flew deep into a huge snow drift that had collected around a small copse of pine trees. A quick attempt to move brought the realisation that he was stuck, with the column he had created in his fall more smooth ice than snow.

It was almost like being back in the aftermath of the avalanche, surrounded by freezing white. Only this time he could clearly see which way was up, as up above him Rhew stood on a rocky outcrop glaring down at him with his one fierce eye.

'Your death is nigh. I will let you freeze. I will not let you enjoy a passing with ease,' he growled in his high whispering voice.

Barry felt totally powerless stuck in his frozen hole, able to see nothing but the glowing blue of the ice fravashi's head, and his red coat against the night sky. His body began to shake in the sub-zero temperatures that had further plummeted as the night wore on. He searched for the flower that Felanne had given him for some sign of warmth, but it had been lost on the mountain like so much else.

Rhew did not attempt to climb down, content to just coldly watch Barry slowly freeze to death in his icy tomb, no hint of emotion upon his face. The silence was deafening, with not a sound to be heard on the silent patch of desolate mountainside.

Eyes closed, Barry tried to imagine he was somewhere warm, perhaps back in the valley he had seen when arriving as his miniature self on the waterways in what seemed like a lifetime ago, or in his warm bed back in Briley Heath. He thought of his books, of the epic sagas he had read and watched in films; the heroes always won in the end, they didn't freeze in isolated mountain holes. He imagined the score that would play to this scene in a movie, an epic but sad piano refrain, for when all was finally lost. Whether through design or because of his now tentative grasp on consciousness, Barry found himself descending into the Oran. His other awareness felt sluggish at first, and he briefly wondered if he had died and his spirit would now drift up to the clouds to be gathered by the Cloud Runners. Looking across at his physical form, he could see the lips turning hypothermic blue, but shallow breaths were still escaping them. Death was close at hand, but not upon him yet.

He drifted up the icy column and stretched towards the black sky. A tapestry of stars twinkled across them, whole galaxies staring down indifferently to his plight. He had fought so hard to come so far, Barry thought with a detached sigh. He drifted up and looked down at the prone form of the ice fravashi, whose single eye remained fixed on his physical form. Able to look at him properly now, Barry noticed how tall the figure was, and with a great deal more muscle than he had first realised. Neither dead nor alive, the creature was trapped in an eternal purgatory. With a sudden thought, Barry decided to free Rhew, to allow him to pass on. It was so simple! Why had he not thought of it before?

He glided down on the breeze to hover directly in front of the personification of evil, who looked straight through him, but he felt unafraid. He could not be harmed.

With lightning speed the ice fravashi thrust out an arm and grabbed Barry's invisible consciousness around the throat. He hung there, choking under the vice-like grip and for the first time when lowered in the Oran, he felt afraid. Below, his unconscious physical body began choking and bucking. 'This is not possible!' Barry screamed to himself.

'I have some news, for you, 'tis tragic: your tricks do not work with creatures of magic. Now you must stare into the face of death, the time has arrived to release your last breath,' Rhew said in an almost silent whisper full of maliciousness.

Barry thrust forward, his insubstantial hand passing through Rhew's chest. He could feel the ancient heart beating slowly and steadily. With a final effort, he deepened the Oran and solidified his consciousness.

Rhew's eye widened in shock. He began to choke as Barry's hand closed around the heart.

'Death is close tonight, but it does not belong to me,' Barry said, though he doubted Rhew could hear, and summoning all his strength, he pulled as hard as he could, bringing the heart with him.

The fravashi, who had roamed the high places of the Shodum Mountains for hundreds, if not thousands, of years gurgled in shock, and with his last breath, a blue shadow escaped his body and drifted upwards to join the stars. The red cloaked body fell forward and tumbled into the snow drift.

Quickly, Barry raced his consciousness back down and began trying to hoist his body upwards. The quickly freezing body was so heavy and even his soul was so very, very tired. The first touches of daylight were beginning to appear on the horizon, the skyline beginning to lighten. Suddenly, a single beam of sunlight bathed him in morning sunshine as the top of the sun peeked just above a mountaintop in the distance. It filled his entire being with a sense of joyous warmth. He pulled with all his might, and his body landed clumsily on top of the snow.

He hurriedly descended back into his body, and his mouth opened in a silent scream. He could scarcely feel his body, everything was so stiff, so frozen. Opening his eyes was even difficult as a thin layer of ice had formed on them. With a soft crack, the ice fell away and his pale grey eyes saw the dawn of a new day.

The scene was beautiful, a layer of mist floating through the valley below as sunshine breathed a tiny bead of warmth back into his heart. It gave him a renewed determination and he began to try and move his limbs. They were horribly stiff, but they began to slightly creak into action.

Beneath him, ahead of the icy snowdrift, was the prone body of Rhew and he began to try and crawl towards it, being careful not to fall again into the drift, which would surely spell the end.

He half rolled down off the drift to land on the firmer ground where the body lay. He suddenly noticed that in his frozen hand was clutched the black heart of the fallen fravashi. It was completely smooth and freezing cold.

With a cry of pain, he pushed himself to his feet, staggered over to his vanquished enemy, and pulled off the long red coat, throwing it over himself. Instantly he felt a swell of warmth. It was made of a fabric unlike anything Barry had ever seen before, like the rustling of leaves and sunshine woven into a silkily flowing coat. Whether it was good or evil, Barry was in no position to turn it away as heat magically began to flow back into his extremities. With the warmth came a return of the pain, but he was distracted as he looked at the body of the ice fravashi named Rhew. In death it had turned to pure ice, that somehow looked both terrifying and regal. Barry wondered if it had captured a modicum of the man Rhew had once been. With a huge heave, he stood the ice sculpture onto its feet, a statue to forever take watch over the spectacular mountainside. He pocketed the smooth, dry and blackened heart for reasons he couldn't understand, and returned to his camp from the night before.

There were still some burning embers glowing in the fire and he stoked it up, enjoying the heat that washed over him. With great reluctance he skinned and cooked the haunch of one of the fallen wolves. Too hungry to be repulsed, he ravenously chewed down the meat, barely noticing or caring what it tasted like. To his starved stomach the hot meat tasted incredible and he felt the strength returning to him, aided by as much melted snow as he could stomach.

With no idea where the road was, and no desire to encounter any more screaming wolves, ice fravashis, or any of the other magical beasts that resided on the mountain, Barry resolved to get to low ground as swiftly as possible. His ruined shoulder was a constant agony, and he used some of the slimy hide from the wolf to fashion a makeshift sling, which offered some relief. He pulled a burning branch from the fire in case of any more wolves, and with that, he pursed his lips and decided to angle downwards through the trees, aiming for the misty valley below.

He encountered nothing as he staggered down the mountain, every step on the steep slope sending jolts through his battered and bruised body. Eventually the snow became less, and the trees grew denser, the ground littered with pine needles as the snow line got left fully behind.

It began to grow much warmer as the morning wore on, but now the coat around him was cool. At one point the trees cleared and he saw a glacial lake in the distance standing on a large, flat area of the mountain. The water was a pale, cloudy blue and he yearned to wash in it and drink the fresh water. He began to angle towards it, but the sight of a splash in the middle of the lake made him stop in his tracks. He remembered Maurice's warnings of Highland silkies, and turned away. He had no inclination to encounter a saw-toothed mountain seal today.

After several hours of walking, the coniferous mountain forest of evergreens began to be replaced by the deciduous, leaf-shedding trees of the lowlands and the air felt easier to breath. Game trails began to appear, and he followed them gratefully, pleased to have a route, no matter how haphazard, to follow into the valley.

The shadows were growing longer when he finally made it to the foot of the mountain. A stream bubbled merrily along, cutting its way between the enormous slopes above. Unable to walk any further, Barry collapsed down on the bank next to it and drank hungrily. The sun dappled bank felt soft and warm, and he decided to stop there for the night. After washing himself down he felt refreshed. Exploring the surrounding woodland and stream he found mushrooms, wild garlic and arugula growing. It wasn't much, but Barry did not have the energy to hunt for his food. The meal he cooked on a small fire was paltry, but with tiredness reaching right to his core, Barry allowed a long dreamless sleep to take him. Dawn was breaking when he eventually woke up. His body felt stiff and sore after sleeping on the forest floor, but his mind felt clearer.

In the stream below he spotted the dark shapes of trout and decided to try something he had heard worked. He lay on his stomach and reached into the water by the bank. There was a sudden movement below as a number of trout burst out of their shaded alcove. But there was one lazy trout that Barry was able to roughly pin to the side. He began to tickle its stomach, and after a minute or so the wriggling, slippery fish became stock still. Quick as a flash Barry grabbed its tail and threw it onto the bank. Unlike the speckled trout he knew from back home, these were striped, almost like zebra. They still tasted just as good though, and breakfast that morning was a lot more satisfying than his foraged, rubbery mushrooms the night before as he cooked up the fish on a hot stone with some more wild garlic.

Feeling sated and rested, he turned his attentions to how to get back to Burroha. He had no idea where he was, which way was home, and in a valley that looked to have been untouched by human hands, no likelihood of meeting anyone who could point him in the right direction.

Peering up at the mountain above him, which disappeared into the clouds, he had no idea where the avalanche had taken him, where he was in relation to the now destroyed viaduct, and no clue where the road was.

Making a snap decision, he decided to head upstream and follow the water as it snaked through the valley, hoping it might lead him towards something familiar.

***

Two days later he was still hopelessly lost.

His clothes were tattered after having to wade through thick bracken on the lower parts of hills and mountains. The night before he had narrowly avoided a bear with pale green fur, which had definitely not featured in any of his lessons, Barry having to let the current carry him down the river for a mile in order to escape. He had a very bad chill from sleeping outside with no covers that kept making him dizzy, it hurt to breathe and his body felt like it was beginning to shut down. Only the long coat of the ice fravashi offered him any protection from the elements, and miraculously remained unscathed.

Tchyglock would have looked for his arrival at sundown the day before, and the Sonphea would most likely now presume him dead. That night he had found a small cave in the side of a mountain covered with shale. He had squeezed through the narrow entrance to the cave, which then opened out nicely and he was relieved to have a night away from the elements. That morning he had woken up covered in frosty dew. His shoulder was now a deep shade of purple that spread right across his chest and down his arm, and had swollen to twice its normal size. Infected looking scabs covered his face, and much of his body too, and they itched uncomfortably.

Laying down on the rocky floor, he began to drift off into a feverish sleep, both boiling hot and freezing cold at the same time, when he heard the sound of voices.

He jubilantly leapt to his feet, delighted to hear some form of human life, a flame of hope leaping inside his wheezy chest. He hurried to the mouth of the cave and saw a small group of soldiers in blood-red chain mail trudging in the valley, just yards below him, illuminated by flaming torches they carried with them in the twilight. They carried a black flag with a red crown upon it and Barry gasped. The flag of Suzerain Cikavac.

'Can't we stop, Sarge? We've been marching for hours,' one of the soldiers complained loudly.

'Private Craddock, you complain more than my wife,' the man leading them retorted. 'But this seems as good a place as any. Craddock, I think you've volunteered for setting up camp,' he added, pulling a low stool from his pack and stretching out his legs. 'Vagel, give Craddock a hand fetching sticks for the tents. Matte and Smir, go and collect some firewood, it's going to be a cold one tonight.'

There was a collective grumbling as the men dispersed, leaving the sergeant and one other seated together.

'This is the most pointless recon mission I've ever been sent on, Sarge,' said remaining soldier said quietly once his companions were out of earshot. 'We've no more chance of finding the Sonphea in these mountains than Craddock has of shutting his mouth for five minutes.'

'I know that as well as you do, but orders is orders, who are we to question them?'

'Until the suzerain starts paying us a proper wage, I feel just fine about questioning the orders plenty.'

'Careful, Desh, that's only a step away from desertion talk,' the sergeant growled. 'Though I can't say I disagree. Sooner we can wipe out the Sonphea the sooner we can all get some rest. I only signed up for a quiet life on a barracks.'

'Pish posh! You signed up because you love impaling the resistance on that sword of yours,' Desh cackled.

'Well I do love that,' the sergeant admitted with a chuckle. The soldiers who must have been Matte and Smir returned with firewood, and a fire was soon crackling merrily, throwing their faces into glow and shadow. The smell of bacon began to drift up towards Barry who was afraid to so much as breathe, but instantly began to salivate.

The relative silence was broken by a commotion from further down the valley within the trees.

'What is all that goddam racket?' the sergeant shouted. 'They'll have every monster down on us in minutes.'

Craddock and Vagel came marching back up the low rise to their camp, quickly.

'Where are the sticks? Seven suns, Craddock, you have to be the worst soldier I've ever encountered, and I've been with Corporal Desh here for years.'

'Oi!' Desh protested.

'Sarge, you need to come and take a look at this,' Craddock said breathlessly.

'What is it? Confused an old tree with a griffin again?' one of the other soldiers said cruelly.

'Say that again, Matte, and you won't see the morning,' Craddock said, loosening his sword in its sheath, as Matte stood up menacingly.

'Calm down, calm down, the pair of you. What's got you so excited, Private?' the sergeant demanded.

'Just down there in the valley, the trees have been crushed and obliterated by hundreds of enormous stones and blocks of ice.'

'So?' Desh said curtly.

'So it looks like it only happened in the last couple of days. Sir, I think we might be close to the Sonphea. The stone looks to have been hewn by the hands of humans.'

Barry's heart was beating furiously in his fevered chest. It sounded like this was where the viaduct had fallen from thousands of feet above. But if squads of soldiers were coming, he needed to warn Xhaffa and Tchyglock immediately. His legs were trembling with the effort of keeping him upright, and waves of dizziness were hitting him from every angle.

'Is what Private Craddock saying true, Private Vagel?' the sergeant asked, lowering his voice.

'Yessir. Saw it wiv my own eyes, din't I. I'd heard tales of an ancient bridge up in them mountains, this could be from that. Had always thought it was just a story, but maybe it weren't.'

Barry was jarringly reminded of Dyn and realised how much he missed his friend.

'This could be big. If we're the squad that found the Sonphea… it'll be even more fun than burning villages,' the sergeant said, his big grin looking haunted in the firelight as the others cackled.

The sergeant suddenly held up his hand to silence them. 'Did any of you hear that?' he whispered, drawing his sword. Barry too thought he had heard a sound, like the snapping of a twig. The other soldiers nodded, drawing their own swords with practised silence.

Barry dared not move as he strained his ears for another sound over the crackling of the fire. What monster would the mountains throw at him next?

The quiet was broken by the sound of whistling. To Barry it sounded like it was coming from every direction. Realisation dawned on the soldiers too late as arrows flew into them. The sergeant rose with a roar and brandished his sword, two arrows sticking out of his arm. Seconds later he looked more like a pin cushion, as tens of arrows buried themselves in his chest and he fell, gurgling briefly before growing silent. The flint of the arrows pinged off the stone around Barry's cave and he dived back inside.

The commotion was over as quickly as it had begun. Barry crawled to the edge of his cave and peered into the gloom. Shadowy figures were descending on the camp from every direction and Barry strained to hear what they said. And then, without warning, there was a cracking of shale from just above him and a figure landed before him.

'What do we have here?' the man clad in black leather said. Before Barry had chance to answer, the man had grabbed him by the collar and thrown him over the ledge, onto the floor below. He landed clumsily on the fallen body of Private Craddock, and immediately rolled and jumped to his feet, drawing his sword.

The figures closed in and Barry whirled frantically in a circle, trying to keep them at sword's length, but there was no strength left in his arm and a wave of dizziness hit him so hard he fell to one knee and vomited onto the ground.

'Barry?' asked a voice that Barry recognised, but could not believe it to be true. Out of the gloom walked a hooded woman. As she approached, she lowered the hood and standing, Barry gazed into the eyes of Zosime.

CHAPTER 19

A Dream and a Story

When he looked back, Barry was unable to recall the journey back to Burroha. He had fallen into Zosime's arms and the rest was a blur of night sky, being dragged on some sort of sled. By the time they reached the halls of the Sonphea, the fever had overcome him and he was completely unconscious.

He dreamt over and over of the princess; she was whispering to him, but he could not understand what she was saying, too entranced was he by her. In the murk behind her he could see flames and enormous shadows, but then suddenly he would be back in The Golden Lion with Tracy Lackey and Micky Hancock. He tried to scream at them to save him, but all they would say was, 'Come back,' over and over. From there he was in the eye of a storm, a swirling vortex of wind whipping around him. Within the tornado appeared the ethereal faces of Tchyglock, Dyn, Zosime, Dead-Nettle and Felanne. 'Come back, come back,' they murmured over and over, their voices being stolen away on the wind. Rhew suddenly appeared like a giant in the dark clouds, his flaming blue eyes piercing through the rain like lightning. Barry shrank back, trying to escape into the ground. 'Child, come join me in the clouds on high, 'tis a blessing, in the end, to die.' Barry screamed but he couldn't hear his voice, only the thudding of the blackened heart in his pocket.

After what felt like an eternity the storm died down and he found himself on a sandy beach. The sun was shining and it warmed his skin. He looked down and it was completely unblemished, his shoulder whole. The sand was hot but not unpleasant, and an azure sea was sparkling before him, small waves crashing softly. Along the beach was coming a figure. He flinched, fearing the return of Rhew once again. But soon he saw that it was a woman, dressed in a simple white dress. Her jet black hair tumbled over one shoulder, her eyes were a dark umber and she had familiar, almost angelic features, and to Barry seemed the most exotic and beautiful woman he had ever seen.

'Princess Luellason.' He bowed formally as she approached.

She laughed and it tinkled like small cheerful bells. 'I think we are past such formality, Barry.'

She sat down beside him. 'Come back to us, Barry,' she whispered into his ear.

'But it is so comfortable here, back there it hurts.'

'There has to be rain to fully appreciate the sun,' she replied cryptically, smiling through expressive lips. She frowned. 'Sometimes I too would rather stay here, but people like you and I, we do not get to enjoy the easy option.'

They sat in silence for several minutes.

'Where are we?' Barry asked.

'Somewhere in between our dreams,' she answered with a shrug of her shoulders.

'Maybe… we could come here together again,' he said hesitantly, blushing.

She laughed her tinkling laugh again, and stroked his cheek gently, saying nothing.

'Come back,' she mouthed, but he could not hear her as the colours began to swirl.

'No!' he cried as her face began to fade with a smile on her lips. The wind again seemed to whisper to him as he felt as if he were falling from a great height.

With a jolt, his eyes opened.

Barry immediately turned on his side but nearly rolled off the edge of what turned out to be the bed he was lying in.

Dark shapes were moving around him, but his eyes were heavy. A cool hand was placed on his forehead.

'Gently, child, it's okay,' a high voice said.

At the word *child* Barry sat bolt upright, convinced Rhew had somehow been revived and come to get him.

'No!' he shouted, trying to reach for his sword but finding only bed linen. The room began to come into focus. He was back in his cave in

Burroha, but a huge raised, soft bed had been brought in, which filled much of the room, and pastel-coloured drapes had been hung from the walls, making it feel lighter and more welcoming. An elderly woman with a kindly face stood next to him, and at the foot of the bed was Tchyglock, looking grave and drawn.

'Now, now, Master Birchwood, it's okay. You're safe now, back in Burroha,' said the woman.

'What? How?' Barry spluttered, feeling disorientated and confused.

'You'll get no answers if you don't lie back down, young man,' the matronly woman said sternly. Barry looked at her as he allowed himself to be pushed back down onto his back and pillows were stuffed under his head to prop him up. Crinkled, kindly eyes looked out at him from a weather-beaten face. She had a huge bosom and large arms and hands, and was clearly not one to argue with.

'Now take a deep breath and try to relax, you have been sleeping for a long time.'

With great reluctance Barry did as he was told, closing his eyes and taking a deep breath. He thought longingly of that beach and the princess as he became increasingly aware of the pain in his body. When he opened his eyes, everything seemed clearer and his brain began to catch up.

He noticed that his arms were covered in bandages, and more were wrapped tightly around his head. The dimness and confusion began to make more sense as he realised he was wearing a patch over one eye, and one arm was strapped across his chest.

He looked at the silent Tchyglock. 'Tell me everything, Tchyglock.' Tchyglock's face broke into a rare, almost fatherly, smile. In spite of himself, Barry smiled too. It hurt his face.

'I am far more interested to hear everything from you,' he said, but at a look from Barry cleared his throat. 'But of course, I will go first.' It was the first time Barry could remember Tchyglock acquiescing to a request from him.

'Do not keep him talking for long, Commander, he needs rest,' the woman said.

'Of course, Anita,' Tchyglock said respectfully, as he sat on the edge of the bed.

'There is not so much to tell,' he began as Anita gently wiped at Barry's face with a wet flannel. 'Early in the trial it became clear that you had been given an impossible task — or so it seemed. When your arm was ripped from the socket by the mountain arrow and falling frozen waterfall, even Xhaffa accepted that he had gone too far and it must be abandoned. When you revealed that you are…' He paused, and let out a big sigh. 'That you are a Küdugar, chaos began to ensue. And when you refused to stop, we all felt completely helpless, certain that you were determined to die,' Tchyglock said bleakly.

'I'm a what?' Barry asked, nonplussed.

'A Küdugar. It is your ability to affect things in the world with only your Oran consciousness. It is an ability only ever known to be possessed by the ancient royal line.' When Barry continued to look unimpressed, he narrowed his eyes. 'Look, Många Världar is a world alive with magic, but only a handful are able to access it and channel it, which different people do in different ways. For example, the warlocks use runes, staffs and spells to bind the magic of the land to their will. Some, like me, use their mind, words and a focus to channel the magic. Anita here uses herbs and plants imbued with the magic of the land and brings it to bear in medicine. Others, like Darvagh, have different ways and means, but the royal family had more magic and power than anyone else, and were able to bend the rules of the world in a way that no others can, like having their shadows do their bidding. To have that level of power is to be a Küdugar, or lord of the elements. It effectively ascends you to the level of royalty.'

'Royalty? Me?' Barry said stupidly.

'He may be a Küdugar but he doesn't seem to be the quickest, Tchyglock,' Anita said with a wink.

'I should have told you before, Zosime wanted me to, but I felt there was enough pressure on you already. Now it is there for all to see. But even after you revealed your abilities in the trial, when the entire bridge collapsed and fell, with no sign that you had survived, we were sure you had perished,' he continued. 'I still held onto some hope, but then the avalanche struck. We all watched from across the chasm as it rolled down the opposite slopes, destroying everything in its path. At that point, the crowd turned angry, directing rage and fury at Xhaffa and the Council. There has been much anger at forcing the saviour into such a trial at such a young age, and with so much pressure that he felt compelled to continue an impossible trial with the full use of only one arm. But to find out that he had lost us both a saviour and Küdugar, well, there is much anger indeed.'

'And rightly so, absolute nonsense,' Anita interrupted, clucking. She poured some jauce tea down his dry throat and he felt its replenishing properties warm his body.

Tchyglock held up his hand as if to say *You see what I mean?*.

'I was caught in the avalanche,' Barry said quietly, still trying to process everything Tchyglock had said. 'It was even more terrifying and painful than the viaduct.' When Tchyglock only looked at him sadly, Barry grunted, 'Carry on with your story.'

Tchyglock cleared his throat again. 'Well after that you were presumed dead. And when there was no sign of you on the evening of the second day, even I must admit I lost all hope. It was… a very difficult time.'

'You have no idea,' Barry murmured, struggling to get comfortable amidst the bandages, scabs and wounds. 'How did Zosime find me?'

'Pure chance. She was leading an operation after we were alerted to a reconnaissance squad of the usurper's soldiers near to Burroha. It was just dumb luck on our part that you were hiding in a cave above them. You passed out when they found you, and the ops team then fashioned a sled to carry you on. By the time they brought you back, you were nearly dead. It is only through the magic and care of Anita here that you were brought back from the brink.'

'You gave us plenty of scares over the past four days, let me tell you that, boy,' she said, putting a hand on him to stop him fidgeting.

'Four days?' Barry exclaimed.

'Your fever only broke this morning,' another voice that Barry recognised said. Maurice appeared out of Barry's blind spot from the eye patch.

'Maurice!' Barry said joyfully.

The Ohjaja's face was grizzled and sombre as he looked at his protégé. 'Last night we thought we had lost you,' he added. 'You were having fits in your sleep, and screaming something… something about a Roo.'

'Rhew,' Barry said quietly, the name still bringing a chill to his bones.

Maurice closed his eyes. 'Seven suns, no,' he breathed.

'What is a Rhew?' Tchyglock asked with unusual softness.

'Not a what... a who,' Maurice replied. 'Rhew is one of the most ancient and terrifying ice fravashis of the Shodum Mountains.'

'An ice fravashi?' Tchyglock exclaimed, looking from Barry to Maurice and back again. 'It cannot be!'

'I think now it might be time to hear your side of the story, young master,' said Maurice.

'Come, Ohjaja, he is tired. He very nearly died even last night, you must let him rest,' Anita said sternly, trying to shoo the two grizzled Sonphea warriors out of the cave.

'Sorry, Anita, but this is important,' Tchyglock said.

'Okay, well make it quick,' she grumbled, 'I'll be back in a minute,' she added, bustling out of the cave.

'We will be as swift as possible and leave him in your very capable hands,' Tchyglock replied. 'Now, Barry, tell us everything.'

Barry talked through a cracked and parched throat, pausing often as Tchyglock fed him some water. He told them of saving himself from falling with his Oran consciousness, of making it through the waterfall and the collapse of the bridge as he shinned across the archway.

'That is a truly incredible achievement, boy,' Maurice said, his craggy, one-eyed face impressed. Barry thought it might have been the first time the training master had ever properly complimented him.

'Please continue, Barry,' Tchyglock said, his face grave.

'Well... then I walked around the corner and the avalanche struck,' Barry said lamely. He went on to describe the experience of being in the avalanche, of the world turned upside down before finally coming to rest miles away from where he was meant to be, and with no sight of the road. He told them of the screaming wolves, and his encounter with the fravashi. At that point, both of the old men sat down, and Barry noticed that Tchyglock's hands were white knuckled, gripping the side of his seat.

'What you are saying is impossible,' Tchyglock said in a whisper.

'Not impossible, old man,' Maurice interjected, 'incredibly improbable.'

'I'm a good many years younger than you, *old man,*' Tchyglock protested, but fell silent at a look from Barry.

When Barry told them of how he used the Oran to defeat Rhew when all seemed lost, their mouths fell open.

'Do you see that red coat on the chair over there?' Barry asked, nodding towards it. 'That is the coat of Rhew. Look in the pocket and you will find his heart.'

Maurice did as he said, and held the smooth, black heart in his palm, his face aghast.

'The Council cannot deny proof like that,' Tchyglock said.

'The coat saved my life,' Barry said. 'Somehow it always gave me some warmth, no matter how cold it was.'

'The coat of an ice fravashi is imbued with an ancient magic. No living man has ever claimed one. I have not heard of someone defeating one since Degfan the Great in the days of antiquity, and that may only be myth.'

'Me neither,' Tchyglock added, shaking his head.

Barry shrugged, which sent knives of pain through his shoulder. He swiftly finished his tale up to the point of collapsing into Zosime's arms. Just like in the story, he began to feel consciousness slipping away from him.

'Seven suns, are you two still here?' Anita cried as she re-entered the cave, carrying several herbs and tonics. 'The boy needs *rest*!'

'We of course defer to your wisdom,' Tchyglock said gently. Before he turned to leave, he looked at Barry. 'What you have done is something truly special, Barry Birchwood. We will talk more when you have slept. Your friends have been desperate to see you, so don't sleep too long.'

'He will sleep as much as he needs to, no more or less than that!' Anita snapped, shooing the two men out.

Maurice turned at the doorway, Barry only dimly able to see him, and pressed the back of his fist to his forehead. Barry smiled and let the darkness take him once more.

CHAPTER 20

The Soothsayer's Omen

The next few days were a bit of a blur for Barry. Anita did her best to keep well-wishers at bay, but a steady stream of visitors made their way past her defences to come and see him in between his increasingly enforced naps.

She drew the line, however, when Dyn rushed in and pulled him into a rough embrace, causing him to wail in pain. Scabs, muscles, frost bite and his shoulder were not yet ready for human contact, and Anita whacked Dyn around the head with a thick bunch of medicinal plants. But she couldn't keep Dyn from hearing Barry's tale.

'They're callin' you Nida Killaer and Bjurg Lak,' Dyn said excitedly one morning after dodging a swing of Anita's broad arms.

'What do they mean?' Barry asked, his curiosity piqued.

'Nida Killaer is Conqueror of Shadows and Bjurg Lak is Mountain King!'

'I don't imagine Xhaffa is too fond of them calling me Mountain King,' Barry said, worried. 'But I don't *hate* Conqueror of Shadows,' he admitted with a small smile.

'That is a seriously cool nickname,' Dyn agreed, 'I wonder will I ever get one,' he added wistfully.

'I can give you one if you want?' Barry said grinning.

'I'm not havin' anything you make up for me! I need to earn one, to go on a mission or summat.'

'Tell you what, I'll trade you my nickname and the trial, for your healthy body,' Barry said, reaching out with his scabbed arms and bandaged hands.

'No chance, mate, clear orf!' Dyn said, screwing up his face.

'I wondered what all the racket was,' Tchyglock said, having silently entered the cave without either of them noticing.

Dyn's blushed instantly.

'Barry, you'll be pleased to hear you can finally leave your cave today.'

'Excellent!' Barry exclaimed.

'There is to be a feast in your name this afternoon,' he added.

'Oh,' Barry said, feeling awkward. 'I don't really want anything like that, I just want to be able to walk about a bit and get some fresh air.'

'I understand, but Xhaffa has commanded it. I think he seeks to curry some favour by publicly celebrating you. Public opinion is not warm towards him at present.'

'Too right!' Dyn said. 'Making Barry do that ridiculous trial 'n' all.'

'Be that as it may, Xhaffa is nonetheless the leader of the Sonphea and we must do as he commands, even if it means being used for his political jousting.'

'Can't we just skip the feast, have a Council meeting and crack on with going to the Cloud Runners?' Barry asked impatiently. 'I thought...' He lowered his voice conspiratorially. 'I thought we were going to head off and do that no matter what Xhaffa said?'

Tchyglock glanced over his shoulder and placed a finger to his lips. He moved closer to the pair. 'There are ears and eyes everywhere under the mountain,' he breathed, barely audibly. He beckoned them to him and walked to the back of the cave. Barry climbed out of bed and suppressed a groan as his body protested.

'I think now, in light of your shoulder injury, our plans must change out of necessity.' He held up a hand as Barry began to interrupt. 'There is no sense in trying to climb the highest peaks in the world when one of your party cannot use one of his arms properly, it puts everyone at risk. But Princess Lahlia Luellason... she is in dire need of rescue, and that, I think is more in the realms of possibility.'

At that Barry fell silent, and worked to hide his delight.

'Word has reached me of the torment she is enduring at the hands of the usurper, and her survival is essential to the cause and the world we want to build. We must hope we are not already too late.'

'When do we leave?' Barry asked.

'How mobile do you feel?'

'I'm fine,' Barry lied.

Tchyglock lifted an eyebrow but said nothing. 'We will leave at nightfall tomorrow following the Council meeting, whether they approve the mission or not. Dyn, find Zosime and let her know to be ready. I think Dead-Nettle would be a useful addition also in light of the fact that your shoulder limits your sword-fighting ability. The four of us will make up the rescue company.'

Dyn had gone from red to very pale. 'What about me?' he ventured.

Tchyglock looked closely at him.

'I would like you to come… if you're ready,' he said to Dyn. Something seeming to be implied that Barry did not understand.

'No problem,' Dyn grinned, bouncing on his feet.

'Very well, we shall meet at my house when the moon reaches its zenith.'

'That's midnight to you and I,' Barry said to Dyn.

***

Barry spent the rest of the morning moving around his cave and gently stretching, trying to bring some life back to his stiffened limbs. The more he moved, the looser he felt. The scabs were itchy, but even his shoulder felt less painful, albeit it in a tightly fitting sling that Anita had insisted he wear. He had discarded the eye patch in irritation, and his torn eyelid felt flimsy, but mended.

It was mid-afternoon when his summons arrived, and three armed guards in the highly polished armour of Xhaffa's guard escorted him to the main hall. Their pace was fast, and Barry's weakened legs and mending toes complained as he trotted to keep up. By the time he arrived at the entrance to the hall he had a faint sheen of sweat on his brow.

Sweat was the last thing on his mind, however, as his entrance to the hall was greeted with a blaring fanfare of trumpets, bugles and applause.

The hall around the refectory area had been cleared and replaced with hundreds of round tables around which most of the Sonphea seemed to have crammed themselves.

As he was led to a top table, people cheered with whoops, whistles and shouts, and brightly coloured flower petals were strewn at his feet like confetti.

Completely unprepared for such a welcome, Barry smiled sheepishly. The noise was deafening, echoing around the hall to form a roaring assault on the eardrums. As he walked falteringly through the masses, he heard calls of, 'The Saviour!' 'Hail, Bjurg Lak! Our Mountain King!' 'Bjurg Lak! Bjurg Lak!' and even, 'Fravashi Slayer!'. As one, those he passed rose to their feet and gave the Bu sign.

As he approached the top table, which was long rather than round like the others in the hall and was set upon a raised dais, he could see the Council sat along it, and either side were bugle players in brightly coloured garb with their instruments triumphantly singing to the roof of the cavern. Xhaffa sat in the centre of the table, his face steely, which he forced into a welcoming smile as Barry stepped up onto the platform.

Xhaffa raised his hands to silence the crowd, and the din immediately fell away.

'People of the resistance, the saviour that the prophecies have spoken of is here,' he shouted.

'No thanks to you,' came one call from somewhere deep in the crowd, which was greeted by titters and many grunts of approval.

Xhaffa's face darkened but he continued. 'The first person in generations to complete the Trial of the Broken Viaduct, he will forever be the last. We have all witnessed the incredible strength, power and determination he possesses as he made his away across the viaduct with a dislocated shoulder, and a rare magic unheard of for an age, unheard of outside of the royal line. But not only that, he went on to survive an avalanche, an attack from screaming wolves, and incredibly, he slayed an ice fravashi.'

'Nida Killaer! Nida Killaer! Nida Killaer!' the crowd chanted thunderously.

'Now he will join the Council of the Sonphea,' Xhaffa continued when the noise died down, 'and tonight we celebrate as in the days of old, one who has completed the trial; a warrior, saviour and the conqueror of shadows, our Nida Killaer!'

'And our Bjurg Lak! Our Mountain King!' came shouts from the crowd, and Xhaffa's face was bleak. He clapped Barry on the back and looked as if he was about to say something, but just gave him a nod full of genuine warmth, and sat down. Barry found himself standing in front of the enormous crowd of bedraggled Sonphea, forced from their homes to live in a cold, damp and dark mountain, all looking at him with hope. The burden of expectation was almost suffocating, and he wished someone had told him he would be required to give a speech.

'Thank you, everyone,' he said hesitantly.

'Speak up, mate!' that same person shouted from the crowd, and Barry felt a surge of irritation towards him.

'Thank you, everyone,' he said again, and nearly lost his balance with surprise as his voice suddenly sounded ten times its usual volume. He cast his eyes around in surprise, and saw a tiny wink from the stony-faced Nox.

'I am honoured by this feast, and by your incredible support.' More roars and cheers. 'I do not feel worthy because although the trial nearly took my life, I have endured nothing when compared to the hardships you have all faced at the hands of the usurper and the giants.' The crowd gazed at him, drinking in his every word. He noticed with surprise that his face had not gone red. 'I am new to Många Världar and I understand the doubts and the fear of who they said I was. I hope now I have earned my place as one of the Sonphea.' He paused, collecting his words.

'I am no mountain king, for you already have the mighty Xhaffa, and I am not a leader, for you already have the fantastic leaders of the Council here beside me.' He paused again and a dead silence settled over the mountain as people looked conflicted. 'But what I do swear is that I will always do what I believe is right, and will give my life to help you take back your homes, your land and restore peace to Många Världar!' He finished triumphantly, and was greeted with an enormous applause from the vast crowd.

A goblet was thrust into his hand by Tchyglock, and he raised it aloft, and the crowd followed suit with a cacophonous roar.

When he turned to take a seat in between Xhaffa and Tchyglock, he was greeted by a mighty clap on the back from the leader of the Sonphea.

'I am sorry I ever doubted you, Barry,' he said in his clear, sonorous voice. 'Can you forgive an old man for getting lost in his vanity and pride?'

'I would have doubted me too, Xhaffa,' Barry said kindly. 'But please don't make me do any more trials.'

Xhaffa laughed, a hearty laugh that rolled from his feet. 'Agreed!'

As the leader's attention was drawn by someone at the other end of the table, Tchyglock leant in and whispered into his ear. 'Very well played, Master Birchwood. There's more of a politician in you than I would have guessed.'

'We all have a job to do, Tchyglock, I don't think mine is to be a ruler over anyone.'

Tchyglock nodded at him, a look of immense pride on his weather-beaten face.

***

Barry woke early the next morning, and for the first time since the trial felt a little more human. Being up and about the day before had helped to loosen his muscles and work out some of the stiffness. His shoulder hurt him less, while his toes and ribs were sore but manageable, and he felt buoyed by the feeling of being accepted by the Sonphea at long last.

He walked down to breakfast with a spring in his step and for the first time since he had arrived in Burroha, people smiled at him and said good morning as he passed.

He was pleased, however, to arrive early to the breakfast hall and have a moment of silence in the pre-dawn gloom to listen to the mountain come to life around him. That morning the cook, who normally refused to so much as look at Barry, gave him an extra cake with a toothless grin.

For the first time in his entire life, Barry had a sense of belonging.

And so it was that later that day he walked into the meeting of the Council with his head held a little higher, and a little less trepidation than the last time he had been there.

When he entered he was given a round of applause from the other Council members, although he noticed that Langellis Mirnok's clapping was far from enthusiastic.

'Welcome all,' began Xhaffa. 'We meet with a different mood to the Councils of recent times, for this time we meet with a glimmer of hope. The saviour whom the prophecies long spoke of has now undoubtedly arrived, proven by acts of unrivalled resilience, fighting prowess and magical power to complete a trial that I can admit with shame we should never have sent him on. But there are positives to take from it; there can now be no doubt as to Barry's abilities or importance to the Sonphea and I welcome him to his well-earned seat at this Council.'

'Hear, hear!' Adger Godfrey chimed in.

'Thank you,' Barry said to Xhaffa and the Council.

'With that out of the way, we must get to business. Tchyglock, your wisdom was not heard when last this Council met, but now let us all hear what you have to say with open hearts and minds.'

'Thank you, revered leader,' Tchyglock said gruffly, and pushed himself to his feet. 'Our cause stands upon the precipice of defeat, of that there is no doubt. Suzerain Cikavac and Iovixa, king of giants, have swept across the continent, and now control all of the lands south of the Noani River, and much of the lands in the east towards the Endless Forest,' he said, his arm sweeping across a giant map pinned to the middle of the table.

'Not content with holding Princess Luellason captive in the Watchtower of Donnau, their forces swept through the border town of Willow-Under-Hill and unleashed untold horrors upon it. Ruling it was not enough for the suzerain, she wished to destroy it. The princess — the rightful heir to the throne of Många Världar — is in dire straits. If she dies, so does the last symbol for which the resistance is fighting. All that stands between Burroha and their forces are the Hills of Cthopsa which, as commander of Burroha, provides me with little comfort. As Barry here can attest to, the crown has squads roaming the Shodum Mountains hoping to find our mountain base. Time is not on our side. The time to take action is upon us, and we cannot delay any further. Two things we must do to turn the tide of fate in our favour. We must rescue Princess Luellason, and we must make contact with the Cloud Runners, to persuade them to join the war on our side.'

There was a stunned silence at Tchyglock's pronouncement, which was soon broken by laughter from Langellis Mirnok. Xhaffa's right hand man giggled uproariously and slapped the table.

'I fail to see what is amusing, Langellis,' Tchyglock said flatly.

'Well… surely you aren't serious!' Langellis said, still chuckling.

'I have never been more serious about anything in my life.'

'Tchyglock, you speak of divine beings as if one can bump into them at the Dog Inn. They are the winged holy spirits of the heavens and do not converse with mere mortals. They are the Cloud Runners, for the clouds are their homes. They are angels,' Sasha Wellbelieve said, matter-of-factly.

'That is assuming that such things exist at all,' Nox added in his deep baritone, his sunken eyes dark and cold.

'You see, Tchyglock. You would pin the hopes of the Sonphea on something that is most likely a fantasy!' Langellis exclaimed.

'I believe you had a similar feeling about my claims that Barry was the saviour, Langellis.' Tchyglock said with a smile.

The smile fell from Langellis's face. He opened his mouth to reply, then nodded in defeat and acceptance. 'You are right, it is just… the Cloud Runners are an even harder reach for my cynical mind.'

'Okay, thank you, Langellis, Tchyglock,' Xhaffa said. 'Your suggestions give this Council a great deal to consider. Both are incredibly high risk, but if successful would have incredibly high rewards.' He took a deep breath, his huge chest rising and falling. He pushed his long, red, braided hair back over his shoulders and gazed around the room.

'Tell us more about your proposal for the rescue of Princess Luellason,' he said finally.

'Of course, sir. It is my suggestion that I lead a small team consisting of Barry, Zosime, Dead-Nettle and the boy Dyn to rescue the princess—'

He was interrupted by a general outcry from around the table. Tchyglock waited patiently for it to subside before continuing.

'We are not yet ready to attempt to overthrow their garrison with an army; we are no match for Iovixa's giant forces. Our only hope is stealth, and I believe this team combines the perfect skillsets to rescue the princess,' he said. 'And I believe myself, Barry, Zosime and the Ohjaja would then be the right crew to launch the mission to the Cloud Runners,' he finished, almost as an afterthought.

'Your mission has the full backing of the southern resistance,' Adger Godfrey said formally.

'And of the Endless Forest division,' Rummy Goliasson added.

'You have the support of the Vemoham division,' Shengju Plu said slowly, 'but I would query the need to take the boy, Dyn, with you to rescue the princess. Surely he would be a burden and in great danger?'

'He would be in great danger, certainly, but I do not believe him to be a burden. I believe there is much more to him than meets the eye, and if I'm right, he would be a valuable addition to the mission.'

Xhaffa leant back in his chair and pursed his lips.

'I will not make the same mistake twice of doubting your wisdom,' he said slowly. 'But you will have one more to accompany you on the rescue mission of the princess.'

'Oh?' Tchyglock said. 'And who would that be?'

'Me,' Xhaffa said, leaning forward on the table and staring intently into the eyes of Tchyglock.

'You?' Tchyglock exclaimed, as there was a collective intake of breath from around the table.

'You forget yourself, Commander,' Xhaffa said, one eyebrow raised.

'Sorry, sir, but are you sure that is wise? You are too important to the cause to risk on such a high risk operation,' Tchyglock fenced.

'Tchyglock is right, Xhaffa. You are simply too valuable to the Sonphea,' Sasha Wellbelieve commented with typical directness.

'Sir, I must say I agree,' Langellis Mirnok added. 'Such a journey would be... difficult for you now,' he added.

'Enough!' Xhaffa snapped. 'I did not become leader of the Sonphea by sitting in dusty rooms. I did it by fighting many battles against the crown, by the fearsome blade of my sword, and by my cunning. And I can do so again. I have grown too fat and soft, dieting on politics and tactics. It is no wonder the people question me; they need to see that I would myself do everything I would ask them to do. That is leadership.'

'Your reputation as a mighty warrior is already secure, there is no doubt of that,' Adger Godfrey added. 'My troops often tell stories of your feats. You do not have anything to prove.'

'I am not so old as you all seem to think,' Xhaffa said sourly. 'There are still many miles left in me, and the strength of my arm has not diminished. My decision is final,' he added with a meaningful look around the table to head off any further objections.

'I notice you did not mention the mission to the Cloud Runners,' Tchyglock said, breaking the silence.

'That I did not,' Xhaffa agreed.

'What say you to my plan?' Tchyglock asked patiently.

'The rescue mission of the princess gives us a tangible success, a huge symbol to the Sonphea that we are taking back what is ours and the tide of the conflict may be turning. But to risk two Council members, one who is our most experienced commander and lord of our largest base, and the other our newly found saviour, not to mention Zosime, one of our most able captains, on a mission based upon myth and legend would be lunacy. No leader would permit such a thing.'

'But we have testimony that Cikavac and her gang of warlocks have harnessed the powers of hell. Only the forces of heaven can hope to combat such a thing!' Tchyglock exploded.

'It sounds like a wonderful idea to me,' Rummy slurred. He looked like he hadn't stopped celebrating from the night before.

'Perhaps our commanders should look at completing the first suicide mission, before attempting another,' Langellis said, clearly only half joking.

'Our special advisor is right. Let us not get ahead of ourselves, we can discuss your Cloud Runner idea upon the successful completion of the rescue mission, Tchyglock,' Xhaffa said, his voice loud and clear.

He looked at the brooding Nox. 'Soothsayer, what say the runes about our mission?'

'I will consult them at first darkness when such forces are most potent, revered leader. It is not far off now.'

'Very well,' Xhaffa said. 'Tchyglock, Barry. We leave at dawn, ready the team.'

Tchyglock looked like he was trying very hard not to argue back, but managed to restrain himself. Barry simply nodded and got lost in thought about the princess as the Council talk turned to Sasha Wellbelieve's report on supply routes from the capital, and the frequency of caravans delivering grain. As he thought of meeting her, he could feel a tingling sensation in his stomach and a fluttering in his heart.

The Council came to a close when food was brought into the meeting hall. Barry noticed that even though it was subject to the same limitation on ingredients that all the Sonphea were a victim of, it had clearly been put together by far more skilled chefs than those who fed the masses in the refectory each day. Barry slipped some of the finer nibbles into his pockets to pass on to Felanne and Dyn, and then enjoyed eating until his belly hurt. As the plates were cleared away, Nox rose to his feet.

From the depths of his thick emerald cloak he withdrew a bowl hewn from blood-red onyx which he placed onto the table. The room grew silent.

Without a word, Nox threw a collection of stones made from blackest jet high into the air. Miraculously they all landed within the shallow bowl with a clatter and the warlock gazed down at them through his wire-rimmed spectacles.

His usual expression of somewhere between forlorn and furious creased into one of concern. Saying nothing, he scooped up the stones and again cast them into the smoky air. Once more he gazed at them with concern.

'Well? What do the runes foresee?' Xhaffa said sharply.

Nox looked slowly upwards and gazed around the room before fixing on Xhaffa.

'The mission will only succeed with the death of one of the company. If none shall fall, the quest will surely fail.'

CHAPTER 21

The Journey Begins

The mountain was still silent and dark when Barry made his way down to meet the others in the company the following morning. As he walked along a particularly dingy and narrow tunnel he was grabbed roughly from the shadows and pressed into a shallow alcove.

'What the—' Barry began before the wind was pushed out of him.

In the gloom he could barely make out the figure pinning him to the wall and breathing into his face, but he could see enough to instantly know who it was.

Nox stood above him breathing heavily, his breath rising in the cold darkness before him. Despite his age there was still a great deal of strength in his arms and Barry gasped and sputtered under the force pushing him against the wall.

'Quiet, boy,' the elderly warlock whispered, relaxing his hold slightly.

'Nox, what is it?' Barry said, massaging his chest. 'Was terrifying us all with your dark omens last night not enough?'

'That was only a part of what the runes foretold,' Nox said, stepping backwards and looking nervously down the dark passageway.

'What do you mean?' Barry asked curiously. 'What else did they say?'

Nox squeezed into the alcove beside Barry and leant into his ear, his breath sour and moist on Barry's cheek.

'You will be betrayed,' he croaked.

'What? Who by? None in the company would betray us.'

'The root of the betrayal, the runes did not illuminate. But the runes do not lie, and neither do I,' Nox said, his face stern and eyes fearsome.

'The mission cannot be stopped. The princess must be saved.'

'Then you must trust no one in your company, and you must not be the one who is slain,' Nox said with greater passion.

'How do you know that I am not the one who will betray the company? I am by far the newest to the Sonphea.'

Nox sighed and rubbed a weary hand across his eyes. He clearly had not slept that night. 'I admit I was sceptical upon your arrival. Tchyglock has many notions, and not all of them well thought through. The cause cannot afford a false saviour; we are already too close to the abyss. But I hoped it to be true, and when you saved yourself with your consciousness during the trial… to be a Küdugar - that is a gift nought but the gods and the royal line possess. I do not believe our saviour is also our betrayer.'

'Thank you, Nox,' Barry replied earnestly. 'I promise to be vigilant. I believe we can succeed,' he said. 'Now I must hurry, I will be late for the departure.' He nodded to the warlock, and left him standing there, a shadowy figure in a dark corridor, who quickly disappeared into the gloom.

The other members of the rescue company were talking in pre-dawn whispers when Barry arrived at the gate to the mountain. Long shadows were cast through the cavern and across the vast iron studded black door from the torches burning low in their sconces.

Dyn was bleary eyed and had a warm hat pulled low over his head, though his large ears still stuck out at the sides. His backpack looked to be almost as big as he was, and he had resisted Barry's efforts to make him pack light for the journey.

Leather-clad Zosime was there also, quiet and hooded, her eyes unreadable and her hair braided and tied back. She had a bow and quiver of arrows slung over her shoulder, but did not appear to have packed anything else. The tattooed Dead-Nettle was dressed in a green cape that flowed from fabric to her tattoos and back again, without being able to see the seams. The gills at her neck were undulating slightly in the moist air of the caves, and around her belt was a sequence of knives and daggers, ending in the sword at her right hip.

Tchyglock looked much the same as ever, scruffy, unshaven and bleak. He was wrapped in a heavy, moth-eaten travelling cloak, and carried a hessian sack in his arms, which he threw down on the floor with a loud clang that echoed through the silent mountain.

'While we await the arrival of Xhaffa, I have weapons for you both,' he said to Barry and Dyn. 'I do not expect us to get by without fighting.'

He handed Barry and Dyn swords. Barry attached his to his belt, which still held throwing stars and a dagger, before drawing the warm red fravashi coat around him. Dyn was swinging his sword back and forth a little wildly as he got used to it, but stopped with an appraising look from Dead-Nettle.

At that moment the leader of the Sonphea appeared. Xhaffa was wearing thin, steel armour, with golden rivets overlapping one another like leaves, and his powerful arms were gauntleted. He looked every inch a king, and Barry was slowly beginning to understand how the increasingly impressive man had become leader of the resistance.

'Well met,' he said, deeply. 'Now that we are all here, I wanted to make one thing clear,' Tchyglock began. 'This mission is highly dangerous and our chances of success are small. Nox last night foretold that one of us would lose our life in the course of the mission. I set little store in destiny myself, but do not hold it against others if they trust the winds of fate. If you do not wish to come, none here shall force you, so please speak up now.'

'Now you've got that pretty speech out the way, shall we crack on?' Dead-Nettle said with no attempt to hide her eye roll.

'None of us is blind, Tchyglock, we all know the risks,' Zosime said firmly.

'Very well, then let us away,' Tchyglock said, his face drawn. He banged heavily on the huge door in the side of the mountain.

It opened with a creak, and they were greeted by the watchman who had been on duty when Barry had arrived in the mountain all those months ago.

'What a party you make,' the chain-mailed guard croaked. 'The hopes of the people go with you,' he added and gave a deep bow to Barry.

'Erm, thanks, Krimor,' he said awkwardly and shuffled past.

As the door clanged shut behind them, they were pitched into greenish gloom. 'Are we travelling by splodgeworm again?' Barry cautiously asked Tchyglock.

He could almost sense the amusement emanating from the commander at his question. 'I'm afraid so, Master Birchwood, but only some of the way as it would be impossible to go against the current in miniature form.'

'Cool!' Dyn exclaimed. 'I've never got to be splodgewormed!'

'It's not all it's cracked up to be,' Barry murmured, not looking forward to another journey being tossed to and fro by giant leaves and twigs.

They squeezed their way down the narrow walkway and reached the harbour where Tchyglock pulled the tobacco tin of splodgeworms from his cloak and cracked it open. With great distaste Barry looked down at the tiny, farting creatures merrily bouncing around the tin and felt his stomach turn.

Tchyglock passed them around, giving each member of the team a splodgeworn. The smell of eggs was unmistakable.

'Alas, I am no fan of splodgeworms myself,' Xhaffa sighed, before throwing his into his mouth and immediately shrinking from view.

One by one they all followed suit, leaving just Barry grimacing down at the wobbly pink blob. With a groan he forced it into his mouth and fought all of his natural impulses to spit it out, and started furiously chewing.

'Decided to join us, did you?' Dead-Nettle said with a grin as Barry appeared, matchstick size, on the ground next to his companions.

Barry tried to respond, but just emitted a very loud burp that felt like it might nearly lift him off his tiny feet.

'You're disgusting, mate,' Dyn said to him, wrinkling his nose, before an even bigger burp erupted from his own mouth. He clamped his hands over his mouth and looked around, blushing furiously as Barry laughed loudly.

'Boys,' Zosime said, shaking her head.

'If you're all done with being children, let's get going,' Tchgylock said and led them to where a collection of tiny wooden boats were floating merrily on the gentle current of the mountain.

'We get boats!' Barry exclaimed excitedly.

'We do, but remember that they weigh much less than normal boats and will capsize very easily,' Tchyglock said.

'It's still an improvement on last time,' Barry said, feeling buoyed.

'What did you use last time?' Dyn asked curiously.

'You don't want to know,' Barry replied grimly.

It was two to a boat, and to Barry's annoyance he was paired with Xhaffa, while Dyn was with Zosime, and Tchyglock with Dead-Nettle. However, he was soon pleasantly surprised to find that Xhaffa was not only a very capable steerer, navigating them cleverly as the stream angled sharply down the mountain and gathered pace, but he was more cheerful than Barry had given him credit for.

'I had forgotten what it is like to be on an adventure!' the leader of the Sonphea exclaimed exuberantly as their tiny boat bounced and spun through a particularly choppy section of the widening stream. Foam and wind whipped through their hair and despite the ongoing pain in his shoulder, Barry had to admit that he was enjoying the refreshing ride through the rapids.

The duo were still whooping as the stream levelled out and led them to a large, glassy lake.

'The pair of you are likely to alert all of the enemy's forces with that racket,' Tchyglock complained as he and Dead-Nettle pulled alongside them.

'Be still, Tchyglock. I have been cooped up and surrounded by my guardsmen for too long, forgive me a little joy at a rare taste of freedom,' Xhaffa boomed, still chuckling.

Dead-Nettle was looking longingly at the water, and saw Barry looking quizzically at her.

'I long to be back in the water, drinking it in through my gills,' she sighed, 'but someone has to help out this old man here,' she said, prodding Tchyglock in the back. Barry's breath caught in his throat, never having seen anyone other than himself speak to Tchyglock in such a way, but the commander just chuckled at her.

'There will be plenty of time for splashing about later, not all of us need to do it now,' Tchyglock said, with a meaningful look at Barry and Xhaffa.

Zosime rolled her eyes, but a completely drenched Dyn grinned heartily at them.

'I fell in!' he announced, looking for all the world like it was the best thing that had ever happened to him. 'Zosime rescued me, she's very strong,' he added, looking admiringly at her.

'Maybe next time I'll leave you and your nonsense in there,' she snapped back at him, but Barry noticed the corner of her mouth twitched ever so slightly.

'When we get to the far bank of the lake, we will be leaving the relative safety of the Shodum Mountains,' Tchyglock said. 'We must then travel overland.'

'Have you arranged horses?' Xhaffa asked.

'Too noisy, I'm afraid. We must travel on foot and by night.'

Xhaffa sighed. 'I suppose the fun had to end at some point.' He turned to Barry. 'Come, let's see if we can beat the others to the far shore,' he laughed. Barry groaned, but let himself get carried by the enthusiasm of the aged warrior.

Although it was not wide, the lake was deceptively long, curving around corners that had looked like the bank from a distance. The mountains either side of them got smaller and smaller, until, when they finally reached the far shore, they were only surrounded by low, rolling green hills. The sun was getting low in the sky, and they were all tired from a full day of paddling. The laughter had subsided as they dragged their tiny boats onto the shale beach and collapsed, exhausted. Barry held his tongue about his sore, blistered hands with great effort. He did not think moaning about sore hands would be becoming of the one meant to save them all.

'We have a long night ahead, we must get as much food and rest as we can, as we set off at nightfall,' Tchyglock grunted as he passed around the small vials of yellow-blue liquid. Barry shuddered at the memory of the fishy taste it had, but kindly decided not to let Dyn know what was in store.

They all rushed upwards, like balloons being inflated and returned to their full size.

'Yuk! That tasted even worse than the flippin' splodgeworm!' Dyn complained, spitting onto the floor and scraping at his tongue.

'Barry, Dead-Nettle, collect some wood, this will be the last time we can enjoy a fire. Dyn and Zosime, see if you can catch us some fish for supper. We all could use a good meal,' Tchyglock instructed. Zosime scowled at being drawn with Dyn again.

Barry ached from head to toe and his legs felt heavy as he sluggishly dragged himself towards the surrounding woods, with an equally bedraggled Dead-Nettle. He noted bitterly that Tchyglock and Xhaffa had sat down and were enjoying a rest.

'You have not fully recovered,' Dead-Nettle said flatly to him as they walked side by side. It was not a question.

'I'm fine,' Barry lied.

'Barry-Bacch, we have been training together every day for weeks. I know how you move, and you do not move freely. Even paddling, your power was limited, I could tell.'

'What do you expect me to say?' Barry asked angrily, stopping and looking at her.

'I would like you to be honest. I can only protect you if I know the truth,' she said earnestly, pushing her long black plait back over her shoulder.

'I'm completely fine,' Barry said crossly, and carried on walking. He stopped when he heard the scrape of Dead-Nettle's sword being drawn from its sheath.

'What are you doing?' he demanded, turning back to face her.

'If you're completely fine, you won't mind sparring with me.'

'We have to collect wood, it's been a long day,' Barry said, gulping slightly.

'Come on, Baz, it'll be fun. Good to work the kinks out of our splodgewormy muscles!' she chided.

'Fine!' he replied, drawing his own sword and covering the wince from the pang in his shoulder with a cough.

Dead-Nettle pounced and threw a sharp overhead stroke towards his shoulder. Barry yelped and dropped the sword.

'I wasn't ready,' he moaned, scooping up his blade.

'Then go again,' she said, no smile on her face now.

Again she swooped, and after only half a dozen blows, Barry again dropped the sword.

'Do you want to go again, or can you just tell me the truth and we get on with our day?' Dead-Nettle asked.

'Okay, okay!' Barry said furiously, angry at Dead-Nettle and angry at his failing shoulder. He slumped against the trunk of an aspen tree. 'My shoulder hasn't recovered yet. My body is sore, but is getting stronger, but I have little strength in my sword arm. I fear it will never return; I dislocated it that many times in the trial.'

His friend sat down next to him and looked at him kindly. 'What you had to endure on that mountain is more than anyone should have to experience, let alone a boy who is only new to our world.'

'I feel broken and weak,' Barry whispered, revealing a fear he'd been wrestling with.

'No one who lives a life worth living gets through it without being damaged one way or another,' Dead-Nettle said softly. 'But the damage doesn't have to define you, only make you stronger. Do you know why I covered my body in tattoos?'

'No, why?' Barry asked curiously, lifting his head.

'When Suzerain Cikavac's forces came to my homeland and poisoned the waters we lived in, the surrounding crops and wild-flower meadows were destroyed, as were most of my people. Our skin was burned by the water, but instead of feeling ashamed, many of us tattooed our bodies, as you've seen with Adger Godfrey. I decided to turn my body into a symbol of the land they ruined, and a memory of my people, because I am proud of what I am and where I came from. The usurper can never take that from me, and when I look at my body I feel peace, because I know how it has suffered, but I know that it will endure, just like Många Världar did before Cikavac and just like it will afterwards.' She looked wistfully into the distance to where the two older men were sitting in conversation. 'Your body will heal, Barry. But do not hide your pain, instead embrace it and be proud of your journey. In the meantime, I can help you learn to become just as strong a fighter with your other arm.'

'Thank you,' Barry said, feeling cheered by his friend's words. 'That feels like a weight lifted.'

'The last thing you need to be doing is carrying a weight on those poorly shoulders!' she chuckled, helping him to his feet.

'One day I'd like to see where you're from,' Barry said as they started gathering firewood.

'One day I hope there will be something to show you,' she replied, and lapsed into silence.

They had just got the fire merrily crackling away, when Dyn and Zosime returned with an armful of fish, Dyn grinning boyishly.

'Wow, good haul,' Dead-Nettle said.

'Dyn is an excellent fisherman,' Zosime said begrudgingly.

'Well, I am from Degwinkle,' Dyn said modestly. 'Sorta goes with the territory.'

At that point Tchyglock finally got involved, expertly filleting the fish and frying them on a hot thin stone. Darkness began to fall ominously, and Barry took the opportunity for a nap while he could.

He felt like he had barely closed his eyes, and the taste of the delicious, salty fish had barely faded on his lips when Xhaffa woke him roughly. The stars were already glittering overhead and a chill had begun to creep in as they broke camp and began the long hike.

They walked in silence that night, following Tchyglock through the rolling Cthopsa Hills, in muddy, boggy valleys, and over wind-whipped summits, as Zosime scouted on ahead in the near total darkness. Around one o'clock it began to rain, seeping into their cloaks and chilling their bones. Barry found that Rhew's cloak was completely waterproof, but it did not stop the rain from soaking through his boots and drenching his socks. From time to time, they would pass the burnt-out shells of farmhouses that had been destroyed by the enemy's forces. The first time they saw such a building Barry made to approach it but Xhaffa stopped him.

'The enemy do not leave anything behind that you would want to see,' he said bleakly.

As the pale grey of dawn began to hover on the horizon the rain doubled in intensity and a fierce wind raged around them, driving it sideways into their cheeks. The company were cold, tired and thoroughly bedraggled when Tchyglock stopped and gathered them to him.

'We will need to stop now the light is coming,' he shouted, his voice being carried away by the storm. 'There is a cave nearby in which we can find shelter.'

'Take us there, Commander,' Xhaffa urged, his long red hair sodden and dripping. Barry thought it must be very heavy on his head.

'Need help finding…' Tchyglock responded as the others strained to pick up the words. The rest of his words disappeared completely.

'What?' Barry shouted.

Tchyglock gathered them closer and they all put their heads together, blocking out some of the wind.

'There is a large boulder which I use to locate the cave. It is white and on the side of a hill. Spread out and report back here in thirty minutes if any of you find it.'

They pulled apart and nodded, and all charged off in different directions, a renewed energy at the prospect of getting out of the rain.

Barry cast his eyes everywhere as he marched up grassy knolls and slid down muddy slopes. He was about to turn back when he spotted a shining white rock, stood alone on the side of a long, gently sloping hill. He let out a triumphant cheer and raced back as quickly as he could, no longer bothering to step around the endless puddles.

The others were already there, Dyn looking particularly sorry for himself with his huge backpack. Only Dead-Nettle looked cheerful, drinking in the rain through her undulating gills.

Barry waved at them to follow him, and as soon as Tchyglock saw the boulder he nodded confidently, and led them along an old game trail on the hill opposite the rock, through a copse of pine trees, and suddenly disappeared from sight.

As the others caught up to where he had disappeared, they saw that hidden behind an outcrop of rock was a narrow opening. They squeezed through it and Barry let out a gasp of surprise. He had been expecting a cold, hard cave, but what they entered was a fully equipped little home. The cave opened up quite widely, and bunk beds lined either side. There was a fireplace carved out of the cave wall, with a chimney above it, and the rocky floor was strewn with rushes and sand, making it soft and comfortable underfoot.

They all let out an audible sigh as the sound of the rain dulled into a regular thrum on the ground outside and they were able to peel off their soaking wet cloaks and boots.

'What is this place?' Xhaffa asked Tchyglock.

'In my younger days, I was friendly with the smugglers in these parts who were keen to avoid some of the heavier import taxes levied when transporting goods from the Llewin Ocean and up the Noani River towards Vemoham. This was one of the useful hideouts for routing their wares to Willow.'

'How friendly with these smugglers were you exactly?' Xhaffa asked, an eyebrow raised.

Tchyglock shrugged. 'I like smugglers. They don't take themselves too seriously, and only do what they do because of overly high taxes. If they didn't smuggle, people would starve.'

'You didn't answer my question, old friend,' Xhaffa said, more sternly.

'I know.' Tchyglock grinned. When Xhaffa's expression didn't change, his grin faded. 'You know who I am, Xhaffa, I do not pretend to be saintly.'

'You are right, I am sorry,' Xhaffa said, his shoulders slumping. 'It has been a difficult couple of days and I am more tired than I recall ever being. I am grateful for such a place to rest, no matter what its original purpose may have been.'

Dyn was already face down, snoring softly on one of the bunks and had not even removed his backpack. It was not long before the rest of them had followed suit, after a fair amount of grumbling that Tchyglock wouldn't allow them to build a fire.

'We are in the territory of the enemy, and their eyes are everywhere,' was all he would say.

***

That evening before they set off, Tchyglock gathered them around.

'Xhaffa has pointed out that you all might appreciate some information on our plan to reach the tower,' he said.

Barry noted it was a strange balance of power on their mission, with the ruler of the Sonphea letting Tchyglock run it, but he did not hesitate to use his power as leader when he wanted to, almost as a reminder.

'We are roughly here,' Tchyglock said, drawing a cross in the sand with a long stick. 'Here is Willow-Under-Hill, and beyond it is the Watchtower of Donnau where the princess is being held. Willow, and presumably much of Paharam, is largely destroyed and the enemy know that we are based somewhere in the Shodum Mountains, so the plains beyond these hills will be closely guarded, above and below ground. We cannot hope to take the direct route to the tower. Adger Godfrey tells us that the kingdom of Fartálch north of the Noani River is completely under the control of the enemy, and we cannot take that route. We must angle north to Khali-Dhūmi, like so,' he said, drawing a line up across the borderline of Paharam he had scratched into the ground. 'Khali-Dhūmi is yet to be properly occupied, and once across the border we aim sharply east to the Endless Forest. From there we journey south to approach the watchtower from the north east, and avoid Willow entirely if possible.'

'What about the poachers?' Zosime asked. 'Their number will only have increased.'

'It is a gamble we have to take. We six can more than match the poachers should we have to.'

Dyn gulped audibly.

'And if we manage to get through the Cthopsa Hills, across Paharam, survive the wild folk of Khali-Dhūmi and the poachers of the Endless Forest, not to mention the other creatures that reside there, how are we to get to the tower, which is protected by giants and the army of Cikavac?' Xhaffa said.

Tchyglock looked at his leader with an unreadable expression.

'Did you expect an easy journey?' Zosime asked, unable to prevent the irritation from entering her voice.

'You forget your place, Captain,' Xhaffa said, not for the first time. His long hair was still wet and he looked somewhat less intimidating, and more bedraggled.

'Sorry, sir,' she mumbled, looking embarrassed.

'There are no easy roads to the Watchtower of Donnau right now,' Tchyglock said. 'The path I... suggest... gives us the greatest chance of success,' he said, biting his tongue. 'We are all committed to this journey now, and we must stick together, for the final step will be the hardest of them all. The details of it, I am still working on, but let us get that far first; there is no sense in worrying about it in the meantime.'

CHAPTER 22

The Northern Escarpment

The next three days looked much the same to Barry as they travelled only at night. As they moved from the Hills of Cthopsa and into the lowlands they were whipped by cold winds blowing down from the north. Often, they would see watchfires twinkling in the distance and Tchyglock would lead them in wide arcs, sometimes for leagues in the wrong direction, to ensure they avoided detection.

Sleep was difficult to come by during the day, often buried under bushes or in holes. Tchyglock had not led them to any more smugglers' caves, much to Barry's disappointment. The group spoke seldom, and when they did the interactions were often irritable. The only thing Barry enjoyed was his daily sparring sessions with Dead-Nettle, where he found he was quickly becoming nearly as proficient with his left hand as he was with his right.

It was on the third day that the endless, bleak plains were broken on the horizon. The land sloped sharply upwards and the first signs of civilisation they had seen for days became just visible, with some brightly twinkling lights blinking high up.

'We will stop here,' Tchyglock said. 'There are watchful eyes at the border of Khali-Dhūmi so we should not progress any further.'

Barry stopped, and Dyn bumped into him from behind, half asleep as he walked.

'Oh soz,' he said, opening his eyes blearily. His friend had shown amazing resilience on the journey so far, with the least training or experience of any of them, and had scarcely complained. Barry did notice, however, that he had ditched most of the contents of his backpack and that his early joy and enthusiasm had gradually ebbed away.

Tchyglock had stopped them on the side of a small mound in the land, where the ground formed a slight lip, giving them an alcove in which to shelter from the wind. Dyn sat down heavily beside Barry as Tchyglock passed around fruit and hard, stale bread.

As had become the case, Dyn always situated himself where he could gaze at Zosime. The pair of them had built a relationship based on Dyn worshipping her, and Zosime finding him incredibly irritating.

As she sat down, she looked over at the two boys, saw Dyn looking at her intently, rolled her eyes and turned her back.

'Baz, I reckon she's startin' to like me,' Dyn whispered to him, rather loudly.

'No, she's not,' Zosime said loudly. 'You can't even whisper properly.'

Barry laughed out loud, and the others of the group looked up at him and smiled. There had been scarce little to laugh about in recent days.

'There's a thin line between love and hate,' Barry whispered quietly to Dyn, and his friend's face brightened considerably, before he went back to gazing at the back of the young captain.

'How will we cross the border?' Dead-Nettle asked Tchyglock as they all wormed into the alcove, their backs against the earthy wall, looking out across the plain as the sun began to come up.

'It is a poorly patrolled border, even in these times. The two northern kingdoms rarely have to worry about folk wanting to get in. I know a path through the northern escarpment that will lead us away from the main border crossing. We should be able to cross in relative peace, and once we do, we can move more freely.'

'In the daytime?' Barry asked hopefully.

'In the daytime indeed,' Tchyglock said, and smiled as there was a collective cheer from the group.

'And hot food?' Dyn asked eagerly.

'And hot food,' Tchyglock agreed, which was greeted by another cheer.

'And a warm bed?' Xhaffa croaked. 'I would give up my position with the Sonphea for a warm bed right now.'

'I cannot promise that,' Tchyglock responded, which prompted a collective groan, 'but I will do my best,' he added to another cheer.

Feeling more cheerful than they had in days, the ragtag troop of Sonphea soldiers allowed themselves to drift off as the sun lifted above the horizon.

***

As they approached the northern escarpment that night it began to loom high above them, curving in on itself. The cliffs were pearly white, and the ground underfoot became increasingly chalky. The walls of the ridge glowed in the moonlight, and stretched for as far as Barry could see. It seemed utterly unpassable to Barry, aside from a wide road that had been carved deep into the precipice, leading to two high, narrow watchtowers marking the border of the ancient kingdom of Khali-Dhūmi.

Instead of taking them to the road, Tchyglock angled out to the right, leading them along the foot of the cliff. After about two hours of walking Tchyglock stopped.

'Here is where we will make our ascent,' he whispered to the group.

They all looked up at the yawning escarpment above them. There was no sign of any route through.

'Fear not, my friends, here there is an optical illusion,' Tchyglock said, seeing their faces. He clambered over a pure white boulder, and scrambled over what looked to be the cliff face itself. He straightened and stood upon an outcrop that had not previously been visible, and the landscape of the cliff shifted before their eyes.

Now, Barry could see a way through the otherwise smooth and unclimbable rock face. There had been a landslide or rockfall at some point, which had tumbled down rocks and boulders in a diagonal line invisible to the casual eye.

'Is this another smugglers' trick?' Xhaffa asked. 'Because if it is, I say bravo!'

Tchyglock winked.

'Before we press on, have any of you been to Khali-Dhūmi before?'

They all shook their heads.

'Well you have doubtless heard the stories. Most of them are true.'

Barry raised a hand. 'I feel like I might regret asking, but what are the stories?'

'Folk up there are wild and strange,' Dead-Nettle said. Barry allowed himself an inward smile at how far he'd adjusted to Många Världar that the woman with gills could talk to him about other folk being strange.

'I 'ear they worship made up gods,' Dyn said.

'Every God is real to the person who believes in it, it is not for us to say if theirs is real or not,' Xhaffa said sternly.

'Yessir,' Dyn said hastily.

'But what you say has some merit, young man. Their gods are many and demand regular sacrifices. The ceremonies are, I hear, quite horrible,' Xhaffa added.

'There is truth to everything you say, but the people are not so bad. To live in such cold temperatures all year round changes a person's perception of the world. The people of Khali-Dhūmi are not uncivilised, and I have found them to be welcoming and great fun if you open your mind a little,' said Tchyglock.

'I sense there's a but,' Zosime said in her dry voice.

'But,' Tchyglock started, 'they can be coarse, sometimes vulgar, and their acceptance of their part in the empire has never been much more than lip service for an easy life in which they get largely left alone. Their religious ceremonies involve human sacrifice, and in some of the more remote parts of the north, have been known to involve cannibalism, but I do not think that will be an issue for us. Their king is Eorlran and he will not be immune to the dangers spreading across the continent. But we do not know what we will find up there. We will move as quickly as possible, but be alert and keep an open mind.'

'You know how you're the saviour 'n' all?' Dyn said to Barry.

'So they tell me,' Barry replied.

'Do us a favour and make sure you save me from becoming a hairy wild northerner's supper, yeah?'

Barry laughed. 'You don't need all of your toes, do you?'

He stopped when he saw that his friend was not smiling.

'Don't worry, nobody is going to eat you,' Barry promised.

'But y'know what Nox said, about one of us popping our clogs. What if it's me getting nibbled to bits in some food-based religious ceremony?'

Barry could not help but laugh, even though it forced an affronted look from Dyn.

'They don't nibble you, they chop you up while they chant and pray,' Zosime said from behind them.

'Not helpful, Zosime!' Barry said. She shrugged but winked at Barry, as Dyn looked horrified.

'Zosime!' Tchyglock called from ahead of them. 'Scout on ahead and check if the border is being patrolled. Dead-Nettle, bring up the rear, and keep those knives of yours loose in their sheaths.'

The two warriors nodded and took up their positions. Zosime, black-clad and lithe, was like a shadow silhouetted against the white rock as she scampered on ahead, disappearing from sight behind a series of large rocks.

They were halfway up the cliff when Barry's head exploded as the vision of Princess Luellason, usually restricted to his dreams, cried out in his mind. 'Help me! I cannot last much longer!'

Dark circles surrounded her eyes and a trickle of blood was snaking its way down her cheek from her temple.

As quickly as her beautiful and terrified face had appeared in Barry's mind, it disappeared. He put out a hand as a whirl of dizziness overcame him. He lost his footing and slipped, rolling down the hill until Xhaffa grabbed him roughly and stopped his fall.

'Barry! Are you okay?' Dead-Nettle cried, catching up behind them, as Dyn came skidding down towards them too.

Barry dusted himself down, feeling embarrassed.

'Nida Killaer, talk to us,' Xhaffa said.

'The princess is in great danger,' Barry said.

'What are you talking about?' Xhaffa said, as Tchyglock came down to join them. 'Tchyglock, I think he has hit his head.'

'My head is fine!' exclaimed Barry. 'It's just it's hard to explain.'

'Try us,' Tchyglock said calmly.

'I keep seeing the princess... in my dreams,' Barry said, flushing. He looked at floor as he saw grins appear on the faces of his companions, Dyn giving him a wink.

'No listen! It's not like that, it's like we can talk. I'm sure that it's real.'

The smiles faltered and began to change to concern.

'You sure you din't bang your 'ed, mate?' Dyn said, putting a hand on Barry's shoulder and looking worried.

Barry shrugged it off and looked at Tchyglock. 'Tchyglock, it's important you believe me.'

Tchyglock was the only one who had not smiled at him, and instead looked deep in thought. He shared a meaningful look with Xhaffa but neither of them said anything.

'Tell us what you saw,' Tchyglock said softly.

'Well, like I say, it's always been when I'm asleep. But just now her face appeared in my head, like it wasn't me thinking it, and she cried out for help and said she can't hold on much longer. She looked exhausted, and her head was bleeding. Then she disappeared.'

'It's probably nothing,' Zosime said. Barry sensed she was trying to be nice.

'But not definitely nothing,' Tchyglock said. 'There are plenty of unexplainable phenomenon's in Många Världar, perhaps this is another one.' He paused and scratched his stubbly beard, squinting up at the top of the escarpment. 'I think we should assume Barry's vision was real. We must throw some caution to the wind and move with as much haste as possible once we reach Khali-Dhūmi.'

'Then let us waste no more time, let's move,' Xhaffa ordered grimly, and with several cracks of his bones, began again up the slope.

It was about two hours later that the group, now sweating and breathing heavily, approached the lip of the escarpment. Zosime was waiting for them, just a slender shadow in the darkness, perfectly still.

'Is it patrolled?' Dead-Nettle asked anxiously.

'Yes, but I don't think it will be a problem,' Zosime said with a small smile.

'Why's that?'

'Take a peek,' Zosime said, and the group commando-crawled and poked their heads above the parapet.

A crude shed was there with a large, open front designed to look out across the cliffs. From within, the sound of snoring could be clearly heard.

'They're both well gone with drink,' Zosime whispered from behind them.

'Then let's move. *Now*,' Tchyglock said quietly but firmly.

As one, the group pulled themselves over the ledge as quietly as possible. Barry clambered up to his feet and looked out from the top of the cliff and was treated to a spectacular view. A bright moon was illuminating the plains below them, giving the land a celestial, blue hue, and a blanket of stars twinkled in the darkness, making Barry feel like space was within touching distance. He wondered how far away the princess was, and felt a pain in his chest when he imagined the pain and torture she was enduring. He wished he could see the view in the daytime, but was snapped out of his reverie by a *psst* sound from Zosime, trying to get his attention.

She called him over to where the others were stood.

'If you're quite done with star gazing,' Tchyglock said drily. Barry scowled at him in response.

The land surrounding them was flat and barren, with a wide track running parallel to the edge of the escarpment. A couple of miles away was a dense evergreen forest, and other than the shack there was no sign of life.

'What's the plan?' Barry asked.

'We will make our way along the track for a mile or two then head into the woods for some rest.' He held up his hand as he saw Barry begin to protest. 'We will go as quickly as we can, but we must take some rest tonight for I do not know when we will next be able to.' Barry shut his mouth begrudgingly. 'From first light we will be travelling hard and fast.'

***

First light came around all too soon, as Zosime shook them awake to a frost-covered forest. Dyn protested particularly loudly. 'Leave it out! I've barely shut me flippin' eyes!' he said grouchily, rubbing his dark eyes and looking particularly ridiculous with seemingly every item of clothing he owned being worn to keep him warm.

The rest of the group chuckled at his complaints, and Barry had noticed that Dyn had the rare quality of cheering people up with his morning grumpiness.

After a swift breakfast Tchyglock got them moving at a fast pace in a quick march, which soon warmed them up in the freezing dawn, and as the sun came up, they arrived at a ramshackle village.

The track had veered inland from the escarpment and the village had been built in a large area of cleared forest. Rudimentary huts had been hewn from logs and mud, and the roads through the village were little more than dirt tracks. The smell of peat fires filled the group's nostrils and Barry thought longingly of warm rooms and hot food.

A pair of shaggy-haired men clad in furs came gambolling out of an inn and began fiercely brawling in the middle of the street. They were both worse for wear and before long seemed to find it too much effort. With a cheery wave to each other, they wound their way off in opposite directions.

'That's the most amicable bar fight I think I've ever seen,' Xhaffa commented.

'I suspect up here it's as much to keep their blood warm as anything else,' Tchyglock responded, and led them down a side street towards the edge of the small village. The narrower the street the greater the smell seemed to be and Barry averted his eyes from the latrine-based debris lining the sides of the buildings. He remembered learning at school about how, during the Middle Ages, chamber pots were emptied out of the windows of houses, and it looked like the practice was still alive and well in this particular Khali-Dhūmi village.

'This place stinks,' Dyn stated bluntly, and everyone was too busy covering their mouths to argue.

At the end of the street were a paddock and stables where several horses were just waking up. Tchyglock knocked loudly on the door of the small house next to the stables.

After a lot of cursing and crashing from behind the door, a surly man with shaggy bed hair yanked the door open.

'Yak ekker shlin?' he demanded in a harsh accent, rubbing his sleep filled eyes.

'Ghul frick galkkas,' Tchyglock responded in the same guttural language.

'Krocca alt,' the man demanded grumpily and began to close the door. Tchyglock blocked it with his foot.

'We're not coming back later. We need horses and we need them now,' he said. Dead-Nettle loosened her sword in its sheath rather loudly, and the man squinted out at them like a mole appearing out of its hole for the first time in days. When he saw the assorted weaponry on display his disposition changed noticeably.

He grunted and pulled the door behind him.

'Come,' he said and led them to the paddock. He began making a series of strange guttural noises and the horses all cantered over to him, nuzzling his big, calloused hands.

After a short while and a lot of haggling , the company trotted out on six of the horse master's finest steeds. Despite their master's appearance, he had taken excellent care of the horses and they pawed at the ground, eager to be off.

They rode slowly around the edge of the village, and once out the other side and back on the track, Tchyglock stopped.

'We have far to go. Let us make haste and feel the wind in our hair,' he exclaimed, and with a yell, dug his heels into his roan and set off at a gallop.

With similarly jubilant cries the rest of them set off after him.

Barry had been embarrassed to admit to them that he had zero experience of riding a horse, and found that rather than enjoying the experience as the others were, he was simply clinging onto his chestnut-coloured gelding for dear life and hoping it kept following the others.

And that was how he spent the next three days as they pushed their horses hard along the southern border of Khali-Dhūmi. The alarm that the princess had raised in Barry's head had proved enough for them to cast off any plans of blending in or subterfuge, and haste was now the key. The terrain was wild, windswept and rugged and their eyes stung in the frigid air of the northern kingdom. They veered away from towns and villages, stopping only when they needed supplies. The people were friendly and welcoming, and the group looked longingly at the frequent log cabins with open fires and dark ales. But there was a steely determination about them now, and the end felt in sight.

One ongoing distraction for Barry was the pain in his legs. The others did not seem to be suffering in the same way, but every night when they stopped, Barry found he could barely walk, such was the pain in his thighs from clinging onto the saddle all day. Between splodgeworming and horseback riding, Många Världar was definitely not Barry's favourite place for travel. It did help to distract from the ongoing pain in his shoulder, however, which he took as a win.

But his discomfort was outweighed by the weight in his heart when he thought of the princess. She had not appeared in his thoughts, either waking or in sleep, since her alarm on the escarpment, and with each passing mile his fear for her grew greater. His feelings towards her confused him; he had never met her, but she provoked in him feelings deep inside that he had not experienced before, and it made him blush and squirm in equal measure.

At midday on the third day of riding the Endless Forest appeared on the horizon under a clear blue sky and Barry felt a surge of relief. The northern escarpment was lower now and the descent more gradual. When Tchyglock reined them in for lunch Barry walked to the edge of the cliffs and looked out.

'Look!' he exclaimed. 'I think I can see the Watchtower of Donnau!'

'Yes,' Tchyglock agreed without looking up.

'It is further away than it might appear. We still have some way to go,' Xhaffa said, coming to stand next to Barry.

'But the end is in sight,' Barry countered. 'And that gives some comfort to my aching legs.'

Xhaffa chuckled. 'You are not the most graceful rider.'

'I'm not the most graceful at anything,' Barry replied ruefully.

'Grace is overrated,' Xhaffa smiled, clapping him on the back. 'But I must confess that I, too, am gladdened by the sight of the watchtower. It has stood watch over the northern plains and forest for eons, a symbol of a united empire. It was a cruel twist of fate when the usurper first took control of Många Världar and imprisoned the princess there.'

Barry looked closer at the leader of the Sonphea and saw there were deep, dark circles under his eyes, he was hunched slightly over and his movements were noticeably stiff.

'Are you okay, Xhaffa?' Barry asked quietly, making sure nobody else could hear.

Xhaffa's face darkened and his back straightened.

'Do not insult me, Master Birchwood, I am still your leader,' he said, eyes flashing. He turned and stormed back to the group, leaving Barry confused and irritated.

Barry swung back on his horse with the rest of the group, and avoided Xhaffa for the rest of the day. He rode beside Dyn, who made frequent jokes about Barry's riding style, something that only Dyn could manage in a way that actually cheered Barry up.

Their journey continued to take them east toward the Endless Forest, at which point Tchyglock finally turned them south and back down towards Paharam.

The forest was quiet, the steps of the horses muffled by the mossy, pine needle-strewn floor. Their pace slowed, and eventually Tchyglock stopped them.

'We are now level with the border of Paharam, and must begin to travel at night once more,' he said grimly. 'Rest now, for the nights will be long.'

Dyn groaned and tried to turn it into a yawn with no success at all. Zosime frowned at him, and he winked at her in response.

'What of the poachers?' Zosime asked. 'They will be everywhere.'

'The darkness of night is the only chance we can give ourselves of going undetected. We will leave the horses behind; they will only attract attention. Rain is coming, that will help to dampen sounds of our movement, but the same is also true of those who will hunt us. If poachers engage us, we must eliminate them. We cannot risk word of our coming reaching the ears of the enemy.'

The true meaning of his words landed heavily on all of them. They sat down, but not one of them slept that afternoon.

CHAPTER 23

Betrayal

Princess Lahlia Luellason sat hunched in the corner of her tower. Her clothes were torn, and deep welts lay angrily across her face and arms; painful reminders of the torment her captors put her through. She could no longer grasp what was dream and what was reality, life falling into the routine of pain, relief, more pain. She clung to life with a paper-thin grasp. For weeks now they had tortured her to the point of madness, determined to break her and turn her to become a voice for the Suzerain Cikavac.

Her dry, cracked eyes opened and she saw that it was dark outside. There were stars high above. It had finally stopped raining.

Without knowing why, she felt compelled to put herself through it, she dragged herself on all fours out onto the rampart. Her body screamed at her, and the scabs on her hands were torn off, leaving bloody handprints across the cold stone floor.

She lay down on her back when she reached the crenelated wall and gazed up at the stars. The night sky made her think of freedom, a freedom she had not known for many years. So much space, it had always given her hope that the Great Almighty would protect her. Now he beckoned her to him. The heavens would grant her freedom and she smiled benignly, at peace with her last great journey.

Her tranquil thoughts were interrupted by the sound of shouts from the gate at the wall surrounding the tower. She turned her head and through a small drainage hole in the rampart she could see the huge gates being heaved open by several burly guards in the suzerain's blood-red uniform.

As they opened, they revealed a single rider cloaked all in black. The gates had barely opened a metre and he charged through them, galloping up the long path towards the tower. The rider was almost at the tower when the small figure of Ainea, the suzerain's seneschal in Paharam, meandered down to greet the visitor.

Until the destruction of Willow, Ainea had been a courteous captor, but since she had been better surrounded by her own forces, she had revealed a cruel streak the princess had not foreseen, and had no qualms in torturing the princess for nothing more than her own entertainment. She dragged herself closer to the edge and strained her ears to hear what they were saying.

'My lady.' The black-clad figure bowed after climbing down from his horse. The urbane voice was faintly familiar to Lahlia but she could not place it and his face was hidden in shadow.

'You'd better have a good reason for coming here, the suzerain will have your guts if you give yourself away,' the seneschal snapped croakily. Years of heavy pipe smoking had left her with a voice like a toad.

'They are coming for the princess,' the man said shortly and Ainea froze.

'What? Who are? When?' she snapped.

'A small rescue company, led by Tchyglock and Xhaffa. I do not know their route, but I feared they would already be here, it was difficult to get away. The warlock, Nox, watches like a hawk.'

The man shuffled on his feet to keep warm and for a brief moment his face was cast into the moonlight, and the silver goatee of Langellis Mirnok appeared beneath his hood. Lahlia gasped in horror.

'How do we know we can trust you? We have received no word from you for an age. You could have turned and this is a ruse.'

'There are spells placed upon me preventing me from revealing much of what I hear. I have risked a great deal to alert you to their coming, you know how important the princess is for their cause. You must ready your defences.'

Ainea laughed throatily. 'Ready our defences? Where do you think you are, Langellis? This is the Watchtower of Donnau, surrounded by guards, above a village where an entire battalion of the suzerain's army is bivouacked, and I'm sure you will have seen that King Iovixa left us with a pair of his giants at the foot of the hill. What match do you think a small rescue party is for all of that?'

'Do not underestimate them, my lady,' Langellis urged. 'Their party includes the one they call the Saviour.'

'Oh, Langellis, the saviour is a thing of myth and legend!' she said derisively. 'I thought more of you than that.'

'I have seen his skill with my own eyes. He slayed an ice fravashi, they are calling him Nida Killaer. This is no trifling rescue mission. Captain Zosime and the master of swords, Dead-Nettle, also ride with them.'

Lahlia could almost hear the seneschal's eyes narrowing as she considered Langellis's words.

'Very well. Come inside and we will make arrangements.' There was a brief, warm glow as the doors to the tower opened, revealing the light and warmth enjoyed by her captors, before the two disappeared inside.

Fury burned in Lahlia's belly like hot lead at the betrayal of one of the most senior members of the Sonphea, and tears of helplessness came to her eyes as she considered the death trap her rescuers were entering.

She tried to alert Barry via their inexplicable connection, but she was too weak and could barely focus a thought. Blood trickled down her cheek and she fought to keep the darkness away, but the stars slowly faded and unconsciousness took her again, as a tear followed the blood in snaking its way down her cheek.

***

'We are only a few miles from the tree line,' Zosime's low voice said from the shadows, making Barry nearly jump out of his skin. Dyn let out a yelp, tripped over a tree root and fell flat on his face.

'Seven suns, Zosime! You don't need to sneak up on us like that,' Dyn grumbled, wiping mud from his face.

'Tell the others,' she told the pair, before the fading sounds of her moving quietly through the forest told them she had gone to range out ahead once more.

Barry passed the word back to the rest of the group who were bringing up the rear. Their journey for the past two nights had been very stop-start, with frequent poacher raiding parties roaming through the woods. The rain had been heavy, and they were thoroughly damp and cold, but it had helped to hide both their scent and the sound of their footsteps. Now it had stopped and the silence was oppressive.

Barry had developed a newfound respect for Zosime, who was an expert ranger and scout, bringing frequent reports back and helping them avoid the poachers on several occasions. It was always dark this deep in the woods; the trees grew close together and after two days of constantly straining their ears for the sound of enemies, all of their nerves were wound as tight as a guitar string. Despite their respect for Zosime, none of them appreciated her sudden apparitions out of the gloom.

After sharing the message in hushed tones, they began marching carefully onwards once more. Barry aimed a playful kick at Dyn's backside as he walked behind him, but in doing so he lost his balance and grabbed a tree trunk to stay on his feet. It was his trip that saved his life as an arrow whistled past the top of his head and pinged off the tree he was hugging.

'Poachers!' he called and as one the group all dropped to the floor. More arrows began to zing through the air around them. There were shouts and calls coming through the trees and Barry was able to identify at least five different voices, all sounding like they were getting closer.

The five of them were lying on the forest floor and pressed up against trees as the poachers closed in. Dyn looked terrified and was seemingly trying to look in every direction at once. Dead-Nettle was pressed against the tree next to Barry, and looking at each other, they both nodded grimly and loosened their swords in their sheaths.

Xhaffa was breathing heavily and he had a slightly manic grin on his face. 'Finally, a chance for a fight!' he said, pulling a nasty looking axe from his belt with one hand, and drawing his sword with another.

'Where's Zosime?' Dyn whispered from between thin lips. 'She has the only bow and arrow!'

'We must assume that we fight without Zosime,' Tchyglock said.

'What do you mean by that?' Dyn exclaimed.

Xhaffa put a finger to his lips to silence Dyn, who was beginning to panic.

'They are coming from every direction, we must each fight our corner,' the leader of the Sonphea said. His voice was every inch the commander. 'Push them back with any throwing weapons, and then defeat them with swords. Is that clear?'

'Aye,' Tchyglock said.

'Aye,' Barry and Dead-Nettle chimed in.

Dyn nodded nervously. 'Aye,' he croaked almost silently.

The poachers were only a matter of metres away now.

'As one,' Xhaffa whispered and held up three fingers. 'Three,' he mouthed silently. 'Two,' and another finger dropped. 'One!' he yelled and the five of them leapt up with a roar.

Barry spun around the tree he had hidden behind. With a bolt of terror, he realised there were more poachers than they had anticipated and they were everywhere. He began flinging throwing stars in every direction, and from the groans and grunts of pain he knew he had hit his mark with some, and saw the dark figures falling to the floor.

The forest had erupted in a volcano of noise, as screams, roars and cries rang through the trees. An arrow pinged off Barry's sword grip, bruising his hip, and with blood coursing through him, he charged at the shadowy figures, drawing his sword as he ran.

He ran full pelt into the nearest poacher before they had chance to draw their sword, and they both fell into a tree. The poacher, a pale man who stank of sweat, banged his head off a thick tree root as he fell and his eyes slid upwards, as he immediately fell unconscious.

Barry leapt up and ran forwards to where he could see Dyn grappling with two poachers twice the size of him. His friend was just about holding them off, but he was a weak swordfighter and was being forced quickly backwards, flailing increasingly wildly.

Barry entered the fray, and even using his weaker, uninjured arm, his skill was not in doubt, but never before had he had the adrenaline firing through his body and the metallic taste of blood in his mouth. The poacher he faced was a huge, muscular man with twice the strength of Barry, but nowhere near the ability.

With rapier like flicks of the sword with his good arm, Barry drew blood from the arms of his adversary, but then two more poachers entered the fray. Dyn and Barry were back to back, working to keep the four poachers at bay but struggling to break through their ranks. The air was thick with the clanging of metal on metal, and Barry danced and darted but could not make any progress, and more poachers were arriving, for some reason focusing on Barry, who continued to try and defend Dyn as much as himself. He lost his footing on a loose stone and fell to one knee. Blows began to rain down on him from the two poachers in front of him and he could barely fend them off, unable to get back to his feet.

Suddenly an axe buried itself in the head of the huge man Barry had been fighting, and Xhaffa appeared behind it, wielding his huge sword with a power that defied his years, his armour glinting in the moonlight.

He swung it in broad strokes and felled another poacher, as Barry and Dyn pressed their sudden advantage and began to wade through the densely packed poachers. Dead-Nettle joined from the right flank and cut into the now funnelled enemy whose roars of triumph had turned to cries of terror. Arrows began to fly at that point, but this time they weren't aimed at the rescue company, but instead at the poachers, as Zosime reappeared, cutting into them from the rear.

Xhaffa was crowing with bloodthirsty glee as his sword chopped left and right, and the pile of poachers began to grow.

The poachers were now screaming and the several remaining turned to flee, breaking out just ahead of Dyn and charging off into the dark forest.

'Hunt them down!' Xhaffa cried. 'We cannot let them escape.'

It made Barry sick to his stomach, but the group knew Xhaffa's words to be true. They could not risk a poacher reporting their coming to the forces surrounding the princess.

Grimly, the hunted became the hunters, and they chased down those who had sought to kill them for payment. Their business of collecting people like stamps revolted Barry, and he especially wished they had not hunted that night, for he knew the blood on his hands would stay with him forever.

The group went about their grisly work of dispatching the stragglers with ruthless efficiency, but when they gathered back together there was a notable absentee.

'Where's Tchyglock?' Zosime asked sharply.

They all cast their eyes around the perpetual gloom of the forest for signs of their leader, but none could be seen. 'Spread out, and tread carefully,' Xhaffa murmured, taking control, his gold-ringed armour streaked with blood and a fearsome look in his eyes.

They all crept outwards, inspecting the forest floor and warily approaching any prone body. There was a tightness growing in Barry's chest. He tried to push dark thoughts from his mind and focus on the task at hand, but the voice of Nox kept slipping into his mind: "The mission will only succeed with the death of one of the company." He shook his head and moved on. Not Tchyglock.

The group were rolling over fallen poachers and Barry was surprised by how down at heel they all looked. These weren't wealthy people benefiting from the suzerain's protection, but poor citizens who had welcomed the suzerain but were now forced to seek a living in a repugnant fashion. He no longer felt angry at them, but instead he pitied them and their ignorance.

'I've… I've found him,' came Dead-Nettle's wavering voice, and her tone turned the tightness in Barry's chest into a vice like grip on his guts. With a sense of foreboding he joined the others in dashing to where Dead-Nettle stood over the prostrate figure of Tchyglock, lying face down on the forest floor, still and unmoving.

CHAPTER 24

Where Giants Walk

'Is he…?' Zosime whispered softly, her distraught face showing more emotion than Barry had ever seen from her. Dyn put his arm around her to comfort her, and to Barry's surprise she didn't object.

Dead-Nettle rolled him gently over and he flopped lifelessly. His eyes were closed peacefully and there was blood staining the side of his heavy travel cloak which was draped across his chest. Barry felt tears beginning to sting his eyes and blinked them back furiously.

Dead-Nettle tenderly touched his neck to feel for a pulse, and her long black plait fell across his face.

As she pressed down on the weather-beaten commander's neck, his hand, without warning, jerked up and grabbed the hand on his neck and twisted it backwards. She let out a yell and fell sideways to try and twist out of the wrist-breaking hold, while Tchyglock whipped a long, slender knife up from within his cloak with his other hand, and as his eyes snapped open, held it to her throat, his long hair hanging wildly across his face.

'Tchyglock, stop!' Xhaffa roared. Tchyglock's eyes were wild and red rimmed as they fell on Xhaffa and comprehension slowly began to dawn on his face. With a loud groan he released Dead-Nettle, let his hands fall back to his sides and released a big breath. 'Mother God,' he gasped.

'Are you all right?' Zosime asked, falling to her knees and putting her hands delicately on the area where the blood was.

'Yes, yes, I'm fine,' he grunted, pushing her off.

The group let out a sigh of relief; he was still his cantankerous self.

'But you're bleeding!' she exclaimed, trying to push him back down.

He sat up and pushed off his cloak. There was no blood staining the grubby shirt underneath. 'Not my blood,' he grunted and stood up.

'What happened, old friend?' Xhaffa asked as they all relaxed.

Tchyglock rubbed the back of his head. 'I managed to take out this fellow,' he said nudging a nearby body with his boot, 'but slipped backwards.' He looked sheepishly around at them. 'The last thing I remember is a blinding white light. I guess I banged my head and knocked myself out.'

'You're going to have a nasty concussion from that,' Xhaffa said, inspecting the back of the commander's head. 'Perhaps you should sit out the next leg, you won't be yourself.'

Tchyglock laughed. 'Nice try, Xhaffa, a herd of wild kelpies couldn't keep me away from our task ahead. You never know, you may even need me,' he said with a wink. He turned to survey the massed bodies of the poachers.

'The real question is why were there so many of them?'

'We must've been unlucky to bump into them near where they had all gathered,' Dyn suggested.

'Perhaps, but I think not,' Tchyglock said. 'Before I passed out I had noticed that the poachers seemed to be focusing their attentions on Barry, did it seem that way to anyone else?'

'You're right, Commander, tens of them had started crowding Barry and Dyn, and nearly succeeded in killing them. Barry's one-armed swordplay was extraordinary,' she said with a glowing smile at him.

'It nearly wasn't enough,' Barry replied. 'Xhaffa saved my life as they were about to land the killer blow. Thank you, sir,' he said earnestly to the Sonphea leader.

Xhaffa waved his hand. 'It was a good little fight,' he grinned, 'but I do share the commander's concern at why they were focused on you two.'

'Maybe they thought we were the weak link?' Barry ventured.

'Or maybe they know that we travel with the saviour,' Tchyglock said.

'But that would mean we have been betrayed,' Xhaffa said, looking shocked.

'It would be the only rational explanation,' Zosime added.

'Who would betray us?' Dyn asked, shocked.

'Who, and indeed why,' Tchyglock said, stroking his stubbly cheeks and looking thoughtful. The others were all looking at each other, trying to suss out who had forsaken them.

'Stop thinking it!' Barry said crossly. 'I can see in your eyes the fear that one of this group has betrayed us. I do not believe any here would do such a thing.'

'The innocence of youth,' Xhaffa said, his mouth tight and wary. 'Zosime, where did you disappear to?'

'I was ranging ahead, as you instructed me to do!' she said furiously. 'I could ask why you insisted on coming!'

'Stop it, both of you!' Barry snapped. 'I did not say we had not been betrayed, indeed Nox revealed to me prior to our departure that the runes had told him there would be a betrayal. But I do not think that anyone here had done it.'

'Go on, Master Birchwood,' Tchyglock encouraged, taking the news of Nox's secret in his stride rather better than the others, judging by the horrified looks on their faces.

'We were all attacked, nobody was left alone by the poachers, they came at us as one, before focusing attentions on me and Dyn.'

'Let's call a spade a spade, it was more likely Barry they were after,' Dyn said deprecatingly.

'If that is the case then the enemy not only know that we are coming, but they know that we have found the saviour,' Xhaffa said despairingly, his face in his hands.

Dyn sat down heavily on the ground and Dead-Nettle leant face first against a tree.

'Then the mission has failed,' Zosime said sadly. 'We cannot hope to rescue the princess. Surprise was our only chance. If the princess dies, so does the ancient magic of her family.'

'No! We cannot give up hope now,' Barry exclaimed. 'The chances were always slim, but we cannot abandon her to the endless torturing of the enemy.'

'It would be a suicide mission,' Xhaffa said.

'Maybe, but the Sonphea is losing. We will never turn the tide of the war without taking some big risks. If we have been betrayed, then it's only a matter of time before they learn the locations of the Sonphea bases. Burroha will fall before long,' Barry said heatedly. 'We have to take the fight to them and we have to do it now, it's our only chance.'

'Barry is right,' Tchyglock said. 'We have hidden in the mountain for too long. If we die, at least we can do it on our own terms, trying to save the last of the royal line.'

Xhaffa began to nod. 'Yes, to go out in a blaze of glory,' he said, grinning.

'It beats sitting under a mountain forever.' Dead-Nettle shrugged.

'We might even make it into songs!' Dyn said eagerly. They all looked at Zosime who had said nothing.

'You're all crazy,' she said, her eyes like slits.

'Good crazy?' Dyn said hopefully.

'That remains to be seen. I'm in, but only to keep you lot out of trouble,' she said, causing the others to chuckle.

'Well as long as I know you have my back, I can rest easy,' Barry said earnestly, and the other members of the company voiced noises of agreement, Xhaffa particularly loudly.

'Now it's settled that we will still aim to complete the mission we must be clever. And there is still a weapon in our armoury that they do not know we possess,' Tchyclock said enigmatically.

'Only a member of the Council could have betrayed this mission and they would know everything,' Xhaffa said.

'Not quite everything,' Tchyglock said.

'What is this weapon?' Barry asked curiously.

'It's Dyn,' Tchyglock answered simply.

'Come again?' Dyn said, standing up, his face skewed in confusion.

'What sort of weapon can the boy possibly be?' Xhaffa snapped.

'Say what you think why don't you,' Dyn said stroppily, rolling his eyes.

'Dynrym Romalliosson is from the city of Degwinkle,' Tchyglock said.

'Is he going to get us out of trouble by fishing?' Zosime said disparagingly.

Tchyglock turned to Dyn. 'Your city was destroyed by the giants, but you escaped. I think there is more to you than meets the eye.'

Dyn averted his gaze and said nothing.

'Hang on, are you suggesting he is one of the legendary Degwinkle Stone Riders?' Dead-Nettle asked as understanding dawned on her face.

Tchyglock said nothing, but smiled.

'But they're just that, legend!' the sword master exclaimed. 'They are just a story they made up in ages past to add to their reputation as a powerful trading town so that people knew their ships would be safe in harbour.'

'Dyn?' Barry asked, looking at his small friend in a new light.

All eyes turned onto Dyn. He looked small surrounded by them all, with his big eyes and even bigger ears.

Dyn shrugged and muttered something, looking away.

'Speak up, boy,' Xhaffa snapped.

'Might be… dunno.' Dyn shrugged again, looking embarrassed.

'Dynrym,' Tchyglock said, putting a hand on his shoulder and crouching down. 'When you said you were able to get some of your fellow people to safety during the attack on your city, you did that by wall riding, didn't you?'

Dyn gave a barely perceptible nod.

Xhaffa gave a roar of approval and clapped Dyn on the back so hard it would have sent him sprawling to the ground had Barry not caught him.

'Sorry, but what exactly is a Stone Rider?' Barry asked, confused.

Tchyglock stood. 'A millennia ago, the people of Degwinkle in the south of Thomwall were already prosperous due to their location at the meeting of the Noani River and the Llewin Ocean. But with their location as an important trading point, people from all over the world, from far distant lands would descend on the city and brought with it many secrets and magics. As they mixed with the people there, these new magics entered the bloodlines of the people of the city. From that was born a rare breed of people unique to Degwinkle who became known as the Stone Riders. These few people who have appeared in the city over the centuries had the ability to defy gravity… to run along walls, and at great speed.'

'No way!' said Barry. 'Why did you never mention it?'

'Didn't really believe someone like me could do summat like that to be honest, mate. Still don't really.'

'Well start believing,' Tchyglock urged. 'Not only can they run on walls, but on anything made of stone, so cliffs, quarries, even some mountains; they can climb them horizontally as easily as taking a stroll.'

Dead-Nettle still looked highly sceptical. 'No Stone Riders have been so much as heard for centuries…'

'They were both prized and feared, and many were cut down by those who did not understand them. But there has long been hope in the city that not all of the bloodlines were destroyed.'

'I could have done with you helping me out during the Trial of the Broken Viaduct!' Barry exclaimed.

'I think we will need some demonstration of this ability, if our mission is to hinge upon it,' Zosime said, looking suspiciously at the young man who had been following her around like a puppy.

Dyn cast his arms around. 'Not a lot o' walls in the forest.'

'Zosime's point is a good one,' Xhaffa said. 'Our only chance of succeeding in this mission is with this apparent talent of the boy's, which he seems to have little confidence in, and which you have kept from us until now.'

'If I hadn't, the betrayer would have told the enemy of it and our chances of success would be even smaller,' Tchyglock pointed out.

'If the soothsayer Nox's foresight is true, then the only way we can succeed is if one of us forfeits our life. I would not have you send a boy to his grave on a hunch,' Xhaffa said, getting louder.

'A hunch is all we have!' Tchyglock said angrily.

'We all knew the cost of this mission, and we all agreed. I'm no different,' Dyn said in a small but defiant voice. 'I'll do whatever needs to be done, and if it's t' get our land an' homes back then so be it.'

'Well said, Dynrym Romalliosson,' Xhaffa said, conceding. 'I apologise for doubting you.'

'No probs, fella,' Dyn said, causing Tchyglock grimace. 'Plus, who's to say Nox got it wrong. We could all be chowin' down on a celebratory feast in Burroha come the end of the week yet.'

'That's the spirit,' Dead-Nettle said, patting him on the back but not looking like she believed it.

Barry smiled encouragingly, but could not help but think of Nox's accurate prediction of the betrayal, and looked at the faces of his companions for what he hoped was not one of the last times.

****

It was hours later that they stood close to the tree line, with the clearing to the ruined Willow-Under-Hill below them, and the Watchtower of Donnau silhouetted against the low moon atop its hill in the distance.

Barry guessed that it was around three o'clock, and the night was at its blackest. Despite the late hour, the clearing was heavily patrolled, with companies of guards pacing every twenty metres. But it was not the guards who had the group's attention.

Rising high above what was left of the town were two enormous figures, the size of which Barry could scarcely comprehend. His mouth fell completely open.

'Giants,' Barry whispered, unable to keep the fear from creeping into his voice.

The giants were huge and shaggy haired, and their hands, the size of tables, rested on the roofs of the highest remaining houses in the town as they peered around with eyes as big as dinner plates.

Their faces flickered in the light of bonfires flaming throughout the village, and one had a huge black beard, while the other had a white-blond goatee. The bearded giant opened his maw, lifted his head and roared. The sound shattered windows and they could hear men shouting and screaming as the giant began to lift up a foot and stomp down around him. Soldiers clad in the suzerain's blood red uniform ran, terrified, in every direction.

Whistles started blowing as captains and sergeants worked to keep their men in position, while the giants cackled at the pandemonium around them. The blond giant spotted an archer in position on a house several streets over who was looking outwards to the tower. The giant leant over with a vast, long arm, and easing his hand up silently behind the archer, flicked him with his finger. The archer's screams ended as abruptly as they had started when he careered straight through the window of a house on the other side of the town.

The giants roared with laughter and stomped their feet in delight, giving each other a high five that sounded like a thunderclap.

'Seven suns,' Dead-Nettle swore. 'What hope have we against such mindless brutality?'

'They didn't need to wreak such destruction on the town,' Tchyglock said sadly.

'They were making a statement of intent against the rebellion,' Xhaffa replied with a sigh. 'Willow's support for the rebellion was a poorly guarded secret.'

Terror was cast over the faces of all of the group, except for Dyn who looked beyond angry. He looked furious.

'We're gonna beat 'em, and beat 'em good. Both of them was at the destruction of my city,' he said, his voice dripping with controlled hate.

Tchyglock beckoned them back a little further into the trees.

'I know you are all tired, and are all afraid, but our best chance is to strike while it is still dark. We have perhaps three hours left before dawn, so we have to act fast,' he said. The group rubbed their weary eyes and steeled themselves. It had been the hardest week of Barry's life; he didn't think he had got more than four hours of sleep in a night since he left Burroha.

'There is no sense in approaching from the village side,' Xhaffa said, focused on the business at hand now. 'We alone cannot face down two giants. We must circle around to approach the tower.'

'There is no tree cover on the other side of the hill,' Barry said, recalling the first time he arrived in Många Världar. 'We would be sitting ducks for any archers or patrols, even in this darkness. The moon is too bright tonight.'

'That is unfortunate,' Xhaffa said, rubbing his grizzled chin.

'Barry is right,' Zosime said. 'If they know we are coming as we believe they do, to approach from the other side would be tantamount to suicide.'

'Our path to the tower lies through Willow,' Tchyglock confirmed. 'We will pass ourselves off as poachers,' he added. 'After our days of travel, we look as dishevelled as even the meanest of poachers, but take a care to cover anything that would make you stand out.'

'They will never buy that!' Xhaffa protested. 'My face is too well known to the enemy, as is yours.'

'We must trust to the darkness and our disguise to get us through. It is our only option,' he said decisively.

'Oh, and whatever any of you do, stay away from the giants,' Tchyglock added, in what Barry thought was an entirely unnecessary suggestion.

CHAPTER 25

Dynrym's Inheritance

The group worked quickly to make themselves look as poacher-like as possible. They rubbed earth on their hands, hid their knives, throwing stars and axes in the folds of their cloaks, leaving only swords and Zosime's bow and arrow on display. They blackened their teeth with dirt and tucked Xhaffa's long red braids inside his clothing. With reluctance he agreed to leave his armour behind in the woods.

Similarly, Dead-Nettle and Zosime had to change their clothing to cover up their leather garb, and Dead-Nettle to also cover as much of her body art as possible which, if spotted, would be a sure-fire giveaway that she was not from Paharam.

'Just follow my lead, everyone. The main thing is to act as if we belong,' Tchyglock said. He rolled his shoulders and led them out of the forest perimeter, walking confidently. The others followed, trying to play the part of forest poachers. Dyn had been selected as the one to play the part of a prisoner and immediately began to overact his part.

'Why me?' he moaned to the night sky and raised his shackled hands. 'An' me just an 'umble peasant an' all. Couldn'ta just lemme go about my own business could you,' he wailed until Zosime punched him, hard, in the side.

'Shut up,' she said through clenched teeth.

He doubled over and retched, the wind completely blown out of him.

'Cruelty to prisoners that is, love, you'll be in for it when I tell your commanding officer,' he wheezed as his breath returned, and hopped out of reach of another punch.

Barry was struggling not to laugh, while Zosime didn't seem to realise that she had, without meaning to, acted her part of poacher to prisoner exceedingly well.

'Oi! Who goes there?' a soldier shouted, as he and his two fellow patrollers nervously held up swords and approached them cautiously from across the clearing.

'We got us a catch!' Tchyglock yelled back at them, pushing Dyn out in front.

'Who are you?' the lead soldier asked suspiciously as they got to the company. He was a blocky man with short legs and dark circles under his eyes.

'Well met, Captain,' Tchyglock said, bowing to the soldiers. 'Name's Patch Varmouth. Been a long night of poaching, but we managed to get this little runt in the end. Off to collect our coin from the Lady Ainea.'

The soldiers relaxed slightly. 'Not much of a haul there, Patch, but every one less makes our lives easier.'

'Truly,' Tchyglock agreed. 'Why is there so much going on tonight? Normally we only deal with the night's watch at this hour.'

'Rumours of intruders afoot,' a twitchy looking young soldier stood behind the captain said. 'The whole base has been called into action.' The captain silenced him with a furious look.

'Intruders eh?' Tchyglock said curiously. 'Din't see much of that in the woods.'

'You be minding your own business, poacher,' the captain replied angrily.

'Don't worry, Cap,' a sharp looking sergeant stood to one side of him said. 'He's only figuring out if it's worth his while to head back to the forest to get some more coin for any imposters about.'

'You're a sharp one, Sergeant, and I'll not hear anyone say any different,' Tchyglock said in the lilting brogue he'd adopted, doffing his cap to the soldier.

'No one who's about would be worth the price of taking them, Patch,' the captain said gruffly. 'Now do yourself a favour and get a move on, this isn't a night for standing around and jabbering like a crowd of fishwives.'

'Right you are, Cap,' Tchyglock said. 'Come on, you rabble,' he added to the group behind him. With a nod at the soldiers, they set off to the village.

None of them dared speak until they reached the perimeter of the village, but they let out a collective sigh of relief when they reached the shadows of the rubble-strewn street.

The roars of the giants were noticeably louder now, and Barry could taste the acrid smell of bonfire smoke drifting through the streets. He tried very hard not to think about what they might be burning.

'A fine start,' Xhaffa said cheerfully, his face creasing into a wolfish grin. Despite the fatigue showing in every line of his face, he looked like he was having the time of his life. 'Now let us go and relieve the tower of its prisoner,' he added eagerly.

Despite the fear sitting in the pit of Barry's stomach, he could not help but smile at the man's infectious energy.

'There is still a long way to go,' Zosime snapped.

'Then let us get started,' Xhaffa said calmly, and they shuffled cautiously through the haphazard maze of streets. When Barry had first come to Willow-Under-Hill all those months ago, it had been quiet, clean and picturesque. Now it was barely recognisable to him, with the rubble of destroyed houses making some of the roads unpassable, and the houses that still stood stared at them through the jagged smiles of broken windows and splintered doors. Dark stains pooled on the cobbles here and there, and an odour of death and decay sat upon the once thriving market town.

Their guise as poachers drew them little attention from the smattering of drunken soldiers or the few wary remaining villagers abroad at the late hour, with Dyn continuing to play the part he seemed to have been born for. The tall, ruined houses, leaning forwards over the road, cast black shadows across the path giving the streets an eerie, flickering darkness from the sooty fires and ever-lower moon.

As they warily turned into a broader avenue, they walked straight into a column of twenty red-clad soldiers, marching with long spears and burnished shields.

'Halt!' the corpulent officer wearing major's stripes who was leading them cried. He had a vermilion complexion, muttonchop sideburns, an enormous walrus moustache and small, watery eyes. He peered out through them with great suspicion at the group. The odour of alcohol was emanating from him.

'Who the devil are you?' he said rudely to Xhaffa, who was at the front of the group at that point.

'Her majesty's poachers, at your service, Major…?' Xhaffa said with a bow.

The major lurched slightly. 'Major Stringer,' he answered, puffing out his chest self-importantly, which caused him to belch. He wiped his mouth with the back of his hand. 'Well, there's a lot of bloody poachers for one grotty lad. Exterminate the lot of 'em on sight, I say,' he said belching straight into Dyn's face. Dyn opened his mouth to reply but Zosime gave a sharp yank on the ropes binding him and he gagged slightly.

'Well, well. You're a fine woman,' the major said, leering at Zosime. 'You know how to keep the rebellious riffraff in check. We're at the end of our shift. How about I let you escort me and the lads back to the barracks,' he added with a thoroughly unsubtle wink. The soldiers behind him roared their approval.

Barry feared Zosime might chop off the major's head right there and then, but it was with remarkable calm she responded.

'That sounds wonderful, Major,' she said winsomely, to more roars from the column of soldiers stretching down the street. 'But I fear Lady Ainea might not look too favourably on anyone who got in the way of us delivering this important rebel to the watchtower,' she said with a longing sigh.

The major choked slightly as his leer turned to fear. 'The Lady Ainea?'

'Yes, the guvnor specifically requested we deliver this prisoner in person to her, it seems he had some standing with the resistance.'

'This little runt?' he said disbelievingly, poking Dyn in the chest, who clearly struggled to contain his fury at the potbellied soldier.

'Well by all means chop off his head and be done with it now, Major, and then we can enjoy getting to know each other right away. Just so long as you're happy to explain it to the seneschal.'

The major lurched backwards a step, and was propped upright by the men stood behind him. 'Ah no, I think some other time,' he said. Then he paused and an idea dawned on his face. 'But we could escort you to the tower, and make sure that you and I don't lose one another,' he said eagerly. At the idea of more marching the faces of the soldiers behind him instantly fell.

'I couldn't ask you to do that, Major, I'm sure I can come and find you afterwards.'

'I won't risk a beauty like you getting away from me,' he said, placing his hands on his large belly. 'Come on lads, *about turn,*' he yelled, spittle bubbling on his moustache.

Zosime threw an alarmed glance at Tchyglock, but there was little they could do. Stealth was now impossible, and instead they found themselves marching at the head of one of the suzerain's own columns, as the major led them towards the heart of the village.

The ground began to shake.

The destruction as they moved to the centre of the village was much greater, with fewer buildings standing and they had to clamber over piles of rubble peppered with the remains of people's belongings. They found themselves on a road that to Barry was vaguely familiar, and it wasn't until he saw the wooden sign of The Dog creaking back and forth in the breeze that he realised the street, which was piled high with detritus, was the one in which he had arrived on his first visit. Many of the buildings were skeletons now, pitted with the bite of arrowheads and torn asunder by the forces of Iovixa, King of Giants. Willow had truly fallen.

The cobbles below them shook and trembled.

They were forced now to climb over the huge chunks of masonry, and they skirted an enormous bonfire blazing in the centre of the street, where soldiers were warming themselves and throwing in — to Barry's profound disgust — books to keep it burning.

'Keep it moving up there,' the major ordered to Barry who had stopped, intent on somehow saving the remaining books. With great effort, he forced himself to avert his gaze and keep on marching.

They reached a fork in the road, and the rumbling in the ground was so great now that slate tiles were falling from the rooves around them, smashing on the floor.

'Right fork!' the major commanded. 'Unless you are eager to become giant fodder,' he added with a toothy grin.

It was an order that Barry was only too happy to obey, as the column hurried down the street. The soldiers held their shields above their heads, but the fake poachers were forced to dart from side to side to avoid death by roof tile. The sound of roaring from the giants was deafening, and Barry knew they must be dreadfully close to the group, but the shells of buildings either side mercifully blocked them from sight.

Seeing the major and his column marching determinedly through the streets led stray soldiers and peasants to leap to the side or disappear down darkened alleyways, and before long they found themselves reaching the northern edge of the town.

The buildings ended abruptly and again they faced a large clearing which was being religiously patrolled by groups of soldiers. Beyond the guards, the land creased upwards into a smooth green hill, atop of which stood, at last, their destination.

Watchfires burned in the darkness, dotted across the hill.

'There must be thousands of soldiers camped up there,' Barry muttered to Dead-Nettle under his breath. She cast him an uncomfortable glance but said nothing.

'Out of the way,' the major grumbled, barging them aside and swaying slightly on his feet. 'I'd better head us up, let's get this over with as quickly as possible,' he said, winking to Zosime. His column looked very disgruntled behind him, and despite his drunken state he was clearly aware of their irritation, as he pulled from his cloak a clear flask filled with a dark brown liquid and tossed it to the men behind him.

'That'll help you get up the hill, lads, just don't let anyone see,' he barked, and chuckled to himself.

'You know how to keep your men on side, Major,' Xhaffa said.

'Doesn't take much to keep that rabble happy,' the major grunted in reply. 'But a drink takes the edge off these dark times for all of us. Now stop yapping and get marching.' He waddled out in front of them, but they soon caught up with him as he began wheezing at the pace he had set.

Seeing Major Stringer, the patrolling soldiers on the hill melted away. He was clearly not someone worth crossing, and Barry began to feel that being frogmarched by the column was working out rather well.

As they climbed the hill, the small watchfires illuminated rows of canvas tents that had been hastily erected, and more than once came calls of, 'Who goes there?' from alert soldiers on the night's watch.

They were perhaps halfway up the hill when there was an almighty crash behind them, followed by bloodcurdling screams. And then, absolute, oppressive silence.

The column halted and turned to see a vast, shadowy tree trunk in the ground behind them, which hadn't been there moments ago. It was as thick as a terraced house and completely blocked the village from view. Barry's head followed the dark trunk upwards, and upwards some more and he gaped in horror as he realised that it was no tree; it was a shin, and the foot had landed so hard it had disappeared into the ground. Casting his eyes slowly around, Barry could see the other leg, planted some fifty yards away.

There was a loud creaking sound from high up and they could see, illuminated by the moon, the head of the giant bending downwards. He stopped several metres above the group, and the face of the blond giant leered down at them. The vast head blocked out the moon, the fires and all thought, as Barry's voice caught in his throat.

The giant smelled of charred meat and metallic blood, and bits of flesh quivered in his teeth, which were each as large as a door, only some had horribly pointed ends.

The heavy silence was broken by the sound of a shrill whistle as the major began blowing furiously on it.

'Get back, Algernon!' he roared, no doubt emboldened by the copious amount he had been drinking. 'You know full well the giants are confined to the town on the orders of the seneschal!' The major's chins were wobbling horribly as he went back to blowing his whistle.

The giant grinned and with a casual hand, swept the major clean off his feet. The major's face was for Barry forever frozen in his mind at the millisecond before he flew to his death. The corpulent, red-veined face was caught in a moment of total surprise before being swept away by the huge hand. The whistles and screams of Major Stringer faded as he flew long and far over the tower and down the hill behind it.

At that point the resolve of the soldiers dissolved, and they began charging in every direction. The giant, Algernon, released a high-pitched giggle, but didn't take his eyes off the rescue company, who had remained rooted to the spot.

'Methinks you do not belong here,' he said to them in a surprisingly polished accent.

'We are poachers, come to collect the suzerain's coin from the seneschal,' Tchyglock shouted. 'We do not want any trouble.'

'There is no need to shout, old boy,' Algernon said calmly as he knelt down with an earth shaking thud and absently polished his nails on his shirt. Then he slowly looked up to fix his gaze on Tchyglock. 'Or should I say, Tchyglock and his merry band of rebels?' He grinned fiendishly.

If Tchyglock was shocked at the giant recognising them he did not show it. Barry slowly withdrew his sword from its scabbard.

It did not escape Algernon's notice and he let out a massive guffaw. 'You mean to fight me with your pointy little stick, boy?' the giant boomed, and Barry quailed under the force of his gaze. 'The coming of the saviour would be terribly brief if you take another step,' he said, his face lowering so that it hovered inches above Barry. 'So often is it the case, that the rumours that run ahead of such people are far more impressive than the person themselves.' He bit his teeth together with a clang that ran through Barry's head, and he fell backwards.

He heard the calls of his comrades and time slowed down, as if he was in the Oran without having lowered himself into it. Before he had time to realise what he was even doing, Barry's consciousness had separated from his body, and as he had done during the Trial of the Broken Viaduct, his insubstantial arm grabbed the hand of his body, spun and flung it at the face of the vast being. He immediately returned to his body, again barely aware of even meaning to, and opened his eyes to find himself hurtling towards one of the orb-like eyes of the giant. He swung up the arm holding the sword, and after raising it just in the nick of time, the blade sank deep into the broad, black, pupil in the centre of Algernon's eyeball, sinking all the way up to the hilt with the momentum he had thrown himself with.

The giant let out a spine-chilling wail of pain and cast his head backwards, which flung both Barry and his sword out of his eye with a grotesque sucking sound.

Barry landed heavily and rolled a way down the hill, where Dyn raced to him.

'Barry, you madman! Are you okay?' he cried, charging towards him, but his words were drowned out by the roars and screams of the giant above them, who was leaping around cradling his face. His colossal legs were pounding craters into the hill and Barry had no time to feel sorry for himself as a giant foot came rushing towards where he lay.

He rolled aside just in time and grabbed Dyn out of the way of a swinging heel which would have split him in two.

'We must get to the tower!' Barry yelled to his friend, who nodded and the two of them began running up the hill.

The others in the group, who had been scattered around the hillside in trying to avoid the flailing of Algernon rallied to Barry's call as he pointed his bloody sword up the slope.

There were barely any soldiers left now, and the group wound their way through the empty watchfires and camps, many of which had been stomped on by Algernon's thrashing around. He was now at the foot of the hill, leaping up and down and sobbing, making the whole hillside shudder. Any soldiers they did encounter took one fearful look at Barry in his fravashi cloak, wielding his sword with his face wildly covered with the blood and fluid of Algernon's eye, and wisely stepped aside.

When they reached the gates to the tower, they found them locked, and on either side of it was the high thick wall that ran in a wide circle around the top of the hill, at the centre of which stood the tower, and the princess.

Barry realised he had barely thought of the princess for some time and his heart quickened at the thought that he might soon meet her.

'You are Nida Killaer indeed,' Xhaffa said to Barry, grasping his forearm and grinning. Sweat ran in streams down his charcoal face, and he was breathing heavily. 'But by the gods, you are crazy.'

'Seven suns, Barry, you must have a death wish!' Dead-Nettle gasped, holding her side. 'But you saved our lives with your bravery, I am in your debt.'

'Nobody is in my debt, and we still have a long way to go,' Barry said, wiping down his face. 'These eye juices smell of sweaty mushrooms,' he said, scrunching his face up.

Dyn laughed at him, but stopped when he saw Tchyglock staring at him.

'What?' he asked innocently.

'It is time for you to demonstrate your talents, Dynrym,' he said with a look at the wall.

'Please, just call me Dyn,' he replied, looking uncomfortable. 'I dunno…' he said, shifting his feet awkwardly.

'It is our only way through. We do not have a battering ram, and time is against us. Algernon will return shortly, likely with his fellow giant, and he will be looking for vengeance. We must get to the princess, and we must do it now.'

'You can do it, mate,' Barry said, clapping him on the back. Dyn gave him a grateful smile.

"Ere, hold this for us,' he said handing Barry a soldier's spear he had picked up somewhere on the hill. He set his shoulders and looked up at the wall, which stood at roughly three metres in height, approaching the foot of it.

With a deep breath he took several steps back, kicked off his boots, and then ran full pelt at the wall. Barry nearly cried out, sure that his friend would break his neck running face first into the wall, but to his total shock, Dyn took a leap at the last moment.

There was no other way to describe it than he was actually running along the wall, the edges of his feet defying gravity. It was like he was surfing across the face of the wall, making his way upwards at rapid pace.

Within seconds he stood atop the wall, and then, face forward, ran straight down the other side.

The company turned and looked at each other open mouthed, except for Tchyglock who was struggling to keep the smug grin from his face. There was the sound of grinding bolts from the other side.

'Goin' ter need some 'elp pullin' this beast open,' came Dyn's muffled voice from the other side.

The group all leaned heavily against the gate as Dyn pulled from his side and the bulky, thick gates creaked open. Dyn's face appeared grinning, but there was no time to congratulate him. The shouts of guards came as they began running towards the group from the tower, wielding an array of weaponry.

'Ready yourselves,' Xhaffa grunted, moving to the front and swinging his axe in preparation.

'Dyn, we will distract these guards, see if you can get to the princess at the top of the tower,' Tchyglock said, speaking quickly and drawing his own sword.

There was no time for any further discussion as the charge of the guards crashed into the group like a wave. But they stood firm, and the air was filled with the clashing of sword on sword. Barry dimly noticed Dyn slipping along the wall in the shadows and away from the battle, but could look no further as the guard he was facing threw what would have been a deadly jab at his chest, had he not parried it at the last moment.

The guards were mostly ceremonial, and did not have the hard-bitten toughness of active soldiers, and the group soon overcame them. Looking around, Barry was delighted to see that none of his group had sustained any serious injuries, although Xhaffa was bleeding from a cut to his forearm.

'Hurry,' Tchyglock snapped to the group, and they ran up the path towards the tower as one. Dyn was nowhere to be seen, which Barry hoped was a good thing.

They ran into the fortress, under a high stone archway, past the now empty gatehouse, and slowed their pace. But as they entered the great hall, it became clear that the building had been abandoned in a hurry. Although braziers burned in the corners, filling the large room with a smoky warmth, chairs were overturned and drawers hung open, spilling their guts of papers and books onto the flagstones below. On the long oak table running the length of the room, two plates of food stood half-finished. The people who had been dining had not expected the company to get this far with the protection of two giants and at least two army regiments.

Zosime picked up a leg of chicken from one of the plates. 'It's still warm,' she said softly.

'Great, I'm famished,' Barry said, walking to an untouched plate.

Xhaffa grabbed his arm before he had lifted a chip halfway to his mouth. 'Do not eat it. It may be a trap.'

Barry dropped the chip like he had been burned and stepped away from it.

'Be on your guard, all of you. Just because the seneschal is not here, does not mean the fortress is empty. If a guard sees you, do not let them cry for help.'

They hurried through the hall on light feet, and ascended the stairs, spiralling round and round as it climbed higher. There were corridors leading from the staircase on various floors and they could hear the sounds of occupation from them, but they moved silently.

Zosime led the way and from up ahead there was a muffled gurgle and the figure of a glassy-eyed guard came tumbling limply around the spiral towards them. Zosime put her head around the corner. 'Sorry, I dropped him,' she said before disappearing up ahead once more.

They reached the top of the stairs, passing several more prone figures who Zosime had dispatched with deadly silence. Barry averted his eyes from some of the grislier deaths they had endured in the name of stealth.

At the top of the stairs was a corridor and at the end was the door that undoubtedly led to the princess. Barry dimly wondered where Dyn was and why he had not reappeared, and felt an uncomfortable churn in the pit of his stomach, as he again thought of Nox's prediction.

The door was barred by four guards who looked far hardier than the ones they had faced from the gatehouse. Their faces bore the scars of battles won and their red chainmail glowed in the light of the single torch that hung in a bracket on the wall.

There was nowhere to hide, and the corridor only allowed two people to stand abreast. Barry nodded to Zosime, and the pair of them gave a roar as they ran down the corridor to the waiting guards. As he ran, Barry flung two throwing stars, while Zosime did the same with a heavy throwing knife. While her knife found the target and one soldier crumpled with the knife between his eyes, both of Barry's throwing stars were blocked by uplifted shields.

He could hear the others running behind them, but there was no way for them to help in such a narrow space, and he and Zosime faced down two against three. Barry made swift work of the first guard, while Zosime felled her opponent with a long knife under the armpit. The remaining soldier lost his nerve at that point, and barged through the door behind him.

He was immediately cast down dead by the bolt from a heavy crossbow which nearly passed entirely through him.

'Blast it,' a woman cursed in a deep voice from where she stood in the room holding the crossbow. 'Hadn't expected one of my own soldiers to come back through the door.' She was small and wearing a long green dress. She had the look of a once beautiful woman who had led a cruel life, ingrained now in the lines around her dark eyes.

Behind her stood two big, heavily muscled guards. One of them stood over the prone figure of the unconscious princess, and the other held a knife to Dyn's throat. Behind the guards stood the familiar figure of Langellis Escari.

'Langellis!' Xhaffa roared when he spotted the man who had betrayed him. Tchyglock and Dead-Nettle pulled him back with great difficulty. 'You cowardly snake! How could you?' he yelled, pulling at the arms holding him back. 'I trusted you,' he finished, his voice cracking.

In the tower the usually silvery, urbane Langellis now looked grey and drawn. He looked like a man waging an internal battle with himself. He opened his mouth but seemed to think better of what he had to say and closed it again.

'Your trust was, it seems, misplaced,' the Lady Ainea croaked with a thin smile.

'It's the first time I've seen you lost for words, Langellis,' Barry said. 'Now I see why you were so keen for me to do the Trial of the Broken Viaduct, you just wanted to get rid of me so you could earn favour with your master here.'

'She is not my master!' Langellis spat. 'I serve Suzerain Cikavac.' He foamed at the mouth with an almost religious fervour and helpless love, any sign of uncertainty gone.

'What did she offer you for your service?' Tchyglock demanded. 'Burroha? Lord of Paharam? A place in her fawning retinue?'

Lady Ainea cackled. 'She offered him more than that, she will give him a place among the gang of warlocks and the power that comes with it.'

Barry saw Zosime trying to skirt slowly around the edge of the room towards Dyn while the seneschal, Langellis and the guards were distracted.

Xhaffa sighed sadly. 'You fool, Langellis. How can you think that the power of warlocks can be freely given? The suzerain has no more power to do that than I do. You gave up so much, for so little.'

'The suzerain has access to powers your tiny brain could not comprehend. You just sit on your throne in the shadows, puffed up with your own importance, calling yourself leader and doing nothing.'

'Perhaps you are right about me. But the coming of the saviour has helped me see the light, and now I am reclaiming my honour. Can you say the same thing?'

'There is no saviour!' Langellis exclaimed, pushing in front of the guards and looking at Barry with disdain. 'Just a bookish child who has relied on luck and the help of his betters to survive. Don't you see, you should parlay with the suzerain, she will reward those who aid her, it is the only way to save the people,' he pleaded, almost longingly.

'I will not be the one to ease your rotten conscience,' Xhaffa said flatly.

'You there, stop.' the seneschal barked, pointing to Zosime with her crossbow. 'Do not think I am a fool.'

'I think we have bandied words enough with these traitors to the empire,' Tchyglock interrupted them. 'Hand over the boy and the princess, and we will spare your blood.'

'You do not speak for me,' Xhaffa said, grating his axe on a hunting knife and looking at Langellis like a rabid dog.

'Perhaps we can come to some arrangement?' the Lady Ainea suggested. Her eyes were like those of a fox, narrow and golden. 'If you put down your weapons,' she added to Xhaffa.

'Remember why we are here, sir,' Tchyglock said softly.

With a great effort Xhaffa slid the axe back into his belt, but did not remove his hand from the haft. He turned to look at Barry who gave him an encouraging smile.

Xhaffa was unable to return it, however, as his entire body jolted as a jewel-handled dagger buried itself in between his shoulders.

Barry spun around to see Langellis, his face caught between self-congratulation and self-loathing, standing, his arm still outstretched from throwing the knife.

<h1 style="text-align:center">CHAPTER 26</h1>

<h1 style="text-align:center">Courage Rediscovered</h1>

Time slowed and blurred, as the face of Xhaffa went from surprise to pain to fury, and he dropped to one knee.

'No!' Barry screamed as he and the others drew their weapons and charged forward. They had barely taken a step, however, when they were thrown back as the entire roof of the tower was swept clean off, revealing a dark sky flecked with the first pale tinges of dawn.

Rock and stone fell everywhere, and Barry flung his body over that of the princess to protect her from the raining debris. The guard watching her lay dead on the floor, a block of stone the size of a pumpkin where his head had once been.

The cause of the explosion quickly became apparent as the still working eye of Algernon appeared above the parapet, and his mighty fist still clutched some of the remnants of the roof he had single-handedly removed.

Barry rose from the princess and looked around at the devastation. Dust-covered bodies lay on the floor. Some were stirring, others were not.

He ran quickly from body to body, first arriving at the Lady Ainea, who was alive but unconscious. Tchyglock, Zosime and Dead-Nettle were both brushing stone and mortar from themselves as they slowly stood, seemingly unharmed. Xhaffa lay prone on the ground, face down. Langellis was also face down, with a visibly broken arm sticking out at an uncomfortable angle, and Barry didn't bother to check if he was alive or dead, instead looking desperately for his best friend.

'Dyn! Where's Dyn?' Barry shouted, but it was lost over the roars of Algernon who was trying to peer through the chaos to see them.

There was a large pile of rubble in the corner just visible through choking, dust-filled air. Barry ran over to it and began pushing the rubble aside. The body of the guard who had been holding Dyn became visible and Barry quickened his pace in removing the stone.

Freeing the guard, he rolled him to one side and saw the peaceful face of his friend.

'Noooo!' he cried, his heart breaking at the sight of the first friend he had ever had. Tears sprung to his eyes that he could not stop and a chill ran across his whole body. He collapsed onto the ground, his forehead pressed to his friends chest.

'Cher doin'?' Dyn's voice choked suddenly.

Barry's heart nearly exploded with shock and he leapt back to see the whites of Dyn's eyes peeking out from a face covered in shattered rock and grime.

'You're alive!' Barry exclaimed, but felt himself being dragged backwards and away from his friend, as the vast fingertips of Algernon closed around his body.

He drew his sword and stabbed the fingers, the wounds little more than pin pricks in the giant's skin, but it was enough to force them to release him.

The dust was clearing now and he could see his friends, like ghosts, covered in white mortar powder, readying themselves for the assault of Algernon.

'I will skin you alive, saviour!' Algernon spoke now with a controlled fury, his one eye just visible over the parapet, as his hand reached in and tried to grab him. Barry hopped and jumped out of the way. He looked past Algernon and his heart stopped.

The shaggy haired giant was striding up the hill, leading the entire army who had regathered and were marching, in file, in their direction. There was no hope of escape.

'Let Xhaffa's death not be in vain!' Barry cried. 'To me!' he shouted to his friends, who stood up beside him.

Even Dyn hobbled over to him, but he was bleeding heavily from his leg and his face was screwed up in pain.

They moved forwards, weapons out, but with another sweep of his hand the giant knocked Tchyglock, Zosime and Dead-Nettle flying into the wall, where they all slid down, eyes closed. Barry prayed that they were only unconscious.

He pushed the limping Dyn, who was too weak to protest, behind him, and moved forwards alone towards the face of the one-eyed giant.

'Go back to Drumban, Algernon, with the eye you have left. I have no interest in hurting you, or anyone else.'

'I am a lord among giants and do not fear an ant, even one that bites,' the giant rumbled and made a grab for Barry, but he jumped out of the way, pulling Dyn with him. The giant's hand closed around the legs of Langellis, who was just coming around.

As he was lifted in the air by Algernon, he screamed in terror and Barry made a desperate grab for the man who had betrayed the Sonphea.

His hands closed around the hand of his non-broken arm, and he looked into the carefully preened face of Xhaffa's special advisor.

'Help me,' Langellis screamed, and Barry pulled with all his might but he was no match for the strength of a giant and Langellis was easily pulled from his grasp.

Algernon saw his fellow giant coming up the hill some four hundred metres away, and threw Langellis like an American football, in a tight spiral that any quarterback would have been proud of.

'Tostig!' he shouted, and the black bearded giant looked up at the screaming projectile spinning towards him. He opened his huge mouth, more akin to a gaping chasm, and swallowed Langellis whole.

He gagged slightly, swallowed heavily and gave his fellow giant a thumbs up.

Barry stood again, and raised his sword, but was pushed aside, to his shock, by Xhaffa. The old leader of the Sonphea's face was grey now, and he reached over his shoulder to yank the knife out from between his shoulder blades. He was propping himself up with the spear that Dyn had earlier carried up the hill, using it as a walking stick.

'Xhaffa, what are you doing?' Barry asked as the mighty leader hobbled forwards.

Xhaffa turned around and gazed lovingly at Barry. 'You are our saviour, Barry Birchwood, for you have saved me from myself and the obscurity of inaction. You are our mountain king, our conqueror of shadows, and the future. Tell them of my final exploits, and remember me when you forge the new Många Världar,' he said, with pride and a deep, choked regret, 'for I will not be there to see it.' And with that and a final battle cry, wracked with pain, he lurched forward with all his remaining power and ran towards the rampart.

'Xhaffa, no!' Barry cried to the man he had come to love and respect.

Hearing the cry, Algernon turned back in time to see the barrel-chested, red-braided man throw himself from the parapet and put all his weight behind the spear which buried itself in the one remaining eye of the giant.

Algernon unleashed an unholy scream as this time, as his eye totally exploded. Xhaffa momentarily hung from the tip of the spear.

He cast a final look back at Barry and his face broke into a smile.

'I found my courage!' he cried euphorically, and pulling his axe from his belt, swung from the spear and into the mouth of the screaming giant.

The giant stumbled around blindly, kicking and grabbing at everything he could, tearing at his chest where Xhaffa was hacking away in his dying act. As the giant stumbled forwards, his mammoth fist unknowingly crunched into the temple of his fellow giant, Tostig, who was running up behind him, immediately knocking him out cold.

Both giants fell down the slope, with a thunderous crash that sent shockwaves through the hill, flattening vast tranches of the army that was pouring up the hill behind them.

Tears were streaming down Barry's face, but he could not let himself get lost in the grief. There was no time to waste.

Tchyglock had woken in time to see Xhaffa's heroic finale, while Zosime and Dead-Nettle were both stirring dazedly. Barry hurried to the princess who still lay on the ground and checked that she was still breathing.

Her eyes fluttered open, and as she recognised Barry's face, she smiled benevolently at him, before unconsciousness took her once more.

He hoisted her over his shoulder.

'Dyn, can you walk?' he asked his friend.

Dyn nodded bleakly, but Zosime staggered over to him and pulled his arm around her neck, helping him.

'Where's the seneschal?' Tchyglock asked darkly. 'She will pay for her sins,' he raged.

But the Lady Ainea was nowhere to be seen, just dusty footprints leading away from the tower.

'There is no time to concern ourselves with her, we must make our escape while we can,' Barry said to the commander, who nodded in reluctant agreement.

The remaining five members of the company limped from what remained of the Watchtower of Donnau and headed down the back of the hill. In the distance they could hear what was left of the army, which had been left in disarray by the destruction wreaked by the giants.

As he walked, Barry's mind took him back to the last time he had been on the same slope, and his heart ached as he thought of the innocence and ignorance he had been able to enjoy back then. He felt like he might never laugh again.

As the group reached the bottom of the hill and the edge of the forest, Barry began to lead them, not into the forest, but in a different direction.

'Barry, stop,' Tchyglock's voice said behind him.

Barry pretended he hadn't heard him.

'Barry,' Tchyglock's voice said again, this time with a warning in it.

Barry stopped and spun around.

'It is not possible,' the commander said flatly.

'What are you talking about?' Barry replied innocently.

'It would seem like a good idea, but the company does not belong in your world.'

'And maybe I don't belong in this one. It is full of fear, and war, and… death,' he choked, fighting back a sob. He gently lay the princess down on the ground.

Tchyglock walked over to him and put an arm on his shoulder.

'Nobody belongs here more than you,' he said kindly and with more warmth than he had ever shown before, and to Barry's great surprise, Tchyglock pulled him into a rough hug.

Before he could help it, he began to sob, floods of tears wracking through his body in a way that he couldn't control.

Tchyglock held him there, as the others watched sadly, tears in their own eyes as they all began to truly feel the loss of their leader.

CHAPTER 27

A Hollow Victory

That night the group sat close together for warmth, deep in the forest, where they had set up a small camp, with no fire, under a deep, prickly, thicket of holly.

They had wrapped the princess in all the layers they had, and spoon-fed water into her dry, cracked mouth. Barry could not stop staring at her, lost in her tormented but beautiful face, and found it hard to believe he now sat alongside the woman who had lived in his dreams for all these months. Dyn's leg had been heavily bandaged, but he had lost a great deal of blood and he slept fitfully on the ground next to her. Nobody had uttered a word in hours as they all brooded on the events that had led them there. Their mission had been successful, but to Barry it felt like a completely hollow victory.

'We cannot go back to Burroha now,' Zosime said finally breaking the sombre silence. 'The enemy will be watching all paths to that base to try and recapture the princess.'

'You are right, Zosime. There is only one path open to us now. We must together climb to the Cloud Runners,' Tchyglock responded glumly.

'We are in no condition to climb the world's highest mountain,' she snapped at him.

'We will return to Khali-Dhūmi to recuperate. The army will not pursue us there while their strength has been so depleted. From Khali-Dhūmi we can approach Paeharra, and climb to the Cloud Runners,' Tchyglock said firmly, leaving no room for argument.

Nobody much liked it, but nobody argued; they were all past the point of caring.

'Tchyglock… I must first return to my world,' Barry said, closing his eyes to the barrage he knew was coming.

'You can't be serious,' Dead-Nettle exclaimed disbelievingly. 'You can't leave us now, Barry.'

'I do not mean to stay there, but I left without a word to my mother. I must let her know I am alive while I have the chance, while I am so close to the crossing.'

The others looked dubious.

'I will return, I won't abandon the Sonphea, but I'm of more use to you without the distraction of worrying about my mother.'

They all just stared at the ground, and the silence returned.

'You should accompany him,' Zosime said to Tchyglock after several minutes.

'That… would not be wise,' Tchyglock said, avoiding Barry's eye. 'But Zosime, you shall go with him.'

'You do not trust me?' Barry said furiously.

'I trust you completely, but I also understand the pull that going home can have,' Tchyglock said sadly.

***

The next morning the two of them readied to leave, as the sun had now risen in the sky.

The princess was still unconscious, looking frail and pallid in the cold light of dawn.

'Thought I'd never get rid of yer,' Dyn said with a grin as Barry said goodbye.

'Didn't want a hop-a-long slowing me down anyways,' Barry replied with a chuckle.

'Enjoy home, bit gutted I won't get to see your weird world, truth be told,' his friend replied, and paused. He stared awkwardly at the ground, kicking the dirt with his unbandaged foot. 'You are coming back right, Baz?'

'Always,' Barry said, looking into Dyn's eyes with total conviction.

Dyn smiled cheerfully, and it buoyed Barry's footsteps as he walked back through the forest, to be returning to his world ready to face it, for the first time, knowing he had friends.

The sky was clear blue and cheerful, and from this side of the hill there was no sign of the tragedy and bloodshed of the night before. Nonetheless, Barry, Zosime and Tchyglock kept to the edge of the trees, wary of any reinforcements Suzerain Cikavac may have sent to the area.

As they neared the gateway, the gentle sound of the harp playing grew louder as they approached.

The Tutelary stood and scowled through his moustache covered beak at the sight of Barry.

'You again, eh? I thought I was rid of you,' he said condescendingly before looking at his companions. 'Ah, Tchyglock too, it has been a long time since you were last harassing me to get through.'

'You've been through before—' Barry started, but was stopped by Tchyglock holding up a hand of warning.

'A story for another time, my boy,' he said. He was somehow softer than before, less the gruff commander. 'Zosime, make sure Barry returns to his mother and comes straight back. I expect you both to return by nightfall when we will make haste to the border of Khali-Dhūmi. We have won the first battle, but the war still lies ahead.'

'Very well, Commander.'

'Barry, make the visit count, I do not know when or even if you will be able to return again,' he said meaningfully. 'Be kind to your mother; being a parent is not as easy as you might think.'

'I will, Tchyglock.'

'Then make haste, boy. The day grows old.'

'Are you ready, Zosime? This may be a bit of a shock to the system.'

'Do not patronise me, Barry. Stop dawdling,' she snapped in reply.

'I'm glad I'm not the only one who finds him dim-witted,' Kepheus smirked.

'All right, all right, you're all as bad as each other. Let's go.' Before he stepped behind the willow tree, he turned to Tchyglock. 'I'll be back, and then… to Khali-Dhūmi and the Cloud Runners.'

He smiled, and stepped forward, back to the now snow-covered secret garden, and home, with Zosime at his side.

Acknowledgements

I wrote *Where Giants Walk* during the first lockdown when the world had become a scary and uncertain place, so having the escape of Barry's fantastical journey became a welcome one. My wife and I welcomed our daughter into the world amidst it all, and I can credit her with waking me up at all the hours of the night and, unable to get back to sleep, I would sit up writing until the sun came up. That schedule was renewed during the editing process, following the arrival of our son two years later!

This book was only possible thanks to the following people: Firstly, my wife Anne, who has been incredibly tolerant of my writing trips and obsessive periods of frenzied writing, whilst remaining my biggest supporter throughout. She is always my first (and most brutally honest) proof reader, and I couldn't do it without her. My thanks also go to others who have cast their expert eyes over the manuscript for me: especially my mother Deborah Williams and old friend Joanna Grant.

I'm indebted to my incredibly talented friend Kieran Mace for his fantastic map illustration you can see at the start of the book, which put to paper exactly what I had imagined, and his fantastic cover designs.

Thank you as always to my family and my Irish in-laws, many of whom have provided some inspiration for names throughout the book! And finally, thank you to you, the readers, for buying, borrowing and recommending my books, it really does mean the world.

Stay up to date with all the latest news from T. S. J. Smith!

X   @jamiesmithbooks

🌎   @jamiesmithbooks

f   @jamiesmithbooks

9 781804 680124